KALEIDOSCOPE

K

KIDS BIBLES REIMAGINED

published in the united states by Rocky Heights Print & Binding

visit us at www.readkaleidoscope.com

kaleidoscope, *kids bibles reimagined*

library of congress cataloging-in-publication data is available upon request
ISBN - 978-1-64911-008-4

cover art by becca godfrey (www.beccagodfrey.com)
special thanks to abigail agan for her editing services

For Anna Lynn and Eliza.
Know what the Lord has done.
For Israel. For us. For you.
Know how the Lord loves.
How powerfully. How kindly.
How beautifully. How perfectly.

WELCOME TO KALEIDOSCOPE

First of all, thank you for picking up a copy of Kaleidoscope! We are glad to have you. In the following pages, you'll experience the Bible in a whole new way.

Kaleidoscope emerged from the need to retell the Bible for elementary-aged children at a level between a "little kid" Bible and an adult translation. In a way, we are a happy medium.

At Kaleidoscope, we are producing single volumes for every book of the Bible. We design them to read like chapter books, so you'll turn pages and look forward with anticipation to the next volume.

But don't let the fact that we are focused on kids deter you if you are a "big kid!" Good children's books are almost always as good for adults as they are for kids.

Get excited! In the pages that follow, you'll see God's fantastic good news. Our prayer is that his kindness, gentleness, and love will melt our hearts and make us more like Jesus.

In over 20 years of Children's Ministry, this is one of the most inspiring tools I have seen to help kids (and their parents) experience the Bible in a creative and powerful way!
-Jason Houser
Seeds Family Worship

What a great resource for older kids who aren't yet ready for adult level learning! As a pastor of a congregation and father of 5 kids, having age appropriate and biblically faithful resources is crucial in discipleship. Kaleidoscope has delivered a great one.
-Rev. Matt Morginsky
Lead Pastor Grace and Peace Church, Denver CO

Kaleidoscope's aim is big — to help kids see how all the stories in the Bible comprise one grand, beautiful story of redemption. As a parent, Bible teacher, and church planter, I can't commend this approach to Bible study enough.
-Amy Gannett
Tiny Theologians

In this retelling of the books of Judges and Ruth, Powerful Kindness will intrigue kids with stories of battles and bravery, teach kids the fallen fickleness of humanity, and inspire them with the power and kindness we find in the Lord. My five and six year old listened intently (I'm shocked, too!) as I read this aloud, and they were excited for each new chapter! Soon enough, they'll be able to read it on their own, and I'm delighted to know that this book will help them see their need for Jesus in Judges and God's provision of him in Ruth. The action and affection communicated in this book is sure to rivet readers and lay a foundation of lifelong love for God's word!
-Caroline Saunders
Bible teacher and author of LifeWay girls' study Better Than Life: How to Study the Bible and Like It

As a mom, I longed for a kid's Bible that would keep our children engaged while offering a faithful account of the stories in Scripture. Kaleidoscope is entertaining, responsible, and gospel driven!
-Hunter Beless
Executive Director of Journeywomen

My son loves reading Kaleidoscope because he learns new details about old Bible stories and some new stories he has never heard before. As a mom, I love how Kaleidoscope carefully explains tricky passages while connecting each story to the bigger story of the Bible.
-Maggie Combs
author of Motherhood Without All the Rules and Unsupermommy

With stunning illustrations, this retelling of Judges and Ruth will come alive for your children while teaching them the history of God's people and the truth about the powerful and kind God we serve.
-Korrie Johnson
@goodbookmom

CREATORS

Emily Pressley is an Instructional Coach and Bilingual Reading Intervention Teacher in Denver, CO. She has a BA from Anderson University in South Carolina and an MA from the University of Colorado. When she's not writing or teaching or reading, you can find her adventuring with family and friends, hiking up a mountain, or cooking food that's way too complicated for her tiny kitchen.

Stephen Watson is an Associate Professor of Art at Samford University in Birmingham, AL, where he teaches courses in design, drawing, painting, and digital art. He has an MFA from the University of Alabama, and is an M.Div. student at Beeson Divinity School. Stephen loves reading, making art, and spending time with his wife and two kids.

TABLE OF CONTENTS

INTRODUCTION

When I was in middle school, my social studies teacher had a poster on the wall:

> Those who do not learn from history,
> are destined to repeat it.

Sometime in the school year, a classmate asked, "Does that mean people repeat actual history, or students repeat your class?"

"What's the difference?" our teacher asked back.

A few days later, another student must have thought she'd have better luck. "Does your poster mean that we will repeat real history, or just your class?"

"What's the difference?" our teacher responded.

That's when it became a game. Another day, another student, "Repeating history or repeating your class?"

"What's the difference?"

Over and over and over again. All year.

The story you're about to read is about a group of people, the Israelites, who didn't learn from history. You'll notice a pattern: the people of Israel decide to make their own rules about what's right and what's wrong. Which, of course, means they make a giant mess of things. Everything turns to chaos, and they finally return to God.

The people beg Him for His help, and God gives them a leader to guide them out of their mess. (This leader is called a judge, by the way, but more on that later.) For a while, the people are at rest. They follow God's rules, and everything seems peaceful again. Then, their leader dies. And guess what? The people decide again to make their own rules about what's right and what's wrong.

Over and over and over again. For about 300 years.

Judges is a difficult book in the Bible to read and study. But every single word God left for us, matters. Even the ones that are hard. So, we'll read and study and learn together. We think you're up for the task!

The pattern in Judges makes it easy for us to think that the people of Israel weren't very smart. But as we read, if we're honest with ourselves, the Israelites' story isn't too different from our own. The messes of sin that the Israelites get themselves into, remind us of our own messes. More importantly, they remind us of our good God, who loves us right in the middle of the mess. His love, and powerful kindness, rescues us...

...over and over and over again. So, let's get started.

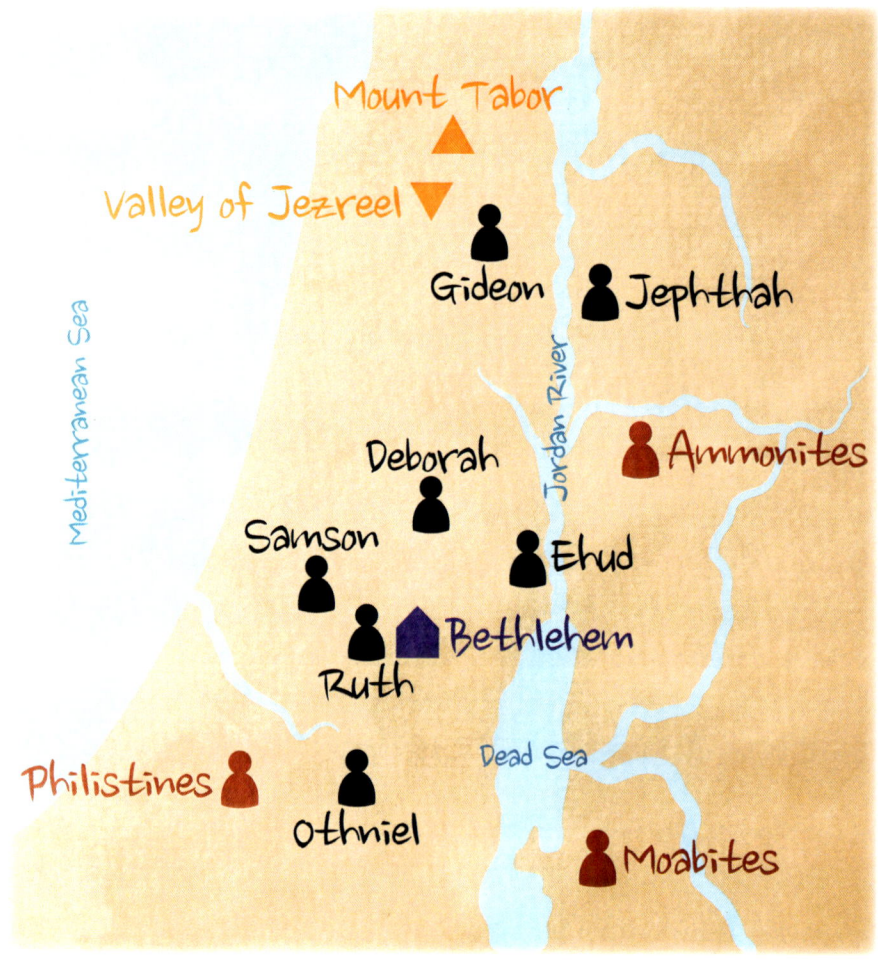

The Judges of Israel
around 1375 — 1050 BC

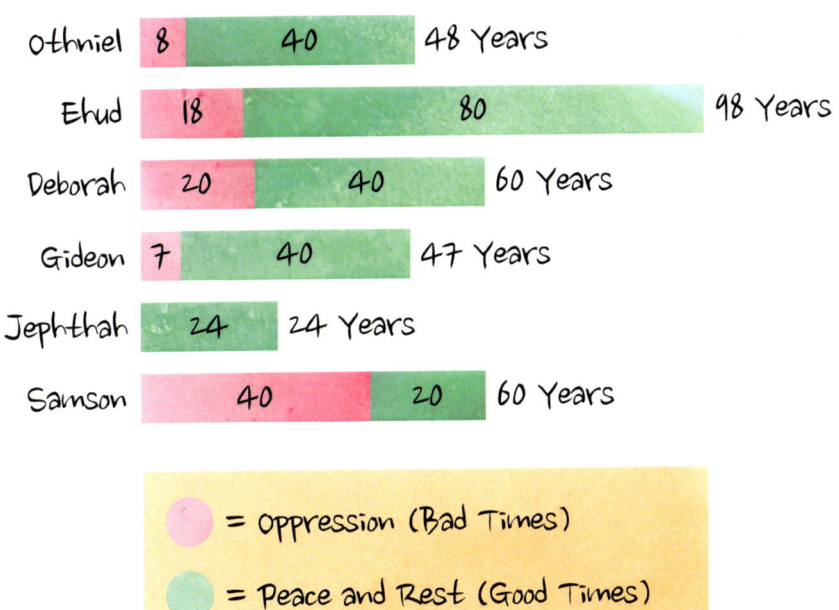

Othniel 8 40 48 Years

Ehud 18 80 98 Years

Deborah 20 40 60 Years

Gideon 7 40 47 Years

Jephthah 24 24 Years

Samson 40 20 60 Years

● = Oppression (Bad Times)

● = Peace and Rest (Good Times)

There were other Judges of Israel, too!
Shamgar, Tola, Jair, Ibzan, Elon, and Abdon

THE PROMISED LAND

JUDGES 1:1-3:6

The Bible is a big book! But it is told in two parts called the Old and the New Testaments. The Old Testament tells the story of God's people, the Israelites. There are laws and battles and seasons of struggle. There are promises and victories and times of peace. Most of all, there is love, shown through God's powerful kindness.

In the Old Testament, you'll find the book of Judges. There, God tells the story of the Israelites as they walk into a land that He had given them. This land was known as the Promised Land.

But this wasn't the first time that the Israelites called the Promised Land "home." You see, hundreds of years earlier, with Abraham as their leader, God's people had already made their home there.

Abraham had a son named Isaac. Isaac had a son named Jacob. Jacob had 12 sons. One of them was named Joseph. All of Jacob's other sons were jealous of Joseph. In their hatred, the brothers sold Joseph as a slave to another country, called Egypt. Slaves are people who are forced to work for someone else, for no pay, and under harsh and cruel conditions.

Joseph and his brothers eventually reunited in Egypt. But, they too would soon become slaves. In His powerful kindness, God rescued the Israelites through a man named Moses and delivered them out of Egypt. They weren't slaves anymore, but they weren't home.

They were nomads, people who wander from place to place without a home. For 40 long years, the Israelites wandered in the desert on their way back to the Promised Land. They suffered in the hot desert sun, day after day. They doubted God's promises. Every day they wondered if they could go home. Every day the answer was the same...not yet. Life was very, very hard.

And that's where our story begins.

After many years, when Moses had died, another leader named Joshua finally led the Israelites out of the desert and back to the Promised Land. A long time had passed since God's people had been home and another group of people, called the Canaanites, had taken over the land.

The Israelites looked around, amazed at the glorious cities the Canaanites had built. These cities were filled with things God's people had only dreamed of owning: breathtaking buildings, captivating artwork, and stories that were written down.

The Canaanites created many beautiful things. But they didn't worship the beautiful Creator. The one true God, the God of Israel, made all things. But the Canaanites believed in many false gods instead. The Canaanites only cared about getting more and more for themselves. Because in their minds, whoever had the most stuff - land, crops, flocks, or children - won.

God knew that if His people lived with the Canaanites, they would begin to love the beautiful things more than they loved Him. They would believe in false gods, and worry about who had the most stuff.

So, God gave the Israelites a command - the Canaanites could not live in the Promised Land. It was the land God had in mind His people.

After God gave this command, Joshua died at the old age of 110. Israel's leaders divided into tribes and spread out in different parts of the Promised Land.

Some Israelites tried to follow God's laws, and some didn't. Most didn't teach their children how God had taken them out of slavery, provided for them in the desert, and guided them into the Promised Land. So when those children grew up, they didn't know God, and they didn't know how God had saved them.

Israel didn't have to wander in the desert anymore, but they chose to wander in their hearts. The longer time went on, the further Israel wandered from God.

The most prominent tribe, Judah, obeyed and began fighting the Canaanites for the land. They asked warriors from the nearby tribe of Simeon to help. For a time, they were winning in the fight against the Canaanites.

But the people of Judah were tired...and afraid. The Canaanites were stronger, and the battle was harder than the Israelites had hoped it would be.

So, God's people decided to make their own rules about what was right and what was wrong. This is called sin. It was the very problem everyone has had since Adam and Eve. Sin causes us to make excuses for things we know are wrong. Instead of loving others, we come up with ways to make sure we are safe and comfortable, even when it hurts other people. Sin separates us from God, and it makes Him very sad.

Some reasoned, "The Canaanites can't be that bad, right? They made all of these beautiful things. Maybe they can teach us how to make them, too."

Others plotted their revenge, saying, "My grandparents were slaves for so long, and they built beautiful cities for other people. Let's make the Canaanites our slaves so they can build beautiful cities for us."

Another group was even more sinister, agreeing, "Let's humiliate and torture the Canaanites as much as the Egyptians humiliated and tortured our grandparents."

The Israelites wanted God's promises and the good things the promises brought. But they didn't want His commands, or the hard decisions those commands required.

So, they let the Canaanites stay in the Promised Land. Some Canaanites stayed as role models or teachers, some as slaves, and some were cruelly abused as prisoners.

God knew that this was not the best plan for His people. He knew that they would soon love what the Canaanites loved.

God had given His people a command to drive the Canaanites out of the Promised Land, but the Israelites disobeyed.

God saw their sin. It made Him sad, and it made Him angry.

In His kindness, God sent an angel of the Lord with a message, "I promised I would rescue you from being slaves in Egypt. I did. I promised I would protect you and provide for you on your journey through the wilderness. I did. I promised I would give you this land. I did. You promised to drive out the people I did not want here, and to destroy the things that would distract you from me. You did not. So, the Canaanites will stay. It will only add to your pain and destruction. You will learn that their ways are not part of my plan for your best."

So, the pattern began. God's people had made their own rules about what was right and what was wrong. And everything became a giant, sinful, sad mess.

Kaleidoscope Corner
Government

A government is the person or group of people who have the power to make the rules in a certain place. From the beginning, God's perfect plan was to be the King of his people, the only one who made the rules to keep them safe. This was called a theocracy.

But God also allowed them to have a human leader, one that they could see. If the leader of a group is a king or queen, that kind of government is called a monarchy. If the leaders of a group are some of the people themselves, it's called a democracy. These three types of government are still used in many places in the world today.

Why was a theocracy part of God's perfect plan for His people? What happened to that plan?

Read Deuteronomy 17:14-20. What were the rules God gave for kings of Israel?

THE FIRST THREE JUDGES

OTHNIEL, EHUD, & SHAMGAR

JUDGES
1:4-8 & 3:7-4:3

God's people would not obey Him and drive the Canaanites from the Promised Land; so they weren't going anywhere, anytime soon. What would Israel do now?

Some of the Israelites treated the Canaanites with hatred, torturing them in ways that broke God's heart.

God told them not to enslave their enemies, but some Israelites made the Canaanites their slaves anyway.

Many Israelites became friends with the Canaanites. They learned from them about how to build buildings or create art or write stories. But they also learned how to live like they did, loving themselves more than they loved others, and worst of all, more than they loved God.

Some Israelites married Canaanites, and as their families mixed, so did their cultures. The Israelites took on the Canaanites' way of life, and their beliefs and religion, as their own. God's own people worshipped the Canaanites' false gods. Did the Israelites remember how they'd wept and prayed when the angel of the Lord warned them about this?

9

Just as the angel of the Lord told them, the Israelites started to see that the Canaanites' ways were not part of God's plan. God wanted a better life for His children.

The people of God found themselves in a mess of their own making. Once again, the Israelites became slaves. This time, though, they were slaves in their own land for eight agonizing years!

The Israelites finally cried out to God for help. God heard them, He saved them, and He gave them a judge.

The idea of a judge as someone in charge may sound confusing. Today we think of a judge as someone who makes decisions in a big fancy courtroom. They answer questions like: *who is the rightful owner of this?* Or, *who has to pay this money?* Or, *what does, or doesn't this law mean?* But in the Bible, being a *judge* meant that you were a leader.

Over hundreds of years, God gave the Israelites 12 judges to lead them. Some judges were famous. Some judges were quiet. Some judges were warriors. Some judges were smart. Some judges were peacemakers and peacekeepers. Some judges were hardworking.

But one thing was true about all of them: none of the judges were perfect. Even still, God used them all to save His people; over and over and over again.

Israel's first judge was named Othniel, which meant "lion of God." Othniel was exactly who you would expect God to pick as a leader. He was from Judah, the strongest and biggest tribe of Israel. He was a mighty soldier, and led his people in a battle against their captors. God gave them the victory, and freed the Israelites from their slavery!

For 40 years, under Othniel's strong and faithful leadership, the Israelites remembered God's promises and obeyed His laws. For those 40 years, they were at peace.

After forty years, Othniel died. Sadly, he had not trained a leader to take over after him. Once again, the Israelites made their own rules about what was right and what was wrong. They sinned against God, and they worked themselves into a giant, sinful, sad mess.

Once again, they were slaves, this time under Eglon, the king of Moab. They were the Moabites' slaves for eighteen cruel, unbearable years. In their distress, the Israelites cried out to God, and He gave them another judge named Ehud.

Unlike Othniel, Ehud wasn't exactly who you would expect God to pick as a leader. He was from the weakest tribe of Israel, called Benjamin. The name Benjamin means "at the right hand," but Ehud was left-handed, which was very rare at that time. People thought it meant something was wrong with you. But as only God can do, and as He often does, He turned someone's so-called weakness into their strength. God had an important plan for left-handed Ehud.

Eglon, the king of Moab, was quite a selfish king and a portly fellow. He ate so much that he couldn't move around very well. Eglon loved when people gave him gifts or flattered him with lots of compliments.

Ehud knew this, so he took a gift to Eglon. Eglon's guards probably checked Ehud for a weapon. But because Ehud was left-handed, he hid his small sword on the inside of his right leg, where the servants didn't check.

Ehud went into Eglon's chamber and presented the gift to the king, telling him, "I have a message from God for you."

Eglon was flattered by the gift and the idea that God had sent him a special messenger. So, he sent all of his guards out of the chamber. Only Ehud and Eglon remained. While Eglon struggled to his feet to receive his "special message," Ehud quickly drew his hidden sword from his right thigh, and with his left hand, killed the king.

Ehud escaped through the palace balcony, locking the doors to the king's chamber behind him. By the time Eglon's guards grew suspicious, Ehud had escaped.

Ehud blew a trumpet to signal for his people on the hills, and told them, "Come with me! The Lord has put your enemy, Moab, right into your hands. The time to defeat them is now."

13

The Israelites followed Ehud, and together, they defeated over 10,000 Moabites and won their freedom. God had sent an unlikely man to save Israel. They were no longer slaves. For 80 incredible years, the Israelites lived in peace under God's protection with Ehud as their judge.

There was also a judge named Shamgar during these early years. We don't know much about him. But, he must have been a great warrior! In fact, he killed 600 Philistines - enemies of Israel - with an oxgoad.

An oxgoad was a long wooden stick with a point carved at one end and a small piece of iron attached to the other. It was a tool meant for pushing oxen along while they were plowing fields, and cleaning mud off the plow.

God showed His power, and His love for the Israelites, by using an unlikely tool in the same way he uses unlikely people or situations: for His glory and their good. Shamgar struck down the enemies of Israel, and saved God's people!

But, as all earthly leaders do, Ehud and Shamgar both died. Just like Othniel, neither of them had trained a leader to take over after them.

So, once again...you guessed it...the people of Israel made their own rules about what was right and what was wrong.

DEBORAH AND THE GREAT BATTLE

JUDGES 4-5

After Ehud and Shamgar died, it wasn't long before the Israelites were again slaves. For twenty terrible years, they served under King Jabin of Canaan. Sisera commanded Jabin's army. He was strong, cruel, and used his power to make the Israelites' lives miserable.

But even though God's people forgot Him again and again, God did not forget them. When Israel cried out to Him for help, He listened. He responded with kindness, and once again trained a judge to save them from their misery.

Under King Jabin, Sisera built a powerful army. In addition to 20,000 soldiers, he had 900 iron chariots. Each chariot was pulled by one or two strong, mighty horses. Chariots often had razor-sharp blades coming off the wheels, which meant no one could even get close, or else they'd get hurt, and might even die! Each chariot had two soldiers: one to drive and one to shoot arrows at their enemies. Everyone thought Sisera's army was unbeatable. So, when Israel cried out for help, they probably hoped God would send 1,000 chariots with 2,000 horses, or an army with 30,000 soldiers, or at least a warrior, to save them.

But instead, God used a woman named Deborah. She was already a leader in Israel; in fact, she was a judge, like we think of the word today. Deborah helped her people by making decisions when there were arguments. She answered questions like: *who is the rightful owner of this?* Or, *who has to pay this money?* Or, *what does or doesn't this law mean?* Deborah was wise, fair, and bold.

One day God gave her a message, and she sent word for a military leader named Barak to come visit her. She told him, "God has given me a command for you. The time has come for us to be slaves no longer. Prepare for battle. Take 10,000 men with you up to Mount Tabor. I will get Sisera's army to come to you, and you will defeat them."

Barak knew Deborah told the truth, and he didn't doubt God's message. But then he thought of Sisera's 900 chariots. Barak thought of each of them being pulled by a galloping horse, while blade-fixed wheels slashed and killed the men he led. He thought of the archers in each chariot shooting arrows with point-blank precision.

Then he thought of his own army of 10,000 soldiers marching on foot and carrying whatever weapons they had made for themselves. Barak was terrified. He said to Deborah, "I'll do what God has told you, but only if you come with me."

Deborah replied, "I'll go, but know this: Because you are too scared to lead alone, the honor of the final victory will go to a woman, not to you."

Together, Deborah and Barak led 10,000 men up to Mount Tabor. Sisera found out that the Israelites were there, prepared for battle. So Sisera gathered all 900 of his iron chariots and the rest of his army to meet them. He thought about his undefeated chariots, his unbeatable horses, and his unafraid soldiers.

Then Sisera thought of his opponents: 10,000 Israelite soldiers on foot. He must have laughed thinking about how the Israelites didn't stand a chance!

But God's mighty hand led Sisera's army on a path that was much too hilly and far too rocky for their chariots. This misstep allowed Barak to lead his men on a charge down the mountain. Every soldier in Sisera's army was defeated: chariot drivers, archers, and foot soldiers.

Sisera saw that he was going to lose the battle and escaped. He ran and ran until he came to a tent belonging to Heber. Heber was an Israelite but was known for supporting King Jabin. Heber wasn't at home, but his wife Jael was. She saw Sisera, breathless and frightened, and invited him to rest in her tent. "Come on in," she said, "Make yourself at home and rest here."

Sisera was relieved. He knew Heber supported the king, and he knew that Barak wouldn't look for him inside a woman's tent. He asked for a drink, and Jael gave him one. Then he asked her to stand guard at the door. Jael agreed and told him that if anyone came by her tent asking, "Is anyone at home?" she would say, "No."

So Sisera, exhausted, fell asleep, thinking he was safe.

What Sisera didn't know is that Jael, unlike her husband, didn't support King Jabin. She loved God, and she supported the Israelites.

That night, as Sisera slept, Jael killed him.

When Barak arrived, Jael led him inside her tent. Barak saw that the last man standing in Sisera's army, Sisera himself, had been defeated by a woman. Just as Deborah had said.

God had heard the cries of His people and had made a way. He delivered them from their captors and had once again freed them from slavery.

Deborah and Barak sang a song of joy:

Listen up, you rulers and kings of the land.
Hear our song for the one true God, the God of Israel,
and make music with us. Sing along!
You, oh Lord, are mighty. Your strength is unmatched.
At Your voice, the earth shakes and
the clouds rain down rivers.
When You march, the mountains leap before You.
You delivered us from our enemies and
brought us into the Promised Land.
But we did not follow Your commands, and war came.
Everything was dangerous, and
we were scared to leave our homes.
You took care of us. You made a way.
You raised up Deborah, a wise mother, as our brave leader.
And You raised up Barak, a strong warrior,
as her faithful helper.
You defeated the soldiers and crashed the chariots.
You sent Sisera to the tent of his enemy.
You raised up Jael, to deliver the final blow.
You saved us. You gave us the victory.
Defeat all Your enemies, oh Lord.
And let those who love You shine like the sun
in all its light and all its strength.

Deborah wisely encouraged her people to live by God's laws instead of their own. And...they did! For forty freedom-filled years, Israel was at peace. Until...

Kaleidoscope Corner
Music and Poetry

The entire chapter of Judges 5 is a song that Deborah and Barak sang together praising God for their victory over King Jabin's army. It's a beautiful example of Hebrew poetry, and one of the earliest-written-down pieces of the Bible, dating to the 9th or 10th century BC. (BC means "before Christ," and is a measure of time by counting the years before Jesus Christ was born.)

The Israelites might have played lutes, lyres, or zithers, instruments common at that time, as they sang. This song not only praised God in that moment, but during a time before many people could read or write, it helped the Israelites remember and tell the story of God's protection to their children, and to their children, and to their children.

In addition to many in the book of Psalms, other examples of praise and victory songs in the Old Testament can be found in Exodus 15, Numbers 21, 2 Samuel 22, and Ezra 3.

Spend some time in your Bible reading the praise and victory songs mentioned here. Do they remind you of any songs you sing today?

Now read a praise song in the New Testament, as well, Revelation 5:8-14. How does this song remind you of the Old Testament songs? What makes it different?

GIDEON & THE FIRE

JUDGES 6

Sadly, Deborah eventually died. Just like the judges before her, she had not trained a leader to take over after her. So again, the people of Israel made their own rules about what was right and what was wrong. Again, they sinned against God and worked themselves into a giant, sinful, sad mess.

During this time, the Israelites made their homes in caves and forts in the mountains. They knew the people of Midian overpowered them. But to survive, the Israelites still had to raise their animals and grow their food. And they couldn't do that in caves or forts. What were they to do?

Every year they came out of their caves to plant. The Midianites were from the desert where crops didn't grow well, and so they would watch all year while the Israelites planted crops and watched them grow. The Midianites watched as the Israelites tended to their flocks of sheep, herds of cattle and, droves of donkeys. The Midianites watched while the Israelites did the hard work of the harvest.

When the harvest was finished, though, the Midianites attacked. The Midianites took all of the food and animals they wanted and destroyed the rest. Nothing remained for the Israelites.

This treatment went on for seven, shameful years. After seven years of destruction and hunger, the Israelites finally cried out for God's help. God had seen their years of sin. It made Him sad, and it made Him angry.

At first, God sent a prophet who delivered a tough message from the Lord, "I delivered you from Egypt. I freed you from slavery. I brought you to this land. I rescued you from every enemy you've had. You promised to love me most and to obey my laws. But you broke your promise."

Many Israelites were starving. But there was one, a farmer named Gideon, who had found a way to keep his harvest safe from the Midianites. As soon as he collected his grain, he hurried it into a winepress, a pit meant to smash grapes into wine. The winepress was hidden and protected from the land around it. There, Gideon was busy separating the grains of good, useable wheat from the useless shells, called "chaff." (Check out the next Kaleidoscope Corner at the end of this chapter for more!)

An angel of the Lord appeared to Gideon in his winepress and said, "The Lord is with you, mighty warrior."

Gideon looked at himself, a farmer of a small piece of land, hiding in a secret pit as he frantically tried to save his crop from his enemies to have enough food for his family. He was confused.

"Sir," Gideon protested, "if the Lord is with us, why am I in this pit? I've heard what the Lord did when he brought our ancestors from Egypt and into this land. But where is He now? The Midianites completely overpower us. He's abandoned us; He's not with me."

The angel of the Lord said to Gideon, "I haven't abandoned them. I'm giving them to you. Go, be strong, and save Israel."

Now Gideon wasn't just confused; he was scared! "Lord!" he cried. "How am I supposed to save Israel?! I am a farmer of a small amount of land from the weakest tribe, and I'm the smallest one even in my own ordinary family!"

"I'll be with you," God promised, "and you'll defeat every single Midianite. All of them together, at the same time."

Gideon didn't understand that because he was speaking with a messenger of the Lord, he was actually speaking with the Lord Himself. "If God is honoring me like this," Gideon said, "please give me a sign that it's really Him talking to me. Wait here while I go make an offering."

While the angel of the Lord waited, Gideon prepared some food. He killed and cooked a young goat. While the goat cooked, Gideon took some flour, made from the ground-up wheat he'd threshed, and adding water, made a flatbread. After everything was ready, he put the meat in a basket. He poured the broth that had simmered around the meat in a jar. He brought the basket of meat, the jar of broth, and the bread out to the angel under an oak tree.

The angel told him, "Put the meat and the bread on this rock. Then pour out the broth." Gideon did as the angel asked.

Then the angel of the Lord lifted His walking stick and touched the meat and the bread with it. Suddenly, a flame blazed from the rock, burning up the meat and the bread. Then, just as quickly as He'd appeared, the angel of the Lord disappeared.

Gideon knew then that he had indeed seen the Lord, and he was terrified. But God comforted him, saying, "Have peace. Don't be afraid. You're not going to die because you saw my angel."

Then Gideon built an altar, a place and focus point for worship, on that rock under the oak tree and called it "The Lord is Peace."

After Gideon had built an altar to Him that night, the true God, the Lord told Gideon to go destroy his father's altar to Baal, a false god. Because he was afraid, Gideon waited until late at night, when everyone was asleep. He took ten men with him, and they destroyed the Baal altar. In its place, they built another altar and made a sacrifice to the one true God.

The next morning, the Israelites asked each other, "What happened here? Who did this?"

When they found out that Gideon was the one who led the mission the night before, they went to Gideon's father, Joash, and demanded, "Bring your son to us! Don't hide him. He has torn down the Baal altar and built another in its place. He has to pay for this; so, he must die."

Joash had built the Baal altar himself. But he wanted to protect his son, and maybe, deep down, he knew the truth about who Baal was, and who God is.

Joash said to the men, "Are you trying to get revenge for your god Baal? If he's as powerful as you say he is, let him avenge himself." The people were convinced, and they agreed. They called on Baal to get revenge for what Gideon had done.

Do you know how Baal got revenge?

He didn't. He couldn't.

God had much more planned for Gideon.

Kaleidoscope Corner
Wheat and Chaff

Have you ever heard the saying "separate the wheat from the chaff?" Separating the small grains of good, useable wheat from their useless shells, called chaff, is a necessary process that's done today mostly by giant machines called combine harvesters. But in ancient Israel, this process, called threshing, was a tedious and time-consuming task. It required patience.

Today, if someone gives the advice to "separate the wheat from the chaff," it means to keep the good and ignore the rest. Can you think of a situation where it would be good to "separate the wheat from the chaff?"

A TRUMPET & A FLEECE

JUDGES 6:33-8:35

Now in the Valley of Jezreel, near the Israelites, the Midianites were camping. God's Spirit came to Gideon and told him to blow a trumpet. When he did, all the people of Israel knew it was time. They journeyed from all directions and gathered together near a spring of water.

Gideon had heard God's voice. He'd seen the angel of the Lord command fire. Gideon saw how God had protected him from his own people after destroying the Baal altar. He knew that the time had come to lead God's people to victory.

But...he was scared.

The smallest farmer from an unimportant family from the weakest tribe of Israel asked God for another sign.

"Look, God," Gideon said, "if you're really going to use me to save all of Israel, do this for me first. I'll put this blanket - this wool fleece - down on the floor of my winepress. If the fleece is wet tomorrow morning, but the ground around it is dry, I'll know what you want me to do."

When Gideon rose early the next morning, he touched the ground all around the blanket. It was as dry as the desert his ancestors had wandered in for forty years. Then he nervously picked up the fleece. It was as wet as the sea that God had parted for those same ancestors! Taking the fleece with both hands, he twisted it, squeezed it, and wrung out a bowlful of water.

All day, Gideon imagined the task before him, and remembered how the Midianites overpowered him and his people again and again, every year, for seven years. Gideon thought, "Maybe the wet fleece wasn't a sign after all. If the fleece soaked up all the dew from the ground, it would make sense that only the blanket was wet. So maybe God wasn't telling me anything after all."

So, one more time, the doubtful, smallest farmer from an unimportant family from the weakest tribe of Israel asked God for a sign.

"Please don't be mad at me, God," said Gideon, "but tonight I'll put this fleece out again. Can you soak the ground around it, but leave the fleece dry?"

And God did.

The next morning, Gideon's bare feet sunk into the soaked ground with a squish. Gideon he worked his way through the mud, and when he picked up the dry fleece he knew the time had come.

Early the next morning, Gideon looked over at his men who were camped near the spring where they'd gathered. There were 32,000 of them. Together, they were planning to battle 135,000 Midianites! But God told Gideon, "There are too many men in your army."

"Too many?!" Gideon must have thought.

The Lord continued, "I don't want Israel to win this fight and congratulate themselves on their strength. They have to understand that I am their strength."

So, Gideon told the men, as God instructed him, "If you are shaking with fear, go home."

22,000 men went home. 10,000 stayed at the camp.

10,000 to battle 135,000.

God told Gideon, "10,000 men is still too many. Take them down to the stream, and I'll tell you what to do next."

So Gideon took the men down to the water and told them to take a drink.

Some of the men plunged their faces straight into the stream to get their drink. Others knelt and used their cupped hands to bring the water to their mouths.

God told Gideon to send away everyone who had put their faces in the stream. After those men went home, only 300 men remained.

300 to battle 135,000.

That night, Gideon didn't have time to ask for another sign. God told Gideon, "I know you're afraid. Take your man Purah, and go down to the Midianite camp. Listen to what they say, and you'll know that I am with you. I will make you brave."

That night, Gideon and Purah snuck down to the camp. It seemed endlessly filled with tents of soldiers. Even their camels appeared to outnumber the very grains of sand on the shore.

As they tiptoed past a tent, they overheard one Midianite man telling his friend about a dream, "I dreamed that a round loaf of barley bread rolled into our camp. It struck the tent with such force that the tent collapsed."

Another friend told the first the meaning of his dream: "The loaf is a symbol for Gideon the farmer, the son of Joash the Israelite. His God is going to give him this whole camp."

Then, just as God had said, Gideon - the smallest farmer from an unimportant family from the weakest tribe of Israel - suddenly felt brave. He worshipped God, and he and Purah returned to their camp.

"Wake up!" Gideon exclaimed to his men. "The Lord has given us the Midianites!" He divided the 300 men into three groups and gave them their battle tools: trumpets, jars, and torches. These, of course, were no ordinary weapons!

"Watch me," Gideon told the men, "and do what I do." Gideon covered his torch with the jar, so that no one would see the light from the fire.

When they got to the edge of the Midianite camp, Gideon blew his trumpet and smashed the jar so that the torch's light shone through. All around the Midianite camp, the three groups of Israelite men did the same.

"For the Lord and for Gideon!" they shouted.

The Midianites weren't expecting this. They were so confused and so scared that they actually attacked each other. Without any of Gideon's 300 men using a single sword, God defeated the Midianites.

Before the battle, Gideon recognized both God's power and His kindness. He worshipped God. After the Midianites were defeated, the Israelites wanted Gideon to be their king. Gideon told them, "I will not be a king here on earth. We have a King in heaven."

But then Gideon did something strange: he collected gold and jewels from what the Israelites had stolen from the defeated Midianites. Gideon used the stolen treasure to made an ephod for himself, which is a type of vest worn only by priests. According to God's laws, Gideon wasn't allowed to make or wear an ephod. But, he did it anyway.

Maybe he wanted the people to look at the ephod and remember how God had delivered them from the Midianites. But whatever his reasons might have been, the people soon loved the beautiful creation, more than the beautiful Creator. Again, God's people began to break God's laws.

But as He always does, God kept His promise, and while Gideon lived as Israel's fifth judge, the Midianites were tamed. For forty restful years, the Israelites again were at peace.

Kaleidoscope Corner
Battles

There are many stories of battles and wars in the Old Testament. Just to name a few, you'll find some in Joshua 6, Judges 7, 1 Samuel 4, and 1 Samuel 17. Many of these battles and wars brought glory to an earthly king, who was temporary and imperfect. As all earthly leaders do, the kings or judges in the Old Testament died. But the New Testament teaches us about our eternal king, Jesus.

In what ways do the earthly judges in this book point to Jesus? In what ways do they remind us that they are not Jesus?

THE THORN BUSH

JUDGES 8:29-9:57

During Gideon's lifetime, he had many children, including 70 sons! Gideon also had a son with another woman who wasn't his wife. That son's name was Abimelech, which meant "my father is king."

Gideon died at an old age and, as you could guess, the Israelites quickly forgot what God had done for them. They made their own rules about what was right and what was wrong, and they sinned and worshipped false gods. They forgot Gideon's story: how the smallest farmer from an unimportant family from the weakest tribe of Israel was used by God to protect an entire nation from their enemies' evil deeds. When the people of Israel began to talk about who would be their next judge, Abimelech decided that it was his moment.

Abimelech was a power-hungry man. He did not want to be a judge of Israel. He wanted to be king.

"Why shouldn't I be king?" he asked his people. "My father has 70 sons who will think they are in charge. They'll all disagree about what should happen, and then we'll be in such a mess. Isn't it better if I am your only leader, instead of having seventy weak men pretend to be leaders, and confuse us all?"

Unfortunately, the people listened to Abimelech.

35

To make sure no one would challenge his claim to the throne, the cold-hearted Abimelech set out to murder all 70 of his half-brothers.

And...he almost succeeded.

The youngest of the 70 brothers, Jotham, got away. Jotham hid until the people were gathering to give Abimelech a king's crown.

Jotham climbed to the top of a mountain and shouted at the people who had gathered, "Listen to me, everyone, so that God will listen to you!"

Then Jotham told a story:

> One day a grove of trees decided that an olive tree should be their king. They said to the olive tree, "You're our king!" But the olive tree replied, "I can't be your king. I'm busy producing olives. That's my job. And I need to do my job because everyone needs the oil that comes from my olives."

> So, the trees decided that a fig tree should be their king. They said to the fig tree, "You're our king!" But the fig tree replied, "I don't want to be your king. I'd have to give up producing sweet and juicy and delicious figs, and I won't do that just to say I'm in charge."

> So, the trees decided a grapevine should be their king. They said to the grapevine, "You're our king!" But the grapevine replied, "I won't be your king. I already have an important job: I make grapes for wine that brings cheer."

> So, then the trees went to a thorn bush. They said to the prickly bush, "You're our king." And the thorn bush replied, "Of course I'm your king! In fact, if you support me, you should come and rest under the safety of my thorns. If you don't support me, stay where you are, and I'll send fire to destroy whatever trees are left standing out there without me."

Jotham told this story to warn the people that crowning Abimelech as their king was a huge mistake. Jotham knew that power-hungry leaders never believed they had enough. He knew that Abimelech would keep destroying anything or anyone who was in the way of him getting more power. Unfortunately, the people ignored Jotham.

Israel crowned Abimelech as their king. For three sinful years, he ruled over Israel. During that dark time, Abimelech made his own rules about what was right and what was wrong.

So did the people.

They put themselves first. They lied, cheated, stole, and were constantly fighting. As Jotham had rightly predicted, Abimelech was determined to destroy anything or anyone who was in the way of him getting more power.

After three years as king of Israel, Abimelech led soldiers on a cruel attack of cities who disagreed with him, just like the thorn bush in Jotham's story. After destroying the entire city of Shechem, and even burning down the temple of his people, he scattered salt where the city ruins smoldered, marking his victory. Abimelech was ruthless!

Next up on his tour of fire and destruction, Abimelech went to a city called Thebez. Many of the townspeople had locked themselves in a strong tower. As Abimelech prepared to storm the tower, a woman on the roof dropped a heavy millstone on his head. Abimelech knew he would die, but was worried that people would remember him as a weak leader who was killed by a woman and her stone. That thought humiliated him so much that with his last words, he instructed his battle servant to make it look like he'd died in a fierce battle instead.

Abimelech did not worship, honor, or fear the one true God. God had not chosen Abimelech to be a leader of Israel. Still, He allowed Abimelech to come to power anyway. God dealt with the darkness of Abimelech in His timing as He raised up another judge for Israel.

Kaleidoscope Corner
Parables

In the New Testament of the Bible, Jesus often told people parables, or simple stories that teach an important lesson about life and faith. There are also some parables in the Old Testament, like the one that Jotham told about the trees choosing a king for themselves, found in Judges 9.
Some other examples of Old Testament parables are:
- The Poor Man's Ewe (2 Samuel 12)
- The Wasted Vineyard (Isaiah 5)
- Two Eagles and a Vine (Ezekiel 17)

Which parable from the Bible is your favorite? What does it teach you about life and faith?

THE MYSTERY JUDGES

JUDGES
10:1-5 & 12:8-15

Five of the six judges of Israel who followed after Abimelech's time as king don't get a lot of space in the Bible. We know almost nothing about most of them, and what we do know is a little bit strange!

In the tribe of Issachar, there was a man named Dodo. Dodo had a son named Puah. Puah had a son named Tola. Tola rose up as the sixth judge to save Israel and was their leader for 23 years.

From Gilead, Jair, Israel's seventh judge, provided peace for Israel for 22 years. He had 30 sons, and they rode around on 30 donkeys.

Jephthah was Israel's eighth judge, and we do know a lot about him. So, we'll come back to him in the next chapter.

Ibzan, the ninth judge of Israel, was from Bethlehem. His 30 sons married 30 wives from outside of their tribe. He led Israel for seven years.

Elon, from the tribe of Zebulun, was Israel's tenth judge. He led for ten years.

From the city of Pirathon, Hillel's son Abdon became Israel's eleventh judge. His 40 sons and 30 grandsons rode around on 70 donkeys. Abdon led Israel for eight years.

Kaleidoscope Corner
Weather, Land, & Farming

Many people imagine Israel to be a vast, dry, hot desert. Some of Israel is covered by desert land, but in other parts of Israel, rivers flow, making the soil around them good for crops. They have a warm dry season and a cool rainy season every year.

People in ancient Israel grew large crops of barley, wheat, beans, figs, grapes, and olives. From those crops, they made bread, roasted grains, wine, and oil. Figs and grapes were sometimes eaten fresh, and they were also dried, to be eaten all year. Smaller gardens provided vegetables during parts of the year. Sometimes dates, pomegranates, and nuts were grown and eaten, as well.

The Israelites during the time of the Judges raised flocks of sheep and goats. The sheep provided wool. The goats' milk was used to make cheese and butter. The Israelites had donkeys and horses to help with transportation and work. In addition to the animals, people raised and took care of foxes, wolves, bears, and even lions could be found in the wild in ancient Israel.

What stories in the Old Testament can you think of that teach us about the land they lived on? The weather they experienced? The food they ate? The animals they encountered?

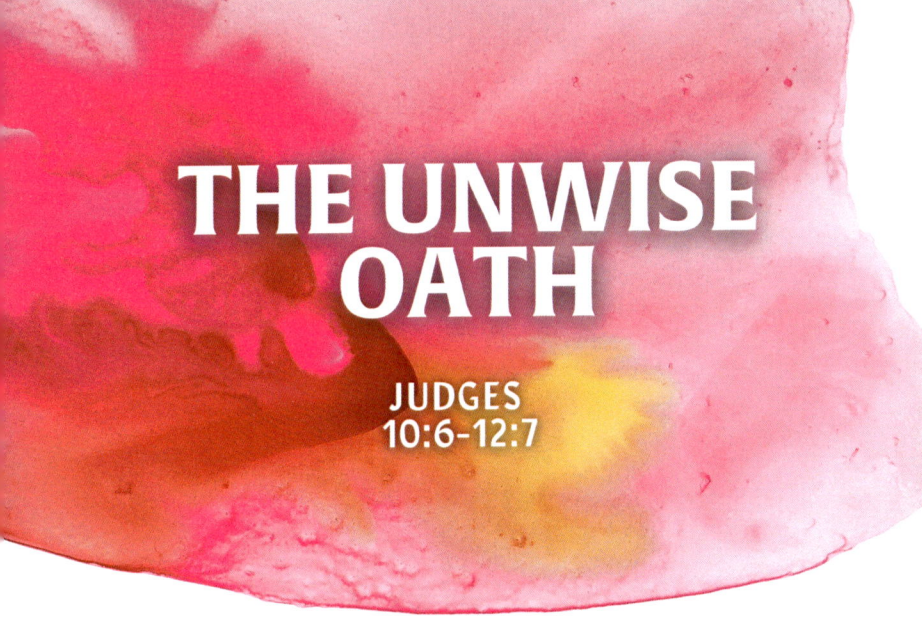

THE UNWISE OATH

JUDGES 10:6-12:7

Back to Israel's eighth judge: Jephthah. Again, the people of Israel made their own rules about what was right and what was wrong. Eventually (you guessed it!), they worked themselves into another giant, sinful, sad mess. They worshipped the gods that everyone around them created and ignored the one true God.

Of course, God saw their sin. It made him very sad and angry. Again, as a good father, God allowed their actions to have consequences. For 18 long years, Israel's enemies defeated them over and over.

Throughout the book of Judges, when things went well for the Israelites, they praised the false gods they'd created. But when things went badly, they begged for mercy - help they didn't deserve - from the real God they'd ignored.

One time, though, they got it right.

When the Israelites again cried out to God for help, this time, they first confessed their sin.

God heard them and replied, "When seven armies from seven nations treated you with cruelty, you called out to me. I saved you, didn't I? But every time I saved you, you forgot me. You wanted my protection and my blessings, but not my laws. Go and ask the gods you've created to help you. Let them save you."

Even though they hadn't lived like it, the Israelites still knew the truth. The created gods couldn't save them because they weren't real. So again, they confessed their sins to the one real God.

They understood that they deserved God's anger, not His protection. They knew they had work to do, so they cleaned the false gods out of their homes, out of their towns, and out of their hearts. Again, they turned back to the one true God.

God watched as His people softened and turned towards him. In His kindness, he couldn't bear to watch His children suffer any longer.

In His power, God raised up Jephthah, a son of Gilead from the tribe also named Gilead, as Israel's eighth judge. He was a mighty warrior, but he was also an outcast. His own half-brothers rejected him because their mother, Gilead's wife, was not Jephthah's mother.

"You may as well leave," they told Jephthah one day. "When our father dies, we'll make sure you don't get anything."

And so, Jephthah left.

But when the Ammonites made it known that they were preparing for a war against the Israelites, Jephthah's half brothers and other leaders from Gilead went to find him. When they reached him, they made a request, "Come and be our commander. We need to fight the Ammonites."

Jephthah replied, "You hated me. You kicked me out of our father's house. Now you decide to come to me?"

The men of Gilead told Jephthah that they needed him. They let him know that if he helped them by commanding their army, and defeating their enemy, that he would be their leader.

Remembering how God had mercy on the Israelites by saving them over and over and over again, Jephthah went with the men of Gilead and became Israel's leader.

Jephthah sent messengers to the Ammonite king, asking, "Why have you attacked us? What have we done to deserve this?"

The Ammonite king answered through the messengers, "When your people came out of Egypt, you took our land. Give it back, and there will be peace."

Jephthah sent them back with a final message, "The land we now have wasn't yours to begin with. It belonged to the Amorites, not the Ammonites. Also, the one true God gave us this land. What land did your gods give you? We've lived in this land for 300 years! Why would you decide to fight for it now?"

But the king of Ammon ignored Jephthah's message and moved toward battle. The Spirit of the Lord came over Jephthah, and he also prepared his men for battle.

God was already with Jephthah, and Jephthah didn't need to do anything but trust. But in his fear and hurry, he made an unneeded vow to the Lord. Jephthah promised, "If you deliver the Ammonites into my hands, whoever comes out of my home first to welcome me upon my safe return, I will sacrifice to you."

Jephthah would soon regret this promise.

As you may have guessed, God did help Israel win the battle. When Jephthah returned home, the door to his house opened, and he remembered his promise.

Out of the door came, not a goat or a sheep as he'd probably expected, but his daughter...his only child.

But instead of meeting her warm welcome with joy, Jephthah remembered his unwise oath to the Lord. He fell to his knees, tore his clothes, and with tears falling down his face, cried, "Why did you have to be the one to come out of our house first? I made a promise to God that I can't break."

Jephthah knew that he had to honor his promise. So, he explained to his only child that she would be sacrificed, not as an animal offering, but in complete service to the Lord. Even though it wasn't the life that either of them had wanted for her, they kept Jephthah's promise. His daughter never married and never had children. She spent the rest of her life in complete service to God.

Israel had won a great battle, and there should have been celebration and joy. But instead, the people of Israel turned against one another. Jealousy over who had more important roles during the battle consumed God's people. The jealousy led to fighting, and the fighting led to murder.

Jephthah was a mighty warrior who led Israel to a great victory. But he was also quick to speak and act, and slow to think and pray. As a result, many of God's people died during the six sort-of-steady years that Jephthah was judge over Israel. Once again, when Jephthah died, the people of Israel made all of their own rules about what was right and what was wrong.

Kaleidoscope Corner
Language

The Israelites from Ephraim were causing lots of trouble for Jephthah. So, Jephthah's men, in order to capture as many Ephraimites as possible, camped out by a stream. In order to cross the stream, anyone who wanted to pass had to say the word stream, which was shibboleth. Most Israelites said the letters "s" and "h" together, making a "sh" sound. But Ephraimites ignored the "h" and pronounced the word like *sibboleth*. So, if someone said they weren't from Ephraim, but then said *sibboleth*, Jephthah's men knew they were lying.

It would be like if today, you held up the letter "z" on a card. An American would say the name of the letter as "zee." But a Canadian would say the name of the letter as "zed." You might not be able to tell their accents apart until you heard them say what letter was on the card. Like *shibboleth*, the way people say the name of the letter "z" can be a sure way to find out the truth about where someone is from.

Your accent, or the way you talk, may be strong, and tell a lot about you, or it may tell nothing about you. What else about your words - and how you say them - tells people what they should know about you?

SAMSON'S MIGHTY RISE

JUDGES 13-15

For 40 fearful years, Israel once again chose their rules over God's rules. They sinned and did evil, and God allowed them to hurt. The Philistines, who lived on the land between Israel's tribes and the great sea, battled the Israelites over and over again. The Philistines had more people and more weapons, so again and again the Israelites lost battle after battle.

During that time, an older couple from the tribe of Dan got a special message from a special visitor. The couple had wanted children, and waited for years, but never had any. Now, they were too old...or they thought they were. But as only God can do, and as He often does - He takes "can't," and changes it to "already did."

An angel of the Lord came to the wife and told her that she would have an extraordinary son. From that day on, she and the son she would soon have were to follow special rules meant for those who did special service. They were to be Nazirites, people set apart for God (more on this in Kaleidoscope Corner at the end of the chapter!).

On the angel's second visit, the husband asked what the angel's name was. At that time, knowing someone's name usually meant that you understood who they were: their family, their beliefs, and their culture.

But the angel of the Lord replied, "Why would you ask my name? It's so wonderful that even if I told you, you couldn't possibly understand."

Then the man and his wife made an offering for the angel. They put some fresh grain on a rock and sacrificed a young goat there. As the couple watched, the fire from the offering blazed through the sky and straight to heaven. The angel of the Lord returned home through the fire.

When the couple saw this, they understood that the angel of the Lord was right. This was all too wonderful for them to understand. They fell down on their faces and worshipped the Lord.

Months later, their son was born. They named him Samson. He grew up strong, and God honored Samson with tremendous strength.

When Samson grew up, he told his parents that he had found the woman he wanted to marry. The woman was a Philistine. What was Samson thinking!? The Philistines were the Israelites' worst enemies. God's law for the Israelites even warned them against marrying Philistines.

Of course, Samson's parents didn't like this idea. But Samson convinced them, and God allowed it. While this marriage wasn't God's plan for Samson's best life, God still used it as part of His plan for the Israelites.

Samson and his parents traveled to another town to meet Samson's future wife. On their way, Samson wandered off from his parents for a while. A young lion suddenly appeared in Samson's path. What was Samson to do?

The spirit of God came upon Samson, and he killed the lion with his bare hands. Samson didn't tell anyone about the lion.

God honored Samson with great strength, and that strength eventually made him famous. But just because he was strong and famous, doesn't mean he was perfect.

Because Samson was a Nazarite, he wasn't supposed to touch a dead body. This rule meant he shouldn't have killed the lion with his hands.

Samson also had an out-of-control temper. Many times, he became angry and destructive. But then he would try to hide his anger, like when he kept his fight with the lion a secret. Samson was not just angry, he was also deceitful.

A little while later, Samson walked the same path from his parents' home to the home of his future wife's family. On the way, he saw the remains of the lion he'd killed. Some bees had built a hive inside, and he scooped out the honey for himself and his family. But because he wasn't supposed to touch a dead body, he didn't tell them where he got honey.

Samson married the Philistine woman, and on the first day of their wedding feast he told everyone a riddle:

> Out of the eater,
> came something to eat.
> Out of the strong,
> came something sweet.

He told those gathered that if they could solve the riddle, and tell him what he was talking about, he'd give them 30 fancy pieces of linen clothing. But if no one could explain it, they would have to give him the clothing.

On the fourth day of the wedding feast, the guests said to Samson's new wife, "We need your help. We don't have 30 fancy pieces of linen clothing to give your new husband, and we won't let him rob us. You have to get him to tell you the answer to the riddle, or else you and your family will be sorry."

So, Samson's new wife went to him, crying her eyes out, saying, "Why do you hate me? You've given my family and friends a riddle, and you haven't even told me the answer. If you loved me, you'd tell me."

Samson wouldn't tell her that day, or the next, or for the rest of the seven-day wedding feast. But she continued to cry and begged him for the answer every day. So late in the afternoon, on the seventh day of their wedding feast, Samson told his wife about the lion he'd killed whose body had become a home for bees. She told her family and friends. Right before the sun set, the wedding guests answered Samson's riddle:

> What could be sweeter than honey?
> What could be stronger than a lion?

Samson was furious. "You tricked my wife, and you tricked me!" Samson fumed as he left his own wedding feast. His anger consumed him. To pay the wedding guests their 30 fancy pieces of linen clothing, Samson killed 30 men. He robbed them of their possessions, and gave the clothes he stole from them to the wedding guests.

Samson stormed away from his own wedding feast, and his wife. So, her father allowed her to marry someone else.

Sometime later, Samson went to visit the woman he thought was his wife. When he found out that his wife had married someone else, Samson again was overcome with rage. To get revenge, Samson caught 300 foxes, tied their tails together, and attached a burning torch to each pair. When he let them loose in the Philistine fields, the fire spread and completely burned up the fields. Their crops of grains, olives, and grapes were all ruined.

This scene was the beginning of a war between the Israelites and the Philistines. In each battle, the Spirit of God came on Samson and gave him strength that could not be beaten. After so many years of the Philistines winning fight after fight against the Israelites, the Israelites finally tamed them! The Philistines realized that even entire armies of their men were no match for Samson. For 20 safe years, God continued to give Samson strength and he led Israel and protected God's people.

But eventually, Samson's weaknesses led to sin, and his sins led him to defeat.

Kaleidoscope Corner
Culture & Religion

In Numbers 6, the Bible explains the special set of rules for Nazirites. They could not drink wine or vinegar. Nazirites could not eat grapes or raisins: any food that came from a grapevine. They could not touch a dead body or visit a grave. And, Nazirites could not cut their hair, so they often wore long braids, or let their hair grow into dreadlocks. They also had to follow special rules about where, when, and how to give offerings to God.

As you read about Samson, ask yourself, in what ways did Samson honor the rules that set him apart as a Nazirite? In what ways did he break the rules? In what ways are we set apart today as those who follow Jesus?

SAMSON'S MIGHTY FALL

JUDGES 16

As time passed, Samson fell in love with a woman named Delilah. When the Philistine leaders heard this, they went to her, bribed her with money, and told her, "We must destroy Samson. We need to know the secret of his strength. You're going to find out, and then you're going to tell us."

So, when he came to visit her, Delilah asked Samson, "How are you so strong? What would it take to defeat you?"

Samson lied, "If someone tied me up with seven fresh strings - the kind used to make bows - I wouldn't be able to get out of them."

Delilah told the Philistines. That night, they brought seven fresh bowstrings to her house. The Philistines tied Samson up while he slept, and then Delilah woke him up. Samson snapped the bowstrings as easily as if they were blades of dried grass.

Delilah asked Samson, "Why have you lied to me and embarrassed me? Don't you trust me? Please tell me the secret to your strength."

Samson lied again, "If someone takes brand new ropes that have never been used and ties me up, I'll be as weak as any other man."

Delilah once again told the Philistines. That night, they brought brand new ropes to her house. The Philistines tied Samson up while he slept, and then Delilah woke him up. He snapped the ropes like they were tiny pieces of thread.

Delilah told Samson, "You're making a fool of me! Tell me the truth. What's the secret to your strength?"

Samson lied again, "If you weave the braids of my hair together with fabric on a loom, and use a pin to secure it, I'll lose all my strength."

That night, Delilah herself tried it. While he slept, she braided Samson's hair together with the fabric on the loom. She secured it with a pin and woke him up. Samson sat up, easily pulling the pin and fabric away from the loom.

Delilah cried to Samson, "Why do you hate me? If you loved me, you'd tell me the truth. How are you so strong?"

Delilah wept and begged day after day, and finally, Samson told her...part of the truth, "Since I was born, I have never cut my hair. If someone were to shave my head, all of my strength would be gone."

Delilah, for the final time, told the Philistines what Samson had told her. That night, while he slept, one of the Philistines paid Delilah and then shaved the long braids from Samson's head. When Delilah woke him up, he laughed to himself and thought, "I'll break whatever they've tied me with yet again."

But Samson didn't know that his strength was gone.

You see, the secret of Samson's strength wasn't in his hair. His strength was God's Spirit in him. He was supposed to be set apart from birth, but in his weakness, he sinned against God. Samson made his own rules about what was right and what was wrong. And so, when Samson awoke, God's Spirit left him, and he was captured.

The mighty warrior and judge of Israel became a slave. The Philistines took out all their anger over the past twenty years on Samson. They beat him, tortured him, and blinded him. They bound his wrists and ankles in bronze shackles and put him in prison. There, he was made to grind grain into flour, a job usually given to poor and weak women. Day after day, Samson lived with the consequences of his choices.

One day, the important Philistines were having a party to celebrate their false god, who they believed had given them victory over Samson and the Israelites. The people came to feast in their temple, and when they had their fill of rich food and drink, they shouted for Samson. "Bring out the failure! He can entertain us with his strength!"

The people cheered as Samson, once a mighty warrior and strong ruler, and now a blind slave, was brought out among them. They didn't know that while Samson had been grinding grain, he had also turned to God. Up until this point in his life, he used the name for knowing about Him anytime he talked about God, "Elohim." But as he stood in front of jeering Philistines, he called on God. This time, Samson used the name for knowing the Lord personally, "Yahweh."

"Lord, You are good and you are powerful," Samson prayed as the Philistines laughed and shouted and mocked and cheered. "Give me strength one more time."

The Spirit of God returned to Samson, and he was overcome once again with great strength. He pushed over the two pillars that held the temple upright, and that day, Samson died along with 3,000 Philistine leaders. They were crushed underneath the temple they'd built to worship their false god.

Samson's family collected his body and buried him in Israel, in the Promised Land, among the people he'd led.

ISRAEL FALLS

JUDGES 17-21

After Samson died, there were no more judges for Israel. For many years, the people of Israel failed to live as God's holy people. As they sinned against God over and over and over again, they fell deeper and deeper and deeper into trouble.

It's hard to find any examples of good choices or right living in the last five chapters of the book of Judges. One man stole from his mother. He returned the money, not because he realized he had done wrong, but because he heard his mother praying a curse over the thief, and he was scared. When he gave the money back to her, she used it to build altars to false gods.

One family kept a priest from doing his job of serving God's people by making him stay in their own home as some kind of good luck charm.

The leaders of one tribe viciously attacked and killed visitors who came to their town. God's people battled each other! Israel was at war with itself.

You would imagine that God's people would have learned by then that disobedience to the one true God always led to chaos. Sometimes the chaos didn't come to pass right away, but it always happened.

In His power and kindness, God had rescued the people of Israel from their sinful and sad messes over and over and over again.

But once again, the Israelites forgot what God had done for them.

Once again, everyone made their own rules about what was right and what was wrong.

And once again, they lived in a mess they'd created themselves.

It may seem like all hope was lost for the Israelites. But God was at work.

BUT GOD...

JUDGES 21:25
RUTH 1:1-2 & 4:16-22

Judges ends on a sad note...

> In those days, Israel had no king.
> Everyone did whatever they wanted.
> The people made their own rules about
> what was right and what was wrong.

Luckily for the Israelites, their story didn't end with the book of Judges. For over 300 years, God's people had worked themselves into mess after mess after mess.

But God wasn't finished with His people. While it seemed like every single Israelite had turned away from God, some still lived their lives remembering God's ways and keeping God's laws. They trusted Him to make the rules about what was right and what was wrong.

The rest of this book is the story of what God did for them and through them. We find their story in the Old Testament book right after Judges. The book is named after its main character: Ruth.

The book of Ruth is one of two books in the Bible that's named after a woman, and it's the only book named after a woman who wasn't from Israel. Ruth was from Moab.

You may remember that when Moab had a lazy and selfish king named Eglon, he made the Israelites his slaves. So, many of God's people would have thought that Ruth was their enemy. Sadly, most of God's people would have at least agreed that Ruth didn't matter very much.

But Ruth wasn't the Israelites' enemy. She wasn't God's enemy. She did matter. She mattered to Naomi, her mother-in-law, and to Boaz, the man who would become her husband.

Even more than that, of course, Ruth mattered to God.

Ruth didn't write her story down for us, and we aren't sure who did. But we are sure that every single word God left for us is important.

We can be sure that God wants us to know her story so that we'll know more of His story.

Ruth reminds us that God is still at work even when we are in the middle of hard things or bad situations. So, while learning about the book of Judges may have made us sad or frustrated or tired, learning about the book of Ruth should bring us joy. Because what was true for the Israelites, is still true for us now:

> The bad news is that the best times
> we have here on earth, don't last forever.
> But the good news is that the worst times,
> the sad messes,
> aren't here to stay.

How does Ruth's good story begin? Well, it starts like all good stories...with a mess.

PROMISE

RUTH 1

As you know, during the time of the Judges, Israel had no king. Everyone did whatever they wanted. God's people made their own rules about what was right and what was wrong. They sinned against God again and again.

For a time, God allowed His people to suffer. Their water sources dried up; their crops withered; their flocks died. They had nothing to eat or drink!

A man named Elimelech finally had enough and decided that it was time for his family to leave Israel. Elimelech and his wife Naomi, whose name meant sweet or pleasant, took their two sons, Mahlon and Chilion, and moved to Moab, a region on the other side of the sea. Moab was full of people the Israelites thought were their enemies, but Elimelech was desperate to find food for his family.

The good news is they did find food in Moab. The bad news is that sometime after the family arrived, Elimelech died.

After Elimelech died, his two sons married women from Moab, named Orpah and Ruth. The family had a place to live and food to eat as they called Moab "home" for about ten years.

Elimelech (dead)

Naomi

Ruth

Mahlon (dead)

Chilion (dead)

Orpah

Naomi probably prayed during those years that her time of suffering would soon be over. She'd lost her home and her husband. For many, it would have been more than they could bear. But sadly, Naomi's bad situation was about to get worse.

Before either of them had any children, both of her sons, Mahlon and Chilion, died.

Suddenly, Naomi, Orpah, and Ruth were all widows. At that time, being a woman without a husband and children meant that you were not just poor but also without much hope. Women, at that time, couldn't own land and didn't plant fields or raise animals. How would they survive? Naomi, consumed with worry by this question, decided that the time had come to return to Israel.

Naomi cared deeply for her daughters-in-law. She knew that she could not take care of them alone. Naomi also knew that Israel was a dangerous place for two widows from Moab.

"Go home," Naomi urged Ruth and Orpah. "Return to your families. Marry again. Have children, and forget you ever met me."

Orpah agreed sadly, and did as Naomi told her. Full of sorrow, she returned home.

But Ruth cared as deeply for her mother-in-law as Naomi cared for her. Ruth had seen, through Naomi, how powerful and kind the Lord was. She couldn't imagine going back to Moab, her old family, and the false gods she used to worship there. Even though she knew that going to Israel would be hard, she promised Naomi:

Wherever you go, I'm going.
Wherever is your home, I'll make my home.
Whoever are your people, I'll call them my people.
Your God, the one true God, is my God.
May the Lord punish me if I don't stick with you- and Him- through death.

So, Ruth and Naomi made the journey back to Israel. "Sweet Naomi!" her friends exclaimed when they saw her. "Is that really you?"

Naomi answered them honestly, and with anger and fear filling her broken heart, she said, "When I left, I had everything. Now as I return, I have nothing. Everything God had given me, He has now taken away. So, don't call me by my name. It doesn't suit me anymore. Call me Mara, because it means bitter, and that's who I am now."

Naomi remembered God's power, but she had forgotten God's kindness.

And so, right when Naomi had lost hope, the first harvest of the year began. Right in God's good timing, Ruth and Naomi arrived home, in a little town called Bethlehem.

Kaleidoscope Corner
Food

Bethlehem means house of bread, and in that part of Israel, crops thrived. At that time, there were two main harvests every year: a barley harvest in the spring, and a wheat harvest in the fall. Both grains were harvested and ground into flour, which was used to make simple breads, such as the one on the following page.

As you and an adult helper make this recipe, watch how basic ingredients like flour and water combine with air to become something more. How does that remind you of what God does for us and through us?

Bethlehem Bread
(makes two flatbreads)

Ingredients
1 cup flour (try whole wheat or barley flour to taste what Ruth would have eaten)
1/4 teaspoon salt
2 tablespoons butter
6 tablespoons water
oil for cooking
honey for serving

Directions
- Wash your hands!
- Mix the flour and salt in a bowl.
- Melt the butter and warm the water together in a pan on the stove, or in a container in the microwave.
- Pour the warm butter and water mixture into the flour, and mix together. (Your mixture won't look quite like dough yet. Don't worry!)
- Dust a thin layer of flour onto a clean table or counter.
- Dump the mixture out of the bowl onto the floured surface, and use your hands to knead the dough. If your dough sticks to your hands, put a little bit of flour on your hands and the dough.
- Knead the dough for two to three minutes.
- Roll the dough into a ball and wrap it with plastic wrap. Then, let the dough rest on your counter for 30-45 minutes. (Or you can put it in the refrigerator overnight.)
- Dust fresh flour on your work surface and unwrap your dough.
- Cut the dough into two equal pieces. Dust the dough and a rolling pin with flour.
- Roll each piece into a thin circle, about 5 or 6 inches across.
- Heat a small amount of oil in a skillet over medium-high heat.
- Wait until the oil is very hot, then put the first flatbread in the skillet.
- After 1-2 minutes, you'll see air pockets (large bubbles) forming on top of the dough. Flip the dough over. Cook for 1-2 more minutes and flip if needed. Both sides should have some golden brown spots. Take your flatbread out of the pan.
- Repeat with the other circle of dough.
- Serve the flatbread with honey for dipping.

HARVEST

RUTH 2

Ruth and Naomi hadn't realized that God had already been working for their good when they arrived in Bethlehem.

Elimelech's extended family still lived in Bethlehem. One of them was a man named Boaz. During a time when most people around him did not, Boaz followed God's laws. He was honest and kind. He cared for the people in his community, no matter who they were. Boaz was a man of integrity, someone who did what was right.

Because Boaz shared relatives with Elimelech, he was also a kinsman-redeemer for Elimelech's family. A kinsman-redeemer is someone who takes care of a family member who has been hurt or wronged. They work to restore the wounded and protect the weak.

Ruth said to Naomi one morning, "I'm going to go find a field to get some grain for us. I know someone will allow me to follow behind them as they harvest. I'll pick up the spare pieces that have fallen."

Ruth was going to glean. Gleaning was not only a custom at that time in Israel, but was also God's law. Gleaning made sure poor widows and orphans would have food. During harvest, workers cut long stalks of grain and tied them into bundles. Landowners who followed God's rules left the corners of their fields unharvested for the poor. They also allowed the needy to follow behind their workers, picking up whatever stalks fell out of the bundles.

When Ruth found a field where the workers allowed her to glean, she got to work right away. She collected as much fallen grain as she could carry. God had led her to just the right field at just the right time.

This landowner was successful, with fields full of rich barley and wheat. He also followed God's laws.

His name was Boaz.

As Boaz approached his field, he greeted his workers warmly, "The Lord is with you!"

The workers cheerfully responded, "The Lord bless you!"

Boaz asked the harvest foreman, "Who is that young woman gleaning behind our workers?"

The foreman explained, "That's Ruth. She's the widow from Moab who came back to Bethlehem with her mother-in-law, Naomi. She asked me early this morning if she could glean your fields. She is a hard worker and has only taken one short break all day!"

Boaz knew that Israel could be a dangerous place for a widow from Moab. So, he went to Ruth and said, "My child, you are most welcome here. Please stay only in my fields. My workers will take care of you. Anytime you are thirsty, take a drink from the jars filled for my workers."

Ruth had set out that morning with a mission. She had planned to work hard, and she hoped to come home with some grain for Naomi and herself. She had also probably expected unkind looks and unfair words from the people she encountered.

But what she got instead was a kindness that overwhelmed her. "Sir," she said to Boaz as she bowed in front of him. "What have I done that you have honored me like this?"

"You have shown your mother-in-law such love. You left your home and your family and your land to take care of her. You've come to know the Lord, the one true God, and I pray He blesses you richly. May you find shelter and rest through Him, as if under His wings."

Then, Boaz did something extraordinary. He invited Ruth to eat with him at his table. She sat at a place of honor, reserved for only the most important people. There, they shared bread with vinegar and roasted grain. Ruth ate until she was full and saved the rest for Naomi.

As she returned to work in the field, Boaz instructed his men to protect her and provide for her. "As you wrap the grain in bundles, make sure to drop some of the best stalks so that Ruth will have something to pick up," he told them.

Ruth worked until the sun set and then brought home the labors of her day, more than 30 pounds of grain. It was almost more than she could carry!

Naomi was impressed and overwhelmed with all Ruth had brought home. "How did you get this much grain?" she asked her daughter-in-law. "God bless whoever was so kind to you. Whose fields were you in?"

Ruth told Naomi all about her day: the promised protection, the invitation to take as much as she needed, the shared meal of honor, the heartfelt blessing, and the unexpected kindness she received from a man named Boaz.

As Naomi listened, something changed in her heart. She began to understand.

Ruth loved Naomi, so she worked to provide food for them.

Boaz loved God, so he kept God's law that allowed Ruth to glean in his fields.

God faithfully blessed the land. He gave the seed to plant, the rain to water, and the sun to warm, so that the grain would grow.

God led Boaz to understand the beauty of His law.

God led Naomi home at the beginning of the harvest, and He led Ruth to just the right field at just the right time. It was a plan almost too beautiful for words.

"May the Lord bless Boaz," Naomi said to Ruth. "He shows honor to those who have died and kindness to those who live. Boaz is a close relative of your late father-in-law and a kinsman-redeemer for our family. Do as he told you. Stay with the women who work in his fields through both harvests."

As Naomi said these things, once again, she began to have hope.

A PLAN &
A FUTURE

RUTH 3-4

Naomi grew worried that Ruth needed someone to take care of her. Naomi knew that Boaz had already honored Ruth greatly. Ruth had gleaned in Boaz's fields for many months, during two harvests. Boaz made sure that Ruth had enough food and was protected. Naomi hoped that Boaz would be the one to save their family. But she was running out of patience. So, she came up with a risky, and maybe unwise, plan.

"Ruth," Naomi said, "don't you think it's time we found you a new husband? We can't live like this forever, and you need someone who can provide you with a home and a family. What about Boaz?"

Naomi told Ruth to sneak down to the threshing floor that night. Boaz would be there with other landowners as they waited their turn to separate the valuable wheat from the useless chaff.

"When he lies down and falls asleep, go lie down at his feet like a servant would," Naomi instructed.

This idea probably made Ruth uncomfortable, but she knew Naomi loved her, so she did as she was told. When she lied down, Boaz woke up and whispered, "Who is here?"

Ruth took a deep breath and bravely answered, "It's me, Ruth. I am here as your servant. Will you be my kinsman-redeemer?"

Boaz, who must have already asked Bethlehem's leaders if he was allowed to marry Ruth, wasn't surprised by what she said. As he had prayed when they first met, he opened up his blanket as if they were wings, to offer her shelter and rest.

"You have brought me joy, and I would be honored to be your kinsman-redeemer," Boaz answered. "But there is one other man who is more closely related to Elimelech. If he wants to be your kinsman-redeemer, then he has the right under our law. I will talk to him about this. If he wants to fulfill his duty, then he will take care of you. But if he doesn't, I promise in front of the Lord, that I want to, and I will."

Before the sun came up, Boaz sent Ruth back to Naomi with her shawl full of barley. Naomi told Ruth that Boaz would have the matter settled that day.

Boaz went the next morning to the other man and asked if he wanted to fulfill his duties. At first, the man thought that all he needed to do was buy back Elimelech's land, so he said yes.

He thought of more land for his crops and a growing fortune. But when Boaz explained that he would also need to marry Ruth, the widow from Moab, the man backed away from what he said. He didn't want to be responsible for Ruth and her mother-in-law, even though that's what God's law required. This man made up his own rules about what was right, and what was wrong, and showed that he cared more about property than people.

As was the Israelite custom, Boaz asked the man to publicly agree to allow him to be the kinsman-redeemer. The man took off his sandal and handed it to Boaz (more on this in the next Kaleidoscope Corner). In front of the city gate, Boaz announced to Bethlehem's leaders, "With all of you as my witnesses, I will buy the land that was Elimelech's, Chilion's, and Mahlon's. I will also marry Ruth, the widow from Moab, so that their family's name is not lost."

The town leaders offered their blessing and a prayer, "May Ruth be like Rachel and Leah, mothers of Israel. May you be a strong pillar of our people and be blessed with a large family." Boaz married Ruth, and she later gave birth to a son. They named him Obed.

Naomi's friends came to meet the child. "Praise the Lord for all He has done for you. Rejoice, sweet Naomi!" her friends sang around her. "When you came home, you thought you were empty. But you had Ruth by your side, who has been more of a blessing to you than seven sons could have been. Even if you'd imagined a perfect life for yourself, it wouldn't have been as good as this one."

Naomi took her grandson in her arms. She laid him down in her lap to look at his precious face. Naomi remembered the times she cried aloud, tears streaming down her face, afraid God had forgotten her.

In those pain-filled seasons she knew God was powerful, but she wasn't sure if He was kind. But God used her seasons of pain to lead her to a life of love. In His perfect timing, the Lord gave her safety and peace and hope and joy.

As Naomi touched her grandson's face, she knew that this tiny baby, whose name meant to serve and to worship, was in her lap because of God's power and kindness.

Kaleidoscope Corner
Culture

In ancient Israel, there was a custom of taking off a sandal and giving it away. This was a symbol that you had entered into a legal arrangement. It was done by the man who agreed to give up his legal right to something and showed everyone who saw, that he understood what he was giving up, and that he agreed to it

How important were sandals in ancient Israel? How does this custom symbolize what the men agreed to? Does this custom point us to someone else, who would give up His right to something?

NOT THE END

RUTH 4:18-22

If Ruth's story ended there, we would see how much God loved her and her family. But the story doesn't end there. God wanted to give us a hint of how he would save the world.

The final verses of Ruth tell us about their family tree:

Perez was the father of Hezron.
Hezron was the father of Ram.
Ram was the father of Amminadab.
Amminadab was the father of Nahshon.
Nahshon was the father of Salmon.
Salmon was the father of Boaz.
Boaz was the father of Obed.
Obed was the father of Jesse.
And Jesse was the father of David.

These verses may not seem very important. But they tell us so much. You see, God's kindness honored Ruth in ways she never fully understood during her lifetime.

These verses tell us that Ruth's great-grandson was David, a shepherd boy who would become a king. David was a king who sought to know and love the Lord. He was a king who tried to keep the laws of the one true God. And like his King in Heaven, David was a king on earth who led his people with power and served them with kindness. He was the king that the Israelites in the book of Judges longed for.

King David's legacy doesn't stop there. David's family was used by God to send His only son into the world. Twenty-eight generations later, in that same little town of Bethlehem, where his grandfathers David and Obed and Boaz had been born, another baby boy was born.

This baby inherited David's throne. His name was Jesus. Jesus was - and is - the final and perfect King. He is the King that our hearts need most.

So in the time of the Judges, when Israel had no king on earth, the people made their own rules about what was right and what was wrong.

Everyone did whatever they wanted...almost everyone.

There was Naomi, who even though she sometimes doubted the kindness of God, she never doubted His power.

There was Ruth, who made a promise to love God and to care for her mother-in-law.

There was Boaz, who obeyed God. He showed honor to those who had died and kindness to those who lived. God blessed them - and us - with a family.

Ruth redeemed Naomi.

Boaz redeemed Ruth.

And for those of us who trust in Him, Jesus redeems us all.

Made in the USA
Las Vegas, NV
17 October 2024

97002954R00219

unhinged comments. I love you all and you had one of the biggest roles in getting me this far.

To my readers, both new and old, who commented and shared with unashamed glee whenever they came across a teaser on social media, thank you.

To my mother, who has no idea about this book, and won't until it surprises her in print at my next book signing....I'm so sorry mommy. Please don't read it. I will never be able to look you in the eye again. BUT if you do read it...maybe you can warn the family away from this one? K. Thanks.

To my editor, at Spicemeupediting. You have saved us all from my horrible grammar. A true superhero I tell ya.

To my cover artist, @indicreates, this is the most beautiful cover I have ever had. Im obsessed with it. I want to marry it and kick my husband out of the bed so it can lay beside me at night. It's gorgeous. It's perfect. It's everything I ever wanted.

Lastly, to my readers again–yes, you deserve a second mention– Thank you for hanging with me as I grow in my craft. I write for me, but I also write for *you* and anyone else who needs an escape from reality every now and then.

thank you

Writing a book is always a huge undertaking that couldn't be completed without the amazing people in my corner. Seriously. When imposter syndrome hits, it hits *hard,* and the only way out of it is a clear, calm lecture about how what I just wrote wasn't as terrible as I thought it was...followed immediately by demands for me to finish that damned sex scene!

The biggest thank you to my lovely Wendybird. This book would not be here without you. It would still be scattered notes on my phone and maybe a few incomplete chapters that would never see the light of day. You were my number one cheerleader who pulled me from doubt and screamed your excitement with every individual chapter I sent you....one measly chapter, one day at a time. Your support for these characters and for my writing as I ventured into my first *adult* spice is how Kai and Eryn got their happy ever after. It's also why Kai is into butt stuff and probably why poor Rani will get the full monty from Ezra. I BLAME YOU.

To my other friends that kept me sane with their eager willingness to listen to my plot ideas and theories, Lizzy, Jenn, Kayla, Tammy, Lauren...you all kept me going.

I did something different and made a discord for my betas this time. To all the girlie pops in there and your absolutely

MW01602228

 Created with Vellum

bonded nightmare

E.M. RINALDI

To the readers who know that sometimes...romance is the plot.

prologue

My worn-out combat boots hit the pavement in a staccato rhythm. I wasn't going to make it in time. Only four days after my eighteenth birthday, and I'd screwed everything up. Again. My breaths were choppy as I squeezed whatever oxygen I could into my lungs, but I'd never run this long before.

The cool autumn air kissed my heated skin as I made it to the top of the hill. Our house sat nestled at the bottom, surrounded on all sides by thick, ancient trees. I increased my speed, nearly stumbling down the steep sidewalk in my haste to reach my parents. I had to tell them what I'd done before it was too late.

Please don't let it be too late.

The hair on the nape of my neck stood on end when I thought about who could be watching me as I ran home. As I ran away from the mistake that might just cost us our lives. My practiced speech played over and over in my head; it was an accident. *I didn't mean to. I'm sorry.* But my remorse wouldn't save us when the hunters came.

A deep burning took root in my thighs as they trembled and were pushed past their limits. Still, I kept running. Not much

further now. Our cute, unremarkable ranch home was chosen specifically for its distance from the humans, while also maintaining its anonymity for being just close *enough*. The hunters wouldn't look twice at it. At least, they wouldn't have if I hadn't lost control today and broke into the mind of a human.

Now, every hunter in the country would zero in on this town to win the trophy kill of the century—the last nightmares. My parents and I weren't monsters, but other supernaturals still feared us. After what I did today, I didn't blame them. I forced myself to stop at the fence that marked our property line. There were still enough leaves on the trees to cover me while I tried to calm my racing heart.

As I caught my breath, I turned my focus outward, tuning in to the frequency that only another supernatural could sense. Power flowed through every living thing, even the stagnant rocks at my feet, and all power registered to other supernaturals nearby. Big or small magicks, it didn't matter. However, only larger magicks could be traced, say, to a small town in the middle of nowhere that hid innocent parents and their careless child.

No power pulsed from inside the house. My dark curls flew past my shoulders as I broke into another sprint. Only a few yards left. I made out my parents' beat-up station wagon in the drive. A good sign. One more yard. The front porch loomed ahead just as I wore a stitch in my side. There was no time to stretch it out. No time to breathe. I had to warn my parents. We had to start packing. We had to leave. We had to—

I skidded to a stop, heart in my throat as I stared at the broken front door in horror. It was ripped off the hinges and leaned awkwardly to the side. My panicked gaze took in more details I'd missed on my sprint over. Mom's flowerpots were shattered—the soil and roots spilling across the entryway. The fence gate was in a similar state as the front door, and the

living room window had cracks spiderwebbed across the entire thing.

No.

My hands shook as I listened for movement from the inside.

Please.

Not a sound. My boots crunched over broken pottery and wood chips, and I froze on the threshold of my temporary home. They were all temporary, but always because we chose to leave them. The devastation before me was anything but a choice. Our living room was in shambles.

The coffee table we'd found at a yard sale was now in pieces on the other side of the room, a strong tell of how the TV screen was shattered. The couch was overturned, and random scorch marks stained the walls and carpet, with no other signs of a fire. It was my mother's crumpled form in the center of it all that sent me to my knees. I crawled to her, ignoring the debris that dug into my skin.

"Mom?" My voice was a broken whisper as I gently shook her shoulder. "Mommy?" She turned her head to look at me, and I let the tears fall in relief.

There was blood in her hair, but it was dry. Bruises marred her face, and I knew she had fought with everything she had. Everything but her magick. My parents were strong enough to infiltrate multiple minds at once, even ones experienced at keeping them out. They could have easily subdued the force that attacked them here, but that level of power left a mark and would have been an alarm to whatever hunters weren't already on their way.

My parents had one great weakness—me. Sobs caught in my throat at what I'd done. I brought the hunters to us, and *I* was the reason they couldn't even defend themselves. Crystal green eyes, the exact shade of my own, looked back at me with a glassy emptiness.

"They took him," she whispered, the words scratchy as if she hadn't spoken for a while. Or had been screaming.

I quickly scanned the room again, heart squeezing for the one thing I'd missed the first time.

My father.

I looked back at my mother with a trembling chin. "Who took him?" I needed her to say it.

A slow blink. "The tribunal."

One moment of panic. That's all I allowed; a single heart-shattering moment of terror for my father before I got to work. I knew what I had to do. We had contingency plans for everything, even this. I stood and grabbed the car keys from the hook on the wall. Supplies. I'd fill the car with the basics, and we'd get the rest as we went.

I raided the kitchen first for non-perishables before stepping over my mother and grabbing a box from the closet. I glanced back at where she still sat on the floor, broken, but...

"Is he alive?" I asked my mother, all business now to keep from falling apart. "Mom!" I shouted when she didn't answer. "Is your bond alive?"

The last bonded nightmares. My parents were lucky that they were fated for one another. There were none of our kind left for me—not that bonds had to be from the same faction, but with the death threat over my head, I had zero chances. I shoved a few jackets and blankets into the box before digging in the back of the closet for the sleeping bags.

Mom didn't answer, and I tried not to freak out. Maybe she was sensing the bond, feeling for what shape my father was in. Bonded couples had a connection like no other. Their very souls were joined. Emotions, energy, *pain*...It could all be shared and felt, like the opposite ends of a lifeline. I had no experience with it, but surely it didn't take this long.

"Is your bond intact?" I forced out, fingers denting the cardboard in my hands. Was my father alive?

"It's still intact." The answer came from behind me, and I whirled around to see my father standing in the door. Haggard, but alive.

My mother made a keening sound and launched herself at him. They both went down, but my father braced himself against the frame and whispered soothing reassurances in her ear. I stood, rooted in the closet as relief flooded me hard enough to crack the fragile pieces of my heart I'd managed to hold on to.

"Daddy," I whispered, seconds away from a full breakdown.

"We don't have much time," he said, his voice as steady as ever. "They will be back, but not yet."

I'd almost killed my parents. Holy shit.

I'd almost killed my parents.

"I need you to keep it together, little nightmare." His arms were still wrapped tightly around my mother, but he stood closer now. I took a shuddering breath, held it, and then let it out slowly. When I nodded, he smiled at me with pride. "That's my girl."

It took some time, but my mother recovered enough to let go. Together, we put the couch to rights and sat silently in the fractured shell of our home.

"The tribunal offered us clemency," my father said, and it took a minute for his words to register.

Clemency?

I stared at the mutilated memories the hunters left around us. Was this what that looked like? A wrecked house and an almost broken bond? They couldn't have just sent a note?

"We've been hunted our whole lives," I croaked. "What's changed?"

My father glanced down at my mother with a sad smile. He

5

gave her a soft kiss on the head, and then met my confused frown. "They found your bond."

All sound ceased to exist as my racing heart drowned out the rest of his explanation. I only heard bits and pieces over the one word cycling through my head.

Bond.

"The oracles announced it."

Bond.

"He's the heir to the witch faction."

I'd never admitted it out loud, but I'd always dreamed of finding it—the kind of love my parents had. They said to find your bond was to find a piece of yourself you didn't even know was missing. It filled a hole, and it fucking sucked to know I would spend the rest of my life with a giant chunk of me missing.

"I won't do it." Something fluttered in my chest. My bond? My breaking heart? It didn't matter. "Tell their precious warlock he can be alone forever."

My parents glanced at one another, communicating without words. I didn't want something like that with someone who would have killed me without a second thought if I weren't fated for them.

"That means you'll be alone forever too," my mother warned. Like I didn't know that I was turning down my only chance.

"I'd be alone anyway," I replied.

I never wanted the tribunal's acceptance, only to be left alone. What would my life be like with a would-be murderer as a bond mate? Not worth it. But...

"What happens if I reject him?" I asked. "What happens to you guys?"

The tribunal couldn't kill me now, no matter what I chose, not without severely weakening a faction heir—even with an

uncompleted bond. But my parents...they could retaliate against them.

"This is your choice, little nightmare." There was no condemnation in my father's eyes. Only love. "Your mother and I will support you no matter what."

I nodded, decision already made. "Then I say, no."

I leaned into my anger to cover the heart-wrenching pain that squeezed my chest like a vise, but it only got worse. The deeper I sank into my decision, the more it hurt. My hands clutched at my shirt as I rode the waves. My parents looked on in pity, but there was nothing they could do. This was my choice. When the pain finally tapered off, only a small flicker of...*something*...remained inside me. I pushed it down until I felt nothing.

one

2 years later

Eryn

A sea-kissed breeze grazed my cheek as I stepped off the stale Greyhound bus. It had taken two days to get here, and the glint of the morning sun off the cresting waves was a welcome sight. Stretching out the kinks in my back, I basked in the still-warm, late-season sun and smiled for the first time since leaving my parents' house.

The ocean. I'd never seen it in person. My gaze followed the rolling waves, mesmerized by how they shattered along the shoreline. Even this late in the season, there were surfers idling just past the break; fellow students most likely. The private beach behind the bus depo belonged to the college and was used heavily by its world-renowned Marine Biology program. Most of it was cordoned off for conservation, but I read in the brochure that a portion was saved for student use.

The small strip of sand led far into the distance where ocean spray gave way to palm trees and ancient brick buildings with

9

polished steeples. Moorcroft University. I grabbed my meager belongings from under the bus and took the first steps toward my new life. My sleeping bag strapped atop my backpack, and duffel over my shoulder, I took the scenic route along the coast. Even out here, there were signs directing where to go and pointing toward specific campus landmarks.

I needed to check-in at Midnight Hall and according to the small campus map, that was on the opposite side from the beach. Meaning it was at least two miles from where I now stood. There were campus shuttles that circled the outer perimeter, but their schedule was too slow. What if I had to run in the middle of the night? Two miles on foot was a long way with someone chasing you.

The sound of the ocean merged with the roaring in my ears. Panic was a default setting for me. It always hovered in the back of my mind, ready to surge forward and take over at the first sign of trouble, and having my main escape route so far from where I'd be staying was definitely not good.

There are other ways to disappear, I reminded myself, forcing much-needed breaths into my lungs. *The bus might not be the best option.*

That was true enough. Being reliant on a bus schedule wasn't the best course of action when every minute mattered in a race for freedom. Stealing a car was another option and very possible for me. Disappearing into the shadows was a specialty of mine. I could easily vanish and avoid capture if I had enough of a head start.

Barely escaping the tribunal meant my family had to go even deeper into hiding, and being idle was never my strong suit. I took my pre-req classes online and learned all sorts of new trades to keep those prejudiced assholes and my potential bond mate off our backs. But after two years of fixing up stray animals

by day and broadening my life of crime by night, my parents had had enough.

They wanted me to have a good life, one not spent hiding and staring at the syllabi of classes I could never take. I was kicked out, in no uncertain terms, to finish my college degree in person. To become a veterinarian. My ultimate dream. But old habits die hard, and a childhood spent running for my life wasn't something I could just quit. I was still in danger, and I had backup plans on top of backup plans in case I was found, but... they were right. Enough was enough. I had to live my life at some point, and if I was careful, I could spend my future fixing helpless animals among the humans until the tribunal assumed I died.

The ancient brick buildings finally took shape as I neared the start of campus. Sand blew across the sidewalk and I slowed my steps to a stop. I strained my hearing, listening for the cry I thought I heard. The ocean on my left was thunderous, demanding the attention of any who dared stand too close, but even its fury couldn't drown out the sound. It wasn't my ears I was using, anyway. The cry rang out again, and I followed it closer to the boardwalk, where a large, two-story building jutted out right along the water.

A massive fence, large enough to stop a truck, marked the boundaries of an outdoor space in the back. One side of the brick walls morphed into wood panels that then connected to the dock, with a ramp leading into the water. There was a garage door there too, perfectly positioned for a boat to be launched and returned. The other half of the building faced a parking lot.

What was this place? Was it part of the college? As I grew closer, more voices joined the first until my head swam with their pain. Whatever this was, there were injured animals behind those walls. My eye twitched as an uncomfortable throbbing took root behind it. I couldn't tune them out—not that I

would, they needed me—but I also didn't know how to get inside and help them.

The mental aspect of the nightmare gifts manifested in a different way for me than my parents. I could still break into minds, human or supernatural, with some degree of success, but last year I realized I could connect with animals as well. Communication outside of vague feelings and jumbled images was impossible, their minds weren't as complex, but it was just enough for me to pinpoint where the pain or illness was coming from.

This open connection drew animals to me like bees to pollen, and I was powerless against their innocent cries and begging mewls. Unfortunately, my gifts didn't include healing, so I had to patch them up the human way...if I could. It was why I wanted to be a vet. What use was this connection if I couldn't fix the problems it showed me?

A metal door beside the fence caught my eye, and I crept toward it. The cries got louder the closer I moved until my hand wrapped around the doorknob. Glancing up, there were no cameras and I sensed no humans nearby. The lack of security made me brave, and before I could second guess myself, I knelt in front of the door and reached for my lock picks.

Some of the cries in my head filtered out. I still felt their life force, but the pain was now locked away behind a muted haze. I worked faster. Picking locks could be tricky if you didn't pay attention. There were small clicks to listen for and brief changes in the gears. It was hard enough to focus with the raucous calls in my head, but now my chest was acting up too.

There was a pressure pressing out from behind my ribs and a flutter that felt odd enough to make me pause. Someone was coming. I swiftly stood, tucking my picks into my pocket just as the door swung open and knocked me back. My butt met the cold sidewalk, sending a shockwave up my tailbone. The weight

of my bags toppled me even further until my sleeping bag was the only thing that kept my head from kissing the concrete. When I tried to sit up, I found myself too heavy to rise, and I lay there, stuck like an upside-down turtle.

That's when I noticed him. He was easily the most beautiful man I'd ever seen. A strong jaw and symmetrical lines, full lips. His hair was three different shades of blond swirled together, with the strands swooping low over one eye in a style that appeared effortless but must have taken at least an hour to accomplish. And those eyes, a strange turquoise to match the ocean.

His shock settled before mine did, and he raised a sandy brow. The action pulled at a crescent scar that started in the corner of his eye and reached the top of his cheekbone. It didn't distract from his beauty. If anything, it added an air of danger I couldn't shy away from despite the panic screaming somewhere in the back of my mind. I was struck by a sense of recognition so strong that my heart stopped in my chest.

How was he familiar? I was sure I'd never seen this man before in my life. His lips started moving, a perfect cupid's bow marked with another scar. This one was tiny and pale white with time. My palm rubbed across my breastbone to try and ease the weird ache. The man cleared his throat, and I realized he was talking to me.

I forced my eyes to meet his and recoiled at the disgust I saw there. Anger radiated off him in waves, and the feel of it didn't match the view I'd spent the last few minutes admiring. I blushed, knowing it was rude to stare, and averted my gaze.

"Predictable," he scoffed.

My mouth dropped and a small, incredulous laugh escaped. Why did all the beautiful ones have to be so conceited?

"Excuse me?" I asked, no longer shy about meeting that glare.

13

"Freshmen aren't allowed in the hospital."

That was all he said before pinning me with another dirty look. Who pissed in his Cheerios? His audacity floored me, but then his words registered, and I forgot about his sour attitude. This must be the veterinary hospital. I read about it online and it was why I chose to pursue my degree here. Students got real-time, practical experience under the watchful eyes of the instructors, starting junior year.

I took in the building with a whole new outlook. That would explain the injured animals calling out to me from inside. And why it felt like a haze settled over some of them. Pain medication diluted the connection. The animosity coming from the grumpy Adonis saturated the air, and my chest gave another throb.

"I didn't know." I plastered on a fake smile. It was the truth, but I couldn't bring myself to do more than admit it, not with that superiority complex staring right at me.

He tapped on the back of the door where an "Authorized Personnel" sign hung. And below that, "No Student Access." So what, I ignored the signs. I wasn't going to let them stop me from helping innocent animals. I didn't care how hard he glared at me. If there had been a sign that said "Hospital" or some other identification of what this place was, I would have given it more thought.

He continued to stare at me, and I stared right back, refusing to back down. He appeared expectant like he was waiting for me to say something else, and my chin rose in defiance. I would apologize for trying to break in once he apologized for knocking me over. He hadn't even offered to help me up. The sidewalk was damp, and my palms were definitely scraped from trying to break my fall.

One of my hands still pressed against my chest, like clutching my shirt would relieve the weird pressure there, but I didn't back down. The V in his brow deepened. My lips pursed.

His fingers tightened on the door until his knuckles went white. I cocked my head to the side.

"Fucking stubborn." With a final scoff and roll of his eyes, he went back inside and slammed the door behind him.

It took a full five minutes for the ache in my chest to ease into a flutter, before resolving altogether. I had to slip my arms out of my bag to stand, and then heave it back onto my shoulders. I glared one final time at the door, and the broody bastard somewhere behind it, then left the hospital and resumed my search for Midnight Hall. Hopefully, breaking and entering wouldn't be required to get into my own dorm.

Thankfully, it wasn't too hard to find. The mass influx of family cars and fathers overloaded with moving boxes was telling. It was the spring semester, but I guess I wasn't the only one who transferred in mid-year. I tightened my hand around the strap of my duffel bag. Everything I owned was in there; a sparse array of clothes, my meager toiletries, and a pillow. My backpack held all I needed for class, with almost all my textbooks being in digital format that I could read on my used kindle. I'd have to do all my assignments and studying at the library on the provided computers, but I would deal.

I didn't need a fancy laptop or a horde of people moving me in to be successful here. Squeezing past the overshow of emotion that clogged the shared courtyard between the dorm halls, I checked in at the small table in the lobby and took the stairs to the third floor with an annoyed grumble. Forty-two steps didn't seem like much, but I'd requested a room on the main floor. Being trapped deep in this maze of hormone-ridden prison cells would slow me down.

However, there was some protection to be found behind a wall of humans. Had to find the bright side somewhere. The carpet in the hall had seen better days, but the doors lining one side were of solid wood. My key slid easily into the lock, and I

got my first good look at where I'd be spending the next six years...hopefully. If I made it through with a high enough score, I could travel anywhere in the country for veterinary school or choose to stay here.

That flexibility was non-negotiable. Would the last two years of undergrad be enough for the tribunal to stop looking for me? Probably not. Which was why I needed the options.

"Are you going to stand there in the door or come in?"

I jumped as the owner of the voice hopped down from her raised bed. There was another on the other side of the room, my side, but it lacked the deep green comforter and throw pillows.

"Jumpy one, aren't you?" The curvy redhead wore a smile that I tried hard to return. "I'm Rani," she said. "Marine Bio major."

I stared hard at the hand she offered for a few awkward seconds before gently shaking it. "Eryn," I told her. "Veterinary Medicine."

A real smile graced my lips then. It was the first time I said that out loud. Despite my less-than-bubbly reception to my new roommate, the vibe of the room was easy and not forced. Rani left me alone to unpack and didn't crowd. It took less than an hour to unroll my sleeping bag on the thin but clean mattress, tuck my backpack under the desk, and put my clothes away. There was still half a closet and one whole drawer empty. I refused to look behind me at Rani's overstuffed half of the room, but I felt her beginning to hover.

"Is your family downstairs with the rest?" she asked, honesty saturating her tone. "Do they need help bringing it up?"

I wasn't a rude person by any means, but the quickest way to attract my suspicion was to ask about my family. Too many probing questions always followed. From teachers, it was to see if I was being abused. From classmates, it was to see how poor I was and where I fell in the social ranking. Rarely ever was it

actually out of the goodness of someone's heart. That's how I justified what I did next.

It wasn't a violation per se. I didn't break into her mind or take it over but rather skimmed her surface thoughts. Color me surprised when I read only genuine curiosity. The urge to push further was strong, but she hadn't done anything to actually warrant the search, and I couldn't afford to broadcast my magick so soon. Or ever.

"This *is* all my stuff," I replied with a stern frown.

Her brows wrinkled in an adorable way that I'd never be able to pull off. I was instantly jealous. "You don't have sheets? A comforter? Toiletries? *Anything?*"

She was one hundred percent authentic, which made my cheeks burn as I pointed to my empty duffel and the school bag. I wouldn't be embarrassed. I *wouldn't*.

"That's all I need for school," I told her, only slightly defensive. "It's worked well enough for me my entire life."

Rani worried her bottom lip and side-eyed my half of the room. She was obviously torn between insulting me or saying what was on her mind. Just as the silence grew too uncomfortable, and I was sure I'd have to get nasty in order for her to drop it, she smiled.

"Well, I have plenty of everything. My parents are worriers, so help yourself to whatever you need."

She grabbed my arm and dragged me to her closet, which was filled to the brim with lotions and makeup, shampoos, and body wash. Scents of flowers, sugar, and citrus permeated the air as she pointed out her favorite products and why I just *had* to try them. By the time she was done, the top shelf of my own closet bore more self-care products and spare towels than I'd ever need, and I'd somehow accepted her invitation to lunch.

"You may be considered an upperclassman thanks to your

credit hours, but this campus can get tricky if you don't know where you're going," she said with a grin.

I watched the spirited redhead bounce from the room like she hadn't just flipped my world on its axis. I'd told her about my online classes and how this was my first time on campus. The fact that she was able to pull anything about my life out of me blew my mind, and I was convinced she used a spell or something. She managed to both confuse me and take me under her wing like I was a lost little chick.

There were no ulterior motives I could sense. I'd know. I couldn't help but scan her mind again in between her comparison of shea butter versus regular moisturizer and when to use each one. With her larger-than-life personality out of the room, I took the time to snoop for anything out of the ordinary. I sensed no power from her but that meant nothing if she wasn't actively using magick or if she could shield herself from me.

My search revealed no obvious witchery or tools the djinn preferred, and we were too far from the water for her to be a siren. My eye caught on the narrow window between our beds, and I sighed. Who knew first-floor rooms were in such high demand? My only escape routes were down the stairs, the elevator, or out of that window.

A drop that high wouldn't kill me, but it would hurt and potentially hinder the rest of my plan if I was too injured. Only if absolutely necessary then. Tonight, I'd mark the other routes and time them. And later, I'd need to practice how long it took from those routes to the bus depot. Obviously, I would have to estimate the window option.

"Are you coming?" Rani popped her head back in, interrupting my thoughts.

A small, but very real smile took control of my lips. I'd never been invited anywhere. Maybe this college thing wouldn't be so bad after all.

two

Kaiden

She's here.

The Commons bustled for the midday meal. Students clustered around tables and the various food stations with oblivious glee. Humans weren't attuned to the subtle dip in pressure that her kind instigated. It was an unconscious side effect of the strength and nature of her power. The mental vulnerability caused by the presence of a nightmare resulted in the uncontrollable urge by the potential victim—in this case, humans—to grow restless.

They couldn't pinpoint the danger, and the result was a louder, more animated Commons as the sheep instinctively reacted. It was interesting, really, and I would have taken more time to study the phenomena if I hadn't felt her. Just like at the animal hospital earlier, her presence was a tug in my chest. I recognized what it was at the first pull, having been prepared to find my bond my entire life. To say I was no longer enthusiastic about the experience was an understatement.

I scanned the room, looking for the girl with a head of dark curls and eyes of absolute fire. The emerald in her gaze glowed when she was pissed; a fact I couldn't tell from the varied portraits I'd collected of her. Finding my little wayward bond was my sole focus these past two years, and I was nothing if not thorough.

"Is that her? Nah, that one's more of a brunette."

I rolled my eyes at my annoying, but only tolerable cousin. "You're drooling, Ez."

He grinned wider. "Not having a bond means I can look all I want. *Shit*, I can touch all I want, too." His fingers strummed atop the table in reflex. "Want me to put in some extra love for you, man?"

"Ez," I warned.

Hearing about his frequent pursuits hit harder now that I had a bond consuming my every thought. Before, it was entertaining, a vicarious adventure to pass the time. Now, it pissed me the fuck off. No amount of half-naked co-eds with perfect tits could compare. My dick was only interested in our bond, and it refused to rise for even the most tempting of distractions, much to my cousin's amusement.

"Not to worry, cuz. When I'm pumping into that luscious ass tonight, I'll put in an extra thrust for you."

"Ezra!"

His cackle was drowned out by the sledgehammer that hit my heart. There she was. She stood in line for the salad bar beside a curvaceous redhead that would make Ez's tongue roll out like a welcome mat once he caught sight of her. I took my time checking out my little bond. Petite but not too short, legs I wanted wrapped around my waist, and those curls that fascinated me at first glance. They were tied off behind her head now, but this morning they'd cradled her face the way my hands itched too.

"Holy shit, that's her. That's definitely her," Ez breathed beside me.

A nod was all I gave him in reply, too busy sizing up my prey. I already knew all I possibly could about this girl. Her favorite color: purple—based on the amount of pictures with her wearing it. Athletic according to her yearbooks and a love for animals. That one was obvious. She had no social media, so it was hard to gain insight into her inner thoughts, but I easily hacked her school records and read all the essays and written projects she had submitted so far.

What I learned was that my bond was a passionate, caring, intelligent woman. Or so I thought; before. Before she denied our bond and chose a life of misery and loneliness for *both* of us. It was selfish and insane. Who chose to live like that? I knew her parents were bonded: didn't she want that connection?

When the oracles made their announcement about Eryn, I couldn't wait to meet her. Then they dropped the bomb that she was a nightmare; a faction all but extinct and feared for their power. I didn't care. A part of me awakened when I heard her name, and nothing else mattered but finding her. Meeting her. Well, we met, and it changed nothing.

I gave her time to sense me coming before I opened that hospital door, but she didn't move away fast enough. Her beauty struck me mute, and I felt like a jackass now for not helping her up. It was wishful thinking for her to be drawn to me as well. Her hungry gaze, I thought, was a sign she was ready to concede. The feel of her eyes on me—I groaned at the memory. Exquisite. But she did nothing. She *said nothing*. No apology, no explanation for why she subjected us to this torture for two years.

It was predictable but somehow still surprising. Her stubborn nature was obvious from her initial denial, but still...I wanted her out of my head. I wanted to forget those lips and that

dimple I glimpsed on one cheek when she smiled. A fake smile, but it counted.

"What are you going to do?" Ez adopted a more serious demeanor, choosing to hunch over the table like we were on a stakeout.

"Watch for now," I told him.

It was also a warning. I didn't want him approaching her and ruining my plan before I could put it into effect. Eryn Montalli was mine, and it was about time she learned it. She moved up the line, and my eyes burned a hole in the back of her head. If I looked a little lower, I could watch those curls bounce just above the curve of her ass. The bond in my chest lunged at the sight, and I gripped my silverware to keep from lurching to my feet and dragging her from this room. She acted like I wasn't here when I knew she felt me. I gave a gentle strum to that connection between us, and she stiffened.

Finally.

She covertly scanned the crowd. It was kind of adorable. To anyone else, her wandering gaze and teeth nibbling her bottom lip could be interpreted as curiosity, but I knew it for what it was. She was looking for me. For the source of that ache in her chest. Those green beauties finally landed on me, and they widened. It was about damn time.

I worked to soften my glare so she wouldn't be too intimidated to approach and apologize. Surely, she must have realized her mistake. A small swallowing of her pride, and we could move on with our lives.

"Fuck." Ez started laughing, no longer worried about being noticed. "Oh fuck, you're in for it, cuz."

My little bond narrowed her eyes and deliberately turned her back to me. She moved toward the damn salad bar like she hadn't seen me. She was *ignoring* me. What the actual fuck? Who did this girl think she was? Back straight and stubborn

chin up, she marched right past me with the attitude of slighted royalty. This princess had no idea who she was fucking with.

"Easy, Kai." Ezra threw his jacket over me to hide the black tendrils of my shadows as they bent the metal in my hands.

I pushed away from the table and stormed from the Commons, choosing not to risk a power surge in front of the humans. The cool air outside did little to ease my temper. What was this girl doing to me? Ez caught up in the parking lot and hopped into the passenger seat of my truck.

"Give her time, man."

"She's had two years of time," I growled. "How much more do you suggest I allow her?"

He shook his head but didn't take my tone to heart. "She's been exiled for her entire life. Two years is nothing compared to that."

I let out a breath and eased my grip on the steering wheel. As usual, he was right. I thought I understood it when she denied me. She'd never really known my world, and who knew what kind of lies her parents had fed to her about it. They were offered clemency, but maybe she didn't believe it.

A future chained up in a room with only her bonded keeping her alive—that was probably what she saw. I didn't blame her for those fears. I was hurt but understanding when she disappeared. Angry when she was later discovered hiding out in some shithole, completing online classes rather than living in the comfort and luxury afforded to her new station once we completed the bond. But now, I was enraged.

"She felt me, I know she did." I let us into the apartment and slammed the door. "Why does she still deny me?"

"Who knows? Women make no sense outside the bedroom," Ez joked, heading straight for the fridge and cracking open a cold one.

He sat on the couch, and I kicked his legs to drop his dirty-

ass shoes off the coffee table. "I didn't spend the last two years creating this human cover and working my way into a position at this university for nothing."

I wasn't lying when I said I understood her fears. She needed time, so I gave it to her. I kept the tribunal off her back and let her decide her future. It was a simple matter of watching her emails to see where she'd apply and then transferring here into a position close to her.

"I've been patient, but no more." Ez said nothing, but I wasn't sure if it was from lack of opinion or because he knew I wouldn't listen.

I thought I wanted to get to know my bond. I planned to use my resources to help her get this useless degree before going home and beginning our lives together. If she wanted to fix animals in her free time, so be it if it made her happy. The tribunal families had pets, too. But now, I wanted to destroy that fairytale.

I wanted to shut down every dream she had about living a quiet life among the humans until she only had me left to turn to. Until she was forced to beg me for forgiveness and take her rightful place at my side. Maybe that was the anger talking, but I didn't shy away from it. I let it simmer and grow until it was a shield protecting my heart from the only girl in the world who could break it. And she didn't even care.

Ready or not, princess. Here I come.

I paced my room. Back and forth in front of the mirror, until I wore a track in the useless rug my mother insisted I buy as I waited for her image to appear. The large mirror over my dresser revealed a smooth surface, not even a ripple.

A shallow, gold bowl rested in front of it, filled to the brim with a fresh batch of moon water and three crystals balanced in the middle—amethyst to open communication, rose quartz to focus on calling my mother specifically, and I threw in a blue kyanite for extra emotional balance.

I needed all the help I could get. My shadows had only just calmed enough for me to venture back out among the humans, and it took an entire afternoon of meditation to get it that way.

"Would you hurry up?" Ez burst into my room with a trailing cloud of cinnamon and ginger, his favorite herbs when he wanted to get lucky. "If we're any later, the only available women left will be the ones too drunk to even know where I'm asking to stick my dick."

I rolled my eyes and lit an extra candle for urgency. "At least you're asking."

"Don't be an ass just because Mommy Dearest isn't picking up. You know I'm big on consent."

I heard the irritation in his voice, along with an undertone of hurt, and turned to him with a grimace. There wasn't a whole lot of choice in my cousin's life and insinuating that he took it lightly was a dick move.

"You're right, I'm sorry. Why don't you go ahead without me, and I'll catch up?" I offered, knowing I wasn't leaving this room tonight until my mother answered.

"That seems highly irresponsible seeing as Ezra is supposed to be guarding you." I whirled around at the sound of my mother's voice and caught the tail end of her materialization. The ripples in the mirror settled into a familiar stern frown. "Sending your protection away was not part of the deal, and I'm sure your cousin is aware of the consequences should he fail."

The room grew ten degrees cooler before I could answer. Frost coated the crystals in the bowl and splintered along the edges of the mirror as Ez's temper filled the small space.

"Hello, Auntie Mira. It's a pleasure, as always."

I didn't need to see him to know his eyes were narrowed in disrespect. His normally dark complexion grew paler the more he fell into his power. I could see my breath in front of me and knew this stare-down would only result in me mopping up the room once all the ice melted if I didn't put a stop to it.

"Go wait in the living room," I ordered. "Mother and I will be done in a moment." Ez left without another word, and I fixed a glare at the mirror. "Why do you do that? Why taunt him just to be cruel?"

My mother glanced down at the large ring dominating the index finger on her right hand, our family crest staring back at her. "My displeasure at you choosing that...mongrel as your second is a known fact," she sniffed. "My brother should have dealt with him as a baby, as our rules demand."

Being half-human, as Ezra was, was a crime in our world. Only pure blood ensured our people remained strong enough to survive, both against the changing outside world and the other factions in the tribunal seeking more than their share of power.

My uncle having an affair with a human was distasteful but not unheard of. That he bred an heir on her, that Ezra was left on his doorstep as a screaming infant for the whole community to learn about...it was shameful for the faction. But it was not "dealing with it" that my mother saw as the gravest insult.

Instead, my uncle named Ezra his rightful heir, even after the full-blooded children that followed, and then I chose him as my second.

"Loyalty can't be bought, Mother, as you're well aware. And Ezra is the only member of our conniving family that I trust not to *accidentally* push me in front of a train to gain a step closer to the family seat." It was an old argument, and one I didn't have time to rehash tonight. Before she could butt in with the lecture I knew was coming, I interrupted her with my news. "I found

her." I didn't have to elaborate on the *her* I was talking about. "She arrived today, and things are more complicated than I anticipated."

"Complicated how?" my mother demanded. She leaned forward, worry morphing her annoyance into a contemplative frown. "Did the djinn already get to her?"

Now it was my turn to frown. "The djinn? What do they have to do with anything?"

"Honestly, Kaiden, I raised you smarter than this. Ask me again why the djinn would be interested in the powerful, *vulnerable,* bond of our faction's heir."

My cheeks heated at her disappointment even as my heart raced in a growing panic. The djinn were our greatest opposition on the tribunal. Power just as strong and ancient as our own, they consistently worked behind the scenes to topple the balance in their favor.

I knew they wouldn't be happy to hear my bond was a nightmare. The combined power our children would inherit promised to keep our faction at the top with theirs for generations to come. Perhaps even push us ahead, something unacceptable to them.

"We haven't seen any djinn on campus, Mother." It wasn't a lie, but it seemed that Ez and I would have to be extra vigilant if my mother was already worked up.

"Then what's the problem?"

I sighed, frustration sending my shadows into a frenzy. I kept them locked away, barely. "She wants nothing to do with me."

"Who?"

"My bond!" I growled. "I saw her today, twice. And both times she denied me. Perhaps her upbringing will be a harder hurdle than I accounted for."

The background noise from my mother's side rose as she contemplated. As the head of our faction, her days were busy,

and I knew this conversation wouldn't last much longer, despite the urgency.

"I'm not going to tell you to get the girl in line because you already know it's what you must do," she said after whatever the distraction was on her side faded. "And I shouldn't have to tell you what will happen if the djinn get to her before you."

I glared at her in defiance. Those conjuring assholes wouldn't lay a finger on what's mine. "That won't be a problem."

"Good. Then I also don't need to mention what will happen to your power if she's taken out."

My jaw ached from how hard I clenched it. My mother knew exactly what buttons to hit. If they killed her, even before we completed the bond, it would weaken me. Perhaps to a point where I could no longer take over from my mother and lead.

But that wasn't what had my shadows once again breaking free and leaving gouges in the wood of the dresser like phantom fists. No. It was the thought of those curls saturated with blood. Of those emerald eyes fading and taking that spark I craved with them.

I let my shadows rage and watched their reflection in the now-empty mirror. I needed to bring my little bond to heel. No more games. No more running. She would be mine before the semester was out.

I blew out a breath and let my shadows sink beneath my skin once more. But first, I needed a drink.

three

Eryn

Tomorrow was the start of classes, but you wouldn't know it by the sounds filtering in from outside. I smoothed out the bunches in my sleeping bag for the millionth time, triple-checked that my backpack was ready to go, and mentally ran through my schedule. My first class wasn't until ten thirty, but I needed to hike to the Commons for breakfast and possibly time the distance from there to the bus depot...and back. There was still a lot to do before I felt even moderately comfortable here.

A wolf howl cut the silence of the room, followed quickly by a chorus of yips and answering calls. A quick glance out into the shared courtyard showed windows opening and more heads sticking out to join the campus...serenade? Round up? I had no idea what to call it. There was nothing in the welcome packet about the potential for students to turn rabid the night before the semester started. The digital clock on Rani's desk read just before midnight as I shut the window and climbed into bed, folding my thin pillow over my ears.

"Absolutely not." The door to our room struck Rani's closet with enough force to send some of her precious lotions tumbling. Not that it bothered her as she flicked on the lights and marched up to me. "As your roommate and new friend, I cannot allow this to happen."

When my instinct to shred her mind to ribbons faded and my heart stopped choking me, I sat up. "I'm not sure I follow."

Did she mean the howling? It was unusual—and annoying —but as a human, I assumed she was used to the idiocy from the others of her species. She rolled her eyes and stripped the sleeping bag off my bare legs before turning to rummage through the drawers beneath her bed.

"Theta Delta Sigma just sent out the pack call. Didn't you hear it?"

A fraternity. Somehow, that made sense. I caught the dark denim she threw at me before it hit my face and warily tracked her as she moved to her closet next.

"I heard it," I replied. "Why is it sending you into a frenzy?"

Perhaps I'd missed something when I declared her human. She laughed at my choice of words and handed me a hanger with a skimpy red top attached. I glanced between the top, the scrap of denim in my lap, and the mischievous grin on her face.

"No." The clothes were dropped, and I clutched my sleeping bag for support.

Despite how easily Rani attached herself to me, I wasn't here to make friends or give in to the hookup culture that saturated the party scene. Been there, tried that. Human friends didn't stick around long when they knew you were keeping secrets, or when your life got too weird. While I hoped my days of running in the middle of the night were over, I couldn't guarantee I wouldn't have to.

As for hooking up, why bother? The few times I'd tried it

were nothing to swoon over. Boring, uncomfortable, and embarrassing were all I had to say about sex. Maybe it was me? The way everyone else went on about how great it was...I was obviously missing something.

"Hello, earth to Eryn." Rani wiggled that red top until the subtle glitter in the material winked. "It's not even that cold out yet."

"It's not the *subfreezing temperature* I'm worried about." I wrinkled my nose. "It's being charged with public indecency."

The top wasn't that bad, actually. I had ample breasts but nothing too outrageous. That skirt, however, would need every single one of its stitches to grow three inches if it wanted to cover my ass.

"Please," Rani pleaded. "Your legs would look incredible, and you can even wear your boots. Edgy."

I would have no choice but to wear the boots. For one thing, they were the only pair of shoes I owned, and for the other, there was *ice* outside. Why did tumbling temperatures mean putting on fewer clothes? Was hypothermia not a thing for humans anymore?

"I have class tomorrow," I mumbled, but she wouldn't accept my excuse.

"The whole campus has class tomorrow."

I shrugged. The whole campus didn't rely on the college for literally everything. They didn't have a supernatural bounty on their heads. I couldn't risk my future and safety over this never-ending need to feel included. I knew better.

"Babe, I'm going to be upfront with you. Okay? I know your life hasn't been easy." She held up her hand when I opened my mouth. "I won't ask questions, and this is the only time I'll bring it up unless you offer, but girl, you can't forget to live."

'It's not unheard of for someone to not like to party."

"It's not. But," she caught my gaze and held it, "have you ever been to one?"

Magick. She had to be using magick. How else did she know? How could she see me so clearly when everyone else saw what I wanted them to? I blushed at how exposed I felt, and Rani nodded.

"One party," she said. "Try a drink. Meet new people. Who knows, you might enjoy yourself." I eyed the outfit she selected, my fingers itching to try it on. "I'll stay by your side the whole time, and if you want to leave five minutes after getting there, I'll escort you back with a smile on my face."

"Fine."

And that's how I ended up in front of a large house with too many windows and drunk humans mingling out of the door and onto the lawn. A steady bass smothered the sound of their revelry. My own body thrummed with it. The frat party resembled one from every movie *ever*, and I was actually disappointed that it wasn't something different.

Rani held my hand and led me inside before we froze. Past the dancing and beer pong, past the couples getting too handsy in the shadows, and straight to the kitchen. It was actually pretty tolerable in here and not that messy. A red solo cup appeared in front of me.

"I mixed it myself," she warned. "It's strong, so baby it for a while. If you want more, I'll get it. Or you. Don't accept anything from anyone else."

I nodded, familiar with the basics of drink safety: don't set it down, keep it covered, those sorts of things. Some of the juice sloshed out as we rushed back to the music for dancing. Even more escaped as I swung my hips and pulled at my skirt to keep it covering all my important parts. An hour passed. Maybe two. Somewhere between a guy asking Rani to dance and my second cup, I realized I was having fun.

I raised my cup with the room—because the song told us to—and startled when a warm body pressed against me. My wide, panicked eyes begged my roommate for help, and she laughed.

"He's cute!" she shouted over the music, then grabbed my free hand and swiveled her hips.

I could do this. It was just dancing. The song switched to a slower beat, and I let it carry me away. This was what I've been missing. I'd never felt more free than in this moment, lost in a crowded room of strangers. The song changed again, and it took me a moment to notice the pressure in my chest.

Standing near the speakers made it hard to separate my body from the music, but when I saw him, I knew I wasn't imagining things. It was like my body had a warning signal for when he was around. His blond hair was darker inside, but nothing could mask that glare. Just like at the hospital and again later in the Commons, I was torn between challenging him or running and hiding behind whatever locked door I could find.

There was something about him that both frightened and excited me. Neither was good.

"Who's that?" I asked Rani, gesturing to where the mystery guy leaned against the wall, watching me.

Her brows rose in shock when she saw who I meant. "That's Kai," she shouted into my ear. "He's a TA and totally off-limits to undergrads."

I frowned. Why was he here? And why hadn't he said that when we first bumped into one another? Telling me to stay away from the hospital made more sense now that I knew he had some authority on the matter. But it didn't explain why he kept popping up wherever I was. The guy behind me grew bolder with each song, and his roaming hands were a little much on top of the anger brewing in my chest.

I drained the last of my cup and pushed away. It was time to leave.

Kaiden

That skirt was obscene. The dark fabric clung to every curve and stopped high enough on her thighs that I didn't have to imagine those legs in my dreams tonight. The meathead behind her was on borrowed time. If he pulled her back again, I couldn't promise he'd still have hands when I was finished with him.

Had I known she'd be here, I would have arrived earlier and put a stop to this before it began.

Ez gave a low whistle beside me. "It's like she's trying to piss you off."

I grunted but didn't quite agree. She was surprised to see me here, that much was clear before her signature attitude slid into place. I watched her point to me and ask her friend something like she wasn't aware of who I was or how her behavior was a blatant show of disrespect.

A few more exchanges with the redhead and my little bond separated from the human to disappear in the crowd.

"Is there a plan?" Ez asked, but his attention was on the brunette eye-fucking him from across the room.

It was fine. My plans didn't require his assistance anyway. I sent him off with a flick of my hand and turned my attention back to the dance floor. A quick scan showed my bond hadn't returned. Only a few minutes passed since her departure, but that was plenty of time for her to get into more trouble.

Her friend didn't appear concerned by her absence. I crossed my arms and leaned back, prepared to wait a little longer. If she planned to return to the dance floor, I would have no choice but

to hold back until she ventured closer to one of the house's many exits. I doubted she'd agree to dance with me, which meant I couldn't exactly steer her in the direction I needed.

Watching her grind on that meathead was also less than ideal. Speaking of...I walked the perimeter of the room, searching for the over-confident sheep that was all over my bond. He was gone as well.

Oh *fuck* no.

I swore on my family seat that if she'd gone upstairs to hook up with that human, being chained up in my room would be the least of her worries. When I circled for a second time and still didn't see them, I took the stairs in leaps, vowing to bust down the door of every room if I had to. Lucky for them, that wasn't necessary.

The second floor was nothing more than a couple hallways with closed doors on either side. I found them tucked at the end of one next to an open bathroom. My bond was pressed against the wall with the entire height of her human date leaning over her. He was close, too close, but that wasn't what had my steps eating up the distance between us.

I didn't care that her fists were pressed against his chest or that his mouth was close to her skin. It was the overpowering scent of lavender that slowly leaked out toward the stairs and how my bond was using the full force of her power so carelessly out in the open that had me ready to take her over my knee.

"Are you out of your damn mind?"

My outrage was laced with a hint of my own power, and I allowed it loose to separate them before anyone else came up those stairs. My shadows were visible, like an extra limb, but the lack of light in this far corner worked in my favor. I wasn't even sure my bond saw them before the human snapped out of whatever trance she had him in.

He was breathing heavily, they both were, but the sudden

disconnect from her power confused him, and I wasted no time. Wrapping a hand around my bond, I grabbed her arm and dragged her away. A spark burned my skin when we touched, but I ignored it, along with the wince on her face at the unexpected sting.

The stairs were clear, but I had to push our way through the front door and onto the street. The cool air jolted her from her docile state, and she finally fought against my hold.

"Let me go!" she shouted, and I hurried us along before someone heard her cries and misinterpreted them for something else.

"Now isn't the time for a tantrum, Eryn. I'd say you've had enough fun tonight, wouldn't you?" She fought harder, and I was forced to let her go or risk dislocating her shoulder.

"How do you know my name?" she asked, out of breath but defiant as ever.

Were we really going to keep playing this game? "I asked your friend," I lied. "The redhead."

She cursed under her breath, something I couldn't make out, and then turned that powerful gaze upon me.

"Why would she tell you?"

"Because I asked."

The bond between us was palpable. It took every ounce of my control to keep it leashed. Was hers as desperate for me? Did it lunge in her chest like it could escape from behind her ribs and draw us together? My lungs couldn't hold enough oxygen, but she didn't look nearly as affected. Interesting. Control that strong yet she couldn't keep her power contained in that hallway?

"If this stare-down is over, I'll be going now."

Not a damn chance. I grabbed her shirt this time. There were consequences for her actions, and she wasn't leaving my presence tonight without knowing every single one of them. Not

least of which being the giant "I'm here" sign she just blasted to every member of our community within a fifty-mile radius. By the way she squirmed in my hold, I figured maybe she wasn't as blind to the consequences as she pretended to be.

"Not so fast," I murmured, and not so gently led her to the secluded alley between the last house on this street and the start of campus. Once safely hidden from prying eyes, I turned on her. "What were you thinking?"

Her eyes widened as she took a step back. "E-excuse me?"

"With that guy back there." I wasn't going to let this go. "Alone. Hands on his chest. Ring a bell?"

She was going to say it even if I had to drag it out of her. I was huge on accountability, and no bond of mine would be allowed to brush off her mistakes.

"I did nothing wrong!" she shouted and pushed me. Actually pushed me. "He followed me up there and wouldn't let go, even when I told him to stop. But I was asking for it, right?"

Wait, what? That asshole *assaulted* her? I stepped back and took a good look at her for the first time. Smeared makeup, a tear in the strap of her top, and *fuck*, there was a bruise on her forearm. She wasn't feeding off him. She was defending herself.

"Wearing a skirt this short means I must want sex, and I'm a tease if I don't let them touch me. Is that what you're saying?"

Her eyes were rimmed with tears, and I couldn't help but reach out to wipe them away. Another jolt went through me when we touched.

"No one deserves to have their boundaries ignored," I told her, my voice a growl from my growing fury. "No, is a complete sentence. Stop, is a complete sentence."

"Oh," she breathed, the fight leaving her in the same breath. That fucker was dead if I ever saw him again. A quick text to Ez might even have it taken care of tonight.

"But," I continued, "there are monsters out there who can't

read the words thrown at them. Letting your guard down while you're *drunk*, and almost—"

"Are you serious right now? Where do you get off trying to lecture me about my choices?" That fire was back, but she hadn't brushed my hand away yet.

As for her question, I was her bond. I was responsible for her safety and well-being. I was the only person in the world with the right to discipline her when her actions put her in danger.

"I'm—"

"Not my father." She set that stubborn chin and glared right at me.

For the second time tonight, she derailed my thoughts. Was she still trying to deny us? I saw no deception in her gaze. This wasn't a game; she was truly pissed. Almost as if she didn't know who I was. I brought up both hands to cup her cheeks and watched her reaction. While it felt like a mild form of lightning ran beneath my skin, aside from an initial jolt, she was unaffected. *Holy shit.* Worse than that, there was no recognition whatsoever.

In fact, I was probably freaking her out. I released her and stepped back. My hand ran through my hair as I thought this through. This changed everything. My plans for our immediate future were on a permanent hold. I could tell her right now who I was, but I risked her running again, and I put in too much work to get us here.

Months of plans were scrapped in a matter of seconds. I needed time to figure this out.

"Umm...well...this has been fun." She started inching away from me, not exactly scared, but definitely hesitant.

My silence wasn't helping. I didn't know what our future held just yet, but I did know I couldn't let her walk back to her dorm alone—not with the power flare she sent up back there.

The djinn would be on her by morning if I didn't lay down some wards to protect her tonight.

"Thank you for the save," she added, still inching away. "But I can take it from here."

"Oh no, princess." I stepped in front of her before she got too far. "I don't trust you to not find more trouble on your way back to your dorm."

Wary morphed back into anger as she hit me with her little fist. "Screw you."

I caught her next swing, enveloping her hand in my own. "Are you offering?" My smirk disappeared when she didn't respond to my teasing. "Relax. I'm going to escort you back and drop you at your door like the perfect gentleman."

The campus was a map of frozen silence, and I was on high alert. Every small sound was a threat to the spitfire beside me. My soulmate who didn't recognize who I was. I saw our earlier encounters in a whole new light. She wasn't being difficult or denying me, she was being herself and standing strong in the face of my, up until now, utterly rude behavior. Pride filled me at the knowledge that she could hold her own.

I glanced at her for the millionth time and cursed as she shivered. That outfit in this weather? I wasn't complaining. In fact, the sight of her ass in that skirt would serve me well the next time I had my dick in hand, but what kind of bond would I be if I let her freeze just to enjoy the view?

"Here," I slipped off my hoodie and held it out to her. "Since your outfit is missing several yards of material."

She stopped walking and stared at the dark cotton like it would jump from my hand to her face if she wasn't careful. It just might if I had to watch her shiver one more time.

"Do I need to assist you?" I offered, stepping closer. She didn't answer. Her brows creased in confusion like she was trying to figure out why I was being kind to her.

I held in a growl at her hesitancy. It was my fault we were off to a rocky start, but watching her stand there in obvious discomfort was a test of patience. Finally, she tentatively reached out and took the hoodie with a tiny smile. Progress.

"Thank you," she murmured, sliding the soft material over her head.

I watched it settle over her, reaching almost down to her knees. The sleeves were too long for her, and her hands disappeared inside them. She looked fucking adorable and somehow sexy as hell. Seeing her in my clothes did something to me, and it was another battle in restraint not to grab her and run.

"You're nothing like I thought you'd be," I told her, and her small smirk made my heart stop dead. Beautiful.

"What, from the ten minutes you've known me and the couple of other times you've stared at me?"

"I didn't stare," I disputed, even though I totally had. How could I not?

"Okayyy," she snorted, teasing me as she resumed walking, leaving me to follow along behind her.

"I didn't stare," I repeated. "I just thought... you looked familiar." There. That was safe.

She glanced back at me, and for one heartbeat, I thought she'd figured it out, but she only frowned and said, "I thought the same thing when I first saw you." She skipped away to the doors of Midnight Hall. One swipe of her student ID, and they opened for her. "But then I realized you were just an asshole glaring at me for no reason."

The doors shut on my laugh, and I waited until her window glowed with a light to tell me she had made it safely. I knew which room was hers already because I'd planned to force her to leave with me. But now, I wanted to see if she'd come willingly. I wanted to woo her and see those eyes light up with a different

fire. Yeah. I wanted her to *want* to belong to me, as much as I now belonged to her.

four

Eryn

The sharp morning air cut through the hoodie as if the borrowed cotton was as thin as a sheet of paper. I should have worn my jacket, but in my defense, I thought it was too bulky, and I'd stand out. The students passing me in the parking lot weren't bundled up like the Michelin Man. Then again, none of them had been out here for the past three hours timing how long it took to run from the Commons to the animal hospital on the edge of campus.

When I woke up this morning three things occurred to me. Front and center, I was never going to drink again. My teeth were so fuzzy, I used a quarter of my toothpaste to scrub them. My head still pounded, even after all the fresh air, and I silently thanked the gods that the first day of classes were, according to Rani, usually a review of the syllabus.

My queasy stomach reminded me of my second realization: alcohol made me careless. I wasn't so wasted last night that I didn't remember what happened. Being cornered in a dark

hallway was bad enough, but I'd been forced to use my power against that jockstrap. A lot of it. Gaining control over his mind was difficult, and I didn't think it had anything to do with his mental constitution.

Alcohol made it harder to manipulate human minds. Lesson learned.

I'd spent the better part of my jog this morning mapping escape routes and fighting off a panic attack at the thought of how soon I might have to put those plans into effect. Any supernaturals nearby would have felt my burst of magick last night. Hopefully, if there were any around, they were too drunk themselves or not of a curious nature. But I couldn't afford to rely on that wishful thinking.

I planned to leave that little slip up out of my weekly email to my parents.

Hi guys, I've settled in great. Campus is beautiful and my roommate isn't a hunter in disguise, oh, and I might have given myself away in less than twenty four hours of being here but I'm just going to pretend I didn't and see what happens.

Yeah, that would go over well.

Another biting breeze blew through the brick-paved corridor, and I hunched over my crossed arms. The lecture hall was only a few yards ahead, but it felt like another mile. The bag on my back offered no protection, and once again the hoodie failed to keep any warmth contained. My skin felt like ice.

It was an unconscious decision to wear it this morning. I'd fallen asleep with it on, surrounded by a rich citrus scent that smelled better than anything Rani had in her closet. I wanted to soak in it, which I guess was why I had yet to take it off. I thought about its owner: Kai. He was...unexpected. Domineering, with a swagger that couldn't be matched, but a kind heart underneath it all.

He saved me. Was he pushy about it and a complete ass for

half of it? Without a doubt. There was something about him, though.

"Eryn!" Rani's chipper shout echoed off the large buildings as she waved at me from the steps of the science building.

We shared this class three times a week, and I gave a grateful sigh that I knew someone else. Two heads were better than one, and I needed all the help I could get on the subject. I passed the 101-level last year fine enough, but it was online, and the teacher didn't care about our comprehension of the subject as long as we completed our modules.

The classroom had amphitheater-style seating, with rows arranged in semicircles and leveled. Rani and I grabbed two seats in the middle near the front and dropped our bags at our feet.

"Don't think I don't recognize that hoodie," Rani whispered, with a smirk of approval. My cheeks burned, and I crossed my arms again like that would hide the evidence.

"I don't know what you mean." I ignored how her smirk grew and focused on arranging my notebook and highlighters. I used all the colors that came in the pack to organize my notes.

Blue meant it was something I already had a strong grasp of. Pink was when the teacher marked something for a test. Yellow was something easily transferable to notecards, and green meant I needed all the help. I really hoped my notes stayed blue this semester.

"Nice try." Rani's reprimand drew a few curious stares, but she ignored them and leaned closer. "I saw you leave with Kai last night, and now you show up this morning in his hoodie. Spill it."

She practically vibrated in her seat. Nothing happened between us, despite how it appeared. Wasn't she the one who told me he was off-limits anyway? She poked my arm with her

pen, then did it again when I refused to acknowledge her. Poke. Poke. Poke.

"Okay, okay!" I growled. "You're relentless."

"Damn straight. Now, tell me all the dirty little details."

I rolled my eyes. "Sorry to disappoint, but there are none. He walked me home; I was cold, and he offered his hoodie. That's it." She pouted, and my lips twitched as I held back a smile. This girl. "I spent the night in my own bed, which is *right next to yours* if you recall."

"Ugh, I know." She settled back in her seat. "I was hoping something happened before I got back. A little smoochy time? No?

She sounded so hopeful. What was it about college guys that made hooking up with them so necessary? Did they have an extra appendage I wasn't aware of? A unique skill set? Was I really missing out if nothing happened with my pushy savior last night? I thought back to how commanding he was. Someone was obviously used to getting his way, but so was I.

Living my life in obscurity, I wasn't used to people paying me much attention, and that afforded me a different type of freedom. I went where I wanted, when I wanted, without having to worry about anything but keeping my magick contained and staying off the supernatural radar. Kai trying to tell me what to do, on more than one occasion now, was annoying but...intriguing.

He was in a constant state of pissed off whenever he was around me. At least, that's what it seemed like, but he also flirted with me last night. I wasn't so naive that I didn't recognize his offer to mess around as more than just banter. He'd have had me out of that skirt in seconds if I was willing. I snorted when I thought about it; him trying to command me out of my clothes. It was ridiculous, offensive, it was...kind of hot, actually.

I was saved from the embarrassment of my own imagination

by the professor arriving. He strolled to the front of the class and set his cup of coffee on the podium.

"Welcome to Organismal Biology 102." His smooth baritone carried easily to even the highest row. "I'm Dr. Carver, and we will be spending quite a bit of time together this semester. Three days a week, for an hour and a half, we will navigate the complexities of ecology and physiology. We will dig into organismal structure and functional genomics. By the end of this course, you will be far more familiar with the causes and consequences of mating and migration systems, immunological defenses, and even knowledge of swim bladders and feathers that will surprise you."

I sat up straighter and clutched my pen to keep it from rolling off the small desk. This is what I was here for. Finally, after two years of useless humanities and math courses, I was about to learn the real stuff. Subjects that would bring me a step closer to my dream job. The subject material wouldn't be easy, but it was definitely doable. Having a genuine interest in it helped, I was sure.

"Many of you are here because this is a required course for your degree. Those pursuing the sciences or conservation, those interested in our illustrious Marine Biology Department, as well as those seeking acceptance to the Veterinary Medicine Program, to name but a few."

Rani and I glanced at one another, our excitement barely contained. We were going to rock this semester. The sound of a door opening interrupted Dr. Carver, and he looked over, then waved to whoever it was that entered.

"Since this course is so popular, and your class is not my only one this semester, I've enlisted the help of my TA. All of your questions, projects, and assignments will be filtered through him. As such, you will find his office hours and email

listed on the syllabus instead of my own. If anything arises that he can't handle, he will forward it to me."

I didn't have to glance down at my printed syllabus to know who the TA was. That telltale tug in the center of my chest told me all I needed before Kai appeared out of the corner of my eye. He casually sauntered up beside the professor, hands in his pockets and that signature half-smile on his face that I'd recognize anywhere.

The fluorescent lights in the room caused the faint scar near his eye to stand out, and it lent him a haunting look as he scanned the room. The professor continued to make his introductions, but I couldn't hear them over my racing heart. Kai wasn't supposed to be here. I wasn't supposed to have to see him again, ever. Gods, I was just imagining him commanding me to take my clothes off. Being forced to interact with him twice in one day was enough to mess with my head, and now I was going to have to do it three times a week?

His eyes appeared more green than blue today, almost aquamarine as they stared at me. Like he knew my thoughts, the corner of his mouth curled in a sensual smile that sent heat zinging down my spine. I crossed and uncrossed my legs, shifting in my seat from the unfamiliar feeling coursing through me. This was more than attraction. That domineering asshole was turning me on, with just a look.

"Why is Kai staring at you like that?" Rani whispered, her head only slightly turned toward me, like she too was ensnared by the intensity that was our new TA.

"He's not," I replied because I refused to believe it. I refused to acknowledge whatever was happening right now.

"Oh, he definitely is," she purred, and I elbowed her to stop before he heard.

How he saw me among the crowd of students was a mystery. We weren't even in the front row. The professor droned on about

his expectations for the next few months while Kai practically undressed me with his eyes. I conspicuously checked to see if anyone else had noticed, but my classmates were too busy jotting down in their calendars and listening to the key dates for assignments and tests. Things I should be listening to but was too distracted to focus on.

Tired of the unfamiliar feelings taking over, I fearlessly returned Kai's stare, determined to make him be the one to look away. I failed. Spectacularly. His gaze was filled with molten hunger as he dipped his chin ever so slightly. I lifted a brow, and his stare flicked to the front of the hoodie, then back up at me. What was he–oh my gods, the hoodie. I was wearing his hoodie!

My face heated, and I gave in, ducking my head to hide from that knowing smirk. It wasn't a big deal, I told myself. It was just a piece of clothing; a soft, borrowed, piece of clothing that should be somewhere on my floor right now, ready to be returned to its owner, rather than being worn. Again—or still— because I had yet to take it off. Fuck.

"Today will be an easy class, and you will be released early after you finish the test," Dr. Carver caught my attention with that nugget of information.

Test? We hadn't cracked open a textbook or discussed a single slide. What could he possibly test us on? The panicked murmurs circling the room told me I wasn't the only one distressed at the thought.

"Don't worry," he chuckled, oblivious to the high blood pressure he caused in half of us. "This is a placement test and won't count toward your final grade. It's only meant to challenge your current knowledge of the subject material and see whether you're ready to take on the intensity of this course."

It helped knowing this grade wouldn't count against me, but I was still nervous. Kai walked up the stairs, handing out a stack

of papers to the head of each row. As the tests were handed out, the professor left us with one final requirement.

"Please turn your test in to Mr. Winmore on your way out. Lastly, on the table beside him is a sign-up form. Each student is responsible for choosing a time that works best with their schedules and must meet with Mr. Winmore to go over their grade from this test. He will point out your strengths and weaknesses and be able to set you up with helpful study materials and groups to get you through the semester. There are no excuses—if you fail it will be because you didn't try."

The test was in another language, or I had suddenly forgotten how to read. Letters swirled and blurred as I tried to read the question for the fifth time. Half the class already finished, and I was stuck here, my mind going in a million different directions. I filled in the little bubble, erased it, then filled it in again. I skimmed my fingers through my hair, and the sleeve of the hoodie brushed my cheek in a waft of citrus.

Peeking at the table by the side doors, Kai was already grading while sporting a pair of dark-framed glasses. When had he put those on? *Focus, Eryn.* I turned back to the last page of the test and tried to just get through it. Calming down was easier said than done when I knew that finishing meant I'd have to approach the subject of my distraction.

He hadn't looked at me in over an hour—not that I was counting—but the thought of drawing his attention again sent the never-ending throbbing in my chest into overdrive. I needed to get it over with. Turn in the test, say nothing about the hoodie, and get the hell out of here. With a sigh, I packed up and awkwardly squeezed past the others in my row who were still working.

I slowly approached the table, my fingers gently shaking. Seriously. What the hell was wrong with me? He was just a guy. Hot as hell with a smile that did things to my insides, but he was

human. I could crush him like a fly with barely a thought if I really wanted to. My mental pep talk carried me the rest of the way, and I practically threw my test into the pile and bolted for the doors.

"Not so fast," Kai chided, without even looking. I froze across from him, one foot pointing at the exit for a quick getaway. "Aren't you forgetting something?"

He finally looked up, put the cap on the red marker in his hand, and gave me his undivided attention. Great. The dark frames around his eyes made the blue pop, and I begged my cheeks to behave and not give me away. No more blushing for the love of the gods. He patiently waited for me to get a hold of myself, but the only thing I could think of was the damned hoodie.

He wanted it back, of course he did. But did it have to be now? It was cold outside, and I had a decent walk ahead of me. The longer I stood there, the more I risked drawing attention to an already humiliating moment. I grabbed at the hem of the sweatshirt and lifted. A deep chuckle stopped me before the material passed my boobs.

"Not the damn jacket, Eryn." Kai's shoulders shook with mirth, and I blinked at how it transformed his face. "The one-on-one, you need to sign up for yours."

"Right," I mumbled. "The meeting. With you."

He nodded, still laughing. "Yes, the meeting with me."

"Alone."

"Alone."

"To go over the grade of this test," I added and blushed when his grin got wider. Damn cheeks betraying me again.

"If I didn't know better, I'd say you were nervous." The entire conversation was barely loud enough to carry to the other students in the room, but the look on his face would definitely give some of them ideas.

I couldn't afford for people to think something was going on between us when it wasn't. The consequence of fraternizing with the TA was probably expulsion, and that would ruin everything. I grabbed the sign-up sheet and hastily scanned it for openings. Crap. Of course, all the good slots were taken. The only ones left were during lunch or late in the evening before the library closed. I scribbled my name beside the late slot, figuring I'd be studying in the library anyway.

Handing the sheet back to him, I glared at the teasing gleam in his eye. "I'm glad you know better. See you on Thursday."

I ran from the room before he could answer with another taunt. The blast of cold air outside was a shock to the system, but no wind reached me tucked at the top of the stairs. Rani didn't look that far behind me when I glanced at her test, I'd wait here, and we could walk to lunch together as planned.

Movement on the other side of the landing revealed an orange tabby with a bent tail. The cat hissed when I took a step toward it, but then gave a pitiful meow and limped away. The poor thing looked a wreck. Was it hit by a car? A fight with another stray perhaps? I crouched low and held out my fingers.

"Pspsps, come here little guy." The cat was unimpressed at my attempt at communication.

It limped further away, heading toward the alley that ran around the back of the building. Careful to only tap into what I needed, I called on my power to try and get a better sense of what was bothering the little guy. Nothing. Frowning, I tried again but was met with silence. That's weird. I'd never had a problem connecting with an animal before, even with pain medicine running through their system. The little one disappeared around the corner but let out another painful cry.

"Hold on, I'm coming," I said, already mentally plotting how I'd catch him. Using my backpack as a carrier might work if he

was a feisty one. Not being able to communicate would make him a little more hostile.

Before I could step off the landing, Rani joined me, complaining about the test and how hungry she was. I listened for the cat, but he was long gone, probably scared off by the sound of another person. My disappointment at failing to help an animal in need was strong. This had never happened before.

"Am I supposed to just leave him?" The idea was enough to make me sick to my stomach. It was *cold* out.

Rani tried to console me. "There are lots of strays on campus, and they're well taken care of. If he's truly injured, it won't be long before the vet students are treating him."

It didn't feel right, but short of forcing her to follow me on a hunt through the back alley, there was nothing I could do unless I saw him again. We quickly hit the Commons and boxed our lunch to go, taking it back to the dorm to eat in front of Rani's TV. It was supposed to be a relaxing afternoon, but then I saw our door.

Some type of sigil was carved into the wood. It was small, too small to be noticed by anyone not looking for it, but I was trained my entire life to keep an eye out for the little details. The sigil was a curved half circle, almost like the letter G, with a string of dots along one side and a couple of strikes through it. I didn't know what it was for, but I knew what it meant. It meant I wasn't the only supernatural on campus. It meant whoever was out there knew *where* I was and was one step closer to learning the truth about *who* if they hadn't already. One day into the semester, and I already messed up. Would I ever learn?

five

Kaiden

The djinn were here. I sensed their magick like a sticky film over campus—it felt like walking through fucking spiderwebs. I hated spiders. They had their purpose, particularly in some strong spells I favored, but the whole eight-legs thing? Count me out.

"Gods," I cursed, stumbling upon another illusion behind the library.

It was too small to register, as were the other illusions we dismantled this week, and therein lay the problem. The djinn were organized and acting under the radar. They were playing smart. Casting an illusion larger than this tabby, or the bunny that Ez found earlier, would alert the supers nearby that they were up to something.

The ugly cat hissed at me and limped under the stairs to get away from the spell I weaved. I smiled. If it was reacting to me, not its intended target, then its caster was nearby and watching. Squeezing the kyanite in my fist, I focused my intent and

allowed the crystal to lead me. A thin tendril of my power speared through the illusion, decimating it before continuing on, slithering along the brick in search of its prey.

"Got you," I murmured and struck. My shadows grew until they wrapped around the djinn like a vengeful python.

Not very intelligent, hiding only a few feet away behind a dumpster, but I guess that was part of the plan. The djinn needed to be close enough to grab my bond once their seriously annoying illusions did their job. Because that's who all these illusions were for: Eryn. Fucking injured animals. *Cute*, injured animals. She wouldn't be able to resist. It was equivalent to a van filled with wriggling puppies.

The djinn had certainly done their homework, and any other time, I might have admired them for it. But they were fucking with something that was *mine*. I sent a text to Ezra, telling him to meet me. It was pure luck that I caught this one tucked behind the buildings like this. The one Ez snagged two days ago was in the middle of the Commons. That almost got messy. Not that this situation didn't have its own risks, getting rid of the djinn without anyone seeing being one of them.

This one was female, with blonde locks that grew more tangled and matted as she fought against my power. Pointless. My shadows were a physical entity when I wanted them to be, but they weren't connected to me any more than Peter Pan's.

"You can't stop us, Alantes!" The djinn spat like a feral cat in a cage. "We will destroy your bond before you and your faction can gain any more undeserved power."

"So, you do know who I am," I purred. "That will make things go a lot smoother for you."

There was never any doubt that the djinn knew who I was on sight. Kaiden Einar Winmore Alantes, heir to the witch faction and bond to the last of the nightmares. Two things my

enemies couldn't stand: I was powerful, and that power was only going to increase.

"We will find her," the djinn continued as if my threat meant nothing to her. "Hiding her here was a mistake."

Hmm. They knew enough about her to lay targeted traps across campus, but not enough to realize they weren't the only ones hunting her. Interesting. What else could she tell me?

"How many of you are there?" I asked. We only knew about three, including her.

There had to be more than that. Underestimating an Alantes was not something I would accuse them of. They knew better. The djinn cackled, a hoarse, deranged sound that echoed off the ancient brick architecture. I squeezed my shadows tighter, trying to cut through the sound, but that only made her laughter more high-pitched. Like a disturbing whistle.

I slapped another shadow over her mouth, but it wasn't enough. If she didn't shut up soon, someone was going to stick their head out of one of the windows to see what was going on.

"Problem, cuz?" Ezra walked up, hands in his pockets and humming like this was an innocent stroll in the park.

My lips twitched at the picture it painted; writhing shadows surrounded an insane djinn across from a laid-back surfer who looked less out of place in an American Eagle ad.

"This one won't talk," I told him. "And we're running out of time."

"Well then, let's see if I can speed things up."

Ez cracked his knuckles, then threw his hands out to the sides. All the windows on the back of the library froze over. The thick layer of ice would conceal our interrogation, even muffling the sound a bit, but it came at a cost. That was a large chunk of magick.

"Ezra," I groaned. "She definitely felt that."

He rolled his eyes, not the least bit bothered at the extra

work he just created for me. "Do you want to know how many of these fuckers are after your girl or not?"

I felt a headache coming on. "Of course I do."

"Then let me do my thing and stop worrying about it. One little blast of power won't send your bond on the run again. You can still stick to wooing her."

"Great Ez. Tell the djinn even more about our plans, I don't think she heard you."

He laughed, and a familiar grin spread across his face, telling me the djinn wouldn't be leaving this alley alive.

"You don't have to worry about the little djinny here spilling your secrets, does he, sweetheart?" The blood drained from her face as he moved closer.

"No, he doesn't. But you..." Ez lifted a brow, and both the djinn's hands were encased in ice. She screamed, "...you should worry."

I thickened the shadows over her mouth as my cousin did what he did best. Ten questions, his favorite game. Our prisoner had ten chances to answer our questions truthfully. Each refusal or lie led to a shattered finger. When Ez ran out of fingers, he moved on to toes, then arms, legs, and so on. It was successful, if not time-consuming. I frowned and glanced at my phone. My last one-on-one for the week was in an hour—with Eryn.

"We need to move this along," I warned my cousin, and then checked the iced windows for good measure. This wasn't a secure location.

When the screaming stopped, I removed the shadow gag. The djinn caught my eyes and held them. Her mouth moved too rapidly for me to track what she said, but when her pupils dilated, I knew she was trying to put me under a compulsion. Stupid. My cousin and I were warded against such psychic attacks. Did she think we were amateurs? I slapped the gag back on her face a second before Ez shattered another finger.

I sighed for what felt like the millionth time. "This is going to take forever."

It didn't take forever, but it did take thirty minutes for the djinn to break and another fifteen for Ez to get all the information he needed. Our unlucky prisoner, with only one frozen digit remaining, had no idea how many of her kind were currently on campus. Honestly, she wasn't a wealth of information. All we learned was that they would keep coming now that they knew Eryn was here.

A fact we were already aware of. I left Ez to clean up and paused at the back door of the library to gain a little composure. My shadows sank beneath my skin with an ease I hadn't felt in days. Knowing I was about to see my bond did a lot to tame them. I felt her. The flutter in my chest told me she was nearby, possibly already at my office. I forced myself to take my time, stopping to grab a coffee from the Starbucks inside before taking the stairs down to the basement.

The TA offices were crammed into the subterranean level as an afterthought. Nowhere near as polished as the floors above, the halls down here didn't have the bells and whistles I was accustomed to seeing on this campus, but they got the job done. Fresh paint, clean carpet, and solid doors; I didn't need much else.

Coffee in hand, I rounded the corner from the rickety elevator I always avoided and came to a complete stop at the sight before me. My bond was gorgeous and especially delectable in a pair of tight leggings and a soft sweater that draped off one shoulder, baring her slender neck and smooth skin.

I observed her for a time, amused at how obviously nervous she was. The bond in my chest was going crazy, so I knew she felt the same. Did she realize yet that that feeling meant I was nearby? She paced in front of my door, stopped, and shifted

from foot to foot, before pacing again. Clearly anxious. I decided to put her out of her misery and traveled down the hall with the silence of a hunter. Eryn spun around just as I reached her, hand on her chest, and I smirked. She definitely felt me.

"Nervous?" I taunted, unable to help myself. Her glare, one of my favorite expressions of hers, was firmly in place.

"Unless you plan to berate me once again for my outfit choice, no. And you never made me nervous," she added, the little bob in her throat betraying her.

I reached around, my arm brushing her bare shoulder, to grab the doorknob and invite her inside. "Then, by all means, please come in."

The office was two inches bigger than a shoe closet, with only enough space for my desk, chair, filing cabinet, and another chair squeezed next to the door. There was hardly enough room to get around to the other side of the desk, and if I stretched, I could almost touch the opposite wall. The close quarters were usually inconvenient at the best of times, but today they were perfect.

I watched her settle in, realize there wasn't enough room to put her bag on the floor, and instead decide to hold it in her lap. Her cheeks were flushed from my obvious attention, and my smirk deepened. It was pure manners that kept me from speaking first. Allowing her to regain her composure had nothing to do with how much I enjoyed watching her squirm. Those rosy cheeks, her nibbling her bottom lip, the vulgar thoughts they created, it was all purely coincidental.

She cleared her throat, bravery gathered for the moment. "I realized I never properly thanked you for helping me earlier this week. So...thank you."

I nodded and clutched the armrests of my chair, unable to speak over the memories. If she knew who that asshole was— the one that dared to try and assault her—she'd know that he

was no longer enrolled here. That he'd just up and left the next morning with no warning or explanation to the university.

She'd been very irresponsible that night, not to say that the pervert's actions were her fault, but her lack of awareness hadn't helped the situation. Drinking without a tolerance, slipping off into a dark hallway alone with no regard for her safety—I still had the urge to spank that luscious ass red when I thought about it.

And it seemed she hadn't learned her lesson. This meeting would end after the library closed to students, making this slot the latest I could offer. The campus shuttles wouldn't be running when she left, which meant she would have to walk back to her dorm, on the opposite side of campus, in the dark. Why the hell had she picked this time slot?

"Have you been responsible since?" I asked her, knowing full well what the answer would be. I was a sucker for punishment, but maybe she was too.

"Excuse me?" I smirked again at her wide-eyed look of surprise. Anger slowly followed behind it.

I leaned back in my chair, hands raised. "I only meant, have you been more aware of your surroundings?"

"You..." Her lips pursed in an adorable frown. "You just don't know when to quit."

I really didn't.

My lack of remorse only pissed her off more. Gods, she was a sight. Her emotions shone through her gaze; she couldn't conceal them there. Her eyes were more jade than emerald, and they practically sparkled with fury. They had me entranced, at least, until she spoke again.

"I love how this amuses you, I truly do," she said. "But I'm only here for the required meeting, and I'd rather go ahead and get it over with so we can move on from this interaction and hopefully never have to repeat it. Ever."

That wouldn't do. I looked down at her file, and the rising panic dissolved as I read over my notes. My little bond wasn't going anywhere. If she wanted to stay in this class, she would be seeing a whole lot more of me.

"Very well," I told her, my excitement in check by strength of will. "Allow me to get straight to the point then. You failed the test."

It was my first time seeing her at a loss for words, and it didn't disappoint—full lips, glossy and open in a perfect little circle. I really was getting too much enjoyment from this.

"What?" she whispered. "Like, there's a few subjects I don't grasp but—"

"No. Failed the whole thing." I didn't want to hurt her, as I knew this would, but she needed the truth. "You're actually behind by a significant amount. Even your grasp on basic molecular foundations isn't as strong as you need for this class."

She slumped in her chair, soaking in the news. I frowned, worried she wouldn't fight back on this. Denial, anger, literally anything to tell me she didn't accept my findings. Then like a switch, she freaked out. Jumping to her feet, she paced as much as the small room would allow; two steps one direction, turn, two steps back, turn, repeat.

"I did so well in the 101 class. Granted, it was online, and the instructor was nonexistent, but *still*. I studied so hard. How the hell can I be this far behind?" The question was directed at me, with her hands slammed flat on my desk, but before I could answer, she was off again. "I won't make the program cut at the end of the year without this credit. I'll be delayed for at least another year. My entire life's plan will be pushed back and..."

Her panicking turned internal as she thought through the repercussions. The color in her face brought on by her earlier anger fled. She sat once more, pale, shaking, and silent. Fuck. I hadn't meant to send her into a spiral.

"Ms. Montalli." She stared at my desk, lost in her thoughts. "Ms. Montalli," I tried again. I could almost sense her anxiety, and our bond wasn't even strong enough yet for me to pick up on her emotions. Double fuck. "*Eryn*," I growled, plucking at the strand in my chest that connected us, and she snapped out of it. "I can help you."

"You can?" she breathed, and some of that color returned.

"I can tutor you twice a week to get you caught up and later maintain your understanding of the material." She nodded, and a relieved sigh escaped. "We can meet here whenever works for you," I offered.

"Tuesdays and Thursdays?" she asked. "Since the class is on the other days of the week, I assume those would be better for you?"

She would be correct.

"Thank you for your consideration." I smiled. "I accept those days. Email me a time after you look over your schedule. We can begin next week."

There was nothing left to discuss, but I didn't want her to leave without some of that fire returning. She stood to go and had her hand on the door before I spoke.

"Princess." At the nickname, her back straightened, and she turned to face me. "This means you'll have to suffer my company each week. Do you think you can do that?"

A small tease. Nothing inappropriate, but with just enough of a taunt to get her going again. She didn't disappoint. She raised her dainty middle finger and followed it with an involuntary grin, she knew what she was doing.

"Somehow, I think I'll survive."

six

Eryn

"Tell me again why we're doing this?"

The skimpy, albeit cute pajamas were a far cry from the last outfit I wore to Greek Row. The little boxer shorts Rani shoved me into were shorter than that skirt, but infinitely more comfortable, and the long-sleeved thermal was the softest thing I'd ever worn. I slipped on Kai's hoodie and the Uggs my roomie threw at me, and the outfit was complete. Cute, but I was about to freeze my ass off. Rani didn't say anything about me still having the hoodie, so I counted that as a win.

"This sleepover is the most important event for the pledges of Kappa Delta," Rani explained again. "And if we're late, I won't sit with you in Bio for the rest of the semester."

Ouch. I clutched my chest and staggered back at the threat, but I knew she was kidding. Maybe. I hoped she was because sitting alone kinda sucked. Pledging a sorority wasn't my idea, it was definitely her thing, but there were a lot of benefits. Connections with alumni that could help me get into the veteri-

nary program being one of them. I just had to make it through these stupid trials to be accepted. And a sleepover didn't sound too bad. I'd never been to one and was secretly excited.

"It's going to be fun," Rani promised and ushered me out the door so we could make the shuttle.

The winter air cut right through the cotton shorts, but the trip to Greek Row wasn't long, and soon, we were once again warm and toasty inside. The massive living room of the sorority house had been converted to a dorm room of sorts with about twenty cots. Each bed had a little teddy bear sitting on it, dressed in a small shirt with a green seashell on it.

I was still apprehensive as Rani and I tucked ourselves in the back near the big bay window. That apprehension grew as more girls arrived. Was it the large group? It had to be. I originally thought that being tucked away in this house, surrounded by humans, would make me feel safer after feeling that blast of power a couple of days ago. I knew I would eventually feel some magick. Supers were everywhere—well, maybe not Antarctica— and it's not like I could completely avoid them forever.

But I hoped to at least last longer than the first week of school. With each new girl that wandered in, I found myself hiding deeper in the corner. Any one of them could be a super; that blonde with the pigtails; or that tall supermodel with the smooth, mocha complexion. I took a slow breath in through my nose, held it, and then let it out. Now wasn't the time to fall into a panic.

Nothing had changed. Even if every single one of these girls was a super, they had no reason to think I was one of them. Blend in. Fly under the radar. My plan was still the same. I couldn't allow my being spooked to ruin everything.

"Don't bother unpacking, ladies. Not all of you will be staying this evening." The president of the sorority— Paisleigh...Kingsleigh...Brinnleigh?– stood at the double doors to

the living room and stared down at us with perfect hair, a full face of makeup, and an obvious superiority complex.

Paisleigh, I remembered now, wore a matching set of Victoria's Secret sweatpants and top. She looked so put together, despite following the pajama dress code set for the night. I looked down at myself and then at the other pledges in the room. We got a different memo. The rest of us were dressed more for comfort than to impress; complete with messy ponytails and blackhead strips for an unfortunate few.

"We're going to complete a little bonding activity before bed," Paisleigh continued, with a suspicious grin. "We promised you dinner after all."

I looked beside me at Rani, but she shrugged, having no idea what was happening either.

"This is called the Dinner Dash, and it's mandatory for further consideration as a pledge." At the whispers, the others were obviously familiar with the event in question. One girl even moaned into her hands and tried to inconspicuously wipe the zit cream off her face. Paisleigh looked on in glee. "I see the reputation of this game proceeds us. We're not allowed to haze anymore, or we lose our charter, so I came up with this instead."

"She got it from a movie!" one of the bubbly sorority sisters giggled. "But our version is actually sanctioned."

Okay, what the hell was the Dinner Dash? If it involved running, I had a pretty good shot at winning, thanks to my fugitive lifestyle, but something told me this wasn't the hundred-yard dash in the backyard of the Kappa Delta house.

"This challenge allows us to test our pledges on their confidence, resourcefulness, and level of attraction. Any girl who completes the dash successfully can consider themselves a probationary sister."

That caused some excited giggles among the pledges, but all I felt was a growing sense of dread. Even Rani was silent and

contemplative. Paisleigh raised her hand for silence, and I didn't trust that calculating glint in her eyes.

"These are the rules; you go as you are, no touch-ups, no changing, not a single brush stroke through your hair. You can't clean your teeth or change your outfit. Any cheating is punishable by an automatic expulsion from this year's pledge class." The girls picking at the products on their faces froze, and true worry settled over them. "Seabird's is a diner on the edge of campus. Each pledge has thirty minutes from the moment I say 'go' to get out there, find a date, and bring him with you to the restaurant."

"Dressed like this?" one pledge whined.

The sisters laughed at her dismay, and Paisleigh nodded. "Exactly as you are. Any pledge who arrives after the thirty minutes is up or without a date will be cut. If your date doesn't stay the whole meal, you're cut. You have permission to do whatever is necessary to secure a date as long as it's legal and doesn't bring shame upon the institution." She paused, letting the rules sink in, as well as the resulting panic. Pulling out a stopwatch, she gave us one final smirk and opened the front door. "Happy hunting, ladies."

It was a mad dash out the door, and the only reason I was in the middle of it was because Rani had a death grip on my arm. We looked ridiculous bolting into the frigid evening dressed as we were, but there was no one else around to take notice. My weird radar tingled. I jerked Rani to a halt, begrudgingly thankful for our little run because it kept the cold at bay. For now.

"Where are all the guys?" I asked, scanning the empty street, finding no one but squealing co-eds in various stages of dress.

"What do you mean?" she panted. "We're supposed to find them."

Our breaths pillowed out in front of us in see-through

clouds. It was cold as shit out here. No dude in his right mind would be out if they didn't have to be. I tilted my head and listened—no music. There wasn't even a party. This was Greek Row, there was *always* a party. I tapped into my magick and listened a little harder, careful not to use enough to register that far. The nearby thoughts I picked up on were shrouded in excitement and nerves. Something about waiting until they made it up the stairs?

"The pledges are going into the houses to find their dates," I said and pointed to where one girl in Mickey Mouse pajama pants ran out of the front door of the nearest fraternity house with a guy in hand, happily trailing after her.

Rani rubbed her arms as a stiff breeze blew in from the ocean. "I heard one girl whisper about how the fraternities were told not to make it easy for us. This must be the resourceful part of the game."

"It's a stupid-ass game," I growled. "I'm not sneaking into a house full of dudes, breaking into their bedrooms, and blinding myself with boxer-covered asses just to get a date."

The last time I was in a frat house, I nearly exposed myself and my powers. My freedom wasn't worth the potential connections Greek life offered. I would get into my program by being at the top of my class. Hard work before dick.

"I don't want to play anymore." I spun around, fully intent on returning to the dorm, cuddling under the warm covers, and possibly stealing one of Rani's ramen packets. Her desperate grip on my arm stopped me.

"Please don't go," she begged. "You don't have to pledge if you don't want to, but they saw us arrive together, and if you ditch it will look bad for me."

Her eyes were pleading. There were even a couple of tears, but I wasn't sure if that was from the cold or if she was just that desperate to fit in.

"Please," she asked again. "I really need to get into this sorority."

I winced. "Fine. But I'm not going into any of those houses. We're going to have to make do with whoever we find outside."

And that was how we ended up closer to campus in the middle of the night, freezing our literal asses off. There couldn't be more than fifteen minutes left of the challenge, and the only guys we'd run across were ones already attached to a pledge. We couldn't even text a friend to help because Paisleigh made Rani leave her phone behind. We might just fail this task.

"Look!" Rani gasped and pointed to where two figures took shape on the other side of the fountain.

We were closer to the middle of campus now. Two dudes wandering in the middle of the night, this far from the dorms or bars was suspicious as fuck. They crept closer, unaware they were being watched, and slowly, their features solidified into more recognizable traits. Tall. Blond hair. Confident stride.

A tingling sense of awareness had me checking out the two strangers a little more critically. One of them had a height and silhouette I swore I'd seen before. The other was recognizable as well, but not as much as the guy on the right. He kind of looked like...That tug in my chest was all too familiar by now. Gods, I couldn't catch a break? Just a teeny one? My groan was like an alarm, and the two guys made their way over to us. Did I seriously just recognize Kai by his *shape*?

"This is perfect." Rani danced next to me, her hips shimming with excitement. "We can take them."

"Your idea of perfect and mine are so far from one another, it's scary."

Moorcroft University had a curse on it. How else could I explain why it kept throwing me and Kai together like two halves of a peanut butter and jelly sandwich? I guess it was lucky that I knew one of the duo now only a few feet away. Kai

could help Rani complete this stupid challenge, and I wouldn't have to feel guilty about being the reason she didn't make it into the sorority.

But that's not quite how it worked out. My frenzied roomie threw herself at the platinum-blond stranger before he had a chance to introduce himself. One quick survey, including a walk-around inspection, and Rani was sold. The stranger crossed his arms, preening with smug satisfaction at the cute redhead's sounds of approval.

Her resigned "you'll do" hit him like a hammer to the face, and that sly grin dropped.

"What do you mean, 'I'll do'?" he scoffed. "Babe, this is top choice. Prime cut. Of course I'll do."

I covered my laugh with my hand. The poor guy. His expression was a sad mix of confidence and outrage as Rani huffed and grabbed his hand.

"Let's not get ahead of ourselves." She gave him a condescending pat on the cheek. "If this prime cut can run, I'll consider rethinking."

The two of them took off, and that's when it registered. I watched their retreating forms with growing horror.

"Seriously?" I shouted. Her answering laugh didn't ease the betrayal.

"At least you know him!"

That wasn't the point. Sighing, I turned back to face the man in question and was met with a glare. Woah. I thought I'd seen him angry before, but this...this was Kai furious. There was color on his cheeks that spread down his neck, and his breaths puffed between us in short bursts. The mini clouds of condensation drew my attention to a small scar. It cut through his full bottom lip in a way that made it tempting to trace.

"What are you doing out here so late and dressed like *that*?" I jerked as if broken from a trance. He moved to take off his jacket,

realized with a glance that it wouldn't be long enough to cover my legs, and chose instead to get me out of the cold altogether.

"What are you doing? Let me go!" I struggled against his grip on my elbow, but just like last time, there was no breaking free.

"I'm beginning to think I'm being tested," he complained, still dragging me toward the parking lot while he pulled a key fob from his pocket.

"Welcome...to...the...damn...club." Out of breath and cold, I stopped fighting as he unlocked the passenger door to a white truck.

I hopped inside without argument and tucked my bare knees up into the hoodie. Kai joined me inside the cab a minute later.

"Nice jacket."

You can't kill him. You can't kill him. You can't kill him.

I settled for a glare instead. That attitude of his was going to get him slapped one day. I hoped by me. The windshield was frosted over with a layer of ice too thick to see through. Kai bumped up the heat to full blast, and we waited.

"Where is your friend taking my cousin?" he asked after a few minutes of silence. He sounded less mad. But only by a little.

"To Seabird's," I grumbled, too exhausted to fight. Heat was finally coming out of the vents, and I held my hands out against them.

I felt Kai watching me, like a phantom pressure on my shoulders. Thank the gods my cheeks were too cold to hold a blush. I counted to sixty, twice, and still felt his eyes on me.

"What?" I snapped.

His gaze touched on my messy bun, passed over his hoodie —*that* got another smirk—then took in my boxer shorts and Uggs. The anger I saw earlier fully faded as he reached a conclusion.

"Dinner dash?"

I tossed my head back against the headrest as Kai reversed out of the parking lot. "How do all the guys on campus know about this stupid challenge, but we had no idea?"

It was a campus-wide conspiracy. And still stupid.

He chuckled and turned right at the light. "Ezra's been roped into a couple already and told me about them. Don't worry, your friend is in good hands."

Ezra must be his cousin.

"And what about me?" I asked, eyeing Seabird's as Kai maneuvered us into an empty spot in their lot. "Am I safe in your hands?"

My body locked up. Why the fuck did I ask that? His answering smile made my heart stop. It was mischievous and a little dirty, and I felt like there was an innuendo there that I missed. Kai hopped out of the truck and came around to my side. Opening my door, he leaned in, bringing with him a scent of oranges mixed with a hint of the coming snow.

I squeezed my knees together, feeling overheated and antsy even with the cool air. Before I could climb down, Kai grabbed my hips under his hoodie and lifted me from the seat. I floundered and clutched at his shoulders as the whole front of my body slid against him. Even once my feet were on the pavement, he didn't let go.

"Always," he finally answered. "But that depends on your definition of safe."

The rest of the pledges and their dates were already seated by the time we made it inside. Paisleigh and the other sisters lost their absolute shit when they saw who I brought with me. Their reactions were honestly the best part of this entire evening.

"Have you gone mental?" Paisleigh squawked, her mouth permanently open in shock. "You can't bring a TA as your date."

"Why not?" I countered. Nothing was mentioned about it in the rules. "All you said was it needed to be an acceptable date.

Which I assumed meant hot." I pointed at Kai—did she see him?

I tried to ignore the absolute panty-dropping smirk Kai wore at my answer. Paisleigh wasn't strong enough to resist, based on the blush working its way across her chest. I felt more than saw Kai turn to look at me and planted my palm in his face to block the sexual rays I was sure were shooting from his eyeballs.

"Don't," I growled. His answering laugh was little more than a rumble.

"B-but he's a TA," another sister repeated. "He's off-limits to undergrads."

Were they still stuck on that?

"The rules didn't say I had to fuck him." Kai jolted beside me. "I was told to bring a date. I've completed the stupid task."

"Actually, it's been way past thirty minutes," Paisleigh jeered, arms crossed. "You failed and are hereby cut from this year's pledge class."

Was she waiting for me to fall apart? I felt nothing but relief at being free. Rani and her date were already seated, so I knew her position was safe. They couldn't penalize her because I missed the deadline, right?

"Come on," Kai said, his voice gentle as he grabbed my hand and threaded our fingers together. "I'll take you to your dorm."

I let him lead me back out to the truck, enjoying the affronted reactions of the Kappa Delta bitches. Rani winked at me while Kai's cousin, Ezra, gave him that universal dude nod—the one with the chin. For once, I wasn't worried about how it would look being seen with the TA or the fact that we were about to be alone in his truck. Again. I enjoyed the warmth of his hand in mine and the butterflies that took flight when he glanced down at me with that soft smile. That right there should have told me I was in trouble, but I couldn't find it in me to care.

seven

Kaiden

The next couple of weeks passed without incident. A tentative routine emerged, where I balanced my busy human schedule with my remote heir duties and hunting with Ez. Searching for the djinn and their traps carried on until late each night, and I was glad I didn't have to take classes this semester to keep up the charade.

It wouldn't leave much time for interrogation. The djinn were still here, but as of late, none were smart or bold enough to do more than lay a trap or two. Thank the gods. Traps were easy enough for Ez and me to dismantle—we were pros at it by now, as well as at finding the source caster and eliminating them.

I had more blood on my hands than ever before, but I couldn't find it in me to be bothered by it. It was worth it. All of it. Every mark against my soul, I'd gladly bear to protect the innocent girl across from me. Her head, full of dark curls, was unbound and spilling across the desk as she leaned over the worksheet.

I didn't have to see her face to know her brow was pinched in concentration and her bottom lip was pinned between her top and bottom incisors. She was a hard worker—a fact I was already aware of—and our weekly sessions were fruitful because of the effort she put into them. It made me proud.

I watched her flip the page and start on the next set of problems, and wondered how long we could keep going like this. It wasn't sustainable, hunting the djinn while she continued, unknowing about the dangers after her, and the bond who was right here, protecting her from them all.

"This equation isn't balanced." I couldn't resist reaching across the desk and brushing my hand over hers as I pointed at the paper. That spark that was always there when we touched had grown stronger. We were in the beginning stages of our bond, and only more contact—more intimate contact—would solidify it. "You need to revise the amount of reactants and products to get the same number of atoms of the given element on each side. Try again."

She scanned the problem but didn't move her pen. I pointed at the unbalanced element, my fingertip grazing her again. A sharp intake of breath, and she looked up. My smile was innocent, and she shook her head before returning her focus to the problem at hand. The plan was working. I wanted my little bond to be comfortable with me.

It was an infuriatingly slow process, one I found difficult to hold on to. Take now, for example, those two small touches made Eryn restless in her seat, her thighs shifting in need and confusion as her mind tried to figure out what her body already knew. What my own body screamed out for. Connection. To drag her over this desk and ravage her until she left here with my mark permanently etched upon her skin. Each day, the bond pulled harder, but not yet. Physically, I knew she wanted me. I could practically taste her need, but mentally, she still resisted.

And the exchanges that came from that resistance...Gods. It was the best kind of foreplay.

"Are you sure you don't mind dropping me off at my dorm?" she asked, packing her bag.

It was an effort not to roll my eyes. "Seeing as how it was *my* idea in the first place, I'm sure."

I locked my office door behind her, and we wound our way through the labyrinth of halls to the parking lot stairwell. She walked beside me with an ease that wasn't there last month when fate continuously threw us together. Now, all our interactions were intentional—at least on my part.

"I was just checking," she mumbled, but dutifully followed me to the truck, which was already warm and running thanks to the remote start.

"Were the past two weeks of me escorting you not enough proof?" I pulled out of the lot but kept the speed below ten. It still only took five minutes to reach her dorm. "I don't know how else to prove to you that I enjoy your company. Maybe I should ask Ezra for a few pointers."

Her laugh was unrestrained and quick, and I smiled, having accomplished my goal.

"Please don't," she said, still giggling. "He's not who I'd recommend you take advice from."

My poor cousin was completely enamored with my bond's roommate. It was almost to the point of obsession, but I didn't think Rani was even aware. She wouldn't give him the time of day, a reaction Ez wasn't used to. Their interactions were a never-ending source of amusement, and my impression of the girl went up every time she sent my cousin packing.

I parked along the curb, directly in front of the entrance to the dorms.

"I'll wait here until you get inside," I told her, even though I didn't have to. It was routine at this point.

Snowflakes littered the windshield, growing heavier as we watched. Eryn stared at them with a wonder I never got tired of seeing; it lit her up from the inside. She cracked the door and shivered, my hoodie doing literally nothing to protect her. Neither one of us commented on my lost article of clothing anymore, it was basically hers now, and as much as I loved her in it, it drove me crazy when it was the only thing she wore besides those ass-hugging leggings.

"You know, you could probably enjoy the snow if you wore something thicker than *that*."

She sighed and pulled back inside the cab to look at me. Her arms crossed as she settled in the passenger seat once more.

"It's not that bad."

"Your constant shivering says otherwise," I argued, jaw clenched.

"I spend like a total of two seconds outside." She threw her hands up in exasperation. "I go from inside, to the shuttle, to back inside, to your truck, to *back inside*. Why would I change the hoodie for that?"

I felt a smirk curl across my lips. "I can give you something else of mine if you'll wear it instead."

"T-that's not why I wear the damn hoodie," she sputtered, obviously flustered. "It's comfortable."

"Right. Whatever you need to tell yourself, princess."

"What's that supposed to mean?"

Laughing would do nothing but piss her off more, but her denial was cute as hell. I pushed back from the steering wheel to lean against the center console and made sure she knew she had my full attention. "I'm not going to spell it out for you."

"Spell what out?"

Now I did laugh. "When you're ready to admit it, I'll be here."

"Admit *what*?" she shouted.

My smile dropped as I stared at her, ensnaring her with a look. I noticed every little reaction; her delicate throat bobbing; the color blooming across her cheeks. She squirmed in her seat as I leaned closer but didn't pull away. Slowly, I reached out to tuck a strand of hair behind her ear, and she shivered again. This one had nothing to do with the weather.

She could deny it all she wanted, but I knew she was affected by me. It wasn't a one-way street. The front of my jeans grew tight as her arousal echoed down the bond to flirt with mine. This was a dangerous game, seeing who would break first. I wanted nothing more than to close the slight distance between us and kiss her until she couldn't form enough thoughts to deny me any longer.

Instead, I cupped the side of her face, my fingers spanning her jaw, with my thumb resting lightly on her lower lip. My dick jumped as I watched her pupils dilate. She held her breath when I brushed my thumb over the plump skin, and her tongue darted out, nearly touching my finger.

I groaned, "That. You know exactly what I'm talking about." I pulled away in one motion and smirked at how she swayed after me, not ready to give up my touch. "I'll see you Thursday for our next appointment."

I sped out of there the second she was safe inside the dorm. Any longer, and I would have chased her up those stairs and taken that kiss she so willingly offered. My alluring bond consumed my thoughts all the way back to the apartment, the entire time I cooked and ate my dinner, and haunted me as I tried to grade the most recent batch of papers.

So much had changed in a month, and all because of her. I lived my life between one moment and the next until I got to see her again. Two days. Hopefully, some djinn were feeling brave this week, and I could distract myself with hunting them. The gentle knock against my mirror broke me from my plans of

informative torture, and I reached over to remove the cloth covering the glass. My mother sat prim and proper in the center, her image taking up the whole frame.

"Hi, Mom."

"Darling," she replied. "How is it going? Have you consummated the bond?"

I rolled my eyes, but not where she could see. My mother hated it. "I already told you, I'm taking it slow. She still doesn't know who I really am."

I felt her annoyance through time and space. It wasn't the answer she wanted to hear. Short of, "I'm on my way home with my obedient bond in tow," nothing would satisfy her.

"The longer you stay there, the more danger you both will be in. The djinn will grow bolder, son."

I was counting on it. The childish illusions they planted were hardly a challenge. And truthfully, there was no way around it anyway. I couldn't think of a way to break the news to Eryn that wouldn't make her hate me or run.

"We're handling the djinn," I told my mother. Did she think we were sitting on our asses all day?

"There's also a growing list of neglected duties that are festering in your absence."

I held in my growl of frustration. She wouldn't move me on her timeline. This was my life. My responsibility.

"My *duty* right now is to my bond. She's more important than anything else." I met my mother's cool gaze and refused to back down. "Sage can handle whatever needs to be done while I'm gone."

She scoffed, "Your sister is far too irresponsible to handle these matters."

"Well, she's all you've got. Easing my bond into our world will take time and careful planning. I foresee a significant step back once she learns my identity, no matter how close we grow

before. Our family is massively responsible for the death of her kind as well as the open hunts on her and her family."

"That ruling was made generations before you or I were even born." This time I let her see me roll my eyes at her overused argument. "Don't give me that attitude, Kaiden. You know our family worked hard to reverse that law long before a nightmare was seen as your bond."

It was true. My grandfather was the first to notice their near-extinct population and recognize what a complete loss of their magick could mean for the rest of us. Times were changing, and humans were becoming more of a threat to supernaturals than the silent war for power between the factions. A healthy population of nightmares could be the turning point if our existence ever became widespread knowledge.

"It doesn't matter, Mom. We haven't done nearly enough. Her people are still gone. Her soul and body are still scarred, and that's on us."

The argument with my mother made it hard to fall asleep. Three cups of chamomile later, and I was still wide awake. It had only been a few hours since I dropped Eryn off, and I wondered what she was doing right now.

It's the middle of the night. She's sleeping you obsessive fuck.

The door to my room burst open and slammed against the wall loud enough to wake me if I wasn't already up. Ezra stood in the hall, a sphere of white quartz in his palm. It pulsed with a harsh glow that cast shadows over my cousin's panicked expression.

"Something's breached the wards on her dorm."

The entire population of Midnight Hall lingered outside, beneath the blinding red lights of the fire engine. The shrill alarm still blared inside the old building, but it was easy to ignore all the way out here. My anxious gaze scanned for that familiar head of curls...there. My bond and her roommate stood

huddled together at the back of the crowd, close to the wall of the neighboring dorm.

Ez moved before me, eager to check over the redhead whose eyes narrowed at his approach. It was a glare of displeasure, and one I mirrored as I watched Eryn standing there in a little pair of sleep shorts, some slippers, and my fucking hoodie. What had we just discussed? I stalked over to her, my anger only growing as realization dawned on her face. She was caught.

"I told you to put something else on." I stopped in front of her, stepping so close she had to crane her neck to look at me. "Your fucking lips are blue."

I shrugged off my own jacket and threw it around her shoulders. Grabbing one hand, I directed it through a sleeve. Her other hand, however, was covering her eyes.

"What are you doing?" I asked when I couldn't pry her fingers off her face.

"I'm avoiding eye contact."

"I can see that." I tried again, but I didn't want to hurt her and gave up. "Why?"

"Because you're yelling at me, and I'm tired of seeing it."

Ezra's laugh turned into a subtle cough beside me. I glared at him. He had his arms tightly wrapped around Rani, his hands vigorously rubbing warmth into her back over the blanket she had wrapped around her shoulders. The scowl on his face told me he was just as upset at the redhead's lack of survival instincts. Instincts she shared with my bond.

I turned back to my own little spitfire. "You can still hear me."

She shrugged, not moving that hand. "Next time, I'll wear headphones."

Smart-ass. There wasn't going to be a next time. "I wouldn't yell if you took better care of yourself." Did she not realize the restraint it took to see her make the same unhealthy choices and

not lock her away in my room until she learned how to properly take care of herself? "I'm sorry," I whispered, gently tugging on her hand again. "Please open your eyes. I'll try to do better if you promise to stop pretending you're immune to the elements."

Her answering laugh was followed by the reveal of the most beautiful green eyes I'd ever seen. It was a punch to the gut, one I welcomed.

"Hi," she whispered shyly.

I shot her a gentle grin and helped her now free arm through the other sleeve just in time for the students to start making their way back inside. We still needed to figure out what had triggered the alarm, both the one to the dorm and the general one that caused the evacuation. But first, I needed to escort my bond back to her room.

"Lending me your body heat during a mild campus emergency does not mean you now get to tuck me into bed, you ass!"

Rani tried to speed walk ahead of my cousin, but he easily kept up with her.

"That part isn't up for discussion, babe. Would you prefer your arms inside or out of the blanket?"

My body shook with suppressed laughter as Eryn and I watched from a safe distance. Rani spun around, righteous fury fueling her every move. She shoved Ez and screeched when he trapped her hands, pulled her close, and dipped down to throw her over his shoulder—blanket and all.

"Put me down, you weird fetish bastard!" Another shriek. "You're not going within five feet of my bed!"

"These delusions of yours worry me," Ez tsked, unbothered by her violent squirming. "We can discuss them once I'm sure this ass is nice and toasty and tucked in the bed that I'm now considering climbing into with you."

Their bickering carried on across the courtyard. We followed but stayed moving at a casual pace so they could work things out

before we arrived at the room. We were the only ones left in the lobby besides the last group of students waiting for the elevators. Eryn slid my jacket off and handed it to me with a quiet "thanks."

She moved to join the last stragglers of students, and I caved, not ready to let her go. I tossed the jacket on a random couch and ushered my confused bond into the stairwell. Crowding her against the far wall, we were tucked to the side of the stairs, invisible from the door. I listened anyway. When no footsteps sounded from above, I looked down and was greeted with an adorable frown.

"What are you doing?"

"We didn't finish our conversation," I told her. "When I see you next time, do you promise to wear something heavier than my hoodie?" I plucked at the offending item of clothing in question.

She huffed, but it was paired with a shy smile. "I guess I should probably return it to you anyway."

That would solve the problem, but when she reached for the bottom of the cotton and started lifting, I shook my head and pressed her further into the wall. Not even an inch separated us as I pinned her arms to her sides with my palms flat against the concrete.

"Keep it. It looks better on you."

That fucking blush.

I licked my lips at the arousal I saw in her gaze before she ducked her head. I couldn't take it. I promised myself I'd wait for her to instigate anything, but if I didn't taste her right now, I wouldn't make it through the night. I used a finger to gently lift her chin. Her eyes flicked back and forth, taking in the scowl I knew I wore. I didn't like losing control.

"What's wrong?" she asked softly.

"I'm mad at myself," I answered, bringing one hand between us and using it to tilt her head back to just the right angle.

Her gaze dropped to my mouth as her tongue dipped out to wet her lips in response. "Why?"

My fingers reached back into her hair and tugged, anchoring her for the storm I was about to unleash. She gasped and arched into my hold but didn't close her eyes. She was daring me; meeting me head-on. Good girl.

"I should have done this earlier," I said, our lips almost touching. "I'll never forgive myself if I miss another opportunity."

This wasn't a gentle kiss, like the ones I'd planned to woo her with. It was a barely suppressed need with a hint of obsession. Her lips were soft and full and so warm as I touched them to my own with a soft slide that had both of us moaning. Despite the urge to devour her, I kissed her slowly, a gentle nip, an easy friction that sent her wiggling against me.

My skin felt too sensitive—like one more scratch of her nails on my scalp would send us both up in flames. I pressed as close as physically possible, my dick so fucking hard it was ready to bust with only a couple of thrusts against her soft belly. Then she whined, and I couldn't deny that plea. Hooking my hands under her thighs, I lifted her and pushed her against the wall, deepening the kiss and languidly thrusting my tongue in imitation of that final act.

Her heat encompassed me, even through our layers of clothes, and I answered with a hard roll of my hips that pushed her up the wall with a squeal. I dragged her mouth back to mine and used it to cover my own groan.

Sweat dripped down my back, and the zipper of my jeans was so tight over the head of my dick it hurt, but I couldn't stop. I couldn't get enough. In the back of my mind, in the small

section still capable of coherent thoughts, I knew our intense reaction was fueled in part by our bond's need to complete.

I felt it heavy in my chest, and I knew the longer we kissed, the more that bond would grow. Potentially to a level strong enough that Eryn would finally notice it. I didn't care. I trailed my lips down her neck.

"Fuck! You don't understand what you do to me, princess." Another moan escaped her, this one a little more desperate than the last. "Make that sound again," I demanded and reached between us.

Her thin shorts were damp and hot, soaked with the evidence of her arousal. I ran my thumb along the seam, adding more pressure at the top. She bit her lip, so I did it again, harder. On the next pass, she mewled against my mouth and tightened her legs around me.

"Kai," she moaned. "Oh gods, please."

"I've got you," I told her, removing my fingers from that sensitive bud and laying my hand flat on her belly, near the top of her shorts. "Do you trust me?"

She panted and squirmed, searching for that missing friction, urged on by her need for release and the bond's influence. We were both lost to its spell, but I refused to let it go further than this. Fuck, I'd stop right now if she told me to. But she didn't stop me, instead, she pulled on my arm to try and direct my hand back to where she ached.

"Princess," I breathed, gently bumping my nose against hers. "Tell me."

Her eyes fluttered open and met mine. "I trust you."

Thank the gods.

My fingers slipped expertly through the slick mess between her thighs. I ignored her nails biting into my skin and stroked with determination, teasing her opening before rubbing firmly against the swollen bud. She was going to feel

me for days after this. I curled my hand, dipping the tip of a finger inside.

Her pussy greedily sucked me in, drawing me deeper until the heel of my palm rested on her clit. She wasn't going to last long. Not as I angled my finger to hit that spongy spot on the roof of her walls. Her fingertips held onto my shoulders hard enough to bruise as she ground herself against my hand. It was like holding a hellcat in my arms, the way she hissed and fought my hold, wanting what I had to offer but wary of its dangerous potency.

"Look at you," I crooned as her inner muscles tensed. "Fuck my fingers, princess. Soak my hand like a good girl."

The cry that left her throat was smothered by my lips. I eased the thrusts of my finger but kept it inside her while my thumb helped her ride out her orgasm. I pulled away from her mouth and let her legs fall, my finger never stopping its strokes against her core. She cried out again as another wave of release rode on the end of the first one.

Her knees buckled and still, the bond in my chest demanded I take more. It wanted her complete submission. It wanted her so weak she couldn't even crawl away as we claimed her on the cold concrete floor. With a pained roar, I forced myself away from her and put as much distance between us as the small room would allow.

"Eryn, you need to go."

Her eyes flashed with shock as she sat slumped against the wall, her chest heaving with deep breaths.

"I—" She shook her head and stood on weak legs. "No one's ever—you just had your—*why*?" A little anger leaked its way past her post-orgasmic confusion. "Why should I go?"

Every second she stood before me, looking so fucking edible I could die from the sight, was another second I lost control. She couldn't recognize the bond yet, so its hold on her waned now

that I no longer touched her, but I remembered with too much clarity how slippery she felt against my fingers. I wanted more. Without breaking eye contact, I lifted my hand to my mouth. The musky scent grew stronger as I tasted the finger I had deep inside her.

A groan escaped. "If you don't run up those stairs right now and lock your door, I'm going to fuck you all over this room. On the stairs, against the wall again, with your ass in the air and bent over the railing until each of my thrusts make you feel like you're going to fall. But you won't because I'd never let you go; not once I bury myself inside you." I took one step and clenched my fists to keep from lunging for her. "Go, Eryn!" I growled, and she flinched. "Please," I begged, softening my voice.

She worried her bottom lip, enough curiosity shining through her nerves to make her wonder if she could take what I offered. Thankfully, her sanity won out, and she disappeared up the stairs without another sound.

eight

Eryn

The basement of the library was a labyrinth of halls that looked exactly the same; same carpet; same shiny brown doors; same plain paint job. I heard rumors that there were tunnels down here, which connected this building to a lot of the older ones on campus, but I wouldn't even know where to begin to look for them.

Not that Civil War Era tunnels were my reason for lurking today. Kai was avoiding me. He canceled our last two tutoring sessions via email, telling me to print and complete the attached worksheets like he hadn't rearranged everything I thought I knew about sex in the fucking stairwell of my dorm.

We didn't even have sex! But I sure as hell had never been kissed like that before. My previous experiences were nice, I guessed, but kissing Kai was like a jolt to the system. Like lightning coursing right underneath the surface of my skin, sinking into my muscles, and taking my nervous system for a joyride.

When he touched me, I couldn't breathe, couldn't think. I

forgot that I wasn't human or that my touch could be toxic to the mental health of anyone unlucky enough to be on the wrong side of my control. It took some serious concentration to keep from slipping into Rani's mind whenever she grabbed my arm or brushed my skin in a hug.

I'd gotten better at it, but still.

Then there was Kai—finger in my literal vagina and my mind was blessedly empty. It was a sign. Maybe Kai was one of those abnormal humans with weird brain waves that disrupted my power. Maybe he was safe from me. I stood in front of his office door and wrung my hands. This could be the worst idea I'd ever had, but I couldn't go another week replaying that night in my head or worrying about whether Kai's change in attitude toward me would affect my grades.

My classes were done for the day, and I usually spent the afternoon and early evening studying or completing assignments. If he wasn't here, I'd go back upstairs and get to work—bury myself in the mound of homework waiting for me. I'd yet to update my parents this week so maybe I'd write that email too.

I wasn't sure what to tell them besides the usual; everything was fine and that I was living the free, fun-filled life they always wanted for me. It sucked that I got to experience all this while they were stuck hiding in some backwoods little town, trying to live a full but inconspicuous life.

We still weren't sure what my rejection of the witch heir meant for them and decided not to test their newfound clemency until *after* I graduated. Just in case.

That was why I needed to buckle down, get my damn degree, and not let some broody blonde with gifted fingers throw me off course.

I raised my fist, knuckles resting on the cool wood. *Screw it.*

The hollow knock cut a harsh tone through the empty hall.

Faint sounds on the other side of the door triggered an unreasonable desire to flee, but then, there he was, standing in front of me with a resigned frown. Some part of me actually expected him not to be here, but he was, and gods, he looked good.

His golden hair was tousled like he'd run his hands through it a thousand times. Those ocean eyes flared when they saw me, then slowly trailed down my body until even the tips of my toes tingled with anticipation.

"Umm, hi," I said, snapping out of it.

He didn't reply, just kept looking at me, and my anger grew once more. He obviously regretted what happened. But so what? I refused to allow him to take it out on me or my grades. I needed his help to pass this class, and whether he liked it or not, he was going to give it to me.

"Nothing to say?" I sneered, then shoved him with both hands. "That wasn't the case after you had your fingers inside me." Another shove. "You couldn't shut up about-"

Voices in the hall rounded the corner, and Kai grabbed my wrists to pull me inside the office. He kicked the door closed behind us, leaving me trapped in the small room with my anger and a guy who wanted nothing to do with me. Nothing was promised, no pretty words were shared, but I didn't peg him for this level of asshole. His glare told me how wrong I was.

"I see you *do* own something appropriate for winter." He scanned my body, arms crossed and hip leaned against the desk.

One week. A whole week of avoidance after warning me away from his feral need to *fuck* me in every way imaginable, and he wanted to talk about my jeans?

"You've got to be kidding me," I hissed and swung a hand at his chest. "You've got." *Hit.* "To be." *Hit.* "**Fucking**." *Hit. Hit.* "Kidding me."

Kai caught my hand before it made contact with his face. His fingers tightened around my arm, sending a shockwave of

tingles up to my shoulder. The corner of his mouth twitched, and there was an answering flutter in my chest. He dropped my arm as if it burned him.

"Turn around," he demanded.

My mouth opened but nothing came out. He didn't smile, didn't tell me he was joking. He did nothing else but stare and wait for me to obey. Still glaring, I turned.

"Put your hands on the wall. Keep them there."

I shivered at the tone in his voice; he'd never spoken to me like that. Bossy and Kai were synonymous, but this was different. This didn't make me want to strangle him. In fact, it did the opposite and made each of my breaths shaky as I placed my hands on the wall beside the door. I felt him step behind me, his chest pressing along my back as he caged me in with his arms planted on either side of my hips.

Every hard muscle of his burned down my body from back to thighs. He nuzzled my neck, inhaling my scent and tickling my skin with his answering breath. I was aware of his lips hovering, but they didn't make contact.

They pulled back to my ear, "Did you think I changed my mind about wanting you? You have no idea the thoughts that keep me up at night." I tilted my head. He chuckled at the invitation, and I snapped my head back straight. "I almost lost control, princess, and you're not ready for the things I want from you."

That wasn't his decision to make, but I said nothing as I watched his hand leave the wall to cup my breast under my thick sweater. The thin silk of my bralette offered little protection as my nipple puckered to a hard point. He rolled it between his fingers, then pinched it hard. I gasped as pleasure zinged down my body, connected by some invisible line to my clit.

My hips twitched back against him. I felt how hard he was and couldn't help but rub against him once more, earning a groan that made me smirk. Two could play at this game. Kai's

other hand left the wall to grab my hip, and he pushed against me harder until I was forced to drop from my hands to my forearms. Gods, why did this turn me on? I wanted more—a repeat of that night.

"What if I want those things?" I asked, pushing back against his weight.

"You don't know what you're asking."

"I'm a big girl," I argued. "I can handle it."

He hummed, but I didn't know what it meant. Did he disagree? A hard knock to my ankle spread my legs as he used his foot to widen my stance. The hand on my hip dipped lower to cup me over my jeans. Gods. The hard ridge of his palm ground against me, using the thick inseam of the denim to cut through the silk of my panties until they were soaked.

My forehead dropped to the wall with a moan. It was both more intense and less than last time. The barrier of my clothes reduced the pressure of his hand, but it also added a different kind of friction. My thighs trembled as he made another slow circle.

"Touch me," I pleaded.

"I am touching you."

With my arms pinned between my chest and the wall, and his entire body crowding me from behind, I was at his mercy. I couldn't grab his fingers and slip them where I wanted. Couldn't twist around to throw my arms around his neck and bring him down for a hungry kiss. I could only roll my hips and beg for him to give me what I needed.

"Let's see how long it will take you to come like this," he challenged, tweaking my nipple again before rolling it between his fingers.

"That's not enough..." I started to argue, and then stopped when the heel of his hand moved. It was different than before, a slower but steadier pace that forced the seam of my jeans back

and forth across my clit. "Fuck," I whimpered and allowed my hips to follow the rhythm he set.

It wasn't enough. The build-up was too slow, making me fear I wouldn't get there at all. My breaths were choppy, and every muscle in my legs was strung tight as I chased my release. Kai's head tucked into the crook of my neck, sending a few delicate curls across my skin. Goosebumps broke out along my arms. I felt him, thick and impossibly hard against my ass.

"Mmm," he groaned. "I can feel your heat against my palm. Are you going to make it?" The whine got stuck in my throat as I shook my head. "I think you are," he taunted, and this time the whine escaped. He chuckled. "But I can be nice. And you're trying so hard."

He popped the button on my jeans, lowered the zipper, and slipped his hand inside. Standing was hard. My knees threatened to give out, but I locked them. Fingers spread over my wet panties and pressed against my throbbing clit. The silk was basically nonexistent at this point. It felt like he was touching me, but he wasn't.

He was still keeping himself separate, and I wanted that last barrier gone. I arched my back and rolled my hips again, trying to get those fingers to slip inside, but that only succeeded in making him still against me.

"Trying to cheat?" He seemed surprised, but not upset at the notion. One finger pulled away and then landed directly on my clit. *Tap.* "Even after I offered to help?" *Tap tap.*

My entire body vibrated. I was so close. "So-rry," I whispered, hoping an apology would get him to move again.

Tap.

"What was that?"

"I'm sorry! P-please, Kai. *Please.*"

I hated begging. I was stronger than that, but in that moment, nothing else mattered than getting him to move those

damn fingers. And oh, he did. His thumb pressed right where I needed, circling around and around. It was almost too much. Another finger slid down to my entrance and pushed inside, despite my panties, and the combination was enough to make me combust.

There was no controlling my hips or how they jerked as I rode wave after wave of toe-curling pleasure. Kai's hips moved too, his whole body wrapped around mine until the shaking stopped, and I could once again register the cool wall on my cheek. The lack of heat on my back told me he stepped away, and a heavy hand on my shoulder turned me around to face him.

He said nothing as he buttoned my pants and smoothed my hair. My body still shook hard enough to make even those little tasks difficult. Our eyes met, and I was satisfied to see he was just as affected.

"Never again doubt that I want you." He reached beside me to open the door, crowding me until I stepped back into the hall. "But until I think you're ready, this won't happen again."

The door shut in my face.

By the middle of the semester, I'd fallen into a comfortable routine; classes by day, studying by night, plus lunch dates and impromptu movie nights with Rani scattered between. I rocked a solid A average, was top of my class already, and just yesterday, I helped an adorable seagull with an aluminum tab stuck around its foot. There were no more random bursts of magick— from me or nearby supers—or embarrassing run-ins with the sorority sisters Rani worked so hard to be accepted by.

All in all, my first semester of college was going exactly as I'd

dreamed. Better. Except for the one dark cloud I was trying my hardest to forget about. An early spring breeze lifted the hair on my neck, and I scrunched deeper into Kai's hoodie. I was pathetic. The rich scent of him left the fabric a while ago, but I couldn't bring myself to stop wearing it.

Dodging a group of guys playing ultimate frisbee beneath the strengthening sun, I ditched the sidewalk and cut across the quad. It was full today. It looked like everyone had the same idea to take advantage of the nice weather this weekend. It was a sea of bare legs, tank tops, and flip-flops as the student population attempted to grow a base tan before spring break. Hopefully, the weather held for the next couple of weeks.

The amount of jackets and blankets lying around told me I wasn't the only one who found this time of year unpredictable. Kind of like a certain guy I knew; hot one minute and cold the next. I swore to forget about him, but it was impossible when I saw him in class three times a week and still exchanged emails about tutoring.

Freaking emails.

"Until I think you're ready, this won't happen again."

I still didn't get what that was supposed to mean. Ready for what? And who the hell was he to decide what I was ready for? I kicked a pinecone unfortunate enough to be nearby and watched it sail into the trees. I was over it. Really. Another pinecone fell victim to how over it I was. A rustle in the bushes followed my latest kick, and a small robin fell out with an outraged *squawk!* The little guy shook his head, ruffled his feathers, and tried to fly away, but one of his wings wouldn't bend correctly.

"Oh gods," I cursed. "Please tell me I didn't hurt an innocent forest creature."

I reached for him, intent on checking him over, but he hopped out of reach, the broken wing dragging alongside him.

"Come 'ere, baby. I only want to help," I cooed in a low voice. Strange. Animals usually loved me, even when hurt. Granted, I had never been the one to cause the damage before. My guilt grew, and I doubled my efforts. He sure was nimble, even with a severe injury. Slowly, I followed him away from the quad and toward the deeper forest. We were still within eyesight of everyone else, and I was sure I looked all kinds of stupid duck-waddling behind this bird with my arms stretched out.

"I'm not going to hurt you...again," I muttered. "Let me help you."

I pushed a strand of my power at him, but couldn't make a connection. Just like that cat by the science building, there was no animal chatter in my mind. Intense reactions like pain were nearly impossible to ignore, they screamed out at me even when I wasn't trying to connect. Maybe this was an old injury. It was possible his wing healed like this from an old break and my pinecone only frightened him from the bushes.

But that didn't fully explain why I couldn't connect to his mind and calm him. With a small burst of speed, I cut him off from the forest and herded him back to open ground.

"I can't catch you in there, buddy. And I really am trying to make you feel better." Anyone else might feel silly speaking to a bird like they could comprehend, but even without magick that was one thing animals were good at, understanding the intent behind the words.

"Is this some kind of nature pilates or have you finally cracked?"

Rani's sparkly purple toes appeared in front of me, passing directly through the injured robin. Before I could do more than gasp, the image of the little bird vanished in thin wisps of smoke–like it was never there at all. Oh my gods. I *had* finally cracked. Who hallucinated a whole-ass bird?

"But seriously, babe," Rani continued. "What are you doing down there?"

I quickly stood and brushed imaginary dirt off my legs. Another quick glance around showed no injured animals, birds or otherwise.

"There was a robin..." I started, but there was no way to finish that sentence without sounding completely mental.

Rani took pity on me and let it slide. The gods knew it wasn't the weirdest thing she'd seen me do. She caught me running from one end of the dorm to the other on multiple occasions. And one time, she watched as I sprinted from my bed in the middle of the night to the bus depot and back with a stopwatch in my hand. She bought my excuse of training for a triathlon, but that didn't make my actions any less weird. Rani looped her arm through mine and made a beeline back across the quad toward the Commons.

"Tell me what the rules are for tonight," she demanded, and I rolled my eyes.

"Study at the library until my eyes cross," I replied. Really, we didn't have to go over it.

"And?"

I sighed. "And then come straight back to the dorm."

"To do what?"

"It's not that bad, Rani," I grumbled. "I know how to—"

"*To do what?*"

She pulled me to a stop just outside the Commons and glared at me. All business. The delectable smells that escaped each time the doors opened made my mouth water. I was starving. My stomach clenched on a wave of nausea when it hit me. How long had it been since I fed? Not on food but on dreams. It was definitely before I got to school, possibly on one of the buses here. That was far too long. No wonder my powers weren't working and I was seeing imaginary animals.

My nausea grew as the panic set in. I risked a flare-out or loss of control if I didn't fix this soon. I needed to find a sleeping human; tonight. My gaze slid to Rani. The thought of feeding off her, now that I knew her, was revolting. Just the thought made me feel slimy and gross. No, it would have to be a stranger. Perhaps someone in the library.

"That's it. I'm going to cancel tonight."

I snapped out of it and shook my head. "I'm all good, I swear." Her side-eye said she was less than convinced, but I couldn't risk her being in the dorm tonight if I didn't find someone to feed from. "I *swear*. I will go straight to sleep. No wallowing over boys allowed. Even though I still argue that imagining detailed ways to dismember someone falls firmly in the "I'm over it" category."

It took most of dinner and the walk to the library to convince her I wasn't going to burn the dorm down by lighting candles and summoning demons to drag Kai to the fiery pits of hell. I managed to forget about my infuriating TA, even while completing the worksheets he sent back with notes. A true feat of strength. The library didn't close for another two hours, and I hoped to find someone passed out deep in the stacks.

My little study desk was tucked away in the back, behind rows and rows of dark aisles and empty group rooms. The perfect amount of privacy. Humans couldn't see anything when I fed, but it would look unusual for me to be standing over someone and touching them for however long it took to fill up. I leaned back in my chair, telling myself I deserved a little rest while I waited. Just a couple minutes. I'd rest my eyes, and then I'd go hunting.

The legs of my chair tipped back a little too far, and I jerked awake to the feeling of falling. Straightening the chair, I rubbed at sandpaper eyes and looked around. The library was darker than usual, only the emergency lights kept the shadows at bay.

Shit. I scrambled to pack my bag, not caring if I bent my note-books. How late was it?

Ears strained for any small sound, I worked my way back to the front doors. Heavy snoring echoed out from one of the group rooms on my left. A janitor sat fast asleep at the table, head in his arms, and headphones on loud enough for me to hear the classical music escaping into his ears. I'd get in trouble if I were caught in the library after hours, but I still needed to feed. Sometimes, things had a way of working out, and I wasn't going to waste this opportunity.

On silent feet, I crept into the room. He couldn't hear me, but humans had a sixth sense about movement and a way of knowing when someone watched them. Even when sleeping. I kept my gaze on the table and observed the janitor out of the corner of my eye. A small piece of exposed skin, that's all I needed. Reaching out, I placed a gentle fingertip on his elbow, the rough skin less sensitive and safer to touch.

One breath. One moment to freak out and worry about being caught, and then I shut it down. I exhaled and pulled on my power. *Time to eat*, I told it. Cautiously, it moved, filling my entire body until I thought the slightest breeze would shatter me and send magick racing in all directions. I inhaled and my power took a bite.

With that first taste came a jumble of images. A beach. Trash cans in the ocean? Another inhale, and the next bite revealed a blurry man with some recognizable features of the human asleep beside me. I hated this part of feeding. I didn't want to see inside this man's dreams, but that's how the magick worked. One was never more vulnerable than when they slept.

The dream transitioned from one random scene to another, as most dreams did, until I felt my magick full and satisfied in my gut. As easy as I came, I left. No hiccups. No accidents. I left

the janitor where I found him, no worse for wear, and turned out of the room...right into a hard chest.

"I'm sorry!" I whispered automatically, and stumbled away.

The man I bumped into chuckled, and the sound sent shivers down my back. Not the good kind. I met his gaze. Rule one of self-defense was to be present, to let any potential attackers know you were aware and *saw* them. Not that this man had done anything wrong, but something didn't feel right.

His dark hair was greasy and slicked back with too much gel. I eyed the open lobby behind him. There wasn't much distance between me and the front doors. I moved to step around the stranger, but he mirrored me and blocked the already narrow route. When he grinned, alarm bells went off in my head, and my freshly replenished magick coiled like an asp sensing danger.

"I'm surprised you've lived as long as you have with how much magick you leak." The stranger closed his eyes and inhaled. When he looked at me again, his eyes glowed yellow, and he smiled. "You weren't hard to find."

Shit.

A hunter stood before me, and a strangled whimper escaped. That made him happy. I backed away, not looking at where I was going. I couldn't tear my gaze away from him. This shouldn't be happening. I was so careful.

"I thought..." The words caught in my throat when my back hit a wall. "I thought the order was lifted," I managed to get out, hoping the tribunal hadn't reinstated my bounty after I denied my bond.

"Oh, it was," the hunter said. "But there are others in power who *really* don't want you to exist. And they pay better."

There were no more questions. The hunter's hands wrapped around my neck and squeezed. It was instinct to fight back, but none of my basic self-defense moves worked. No amount of

kicking, pinching, or scratching brought oxygen back into my lungs. My vision blurred and black dots appeared at an alarming speed.

"Almost done, nasty nightmare."

I forced my eyes to stay open and gripped his wrists until my nails drew blood. He laughed at my attempt to break free, but that wasn't the plan. Eye contact and skin-on-skin were all I needed to strengthen a connection. Unleashing my power would only reveal my location to the other hunters, but I had no choice.

It was this or die, and I chose life. The full force of my magick slammed into him. It weaseled its way around his mental barriers, finding little cracks and holes to squeeze through until his mind belonged to me. A single thought made him release me, and I fell at his feet, gasping and clutching at my raw throat.

I needed to move. That blast of power was strong enough to be heard two states over, and my hold on his mind wouldn't last forever. With weak legs and hazy vision, I stumbled deeper into the library, heading for the one place I felt safe. The door to the basement opened under my featherlight push, and I inched down the stairs. Each breath into my damaged throat felt like fire, but it was slowly getting better. Or maybe I was just getting used to it.

I forced my feet to keep moving past the TA offices that I knew couldn't help me, but that one door gave me the wave of strength I needed to make it to the exit. A huge sign blinked red above it. Before I could reach it, a beefy hand wrapped around my hair and yanked me back.

"Naughty tricks," the hunter crowed in my ear. "It's not nice to play in other people's minds, nightmare."

He pulled harder on my hair until I thought my neck would snap. That was probably his plan. The tiles of the basement

ceiling stared back at me in a boring gray; the last thing I would see on this earth. I wished it was the trees. The night sky with swaying branches would have been a nice vision to go out to.

"Let her go."

I stiffened at the new voice, and it pulled at the hand in my hair, sending tendrils of fire across my scalp. I clutched at the hunter's hand to ease the pain, and my chest throbbed in retaliation. The temperature in the basement plummeted until my breath puffed out in front of me, toward the ceiling. The hunter laughed and tugged me closer, wrapping an arm around my waist.

"You're too late, Alantes," the hunter taunted. "One twist of my hand and your pretty bond is a sad memory."

The threat to my life went over my head, even when that grip pulled my neck at a harsher angle. One word circled my mind above all others: above the very real risk of death even. Alantes. That was the family name of my bond. He was here?

"Now, Ez!"

Three things happened in quick succession. The first was the hunter's screams. They were horrific and shrill, something that reminded me of the sounds wounded animals made in the throes of death. The second thing was my freedom. The hunter's hold on me disappeared completely, followed immediately by the thick scent of blood and more screaming. My head now free, it snapped forward and the rest of my body followed, throwing me right into the arms of the third thing. I looked up at my savior and locked eyes with a familiar aquamarine gaze. Alantes. My bond. Or, as I knew him, *Kai.*

nine

Kaiden

I tightened my grip on her forearms as the confusion clouding her gaze slowly cleared to recognition. My expression stayed artfully blank, despite the growing guilt beating the shit out of me from the inside. She was going to hate me. Already those green eyes burned, and as much as that look turned me all the way on, in this instance, I knew it didn't bode well.

We stared at one another, her piecing together my deceptions, and me taking stock of any injuries the damned djinn might have caused. The red marks around her throat sent the bond in my chest on a rampage. She was hurt. Unconsciously, my finger drifted toward the bruises forming where the djinn had assaulted her.

"Don't touch me," she spat, pulling her head back as far as she could, despite the pain it obviously caused her. "Don't ever touch me."

My jaw clenched at the disgust dripping from those lips, and I couldn't help but strike back. "Too late for that, princess."

Her screech of rage was a sight to behold. She wanted to kill me, I could tell, but she wasn't out of danger yet. Ezra worked on the djinn behind her, trying to extract all the information he could before finishing the job. Lost to the pain and knowledge that death was near, the djinn lunged at Eryn, his bloody, frozen stumps reaching.

"Ez!" I shouted while simultaneously pulling Eryn close.

She spun, trying to run, but I had a solid hold. Her back met my chest hard enough to knock the air from my lungs, but I held fast. Ezra got to the djinn before he could crawl any closer by stomping on one of his frozen legs. Everything below the knee shattered, and the guttural roar that left the djinn nearly shook the foundation.

"Gods!" Eryn shouted, fighting against my arm around her waist. "What is wrong with you people?"

Did she expect us to talk to him? Better yet, did she expect him to actually answer without us forcing it out of him? She tried kicking back at me, but was too close to do more than stomp on my toes. That shit hurt, but nothing in this world would make me let go. Not with danger so near.

"Get off!" she cried, fighting even harder.

"Not quite yet. When you calm down, I'll let you go," I told her, and meant it.

I didn't want her to hate me more than she already did, and trapping her here wasn't doing me any favors. Ez was almost done; only the cleanup remained. I met his amused grin over Eryn's head and fixed him with a glare. The temperature plummeted again as Ez worked to freeze the rest of the body. Once encased in ice, he began smashing the djinn to pieces. The frozen shards were easier to clean than pools of blood—easier to hide as well, you just needed a broom.

"You godsdamned..." She twisted and hit me with an elbow. "Fucking...lying...ass turd!"

Eryn managed to get an arm free during her creative tirade, and I bit my lip to keep from snickering. Ez wasn't as good at hiding his delight, and we both had a front-row seat to his belly-shaking laughter.

"You mother—"

"That's not calm, princess." My other arm came up from her hip to cross her chest. Her entire body molded to mine, her tight little ass fitting snugly against my dick. It was impossible to ignore what that did to the bond, but I did my best. "Calm," my head dipped, and my lips skimmed her ear, "down."

I didn't expect her to listen, but she did. She froze, going as stiff as a statue, and I pulled away an inch to give us both a little space. Only my arms touched her, but there was no escaping the heat trapped between us. The tension. I was tempted to let her go just to see what she'd do.

"She's got shifty eyes, cuz," Ez warned, proving me right.

She was up to something. If she'd calm down like I asked, we could talk this all out. I took an educated guess at what kinds of thoughts were running through that pretty little head—probably the worst things her imagination could conjure. I wanted to ease those fears. Nothing had to change. We could still take our time getting to know one another.

"I'm calm," she ground out, in a way that told me she grit her teeth to admit that lie.

And it was a lie, but I decided to see what she would do anyway. The second my arms loosened, she threw herself away from me. That stung a little. Only a couple weeks ago, I had to shut a door in her face to keep her away. I was sure that moment wasn't helping my case now either.

"Go find a broom, Ez. Or one of those industrial vacuums," I suggested, but he recognized the order.

I couldn't risk Eryn gaining control of him and using his power to escape before we had a chance to clear the air. Ez sent

her a shit-eating grin before heading back the way we came——down the old tunnels. We never would have made it here in time without them. His magick lingered a while, to keep everything frozen, and the cool air did nothing to staunch the fire Eryn tried to set on me with her eyes alone.

If looks could kill...

I took the opportunity to check her over again and noticed with smug satisfaction that she was wearing my hoodie. There was hope for us yet. Her bare legs in those small shorts were fine for the warming weather outside, but I knew she had to be uncomfortable down here in this makeshift freezer.

"Say something."

"You're an Alantes," she replied, spitting the name like it tasted vile. "I thought your last name was Winmore."

I dipped my head. "That's one of my names."

It was my father's family name, but I didn't share that bit of information; not when she looked one wrong breath away from bolting. My magick awakened at the thought of a chase, and I leashed my shadows lest they spook her even more. They were ready, waiting. They swirled inside me, eager to come out and have a taste. She took a small step back, perhaps sensing my thoughts.

"My first name is—"

"Kaiden," she whispered, and my gaze softened at the break in her voice.

I fucking hated lying to her. I thought it the best plan at the time.

"Kai for short," I confessed.

Her delicate hands opened and closed at her sides, and she shivered again. Catching me staring, she crossed her arms and jammed her hands into her sides, hunching until her shoulders were tight. At my first step toward her, she went unnaturally still.

I opened my palms in a sign for peace, and she watched them, blinking.

Fuck, was she going into shock?

The attack, the reveal, watching Ez torture and mutilate the djinn...it was too much at once. I listened harder to that faint bond between us, unsure if the fear I felt was hers or mine. We still had a weak connection, but our more recent sexual contact helped it along a tiny amount. I ran a mental finger against that shimmering thread in my chest, and she snapped, bolting for the short stairs at the back door.

"Shit."

I released my magick, directing my shadows to softly wind around her before she reached the exit. She lost it, fighting, screaming, and falling further into her fear the closer I reeled her in. As an extension of myself, I knew the shadows weren't harming her, but nothing I said got through that shield of panic she wielded.

"Easy. I'm not going to hurt you." I moved in front of her, blocking out everything else. She may hate me, but there was a small kernel of trust we built, and I leaned on it now. Cupping her face in my hands set her off again. "Okay, okay. Look, I won't touch you." I held my palms up. "See? I can't hurt you, princess. *Please*."

Her chest rose and fell under my shadows, but she finally stopped thrashing. I matched my breaths with hers, hoping to sync our breathing, and it slowly brought her down.

In. Out. In. Out.

"I don't believe you," she said, sounding a little more like herself.

"Bonds can't hurt one another," I replied. "Go ahead and try." I met her gaze. The little wrinkles on her forehead deepened, and a bead of sweat rolled down her temple. I raised a brow. "You can't, can you?"

"You're using your power against me," she accused with a frustrated growl.

"But I'm not hurting you," I argued. "If there were any intent to do so, it wouldn't work. You can get into my mind at any time, even control my body if I choose to allow it, but that's not what you planned, was it?" She glared. "I assumed as much."

"You'd let me into your mind?" she asked in disbelief. "Willingly?"

"You're welcome anytime, princess," I purred. "But be prepared for the images you see in there."

Her mouth opened and then closed. She hadn't expected my honesty, but I had nothing left to hide. My shadows dissipated, leaving her confused and unbound in front of me. I gestured toward the exit.

"You've had a rough night, and I really don't want you to hate me. Why don't you get some sleep, and we can discuss...all this, later?"

Once again, I caught her off-guard. Did she expect me to throw her over my shoulder and drag her into my lair? I wasn't ruling that option out, but this open truth we had going was the better route in the long run. Besides, I had a feeling I'd be choosing the other option eventually. This girl couldn't stay out of trouble. Eryn took a few cautious steps, and when I didn't try to stop her, she slammed into the door and disappeared.

"You think that was a good idea?" Ez stepped up beside me, dragging along that big vacuum I hoped he'd find.

"What do you mean?"

He sighed and hunted for an outlet. "She's going to run."

Oh, I counted on it. I'd been watching her this whole semester, the wards on her dorm telling me each time she stepped past their threshold. I tracked her every trip to and from the bus depot, the calculated hikes through the forest, and I

knew which cars in the student lot she'd likely hit first if she planned to hotwire one and leave that way.

There was no escape. My little bond was just going to have to get used to me being around. She ensnared me, enchanted me with her wild curls and soft mouth. I'd had a taste, and I wanted more. A lifetime more.

Eryn

No, no, no.

I flew out of that basement with the kind of speed one only accomplished in times of true fear. Literally running for my life, my worn boots ate the distance between the library and my dorm like there wasn't nearly a mile separating them. Hunters *and* my bond? How had I messed this up so badly?

Grisly images of the hunter's contorted, frozen body mixed with the sounds of his screams courtesy of Ezra—not just your average manwhore, but my bond's cousin. Fuck. Here I thought I was being so careful–not using my magick, laying low, *finally* living my life—and I was playing right into his hands.

"I'm such an idiot."

The sharp turn around the back of Midnight Hall nearly wiped me out, but I skidded across the gravel and straightened in time to slam into the front doors. The night monitor at the desk stared at me through the glass in shock. I scanned my ID and made for the stairs before he could say a word. Once again, I cursed not having a room on the first floor.

Living among the humans didn't hide me as I thought it

would. Kaiden found me easily enough, and his cousin was over here often to harass my roommate. How much of that was planned? Did Ezra even like Rani, or was he using her to keep an eye on me? My throat tightened enough to make me gasp as I thought through every interaction this semester. Kaiden knew who I was from the moment he knocked me over at the animal hospital.

He'd known as I sat there and drooled over him, and he'd known later that night at the party when he insisted on walking me home. I thought it was him being kind, but he was just trying to see where I lived.

"Great job, Eryn. Way to play it smart." I cursed myself as I changed into my warmest clothes and dug under my bed for the duffel I kept packed with emergency supplies in case I had to run.

After a moment's hesitation, I ripped off Kai's hoodie and threw it at the window. The soft cotton was a comfort to me, but just the sight of it made me want to throw up now. Kaiden must have laughed at me every time I wore it, seeing me flaunting his ownership with no clue. A final glance was all I allowed of all the things I'd have to leave behind and the memories I'd built with my first real friend.

I thanked the gods Rani wasn't home tonight but hated to leave her with no explanation. It was easier this way. Dawn was still a few hours off when I made my way across campus for the second time. My head was on a swivel, turning this way and that at every small sound. Kaiden wasn't going to let me go, and I refused to be caught again.

The student parking lot was stagnant; empty cars lined up as far back as I could see. I quickly scanned the rows for the few older models I kept an eye on, knowing they were less likely to have an alarm. I found one of them tucked in the corner only

two spots away from where it normally was. I'd just reached the sedan, my hand curling around the driver's side handle to check if it was locked when a voice came out of the darkness.

"I told him you were going to run." Ezra casually strolled up from somewhere to my left and sat on the hood like it was a sunny afternoon, and this was an everyday conversation. "Surprisingly, my cousin wasn't upset at the idea. He seems eager for the chase."

I ripped my hand away in case he got any ideas about freezing the door and took a few steps back. There would be no outrunning him, but I'd be damned if I let him drag me back to his cousin.

"I told him you'd likely steal a car since the buses didn't run for another few hours and..." he spread his arms wide. "Here I am."

Was this a game to him? I snorted. Of course, it was. If I hadn't seen him torture and murder a hunter myself, I'd argue he never took anything seriously in his life. He watched me side-step my way between the cars, like a cat enjoying how its prey panicked before it fled. I was going to have to use my power again. Somehow.

Without skin contact, I doubted I'd be strong enough to break through his mental barriers. But I also didn't want to get close enough to touch him. A quick peek down at his hands. They were relaxed against the hood of the car, but that could change at any second. Maybe I could trip into him and use the distraction to slip past his defenses?

"I see you plotting, and it's not going to go how you think it will," Ezra smirked, and the temperature dropped a few degrees. "But I dare you to try."

Dammit. At my obvious distress, the blond warlock took pity on me. At least, I hoped it was pity and not some sick game. He

hopped off the car and held an arm out to his side, inviting me back toward campus.

"Go back to your dorm," he ordered with a smile. "Neither of us wants to chase you all night. Well, *I* don't, but my cousin has no plans to whisk you away and lock you in a tower. In case you were worried about that."

Yeah right.

"Why should I believe you?" I asked, still staying out of reach as I squeezed past him.

"Do you have any other choice?"

Good point. Still, I let him think I'd obey. I'd go back to the dorms, he could even follow if he wanted, but there was a back door that led to the walking paths behind Midnight Hall, which connected to the hiking trails in the National Forest that bordered that side of campus. I had more than one way to disappear.

Ezra did follow me for a bit but stopped in the courtyard when he saw me badge into the dorm. I ignored the night monitor's annoyed frown and ducked past the elevators to the service hall. There were a few doors back here, mainly to the janitor's closet and a storage room, but the last one at the end led outside.

A gentle crack of the door, a swift look around to make sure Ezra wasn't lurking, and then I bolted. I didn't get far. It wasn't Ezra standing in the middle of the path, arms crossed, and face set in a scowl. My heart gave a heavy *thump* at the sight of Kaiden bearing down on me. I froze.

"Go back to your room," he demanded, stopping a hair's breadth from me.

I had to look up to meet his gaze and wished that I hadn't. Why did he have to look so good? Gods, it was an effort not to wrap myself around him despite knowing who he was. I wanted to kiss him and punch him in the same breath. Instead, I trembled in silence, trapped between emotions with my mind too

scrambled to act. He gently nudged me with a shadow, and I jumped at the feel of it. It felt like him, but...colder.

"Inside, princess. Enough has happened tonight. We can talk tomorrow."

Talk? He thought I wanted to talk? Stab, yes. Scream, yes. Run as far away as I could and hide until he couldn't find me? With every fiber of my being.

"You don't tell me what to do, Kaiden." I balled my fists at my sides to keep from touching him. He already proved he was immune to my magick, anyway.

"Wanna bet?" he mocked, and a single shadow left his hand to wind around my waist. "I'm responsible for your safety, and there are djinn scouring this campus for you as we speak."

More hunters? Fuck, that complicated things but it didn't make it impossible.

"We're not bonded, Kaiden—"

"Kai," he demanded. "It's Kai to you."

I glared. "*Kaiden*. I rejected the bond. You have no hold over me, so let me go."

His answering chuckle was dark, and he certainly didn't let me go. He and his shadows backed me up against the brick building and pressed forward until I thought I'd drown in his scent. My knees trembled at the close contact, and I felt his dick twitch against my belly, but he kept his hands to himself. His arms bracketed either side of my head as he leaned in close.

"You act unaffected, but I know you're attracted to me. I can tell." I scoffed and his grin grew. "You quiver whenever I touch you."

"It's from disgust," I said through clenched teeth.

His eyes narrowed, and his fingertips were like a ghost's touch on my chin as he tilted my head back to meet his gaze. I fought off the reactions he accused me of, but I couldn't hide it all. His satisfied smirk made the muscles in my tummy clench.

"I don't think it is, princess," he whispered. One hand left the wall to graze my side on its way down to my hip. His fingers flexed and squeezed. "Tell me, are you wet for me right now? I bet you are."

I locked my jaw with a stubborn glare. My body may have betrayed me, but that didn't mean I would give in. His other hand left the wall to wrap around the back of my thigh. Before I even registered what was happening, he lifted me and tucked his hips between my legs. The hard length of him now pressed against my most intimate place, and he groaned into my ear. My fists clutched at his shoulders, simultaneously pulling him in and weakly pushing him away.

"I've got you," he promised, pressing even closer. "I won't let you fall."

I bit my lip against a yelp as he rolled his hips. Slow, calculated motions meant to torture and tease. His chin tilted down so he could watch me, but he didn't try to kiss me, didn't allow our skin to touch at all. The fight slowly left my limbs as sparks of pleasure radiated from between my thighs.

He spread my legs wider, allowing a more solid connection, and I threw my head back with a cry. Gods, how was he able to do this so easily? My entire body vibrated with the need for him to touch me when only minutes ago, I wanted to get as far from him as possible.

"I could take you right here, like this." My thighs tightened at his absolute confidence. "I could slide my cock so deep inside you, you wouldn't be able to climb off. I could lean you back and slow-fuck you until your eyes roll back, and your voice goes hoarse from screaming, until your juices drip between us to soak the ground, until our bond snaps into place so hard you'd never even think of leaving me again. Because guess what?" Both his hands moved down to grab my ass, squeezing and kneading me

closer as he increased the strength of his thrusts. "You didn't reject the bond."

My eyes flared wide, but only a whimper escaped my mouth. There was a tingling starting in my toes that warned of the pleasure to come. I shook my head to deny his words, the only argument I could put up right now with my release so close.

"Oh, you denied it, princess, buried it down so far you didn't even recognize me, but you didn't reject it." My legs shook, and he gripped my ass even harder. His thrusts sent my shirt up my back, and the rough brick scratched my newly-exposed skin. I didn't care. "That's it," he crooned. "Feels good, doesn't it?"

His hips froze, and I cried out at the sudden stop. He dropped one of my legs and held me tight while I settled on one foot. I was still open to him, but those powerful hips didn't push against me anymore, and I glared. I was *right there*. He had to know how close I was.

"I won't force you to complete the bond, and I don't have time tonight to argue for you to believe it. I could have taken you, but I didn't. I'm not the bad guy you think I am."

"I'd say working me up and leaving me like this is the opposite of good," I panted.

His grin turned downright wicked. "Do you need to finish, princess? Let's see what we can do about that." The hand on my hip stretched and reached until his thumb pressed right on my clit. "I couldn't make you feel like this if you rejected the bond."

His thumb rubbed in hard circles; one, two…and I fell into my release. Shockwaves of electricity stemmed from his hand and spread down each of my limbs. The muscles in my stomach tightened until almost painful, and still, it kept going. When it finally eased, Kaiden held me close to his chest and carried me back inside, all the way up to my room. He left a soft kiss on my forehead, the only touch on my skin he allowed tonight, and stepped away.

"We have a lot to discuss," he said, taking another step back from where he set me on my bed. "Don't leave this dorm until class on Monday. I'll know if you do."

I glared, some of my attitude coming back now that we had some distance. "And what if I choose to ignore your orders?"

His smile dared me to try. "My hand on your ass won't feel as pleasurable as what I just did to you. That I promise."

ten

Eryn

I made it a day before sneaking out. One whole day alone in my dorm, and I lost my mind. I still hadn't processed the emotions of finding out Kai was my bond, and that, combined with my already raging anxiety, made it impossible to stay inside for another second. Rani was away at the sorority house all weekend, and there was nothing on TV to distract me.

To top it all off, the knowledge that hunters were gathering, and I was stuck here while they sniffed me out, trapped in this little room like a lamb for slaughter, frightened me more than knowing they were out there to begin with. A small voice in my head whispered that Kaiden wouldn't let anything happen to me, but I knew better than to trust that voice. Sure, he wouldn't let the djinn kill me, thereby weakening himself in the process, but that didn't make him the good guy he claimed to be.

He was playing the long game, pretending to be kind while trying to earn my trust so he could better control me and force the bond. So, he wouldn't physically force me, great. That didn't

mean manipulating my mind to get the same outcome wasn't just as bad. It was worse, actually. Enraged at the idea that anyone, even my supposed other half, could have such sway over my sanity, I decided to go ahead with my plan for escape.

I'd been formulating one for several hours, and it all came down to the *how*. Kaiden said he would know if I left my dorm, which meant the doors had to have some kind of spell or trigger on them. He'd definitely been here enough times to lay one...or two. So, the window was my only option. I slid the glass up and peered down into the empty courtyard. It was a long drop, enough to kill a human, and definitely not something I would have been able to do earlier in broad daylight.

Most of the weekend parties happened off campus, and I only saw a few windows with their lights on. It was now or never. I looped my duffel over my shoulder, slid my legs out, and let myself fall before a student or staff member stumbled upon me. The drop felt longer than I expected, and I didn't properly brace myself before landing.

"Motherfu–ouch *ouch*."

I hobbled closer to the brick wall and tenderly felt around my ankle. It was warm to the touch and already swelling, but I didn't think anything was broken. Thank the gods, but it was still a miserable walk to the student lot. The entire time I worried about how I was going to let me parents know about this latest fuck up.

Did I have time to stop and send an email? I shook my head. Stupid. Of course I didn't.

I needed to focus on getting out of here and back to my parents before Kaiden found out I was missing. Again. A small voice in the back of my head screamed that I needed to warn them about the hunter too, *that* was the biggest danger. But stopping to find a public computer would put them in more danger than just running to them now.

Not for the first time I cursed their choice to not have cell phones. They were too easy to track but dammit they had benefits that would really help right now.

Ezra was nowhere in sight this time as I made a beeline for the same sedan I scoped out a couple nights before. I doubted Kaiden nor Ezra expected me to be out here again.

Still, I moved as quickly as possible. A quick jimmy down the window, and I got the driver's door unlocked. A little more finagling with my trusty screwdriver, and the wires beneath the steering wheel were exposed. A couple snips with my wire cutters, some sweet love with the copper lines, and I'd be good to go. I slid back out to the asphalt, the weird position already putting a kink in my back and reached for my duffel...only it now sat between a pair of high-heeled shoes.

I followed the scuffed pumps up to a pair of dirty skinny jeans, paired with a torn blouse. The raven-haired woman wore a feral smile—one I shouldn't have been as familiar with as I was. Shit. This hunter seemed broken already. Her right hand was held close to her chest with chunks of it missing. What was she doing here? Fuck, how did she find me so quickly?

My instincts screamed at me to run, to jump in the car, hit the gas, and not look back, but I needed that duffel. It held all the basic necessities for going on the run; clothes, some food, and a wad of cash that I wouldn't get very far without.

"This makes it all worth it," the hunter laughed, and her cruel smile sent a shiver down my spine.

Her deranged eyes widened and began to glow. There was a change in the air, like a shift in the natural current around me, and I knew she was drawing on her power. I gathered my own in defense. We weren't making contact, but the hunter's mind was fractured, that much was obvious to me. I could sense the bleeding, jumbled mess from over here, and I pounced before she could make her move, my mental claws sinking deep.

I tunneled into the hunter's psyche, hammering home the only thought I could formulate in my panic; go away. Her knees buckled, and she dropped my duffel. I cautiously leaned forward to grab it, keeping an eye on her shredded mind, when a dark shadow speared its way through her chest. The hunter collapsed in front of me, revealing Kaiden behind her, looking every inch the vengeful god who wasn't above smiting those under his protection.

He glanced at my duffel, trapped beneath the hunter's legs, the open car door with the steering wires hanging out, and shook his head.

"And here I thought our last conversation went so well."

"I don't belong to you, Kaiden. You can't tell me what to do," I snarled.

"We both know that isn't true, princess. You belong to me as much as I do to you." He stepped forward to grab my duffel and sling it over one shoulder.

My heart pounded away in my chest, and I wasn't sure how much of that was from fear and how much was the bond Kaiden claimed I didn't reject. From the other side of the now-useless getaway car, Ezra approached, whistling at the pool of blood forming around the fallen hunter.

"Sorry, cuz. That one got away from me." He glanced at the scowl on Kaiden's face and then over at where I now stood at the hood of the car, trying to inch away. I froze. "I'll let you deal with *that* while I take care of clean up."

Kaiden nodded his reply, then looked back at me and pointed a finger toward campus. "Back to your dorm. The kind of conversation we're about to have is better dealt in private."

I swallowed. "What kind of conversation?"

He smirked, but there was anger beneath it. "Discipline," he clipped. "Now walk."

I tried to keep my back straight and my knees from

wobbling, even with a twisted ankle. I refused to let him see my nerves. This wasn't a conversation I wanted to have, especially while he was angry. He told me bonds couldn't hurt one another, and I held onto that with everything I had.

"Stop," he called. My arms circled at my sides as I stumbled and tried to keep my weight off that bad ankle. "You're hurt."

No shit, Sherlock. I kept my mouth shut, though. He was mad enough already. He moved closer as if to pick me up, and I hopped backward. No way was he touching me right now, I didn't care how much pain I was in. I'd rather walk on glass. He didn't look happy about it, but he let me continue on my own, at least until we got back to the dorm.

I was a panting mess, my forehead damp and chest heaving as we stopped in the courtyard. Kaiden looked up at my open window, down at my pathetic mess of a self, complete with throbbing ankle, and growled. He swung me into his arms before I could protest and carried me the rest of the way in silence.

Once inside my room, he set me down and locked the door behind him. The tension shot to smothering levels with that action alone, and it only got worse as he laid his leveled gaze on me.

"Turn around, put your hands on the desk, and bend over."

My body locked up. He couldn't have just said...he wanted me to do *what*? His hand twitched at his side, and I blanched. Oh gods, he threatened to, but I didn't think he'd actually *spank* me. I leaned away from him, reluctance in my every move as I reached behind me to grip the desk he wanted me to present myself on. That wasn't going to happen.

"You have two choices, princess. The first, you can take your punishment like a good girl and keep your freedom. I'll go easy on you since you seem to be new to the concept of discipline." He smirked at that and moved on. "Option number two is, deny

the punishment you've earned, but move in with me where I can keep a better eye on you."

My mouth dropped. "W-what? You can't do that!"

He crossed his arms and leaned against the door, taking me in. My breath hitched under his gaze as I thought he might decide to punish me regardless. But he spoke softly instead.

"If you trust me enough for this, I can move forward in good faith that you've learned your lesson, and as such, I will allow you to maintain your freedom. By refusing the punishment, you're telling me you refuse to admit that putting yourself in danger is wrong. Your consequence will mirror the behavior you choose."

I gripped the desk behind me even harder, my nails peeling the varnish. Either option sucked. I'd never been spanked before but...it couldn't be that bad, right? I wasn't sure how much freedom he meant to give me if I couldn't even leave my dorm, but it was better than the alternative—being trapped at his place. It didn't mean I wanted him to hit me though.

"Will it hurt?" I instantly wanted to take it back. That was a stupid question. Of course it would hurt. The better question was, could I stand it?

Kaiden's eyes softened, and he uncrossed his arms. He didn't move to touch me, but the small action made me tremble regardless.

"I'm not going to *break* you, Eryn. That isn't the purpose of this." He looked me in the eyes, ensnaring me despite my desire to hide. "It will hurt, but it's nothing you can't handle. And honestly, I think a part of you is craving a little discipline."

Now he was talking flavored shit. Craving it? Was he insane?

"The choice is yours."

Oh gods. Was I actually about to do this? Slowly, I released my death grip on the wood and stood straight. Kaiden nodded, seeing that I'd reached my decision.

"Hands on the desk, princess."

Slow breaths. My palms met the cool surface, and my shoulders hunched up around my ears when I felt him move behind me. Stomach rolling, I waited for the first smack like a condemned prisoner trying to anticipate the executioner's ax. Was it on this breath that he'd strike? What about the next one? His large hand rested on my ass over my thick leggings. A warm, soft touch that was far from what my imagination conjured.

"We'll stick to five since it's your first time," he said, his voice close to my ear, but I kept my head tucked. "One for disobeying my order to stay here, one for putting yourself in danger, one for doing it despite knowing what was hunting you, and two for hurting yourself in the process. Are you ready?"

I think I nodded, but honestly, I was locked up too tight to know if I moved or not.

Kaiden sighed behind me. "I need the words, Eryn."

I was trying my best to not lose my shit. It took all my control to *allow* this to happen in the first place. Now he wanted me to talk about it? Some of my earlier fear bled into anger. His level of audacity was astounding. I kept my mouth shut and waited for the first blow. My entire body shook. I knew he could see, but I wasn't strong enough to hide my fear, keeping silent took everything I had. The anticipation was agony, and I found myself attuned to every little sound.

The soft brush of fabric behind me hinted at movement. The quick change in the air around me, and the growing warmth at my back confirmed it a second before Kaiden's body pressed up against mine with a growl. I jolted at the unexpected, gentle way his arm wrapped around my waist. He pulled me snugly against him while he nuzzled his face into the crook of my neck.

The feel of his lips on my skin was like an electric shock, and I stood frozen, unsure of what was happening.

"What are you doing?" I asked, breathless. His lips made

another pass down my neck, causing goosebumps to sprout in their wake.

"I've changed my mind," he murmured, and then pulled back until his warm breath tickled my ear.

He'd changed his mind? The hand that was on my ass now squeezed my hip, as if to reassure me it didn't plan on causing any pain tonight. Kaiden pulled the chair out beside me, and that hand slid down my thigh, scooped under, and pulled outward.

"Here," he said, lifting my leg a little higher. "Rest your knee on the cushion. You really shouldn't be putting any pressure on that ankle."

I allowed him to guide me and sighed in relief as the stabbing pain in my leg lessened.

"I don't understand." I tried to turn around, but his arms wrapped around me again and halted my movement. "Aren't you going to..." I swallowed. "I thought you were going to punish me."

I felt him sigh into my hair. "I had every intention of doing so, but as it turns out, I don't want you to hate me."

That was unexpected. I didn't think he cared enough about my side of the bond to actually pay attention. Wait, did this mean I had to move in with him now?

"You're not mad anymore?" I asked, testing the waters, and he chuckled.

"I'm furious," he admitted, and his arm tightened around my waist. "I don't like when you put yourself in danger, and you obviously can't be trusted to take care of yourself. So, for the foreseeable future, I guess you're stuck with me as your permanent shadow."

As my permanent..."What?"

Him laughing over my lack of freedom was really starting to

piss me off. His chest shook against my back, and I wanted nothing more than to stomp on his foot to shut him up. He was *not* going to follow me around. That was worse than his idea to spank me. Better than being forced to live with him, but only barely.

"I'd rather you hit me," I grumbled, and that set him off.

When his laughter was under control, he started nuzzling my neck again, like he was reassuring himself I was still here.

"Too bad," he whispered, seeming content to just stand here and hold me. "Now that I know you'd like it, it's not a proper punishment, is it?"

There he went again, spouting nonsense.

"Like it?" I stiffened. "I'd rather get it over with than have you follow me, that's all. Who the hell would like something like that?"

His chuckle was deeper this time, knowing, and it raised the hair on my arms. The hand that helped my knee onto the chair branded my thigh with its warmth. I shivered as it moved higher up my leg, zeroing in on that central part of me growing more wet with every puff of breath against my skin, with every flex of his arm moving from my waist to my chest. How did we always end up like this?

"A little pain mixed with your pleasure is nothing to scoff at, princess. It can heighten sensations to a level that mere kisses and gentle touches can't get you to."

As if to prove his point, Kaiden captured one of my nipples between his fingers and gave it a gentle roll. My back arched when he tugged on it before rolling it again. Tug and roll. Tug and roll.

"Pleasure can be slowly built," he explained, never ceasing his movements. "It can be layered and stoked." His mouth trailed soft kisses from my ear, down my neck until he reached the sensitive spot where it met my shoulder. "Pleasure can grow

and rise like an uncontrollable flame if tended properly, but even something that powerful needs a spark."

The fingers on my nipple suddenly pinched, squeezing the already tender flesh until it hurt. I twisted in his hold, but Kaiden held me fast, whispering words of praise in my ear. When he finally released the aching tip, a rush of warmth flooded my chest on a one-way track to merge with the throbbing between my legs.

"The key is balance," he explained and switched his attention to my other nipple.

My hips rocked, needing that next layer he spoke about, and his hand cupped me over my leggings. The heel of his palm pressed hard, and my head fell back against his shoulder as a breathless moan escaped into the dark room.

"That's it, princess," he nipped at my neck, adding little sparks of pain to my growing pleasure. "Ride my hand. Chase it. I'll help you get there."

I hardly understood what he was saying, but I got the gist of it well enough. My body leaped forward, overriding my mind in its hunt for more. More fire. More friction. More *everything*. I rocked my hips against his hand, using what he offered to push myself higher and higher until I hovered on the edge. My head thrashed against his shoulder. Why wasn't it working?

"Easy," he crooned, and his hand ceased its torture on my nipple. I whined at the loss. "I said I'd help you, and I'm going to do just that."

He shifted to the side and brought his hand down on my ass with enough force to sting. I yelped, thrusting my hips away from the sudden pain and right into his palm. He ground circles against my clit, and I was a goner. It was pleasure and sin, both fire and ice that ran through my veins when I detonated. My knee dug into the chair in an effort to keep me upright, but

without Kaiden's support, I would have been a puddle on the floor.

There was no way my legs were going to support me for much longer. Figuring out what to do next wasn't a problem, because Kaiden swooped me up in his arms and gently deposited me on my bed. I stared at the ceiling and caught my breath as I heard him rummage through Rani's mini fridge. There was a war inside me. Anger fought with fear, pain with confusion, and beneath it all was a weird sense of accomplishment.

Despite my very vocal desire to be free of him, Kaiden had somehow managed to burrow beneath my skin. I felt him there, in that bond I'd tried so hard to deny. It pulsed in my chest like a newborn star, all shiny and proud. I couldn't even blame him. At no point in any of our interactions did I tell him to stop. I chased after my own pleasure with as much enthusiasm as he had giving it to me.

What was I doing? Tears built behind my eyelids, waiting for a private moment to be set free. I blinked them away and watched as Kaiden turned around. He held a small ice pack and quickly wrapped it in one of Rani's many hand towels.

"It's for your ankle," he said and carefully laid it across the injured joint. "It doesn't appear broken but if the swelling gets worse, I'll take you to the health center for an x-ray." He paused like he was unsure of how to say what came next. "Please stay inside tomorrow," his tone could be considered polite, but I recognized an order when I heard one. "Ezra and I will have the current problem handled by classes on Monday, and we can worry about the rest then."

"The rest? You mean like my supposed freedom?" I glared at him, the anger an easier emotion to hold on to. I didn't care if he was being nice. He was still the enemy. His sigh was a tired one, but I refused to care. This was my life he was trying to control.

"I fully intend for you to finish your degree, with the knowledge that it will give us at least another four years to figure...*us*...out."

I side-eyed him, hard. "You're going to let me become a veterinarian?"

"I never wanted you to be unhappy, Eryn," he swore. "I only ever wanted a life with you."

Gods. That one hit me right in the heart. He was either very good at manipulation or he was telling the truth. The problem was, I didn't trust him enough to know the difference. Having a bond who saw me as his equal was the best possible outcome. It was the dream. Happiness. Fulfillment. *Love?* It was everything I ever wanted, and he was dangling it in front of me.

Did I take the risk and trust him? By doing so, I'd be going against everything I'd ever known and every painful experience life had shoved down my throat. Everything I'd been through wasn't a lie. What the tribunal did to my parents in his name wasn't a lie. I stared at the blond warlock in front of me, seeing both my fated bond and the guy who made me smile more these last months than I ever had before. The question was, which one was real, and could I risk the danger in finding out?

eleven

Kaiden

Her ankle wasn't broken, but days later, it was still a little swollen. I was tempted to risk her wrath and carry her to this next class; the pain on her face was enough to drive me insane. Not that she cared. The princess wouldn't even let me carry her books. *Her books*. It's like she was afraid that me touching her things was contagious.

That was bullshit of course. The bond couldn't be deepened through material objects. Physical touch, attraction, the meaningful development of feelings... all of that was required. I'm sure a bond could be forged from coupling alone, but it wouldn't be a strong one, and I didn't want to be shackled to a stranger for my entire life any more than she did.

I didn't know how to make this better. Give her space, and she'd be vulnerable to the djinn. Protect her, and she hated me. I sighed as we passed the library. Almost to class, and she hadn't looked at me once. Rani walked beside Eryn, like most morn-

ings, and her narrowed gaze bounced between us as she sensed the mounting tension that no amount of pretending could hide.

"What did you do this time?" she asked me, twisting just enough to catch my eye.

I shrugged. What was I supposed to say? I snuck a peek at my silent bond, but she didn't add anything. Her pace quickened despite how painful I was sure it felt on her ankle, but I held back an order for her to slow down.

Rani huffed. "Typical male response. You must have done something because my girl is more pissed than usual."

I smothered a smile at Eryn's reaction to that bit of truth. Her anger with me was a difficult hurdle, but not impossible, and it was surprising to hear that her feelings toward me filtered into moments when I wasn't around. That meant she thought about me. Whether that extended anger was good for me or not remained to be seen, but I clung to optimism.

"And what's up with the mood swings?" Rani continued, throwing her hands in the air. "You go from ignoring her to following her around like a lost puppy."

"I prefer guard dog, actually," I smirked when Rani glared. "Why don't you ask her? I've made myself clear on what I want from her. She's the one lying to herself. And me."

As I knew it would, my comment struck a nerve, and my bond growled. Shoulders hunched, she tried to limp faster. Thankfully, the doors to the classroom were in sight, and we reached them before the overwhelming urge to throw my injured bond over my shoulder reached uncontrollable levels.

"Can you grab us some seats?" Eryn asked, then handed her bag to Rani. "I need to have a word with him."

"I'll bet you do," Rani sing-songed then disappeared into the thin trickle of early arrivals.

I tried not to let Eryn's reluctance get to me. Really. Our fledgling bond was weak, but there. She had feelings for me

even if she denied them. I just had to encourage her to give those feelings a chance.

"*We* aren't going to happen."

Well, that wasn't the direction I had in mind.

"I appreciate the protection, I do, but you shouldn't expect anything from it," Eryn warned.

She thought I was doing this for a reward? I didn't care if she denied the bond for the rest of our lives, I'd still protect her. The very thought of anything happening to her made me sick. I couldn't imagine a world without her in it, even if it was nowhere near me, not after meeting her.

"I don't expect a single thing in return for my protection. That's not how this works," I growled, leaning closer so we wouldn't be overheard. "I'd be right here, defending you, even if you never let me touch you again."

"Good." Her eyes widened and she swallowed, some of her earlier bravado fading. "Because you're never going to touch me again."

Her gaze dipped to the side, and I smirked. Liar.

"We'll see."

Pink bloomed on her cheeks. "I mean it. We're not bonding. I don't trust you."

The smirk left my face. I didn't care how long it took for her to accept the bond. I could be patient. But her not trusting me? Not okay. Without her trust, I was nothing more than an over-bearing creep—one with completely honest intentions, but a creep all the same.

"You will," I swore, and her eyes lifted to mine once more. I tried to let her see how much I meant it. "One day, I'll be worthy of your trust. That I promise."

Ezra was on guard through dinner, so it was hours later before I returned to campus. My stomach lashed at me, pissed I hadn't fed it yet, but it could suffer a little longer. Once I saw

Eryn safely back to her dorm, I'd head home and order a pizza or something. Nothing like processed grease to get me through a night of grading papers.

I approached the Commons, prepared to suffer through the smells of food I didn't have time to sit and eat, but was pleasantly surprised to see my bond waiting for me out front. My brows rose, and I scanned the immediate area. Why the fuck was she alone? A flash of platinum blond hair in the window showed an eagle-eyed Ezra watching from a safe distance.

I scoffed. Pussy.

Ever since Rani flambéed him for following them around, he'd taken a more covert approach when there wasn't a legit reason for him to be there. I quite simply didn't care what anyone else thought. The only opinion that mattered belonged to the beautiful woman with dark curls scowling in front of me.

Her arms were folded tightly across her chest, and she walked away as soon as I was within reach, but there was no cussing today. That was a point in my favor. The sun set over campus; slowly, like it was stretched in time. The golden light hovered as we walked, and the warmth it provided felt nice on my skin.

It was hard to keep a bad attitude in the sun, and some of the tension eased from my bond's shoulders. The slow stroll was also easier on her ankle. Small victories.

"I'm not quiet."

"What?" I laughed. That came out of nowhere.

"I won't obey you," she continued. "You should find someone willing to do what you say because I'm not that girl."

Ah, so that was her plan then? Her fury didn't scare me away, so she thought to use reason. Too bad her reasoning was faulty. I didn't want a quiet, timid little bond to boss around the bedroom. I wanted the spirited hellion beside me; someone

strong enough to be my partner...who I also wanted to boss around the bedroom.

"What's this?" I chuckled. "You're trying to convince me to find another bond? It doesn't work like that."

"I'm poor," she insisted, knuckles white as she gripped the strap of her bag. "I don't come with any assets to further your family's position of power."

That was a lie, but perhaps one she wasn't aware of. Her very nature improved my family's political position because our children would be powerful. That wasn't why I wanted her. She wouldn't believe me if I told her, but if she needed that reassurance, I'd be damned if she didn't hear it from me every day.

"Princess, I wouldn't care if you were human."

My mother would, along with most of my family. Definitely the tribunal. They could honestly all go suck a dick for all I cared of their opinions on the matter.

"Now I know you're lying," she snapped. "There's no greater shame to your precious pedigree than tainted blood. Even I know that."

She wasn't wrong. Prejudices in our world ran deep, but she needed to know one thing about me if nothing else—I didn't agree with half of our society's practices. That was why I needed a strong bond. I needed someone to stand at my side while I fought for change. The second I inherited my family's seat, I planned to shred the tribunal to its core and shake things up. Along with the support of others I knew who shared my thoughts.

There were a lot more suffering in our world than just her kind. The sirens specifically had it bad right now. Our community was on the verge of imploding if we didn't change our ways. I glanced down at her, so innocent to the darkness of our world, and yet the direct victim of it as well. I didn't want to fight with anyone else at my side.

"Say that thing about tainted blood to Ezra, and he might just freeze your head."

"Don't tell me, he's an ally?" she snorted. "'Humans are friends, not food.' Yeah, I can see him lobbying the tribunal to forgive him the number of co-eds he's hooked up with on this campus alone." I cleared my throat, and she rolled her eyes. "Oh my gods, he's already tried that, hasn't he?"

"No," I said, slowly. "He couldn't get a meeting with the tribunal if he begged."

"I find that hard to believe," she muttered. "Isn't he your cousin?"

"And half human."

She stumbled, and I instinctively reached out to grab her arm. A slight pulse went from my fingertips on her skin to the center of our bond. When she didn't immediately push me away, a knot eased in my chest.

"Ezra is half human?" she asked with disbelief and a little awe on her face.

It was the first time she'd looked straight at me without a scowl for days, and I soaked it in. Her green eyes looked tired, but not churning with hate. Those delectable lips weren't twisted in a sneer but slightly parted. Gods, she was beautiful. I wanted to keep her there, looking at me like that for as long as I could, so I told her about Ezra and how he was hated by my mother and his siblings but beloved by me and his father. He was loyal and my best friend.

The rest of our walk was amicable and silent as she pondered all she learned. I could tell I'd changed her view of me, somewhat. I wasn't stupid enough to think it fixed anything. We stopped outside her door, and I waited for her to safely step inside. Just when I thought the night would end on good terms, she opened her mouth and shattered my peaceful illusions.

"Rani and I are going to the Kappa party tonight, so don't be surprised if whatever alarm you have on this room goes off."

Son of a bitch.

I pushed my way into the room and slammed the door behind me. She stumbled back with a hiss and balled her fists, ready for another round of our never-ending war.

"No."

I tried to keep the anger out of my tone, but that was tough. My arms were crossed as I leaned back, anything to keep from reaching out and bending her over my knee like I'd already threatened and failed to do.

"It's the start of spring break. Do you honestly expect me to stay here for a *week*?"

"There will be too many people," I argued. "Ez and I can't properly protect you."

Her entire face heated as her eyes narrowed to dangerous slits. "You act as if I'm powerless. I'll be surrounded by humans, plus you and Ezra can be there like proper stalkers to make sure nothing goes wrong."

"No."

She tilted her head, lip curled. "You can't stop me."

I met her challenge with a grin. "Wanna bet?"

Her fingers curled, and I knew if I let them anywhere near me, they would be around my neck. Any other time, I'd be open to try it. That simmering fire was attractive as hell, but being murdered wasn't on my list of shit to get done today.

"This won't work if you don't see me as an equal."

It would work even less if she's dead.

"I do see you as an equal," I countered, but my argument wasn't as solid as hers, and I knew it. "I'd be just as restricted if a kill order was put out on me."

"Bullshit," she spat. "You see me as this little doll that you hover over for fear of someone taking it away from you. I'm a

living, breathing person with her own wants and emotions, Kaiden. I'm going to the party tonight. I'm going with Rani. And you're going to have to deal."

I ground my teeth, not so full of myself that I couldn't see her point. That didn't mean I had to like it.

"Fine," I conceded. "But you need to be careful. Don't wander off on your own, and if Ezra or I say it's time to go, no arguing. You go."

"Deal," she smiled, but I couldn't enjoy the view.

I had a feeling about tonight...that everything was going to change.

The clearing for the base of tonight's party was as secured as it would ever be. Ezra and I laid a few traps around the perimeter —nothing deadly to humans—that should deter any wandering djinn from trying an illusion. There was nothing we could do about the rest of the checkpoints though, and that put me in a mood.

Well, that and not getting my pizza.

I watched a group of Greek Life staff set up the drink tables. It was sodas and water, but I knew for a fact there were a few kegs hidden deeper in the woods for when faculty wasn't looking. Team tents were erected and decorated with their corresponding colors, and I frowned at the purple bandana I was forced to tie around my arm.

Ez had one too, but he was far more excited about it than I was.

"This is the most juvenile thing I've ever taken part in," I grumbled as my cousin swaggered over from somewhere to my right.

"Let her have her fun," he said with a wide grin. "The Zombie Run is actually pretty great."

I sent him a strong side-eye. He would say that. This shit was perfect for him; capture the flag with screaming, half-naked girls, and plenty of dark corners on campus to get lost in. The wide surface area of this game was what concerned me the most. A party in the woods was easily defendable. A party across the entire college campus was a recipe for disaster. We had to be on our game tonight. No mistakes. Nothing and no one got close enough to my bond to hurt her.

"Are you sure this is the best plan?" I asked for what felt like the hundredth time in the past two hours.

He nodded at his matching bandana. "Being a hunter will allow us to follow her and stay close without suspicion. A zombie or spectator would have no reason to always be around."

This stupid-ass game.

"And the tasks? Won't we be split up for those?"

I didn't like the idea of playing, but if it was the only way to protect her, I'd do it. Eryn had been through a lot this past week, and she'd put up with me and my rules better than I thought, considering how it all started. She deserved some freedom.

"I flirted a little with the blonde in charge of assignments," Ez grinned. "She knows to put us in your girl's group."

That was that. We would shadow Eryn for the night. Going where she went and keeping an eye out for another attack. I was confident this clearing was safe, and hopefully, she wouldn't have to leave it more than once. Perhaps this bit of freedom would soften her toward me as well. A man could only hope.

twelve

Eryn

The moon was already high in the sky and shining through our window when Rani finished with me. I had to admit, we looked kinda hot in our purple biker shorts and tank tops. We both pulled hunter cards, so purple bandanas were artfully folded and tied around our biceps. From what I'd heard, zombies wore white bandanas on their heads. If either of us got "bitten," we had to return to our team tent, register as infected, and trade in our bandanas. The last team with their hunters alive won.

"Wait!" Rani called and pulled me back into the chair. "I forgot your eye makeup."

I obediently sat, but my knee tapped in anticipation of finally getting out of this room and away from my permanent shadow.

"So, what's up with you and Kai?"

I jerked at the unexpected question, and Rani scolded me for moving.

"No idea," I grumbled. Was *complicated* an answer?

"Lies," she scoffed. "You obviously like him."

It was on the tip of my tongue to deny it...but I didn't. Denial wasn't a land I wanted to be accused of living in. Besides, liking Kaiden wasn't the problem.

"Okay, I do like him," I admitted. "I'm just not sure I should get involved with him. It won't work out."

"Open." I blinked up at Rani and then closed my eyes again when she dipped her brush in more eyeshadow. "Why wouldn't it work?"

I wished there was an easy answer to that.

"He's...controlling." To put it mildly.

Rani paused, her hand hovering over my cheek. "In what way?" she asked. "Tie you up and bend you over, or cut you off from family and friends controlling? Because there's a difference."

I didn't know how to respond. Both were true but not for reasons she would understand, and I couldn't explain. She took my silence as a red flag and put the brush down.

"Has he hurt you? Or is he threatening you? I don't care how hot he is, I have access to a boat, and can make his body sink to the bottom of the ocean before he can say fish food."

I smiled at her unquestioning defense of me.

"No, nothing like that." She relaxed and reached for the makeup once more. After another minute of silence, I tried again, "He's always there. Watching me, touching me, wanting to carry my books and walk me to class like an invalid." Okay, that didn't sound all that bad, but I wasn't explaining it right. "He wants more from me than I can give him."

"Have you told him that?"

So many times.

"Yes."

"And?" she prompted.

Makeup finished, I got up and paced the small room while Rani cleaned up.

"And he says he's content to wait until I'm ready to discuss 'us.'" I grimaced, and Rani laughed, like what I said was adorable.

"Honey," she said with a soft smile. "If he's making his intentions known and not pressuring you to fulfill them, then I'd say he's being downright chivalrous. Has he tried to kiss you? Or touch you in any way that can be seen as more than friendly?"

"Not since..." I blushed, remembering the last time he touched me, in this very room. "Not since our last conversation about it."

"Then, what's the problem?"

I groaned and threw my head into my hands. That was the problem. The more I was around him, the more I wanted to give in. Was that a bad thing? Normally, I would say no. But our situation was unique and not one I could share with my human roommate, no matter how badly I wanted her opinion. I settled on a shrug and hoped that the guilt of lying to my only friend wouldn't eat me alive.

The party was in full swing when we arrived, but we still had time before the main festivities began. I followed Rani to the purple tent to sign in. As the last to arrive, we were assigned to one of the last missions. That didn't bother me. I still didn't quite understand how it all worked yet anyway. Before being released to mingle and wait our turn, we were outfitted with a Nerf gun and a bag of large marshmallows. My face must have given away my confusion because the guy behind the table laughed.

"The Nerf gun is for the zombies. Three shots equal a kill or just one to the head."

"Then what happens?" I asked.

"The zombie has to sit out for fifteen minutes before they

can reanimate. Thirty minutes if you hit them with a grenade," he said, pointing at the marshmallows.

With those strange instructions bouncing around my brain, I followed Rani into the trees. String lights dangled between branches, giving the whole area a fairytale glow. With beer. The kegs were hidden out here, but I wasn't in the mood for alcohol tonight. My freedom was precious, and I didn't want to risk it by giving Kaiden an excuse to lecture me about safety.

Speak of the devil, I saw him and his cousin making their rounds. We made eye contact, and he nodded but didn't approach. *That* was surprising. I thought for sure I'd have to hide in the shadows all night to avoid him. Smiling, I limped deeper into the crowd with confidence; knowing they were around and willing to protect me went a long way. A fallen log presented itself as the perfect bench, and I sat on it. There was no reason to push my ankle past its limits.

"Oh, great spot, girl." Rani shimmied her way over, beer sloshing out of her cup. "We can watch everyone from here."

To Rani, everyone meant the hot guys walking past to get to the keg. None of them appealed to me, and I tried not to think too hard about why that was. A few returned my roomie's flirtatious smiles, but only one was brave enough to approach. He held two juice bottles, swiped when the sister watching the drink table wasn't looking, I'd bet, and shyly winked as he offered one of them to me.

"Don't worry, it's sealed," he said when I didn't reach out to take it.

I *was* thirsty. I accepted the bottle and was relieved to see he wasn't lying.

"Thanks." I smiled and took a few sips. "I don't know if I should be accepting gifts from a rival team though."

His brows rose in shock. What? Did I do it wrong? Rani

made flirting seem so easy. Just when I was about to dig a hole and bury my head in it, he let out a strained laugh.

"You mean because I'm on Team Green?" His white teeth were a little too bright in this light, and it was another strike against him in my opinion. "I don't mind helping another team win if it has such a beautiful hunter."

Rani elbowed me when I didn't answer, but what was I supposed to say to that? I really was bad at the flirting thing. Thankfully, a whistle blew, signaling the next mission, and our number was called. I turned without another word and started my slow limp to the clearing.

"Hold up!" the guy called out. "Aren't you going to finish your juice?"

I frowned. Was he into saving the earth or something? Maybe he wanted to recycle the bottle. I chugged the rest of it and tossed him the plastic.

"Go nuts," I told him, then turned to catch up with Rani.

I didn't know what I expected from the missions, but me sitting in a shopping cart while our group maneuvered across campus wasn't it. Granted, my ankle made me the perfect prey, and Rani refused to let me get eaten. Neither did Kaiden. He and Ezra were magically in our group, not that I thought it a coincidence.

My stomach hurt as we made our way over uneven brick. Rani pushed me in the cart while the others flanked us with their guns at the ready. It was a funny sight. I held my bag of marshmallows close, tempted to eat one, but the churning in my gut was growing worse the closer we got to our checkpoint. The ancient tree was the marker for the center of campus, and an obnoxiously pink hippo piñata hung from its lowest branch.

"Someone grab it and let's go," Kaiden ordered.

No one questioned him. It was like they all subconsciously decided he should be in charge. The sight of the bright pink in

my lap was enough to kick-start my nausea. We needed to finish this mission quickly. I was obviously coming down with something. The way back was clear until we passed the liberal arts building. A giant horde of half-drunk zombies waited for us and charged the second we came into view.

"Shit," Rani giggled. "They really want that piñata."

The piñata that *I* was holding? Great.

We ran for it—well, the others did. I threw marshmallows from the cart and tried not to throw up. 'Dead' zombies littered the path, picking at grass until their time out was up. Half of our group had to remove their bandanas and switch them when we got back to the tent. Me, Rani, the guys, and a handful of others were the only ones to make it through unscathed. Us and the hippo. I couldn't see the clearing, but I heard the music and it wasn't much further. Too bad that was still too far for my poor stomach.

"Stop," I called out. "Stop the cart."

Rani slowed and leaned over to see what I needed just as I dipped my head over the side to hurl. Cool hands gathered my hair at the base of my neck, and I didn't need the tingles on my skin to tell me it was Kaiden. Another round nearly toppled the cart, but it stayed on four wheels.

"Are you okay?" Kaiden whispered, anxious eyes scanning my face.

I wiped my mouth with the back of my hand and nodded.

"Maybe it was that fish you had at dinner," Rani suggested, resuming our trek at a brisk jog.

Whatever it was, it wasn't done with me yet. By the time we made it back to the clearing, I needed help getting out of the cart. My legs felt like hot Jell-o, ready to melt and drop me to the ground. I stumbled away and threw up again behind a tree. Gods, I felt like shit. My head swam and shivers racked my body

in waves. I barely made out the conversation taking place around me.

"Are you sure? I would do it, but Pasliegh is being a bitch and wants me on clean up."

"I'm sure." That was Kaiden. "I'll take care of her."

Then I was being lifted, and it all went black.

Kaiden

I knew tonight was a bad fucking idea. Ezra raced ahead to open the back door of my truck. Moving as swiftly, but gently as I could, I lay my bond across the back seat. She looked so weak. Vulnerable. Her forehead was beaded with sweat, and her scrunched face told me she was in pain. Fuck. I hopped behind the wheel and slammed the door shut. Ezra barely had enough time to climb in the back with my bond before I tore out of the lot.

"I don't like the look of this, cuz." He placed partially frozen fingers on Eryn's skin, trying to cool her. "The fever is rising too fast, and she's starting to twitch."

"Check her pupils," I ordered, and floored it through a red light.

The apartment was in view when Ezra cursed.

"Blown," he shouted. "This isn't the stomach flu."

No. It was poison, and I had a pretty good idea of what kind. Gathering my bond back in my arms, I took the stairs two at a time and nearly broke my own door down rushing to get her inside. Antidote. I needed the antidote. But first, I needed to

bring her body temperature down. Nothing would do shit for her if her brain fried inside her skull first.

"Ez!" I shouted from the bathroom.

I ran the faucets lukewarm and laid Eryn inside the tub fully clothed. The second she was out of my arms, her eyes flicked open, and she leaned over the side. I jumped out of the way as she was sick once again and growled when she slumped unconscious the second the heaving stopped. Ezra slid into the bathroom, his arms laden with supplies.

"I wasn't sure what we needed," he panted. "Fuck, she doesn't look good."

"Save your opinions for when I ask," I snapped. "Go into the kitchen and boil the following: moon water, kola leaf, St. Mary's thistle, and a clear quartz."

He ran to do as I asked while I lifted my bond from the water. She seemed almost peaceful now, but I knew the worst was yet to come. Carrying her across the hall, I placed her on my bed, not caring if she soaked the sheets. The wet cotton would help keep her cool, and that would further stave off the other symptoms. For now.

Nightshade poisoning was no joke. That had to be what this was. Nothing else affected a nightmare as strongly. How the fuck was she poisoned? I had my eyes on her the entire night. Ezra returned with a vial in hand—magically cooled for immediate use. I thanked him with a nod and uncorked it. Pushing a knee into the mattress, I leaned over my bond to gently lift her head enough for the antidote to trickle into her mouth. The second the vial touched her lips, it all went to hell.

"Shit. Ez!" I shouted over my shoulder. "Get over here and help me."

Half the antidote soaked the pillow beside Eryn's head, and I worked hard to protect the rest as she thrashed beneath me. Her eyes were squeezed shut, and the rest of her face was contorted

in fear. Fuck. The poison was progressing faster than I antici-pated. How much of it did she ingest?

"Quick, get her legs!" I instructed, then narrowly dodged a heel to the ribs.

"What the fuck is happening to her?" Ezra panted. He pinned both her legs to the mattress with genuine concern.

I wasn't the only one disturbed by this new development. I hated seeing her like this. Hopefully, once the antidote kicked in, she would calm down and her body could rest.

"My guess is hallucinations," I responded and barely missed a clawed hand coming for my face. I wasn't fast enough, though, and her nails raked the skin of my neck, drawing blood. "I'm sorry for this, princess."

I released my shadows, and they leaped to do my bidding. Like gentle restraints, I bound them across her chest and shoul-ders, pinning her arms to her sides in the process. Without wasting another precious moment, I forcefully gripped her chin with one hand and poured the antidote down her throat with the other.

She sputtered and coughed, but the cool liquid went down, and I breathed a sigh of relief as it took root. The thrashing stopped, and Eryn's brow smoothed out in the first look of peace I'd seen on her face since we carried her from the party.

"Was it enough?" Ez asked.

He gently released her legs, and I called my shadows back. I sat above her for a few more minutes, just in case, but the worst of it seemed to have passed.

I sighed. "I think so, but let's brew another batch just in case. She shouldn't have reached the hallucination stage so swiftly."

"You're worried she's ingested too much."

I nodded. "Or she's having an adverse reaction to the poison on top of everything else."

Fuck. My bond was *poisoned*. My guilt ate at me through the

night while I kept watch. Ezra easily brewed another batch of the antidote while I scryed Mother to fill her in on all that had happened. To say she was disappointed in me would be an understatement. My failure to protect my bond was glaringly obvious, and no one felt its repercussions more than me. Or Eryn.

After turning down my mother's offer to send the family physician and her multiple attempts at getting me to come home, I did concede on one thing: my bond was to live here, with me and Ezra, for as long we remained at this school. I sank into my plush two-seater on the opposite side of the room, head throbbing.

She would hate me even more after this, but at least she'd be alive. Her soft rustling on the bed grew more frantic, and I worked to ease my anxieties. I wasn't sure how much of it could leak down the bond with her defenses down like this. She needed peace, not the burden of my stress. More rustling and quiet murmurs broke through the darkness of the room.

A night terror? I easily made my way toward the bed, familiar with my room even with the low visibility. Something scrunchy and dark flew at my face, and I caught it before it made contact. It was soft, like cotton, and a little damp. Her shorts? I tossed them to the side and looked up just in time to watch her wrestle with her top. The few beams of moonlight that reached her from the open window showed my half-dressed bond twisting to try and escape her damp tank top.

She was breathtaking. Pale, unblemished skin nearly shone under the moon's glow, like it was embedded with crystal. From the curve of her breasts to the soft roundness of her belly, she radiated beauty. Much more potent than a siren's call, nightmares really did bloom at night: like a midnight flower. Her growls turned frustrated as her top got stuck over her head. It was enough to break me from my trance.

"Easy. Let me help."

It was a struggle because she still appeared to be out of it and was fighting rather than working with me. In the end, one tank top was no match for the two of us, and it joined its companion somewhere on the floor. Now I had a new problem; Eryn was half-naked. Wearing only a bra and panties, she sat and stared at the foot of the bed, her eyes glowing softly.

"Eryn?" I slowly reached out to cup her cheek and hissed when I felt how warm she was.

If the antidote were working properly, she wouldn't have a fever. Godsdammit! At least it wasn't hallucinations again, and maybe this time, she would take the antidote without fighting. I let out every colorful curse I knew and reached for the new vial on the nightstand.

"Kaiden?" I froze, my hand around the small glass and looked back. Eryn faced me now, her clear gaze finding mine in the dark. "What's h-happening?"

Her stutter was more from the fever than the surprise of waking up in a strange bed, I hoped, but I still moved cautiously.

"What do you remember?" I asked, then gently settled a little closer, until I could make out more of her features.

"We were at a party," she started but paused with a frown. "I-I was sick."

"Bit of an understatement, but keep going, princess."

"That's it," she whined. "I remember being sick, and t-then nothing."

It wasn't unheard of for poisoned victims to not remember the aftermath. What I needed was the memories before the symptoms started. Did she still have those?

"You were poisoned," I told her. "Nightshade. And a lot of it."

She didn't answer. The silence stretched between us so long that I wondered if she heard me.

"Eryn?"

"I was poisoned." It wasn't a question, more a statement of disbelief. "I was f-fucking poisoned?"

I couldn't help but grin. If she could be angry right now, then things weren't as bad as I originally thought. She did still have a fever, though, which meant the poison wasn't done with her yet. We had to stay ahead of it.

"Trust me, I've been angry enough for the both of us, but right now, I need you to drink some of this."

I offered her the vial. and she took it from me without argument. Almost.

"What is it?"

"So little trust in me. And after I just saved your life," I teased.

"Kaiden," she warned.

"*Kai.*"

She growled, but with her shivering it sounded like an irritated kitten. Adorable.

"*Kaiden,* what is this stuff?"

"The antidote," I replied with a sigh. "Take half, and it should ease the fever."

She obediently followed my direction, thankfully, and handed the half-empty vial back to me. There were a million questions I wanted to ask her about what happened before her symptoms took over but now wasn't the time. She'd had a rough night and morning wasn't far off. I told her to get some rest and returned to my place on the loveseat before she could comment about me being in bed with her.

Sleep was out of the question, there was too much circling my brain, but it surprised me when an hour later, she hadn't succumbed to her own exhaustion. Her restless movements and soft groans of discomfort should have eased by now.

"I can hear your teeth chattering from here," I told her and stood. "Why didn't you tell me you still had a fever?"

"You gave me the a-antidote," she replied. "I assumed it needed time to work."

That shit worked faster than Tylenol. If she hadn't kicked the poison yet, we needed to try something else. Something I was almost positive would make her want to kill me.

"That was your second dose," I explained while lifting my T-shirt over my head.

"W-what are you doing?"

The tremble in her voice wasn't from the fever this time. I stood in front of the window, so I knew she saw me unbutton my jeans and let them fall to the floor. Clad in only my boxer briefs, I stepped toward the empty side of the bed.

"I have only one dose left, and while Ezra can brew some more, I don't think it will solve our problem."

"Y-you don't?"

I picked up the still-cool vial and glanced over at my bond. She looked so small, huddled behind the covers as she was. I didn't want her to fear me, and pushing our bond was the last thing I wanted to force her into, but I didn't know what else to do.

"Not by itself," I admitted. "The antidote needs a little help from our bond."

I actually heard her gulp, and her fear hit me like a bucket of ice water. I was resigned to the plan, however. Something had to give.

"W-we–" she started, and then went silent. Her breathing picked up when I set a knee on the bed, but she didn't bolt. "We don't have a bond."

She had a point, to a degree. Our bond was nothing more than a seed, but it was there. We just had to convince it to bud a little.

"You know that isn't true," I coaxed, still slowly moving closer. "The bond is there. We have to strengthen it...a tiny bit."

I wasn't going to force her to complete it; that wasn't what we needed. Just a little nudge. Only enough so she could borrow my strength to heal. It was more than I wanted to push her into. I'd avoided touching her for the most part because I wanted the bond to grow organically. I wanted her to *want* it. Now, I was taking even this small choice from her.

"H-how?"

I was close enough to see the slight tremble in her shoulders, and the way she nervously bit at her lip. That she wasn't outright bolting from the room was a good sign. Then again, I hadn't told her my plan yet. Slowly, so I wouldn't spook her, I brushed a fingertip over her cheek and traced it down to her mouth, where I freed that bottom lip.

"Skin to skin."

thirteen

Eryn

The moonlight didn't hide a single detail. His broad chest was toned with enough muscles to make me take a second look. A light dusting of hair started just beneath his navel and danced an enticing path beneath the band of his briefs. I ripped my gaze away and looked up.

Kaiden's usually tamed locks were wild and unkempt. The soft strands tempted me to touch as they fell over one eye, hiding the scar there. I kept my hands clenched in my lap. *Focus.* He spoke again, saying those same words—skin to skin. My pulse kicked into a gallop at the idea, and my stomach rolled along with my next shiver.

I wanted this to stop—the pain, the nausea, feeling like I was about to shake right out of my own body. The antidote was obviously not working, that wasn't a lie, but maybe I hadn't taken enough of it. Was jumping to this extreme really the only option? I turned my head to break Kaiden's stare. His thumb slipped from my lip, leaving his hand hanging between us

before it dropped down to the bed. My gaze caught on the half-empty vial he held.

"C-can you ask Ezra to make more, please?"

Kaiden's head cocked to the side. "I can," he said slowly. "I was going to regardless, just in case, but that won't help us right this moment."

He settled more solidly on the bed, leaning closer in the process, and I nearly fell on my ass as I scrambled off the other side. My bare feet met the cool hardwood, and my knees almost buckled at being forced to abruptly take my weight. I locked them. With more space between us, I felt a little more in control.

We could figure this out. I appreciated his worry, but I was sure there was another solution to my...predicament. My stomach clenched, and I bent in half at the pain. Okay, that hurt. Groaning, I crossed my arms over my waist and rode out the responding shivers.

"Eryn—"

"No!" I held out a hand and took a deep breath. After another moment, I straightened. "It's passed."

Kaiden's expression hardened as he slipped off the bed in one fluid motion. Definitely smoother than my attempt. He rounded the bed. Each step closer, I mirrored with one step away, until I felt the dresser dig into my back.

"This isn't really up for discussion," he warned, blocking my attempt to flee to another part of the room.

Gone was the gentle-talking TA I'd gotten to know these past months. Standing before me now was the stubborn warlock who refused to let me run. His jaw was set; there was no talking my way out of this. My eyes darted to the door on my right. I could reach it, if the next round of stomach cramps didn't take me to my knees. Even now, my symptoms were worse, and I shivered despite the sweat beading on my brow.

I glanced back at Kaiden. Yeah, I could make it to the door,

but out of the apartment? Escape? I wasn't so sure. Still, I had to try something.

"Don't even think about it," Kaiden growled, legs spread and shoulders back. He was ready to rush after me and take me down if he had to.

Dammit.

"P-please Kaiden." My teeth chattered. "I don't w-want to do this."

"I know."

He was right in front of me now. The heat of him did nothing but battle with my rising fever. So close. He was so close. I swore each of the hairs on my body rose and reached for him. We weren't even touching, and the bond between us was palpable. Like my body knew what it needed—what it wanted—and holding out became harder by the second.

"We won't complete the bond," he promised. "I won't touch you anywhere that's covered."

I glanced down at my lacy bralette and matching panties. Too exposed. Peering over at him, I got an eyeful of tanned skin only restrained by a dark pair of boxer briefs. A tight pair. There was little left to my imagination as I stared at the growing bulge in the front. Kaiden groaned, and that bulge twitched. I sprang for the door without thinking.

"Seriously?" he sighed, arms catching me and caging me in.

His forearm hit hard against my hips and lower stomach, sparking a new wave of nausea. When it eased, my back was once again against the dresser, and less than an inch separated us. He lowered his head, cool breath mingling with mine.

"What are you really afraid of?" His lip curled. "If forcing you was what got me off, we wouldn't be here. We'd already be bonded."

I felt the truth in his words, but that couldn't eliminate years of fear. How did I tell him that I was scared of everything?

Creating a bond that I couldn't escape from. Letting down my walls and paying for it later. Falling for him and the hope he sparked, then having it all ripped away at the last moment. I was terrified that the future he promised wasn't real.

I fought to get away, but he was there, holding my hips. His grip was tight, punishing, as he dared me to look him in the eye.

"Face it," he commanded. "Face the fear, and let me help you."

I really didn't have a choice. The symptoms were beyond worse in the short time we argued. My nausea was constant, my entire frame shook, and my head felt like it was about to explode against the back wall. But my fear was rooted just as deep. With the little strength I had left, I pushed against his chest, ignoring how even that small touch sent sparks up my arms.

There was no moving him. I only wore myself out trying. Kaiden sighed and reached down to catch me behind my thighs. The world spun as he lifted me up, holding my legs on either side of his waist. Instinct had me kicking and fighting to squirm my way down.

"Let me go!" I shouted as he spun us toward the bed.

No amount of hits slowed him. Two steps, and I was flying again. My back met the soft sheets with Kaiden climbing right over me.

"I'm going to save your life whether you want me to or not."

He straddled my hips until his knees dug into my sides, keeping me pinned. I thrashed anyway, panicking with every second I couldn't break free. Inside my chest, the bond flared.

"I don't trust you!" I screamed.

"Obviously!"

I flinched at Kaiden's tone, and he blew out a breath, softening his face. The air was charged, but I felt the fight slowly draining from me. Everything hurt, and I was so, so tired.

"I know you're scared," he whispered. "But I refuse to let you

die just because you're afraid of our bond growing stronger." His large hand cupped my chin and pressed down until my mouth was forced open. "Drink."

The last of the antidote poured past my lips and cooled some of the fire ravishing my body. But just like before, it wasn't enough, and I knew what came next. Faster than I could counter, Kaiden rolled off me and pulled me onto my side. He tucked me against him, tight. From back to thighs there was no part of him I didn't feel.

I hissed at the overwhelming shock of it. Like being dunked into ice water, my system was overloaded. Warmth grew in my chest, impossible to ignore, but it wasn't the fever. Our bond slowly cracked one eye and awoke. I knew Kaiden felt it too. His soft gasp brushed over the back of my neck, and his dick grew hard against my ass. I rolled away, reaching for the side of the bed, but Kaiden threw a long leg over mine, pinning me even more.

"Have I ever hurt you?" he asked into the dark.

I shook my head. Never, but I couldn't form words over the wash of emotions battling inside me. He pressed his lips to the skin behind my ear. And my heart rate spiked.

"Have I forced myself on you? Even after feeling you slick against my fingers and ready in my arms?"

"No," I croaked.

"Then trust me to control myself now."

Trust. He made it sound so easy. Sickness and fear reigned over my senses, but Kaiden fought them with gentle touches. His fingers brushed through my hair until the tension in my shoulders eased, and I sank into the mattress. He took his leg off me but wrapped an arm around my middle and tugged me deeper into the curve of his body.

His shadows continued those calming strokes until the fight left me completely.

"I could never hurt you, princess."

With his lips nuzzling my neck, his words followed me into unconsciousness, and I swore the bond smiled.

I was on fire. My entire chest, my thighs, even my arms were smothered in the flames. I clenched my eyes tightly, fearful that the fever had returned, but after a few tense moments, I realized the heat wasn't coming from inside me. Blinking against the thin strip of daylight, I was greeted with a wide expanse of tanned skin peppered with scars and warmth under my palm.

What the...?

The chest under my cheek rose and fell in a steady rhythm, and it took every ounce of my control to not freak out. A quick stock of my body was enough to send me right back to the edge. I was wrapped around Kaiden like a freaking octopus. Well, we were actually wrapped around each other, but that was *my* leg thrown over his like a sneaky parasite.

Shit.

Another heart-stopping moment passed, and when my squirming didn't wake him, I wiggled my ass off the bed and onto the floor. Popping my head past the mattress, I kept a critical eye on him while blindly searching for something to wear. Escaping in only a bralette and panties wouldn't get me far unnoticed.

My fingers caught on cotton, and I pulled the dark material on without thinking. It was a T-shirt—*his* T-shirt–but it fell to mid-thigh and covered all the important bits. I didn't have the time to be picky. The bond told me he was still in a deep sleep, but who knew how long it would last?

He had to be beyond exhausted after spending the past

twenty-four hours fighting to keep me alive. I paused in the doorway, guilty. The strong presence in my chest promptly reminded me why I had to get out of here. Already I felt different. The bond inside me was awake, and there was no more denying it.

I hadn't rejected it years ago, like I thought and no amount of willing it to disappear would change things back to how they were. The process had begun. It would either fade with time and distance or grow until completed. And *that* wasn't going to happen. My body demanded I crawl back in that bed and curl up beside Kaiden like a lizard around a warm rock.

I fought the urge and stumbled into the hall, making sure the door closed behind me without a sound. I had to get out of here. The stairs didn't creak, and all was quiet as I cautiously moved past the open kitchen and living room toward the front door. Downstairs was cool and dark. Long curtains covered the windows, but daylight fought to be seen around the edges.

There wasn't a single alarm as I snuck out. It was really anticlimactic, but I wasn't going to complain. With each step I took from the apartment, I grew more plagued with confusion and worry. Was I making the right choice? I was so confident inside, but now, doubt grew like a stubborn weed. There was no shaking it.

The feeling wasn't overwhelming, my resolve to escape was stronger, but...it was almost as if the emotion wasn't mine. I laughed. Who else would it belong to? Scanning the parking lot, I tried to orient myself and figure out the quickest route to campus.

"I guess it was too much to hope that our bond would change your need to run."

My chest thumped with humor that definitely wasn't mine, and the implication of what that meant was enough to urge me

into a sprint. That humor swiftly turned into annoyance as heavy footfalls sounded behind me.

"Stop!" Kaiden shouted, and I caught a glimpse of his shadows out of the corner of my eye. He was almost close enough to use them. "I will tackle you to the ground, princess!"

He would. I felt his conviction.

I tamed my fear enough to stop running and spun around to face him. His chest rose in heavy breaths as he took me in, braced for battle before him. A pair of dark sweatpants hung low on his hips, and he was barefoot as he moved in.

"Now that you got that out of your system, can we walk back? I hate running first thing in the morning."

Technically, it was more like midday, but that wasn't what I wanted to argue about right now. I held my ground as he kept coming, forcing a glare to my face despite the nerves eating me up inside.

"Short of throwing me over your shoulder, you can't make me go back with you."

There. Let him know he had a fight on his hands, and I had no plans on returning anytime soon. I needed space, my own bed, and time to figure out just how much things had changed.

One blond brow rose as he closed the distance between us. "Oh yeah?"

Wait. Why was he smirking?

I stumbled back, hands raised. "I didn't mean that how it sounded. It wasn't a challenge."

Even feeling his emotions wasn't enough warning.

"Too late." He lunged for me and tossed me over his shoulder. "I accept."

There wasn't much energy in my reserves to fight him off, but I did at least try. Unfortunately, I was locked back inside the apartment and pressed against a wall before my head even

stopped spinning. Kaiden had a grip on the front of his borrowed shirt and pulled me forward.

I drew in a sharp breath. "What are you doing?"

The aquamarine in his eyes glowed, ensnaring me.

"Every time I say something that pisses you off, your eyes widen just a little. Did you know? That's your tell." His hand worked its way up my neck to cradle my jaw, leaving sparks in its wake. He leaned closer. "You like it." That hand moved further until his fingers rested on either side of my throat. Not squeezing but holding me still. The bond fluttered, pleased with his attention. "I know what I want, but how about you? Are you done lying to yourself?"

He rubbed his nose against mine, and my breath left me in a gasp.

"You're insane," I whispered, and he chuckled.

"Liar it is."

I broke free before the bond urged me to do something stupid like kiss him. The manhandling usually set me off, but that anger was missing now. Maybe I was getting used to it because I felt a whole slew of emotions that were inappropriate. There were nerves and borderline panic, but also arousal so strong it made me breathless.

Kaiden lowered his head again as he watched me cycle through each emotion. He said nothing, but his brows rose in surprise when the arousal won out and bloomed in my chest. He chuckled, and my eyes widened. Was he...Could he feel my emotions too? My missing anger returned with a vengeance.

"Stay out of my head," I growled.

"I'm not in your head."

Semantics.

"Then stay out of my...chest," I countered.

His eyes immediately dropped, and a tendril of heat slipped down the bond, making me blush. Gods, this was impossible. I

barely had a hold on my own emotions around him, and now I had to juggle his as well? His hunger grew as he scanned my bare legs before bringing his gaze back up to meet mine.

"You look good in my clothes." His voice was deeper, almost a purr, and it felt like a caress.

I crossed my arms to keep from reaching for him. "It was the first thing I grabbed to cover up."

Truly. This was not like the hoodie situation. I wasn't wearing his shirt because I wanted to. It was necessary. That's all.

"And you were going to what...run all the way to campus naked but for my shirt?" I scoffed at his possessive tone, but he kept going, "I don't know how I feel about others getting a glimpse at what's mine."

"Don't start with that territorial bullshit," I said, pushing at his chest. "Nothing has changed."

He gripped my wrists in a firm but gentle hold and crowded me against the wall, one of his legs slipping between mine. From our hips up, there wasn't an inch between us to spare.

"I'm being who I've always been when it concerns you. You *are* mine. That bond flickering in your chest only proves it."

Panting. I was actually panting like a bitch in heat. I felt him, both inside and out, and it was enough to short-circuit any argument I had. He wasn't really touching me, not like *that*, but gods did I want him to. The attraction was on another level thanks to that damn fledgling bond taking up too much space in my chest.

I felt all of his desires like a battering ram against my defenses. It was impossible to hide from it. I couldn't push it aside. Couldn't bury it or find my way out. Fear and desperation simmered beneath the bond's influence, and suddenly, like a breath of fresh air, it disappeared. Kaiden backed away with it.

"How did you do that?" I asked, a little dazed.

It was quiet on his end like he flipped a switch and shut it all

off. I searched hard, but it was only me and my own emotions left.

"Immense self-control," Kaiden replied. It sounded like he was struggling, but he kept the bond shut down. "Come. Let's have some breakfast and discuss what's going to happen now."

My mind was clear, and I had him to thank for it. I also had him to thank for saving my life, which I still hadn't done, but if he somehow thought all that meant he now had a say in my future, he was in for a rude awakening.

fourteen

Kaiden

I held my breath all the way to the kitchen. I felt her irritation and expected it, but I wasn't sure if it would lead to another chase across the parking lot. I fucking hoped not. It wasn't a lie that I hated running first thing after waking, especially today. My heart got enough of a workout when I woke to find my bond missing from my bed.

Eryn sat silent at the large island, looking sexy as fuck in my shirt. Her emerald eyes tracked my every movement as I gathered the ingredients to make breakfast. I wasn't trying to show off, but I made a mean omelet, among other things. Cooking wasn't too different from preparing a spell, and I was proficient at both.

Once the cheese melted enough, I folded the egg over the ham and peppers, slid it onto a plate, and set it before the enchanting woman still glaring at me. Her eyes widened at the sight of my latest masterpiece, and her stomach grumbled its demand that she dig in. I chuckled at her expression—a mixture

of hunger and stubborn denial—and added a tall glass of water next to the plate.

"Eat up," I said. "We have a lot to figure out."

"It's huge." Her scowl was adorable, more of a pout in my opinion, but I didn't voice that out loud. My smirk only fueled her irritation, and she dug in before I could play off her words. "Shut up."

"You've had nothing but antidote in your stomach for twenty-four hours. You have to be starving."

She didn't deny it. She also didn't say anything about how awesome the omelet tasted, but that was okay. I knew it was. I went to work on my own breakfast, and finished before she even made it halfway through hers. Pushing the plate away, she leaned back in her chair with a slightly less intense stare.

"Keep going," I demanded, and instantly, her scowl returned. Tough shit. She needed to eat. "I won't tell you again," I warned. "Next step is feeding you myself."

There was a hint of curiosity from her side of the bond. It was smothered in fury, but there. She was beyond stubborn... and apparently liked it when I got bossy. Interesting. Also good for me, because I had a feeling she'd call me that more than once in the near future, and not just about her eating habits.

I grinned. There was nothing I'd love more than to boss her around the bedroom...once she let me cross that line. Perhaps that line was closer than I thought if she kept sneaking glances at me like that.

"I literally came back from the dead less than twelve hours ago. Give me a break."

I glared, but she glared right back, the magick in her gaze flaring. Sexy as fuck. After a tense stare-down, she picked up the glass and drained the water. Better, but we'd work on it.

"You *will* finish your lunch."

She scoffed. "What makes you think I'll still be here for lunch?"

I stiffened, knowing I had a battle ahead of me. There was no other option. This was the only plan Ez and I could agree on that would actually work. She was going to hate every part of it. I eyed the front door, hoping she didn't bolt again, and Ezra took that moment to come yawning down the stairs in nothing but a ratty pair of basketball shorts.

If he noticed the tension in the kitchen, he didn't comment on it. He did, however, help himself to Eryn's half-eaten omelet.

"Dude."

He stopped, his fork halfway to his mouth, and blinked up at me. "Wha?"

"It's fine," Eryn said. "I told you I was done."

Ez went back to eating like he hadn't just stolen my bond's breakfast, finished or not. I sighed and planted my hands flat on the island. Hopefully, with Ez here, we could contain her rage. Half asleep or pumped with adrenaline, Ez was a force to be reckoned with and great backup. I gave Eryn my full attention once more, and she straightened in her chair.

"Back to what I was saying." From the corner of my vision, Ez slowed his eating, finally clueing in to what was happening. "You'll be here for lunch, dinner, and every meal thereafter because you live here now."

Dead silence. I don't think I heard her breathe for a good twenty seconds. And then...

"What! You can't decide where the fuck I live, Kaiden."

"I can. And I have."

Ez snorted, but I ignored him. Eryn had my full attention. I sensed the absolute storm surging on her end of the bond. Confusion. Fear. Anticipation. Desperation. And through it all, a clean slice of rage.

"Well...No," she sputtered, and my head cocked. I expected more than that.

"No?"

"*Fuck,* no. You don't own me, and I refuse to stay here a second longer while you spew this bullshit."

She vaulted off the chair and sprinted for the door. There it was. I was only mildly surprised. She was no match for the both of us, so running was her only option. And her forte. She wrapped her hand around the doorknob and yelped, yanking it away, then spun and glared at Ezra, who was whistling while putting his plate in the dishwasher. My lips fought a smirk. He didn't have to freeze it.

"You could have phrased it a better way, man," he told me, and I shrugged.

"I prefer the direct approach. There's no room for confusion."

"I'm still plenty damn confused!" Eryn shouted, hands on her hips, which lifted my shirt high enough to give us a glimpse of her panties.

Fuck. What was it about the top of a woman's thighs that was so damn attractive? I glared at my cousin. He grinned but respectfully looked away.

"What about this confuses you?" I asked her. I truly thought I was being straightforward enough.

"The part where you get to decide all on your own *any* bit of my future!"

Ez laughed and clapped me on the back. "I'll let you handle this. I've got patrol."

He dipped back upstairs without another glance at my half-naked bond. Smart man. She was absolutely delectable right now, all pissed off and puffed up like a feral kitten. Her cheeks were rosy, and her eyes sparked with a subtle green glow. And those legs. Fuck me, I loved it. If she thought her anger a deter-

rent, she couldn't be more wrong. I subtly adjusted myself behind the island.

"You almost died," I said. "Someone poisoned you, somehow, in front of the entire Greek society, and *me*. And. You. Almost. Died."

"And?"

Was she fucking serious?

"And? You may have no sense of self-preservation, but I have enough for the both of us. You're not leaving this apartment until I know we can keep you safe. If I have to lock you in my bedroom to make sure that happens, so be it."

Oh, that really set her off. Power surged down our bond, but it didn't affect me. I was glad Ezra chose to go upstairs, though.

"I have classes!" she screamed, dousing the air with the scent of her magick. "A roommate. A life! I can't just disappear, there will be questions."

We'd already thought of all that, and temporarily, it wasn't a problem.

"Then I guess it's a good thing spring break just started, and we have a week to figure it out."

With a disgusted sound, she stomped away from the still-frozen door and up the stairs. I followed. We were far from done with this conversation, but she slammed the door to my room —*my room*—in my face. I sighed and rested my forehead against the wood. She needed space to calm down. I could give her that at least. Trudging back to the living room, I readied myself for a long wait.

The afternoon passed in quiet torture. I roamed my apartment like a zombie; barely cognizant, but highly aware of my prey

nearby. Shuffle into the living room, straighten up the coffee table. Shuffle to the dining room, clean another table. Back to the living room to clean under the couch cushions. By the time I wiped down the counters in the kitchen and started dinner, I was ready to bound up the stairs and demand my stubborn bond get her ass down here and stop acting like a child.

The hair on my neck rose as the wards around the front door activated. Ez strolled in, fresh from patrol and already salivating over the sauce I had simmering on the stove.

"Homemade lasagna?" He smirked. "Trying a little hard there, cuz, don't you think?"

I ignored his teasing and stirred the pot again so it wouldn't burn. He wasn't far from the truth. Only, I wasn't trying to impress her this time.

"I was hoping the strong aroma would bring her downstairs," I grumbled while draining pasta water.

She missed lunch and had only eaten half of her breakfast. If she allowed herself to grow too weak, she'd relapse. My worry was held in check only because I could sense her health through our bond. I tried to give her privacy, which was why I only snuck a few peeks.

"The cold shoulder. Harsh." Ez swung onto the counter, ignoring the perfectly good stools on the other side of the island.

"It won't last much longer," I swore. "She will eat."

"I'd take your quiet over the day I've had."

I took in my cousin, assessing him for any injuries or signs that his patrol had gone awry. He'd call if things were too bad, but it was possible that with Eryn here, he had taken on more than he could handle.

"Relax, dude. There wasn't a djinn to be found. Not even an illusion for some mild entertainment."

"They're waiting to see if the poison took," I noted. "The second she's spotted around campus, the attacks will resume."

I began layering the lasagna. Pasta, meat, ricotta, sauce. Pasta, meat, ricotta, sauce. It wasn't calming me down. Fuck. This was only a temporary reprieve. They wouldn't stop coming, not until the bond was complete. Probably not even then, but she'd be harder to kill, and hopefully tucked away under the protection of the faction by then.

"She was right, though," Ezra said, interrupting my internal panic. "We can't keep her locked in here indefinitely."

I knew that, but what else was I supposed to do? Even with our protection, she nearly died. My silence was enough to tell Ez what I was thinking. He knew me well.

"Let her go."

Maybe not that well. I dropped the ladle of sauce, sending blood-red splatter across the stovetop. Fitting. His idea was guaranteed death for her.

"That's the literal worst idea you've ever had," I told him, vigorously wiping at the mess.

"I didn't say let her go defenseless," he argued, humor drenching his tone. I was so glad he took this seriously. "We keep guarding her, of course, but closer than before, and with a crystal to warn her of poisons this time."

That was more like it. Still a shit plan, though.

Lasagna stacked, I smothered it with cheese. Ez let me think through his suggestion. It would allow her some freedom, but it was still dangerous. Too dangerous for my liking. Unfortunately, unless we took out every djinn or the leader of their faction who sent them—which would declare open war—they'd keep coming. This was going to be a long four years.

"There's one other problem," Ez hinted. I slid the lasagna into the oven, set a timer on my watch, and then turned and braced myself. My cousin rubbed the back of his neck, a guilty look on his face. "Rani cornered me on campus and went all Rambo, demanding to know where her friend was."

"She cornered you?" Yeah, that was hard to believe.

"Well, I allowed her to corner me." I rolled my eyes. "What? It was the first time she willingly talked to me."

"And how'd that go for you?"

He winced. "She accused us of kidnapping. Which wasn't far from the truth."

"Ez…"

"She said Eryn hasn't been at the dorm, and with no cell phone, she has no other way to contact her. We were the last ones to see her, and she basically accused us of holding Eryn captive. She's pissed, cuz. I tried telling her that you and her girl finally hit it off, but she's not buying it." At my string of curses, Ez grinned. "She's vicious. It's kind of hot."

My pulse pounded in my temples, a sure sign of an impending migraine. I liked Rani for my bond. Her tenacity and fierce protection of Eryn was a giant green flag for me. But in this instance, it was a big problem. I wouldn't put it past the redhead to take this to the dean and bring far more attention to our situation than was safe.

"Eryn needs to contact her roommate and sell the story," I groaned. That wouldn't be easy to convince her to do. I glanced at the timer on my watch. Just under an hour, plenty of time to convince her. I hoped. "Let's go tell the princess to lie to her friend."

My door was still shut. And locked. But it was *my* room, and if I wanted in, I was going to get in. I broke the handle, with a little help from Ez, and prepared myself for a wave of her wrath. Only, she was nowhere to be found. Across the room, the balcony door was open, the curtains swaying in the early evening breeze. Ezra's laughter couldn't drown out my, "Are you fucking kidding me?"

She escaped. Again. And she scaled a three-story rose trellis to do so.

"Why isn't there a ward on your balcony?" My cousin asked between more fits of laughter.

I *thought* I had a good enough reason.

"Anyone dumb enough to try and attack me in my space is asking for the consequences."

Ezra turned purple he laughed so hard.

"Gods," I cursed. "I never imagined she'd climb the fucking shrubbery to get away!" I spun and headed to my dresser, filling my pockets with anything I could need in case we had a fight with more than my bond on our hands. "How long has she been out there?"

It can't have been too long if even Rani hadn't seen her yet.

Ez sobered at the question. "They're going to know she's alive."

Exactly. Fuck. I opened the door to my side of the bond, filling our connection with nothing but her. It was time to go hunting.

fifteen

Eryn

I wasn't running...exactly. There was no point. That throbbing in my chest meant Kaiden could find me anywhere in the world if he was close enough. I just had to get out of that apartment. I felt trapped, in more ways than one. Kicking dirt and pebbles out of my path, I continued my hike along the rising cliff face.

Campus wasn't where I wanted to be right now. Nature. Open space. Freedom. That's what I needed to think it all through. I didn't want this, that was the main argument overwhelming my mind. Was I grateful to be alive? Of course, I didn't want to die. Kaiden vehemently cared for my well-being and that was...nice. Okay, it might make me a little giddy inside, but I shut that shit down fast before it spun out of control.

The fact remained, no matter how or why it happened, I hadn't wanted to initiate this bond. I felt him all the time now, even with his emotions locked up. It was like a phantom stranger in my chest. This wasn't how things were supposed to go. I had a plan and a future I was working toward, which didn't

include being locked away in close quarters with a man I fought tooth and nail to keep my hands off.

Kaiden was attractive and kind—when he wasn't being an ass. That didn't mean I was willing to throw everything away. He claimed he wanted my happiness, for me to pursue my goals. How much of that was lies to get me to bond, though? How much would change now that the threats against me almost succeeded?

Gods, and what did I tell my parents? I wasn't even sure saying something was a good idea. Better to let them stay safe and in hiding while we figured out how to stop the hunters ourselves. I could handle Kaiden on my own.

The dusty trail ended at the peak of the cliff, a wide area overlooking the tumultuous ocean far below. Mother Nature wasn't the only one unsettled right now. That connection in my chest fluttered, and I knew my time was up. I stepped closer to the edge—away from that feeling—soaking in my last moments of freedom.

Small rocks crumbled and fell over the side as my toes cleared solid ground. Cool shadows, obvious even in the fading sun, wound through my legs and up around my waist. I rolled my eyes and turned to where Kaiden stood off to my right.

"I wasn't going to jump."

He warily stepped closer, hair in disarray and hands clenched at his sides. His gaze briefly glanced over the edge, and his jaw tightened.

"I can never be too careful with you. You're unpredictable."

I watched his throat bob as he swallowed. His shadows reeled me in until I stood in front of him. Both my feet back on solid earth, he sighed, and the tension left his shoulders.

A little of the Kaiden I was used to seeing returned. "Scaling the trellis? Really?"

His shadows guided us toward the trees, still in view of the ocean, but at a much safer distance.

I looked away. "It was better than being tackled on my way out the front door."

"My shadows and the new wards would have stopped you. No tackle necessary...unless that's something you're into."

I scoffed but couldn't fight a small smile. He was teasing me. I'd take that over yelling and threatening punishment any day. "You don't stop, do you?"

"Just being honest." He winked.

We watched the ocean and the setting sun in a peaceful silence. Our hearts beat softly and in tune, that detail didn't evade me, but rather than send me into a spiral, it was comfortable. Definitely less frightening than I built it up to be. Kaiden's shadows retracted, but a few lingered around my legs, brushing lightly against me like they couldn't help themselves.

"Give me a week." His voice caught me off-guard and I turned to him with eyes slightly widened in surprise. "The rest of this week to figure out how to keep you safe. Please."

"I can't be your prisoner," I told him.

He sighed, and true remorse shone in his eyes. Enough light reflected off the ocean that I could still make out the creases around his mouth as he frowned.

"I'm sorry I made you feel like that for even a second," he whispered. "But it really is too dangerous right now."

A little of his honesty and desperation leaked through the bond. I knew he believed that—but when would it end? Wouldn't we always be in danger? Him a faction heir, and me the last nightmare. He *was* trying. I could at least meet him halfway.

"One week," I agreed. "At the end of spring break, whether you've figured it out or not, I'm going back to class." He stiffened

and I added, "But I'm open to finding ways of doing it safely." I wasn't a complete idiot. Someone was actively trying to kill me.

He relaxed. "I ask for nothing more."

Yeah right. "Really? Nothing?" My head tilted. *Bullshit.*

His grin was slow and seductive. "Not yet. But you'll fall for my charm soon enough."

I laughed, but deep inside I worried he might be right.

Ezra was staring at me. I blinked my bleary eyes until they cleared and revealed what I thought I'd hallucinated. The lean, bleach blond stood on my side of the bed with a dirty grin and a blaring cellphone in his hand that he ignored.

"Looks like things are working out better than I thought." His grin widened as the arm around my waist tightened.

Kaiden pulled me against him, his hand flat and warm on my bare stomach. At some point in the night, all the pillows I shoved between us so this exact situation *wouldn't* happen, ended up on the floor, and my ass found its way against Kaiden's dick. I blushed as I realized it was an early riser.

"Go away," Kaiden grumbled, burying his face in my hair. "It's not my morning to make breakfast."

Gods, he was a *snuggler*. Ezra chuckled at my futile attempts to break free. Every morning. I woke every morning with some part of Kaiden touching my body: my very overheated and very aware body. Damn, this bond and its endless campaign to click us together like a horny set of Legos. As I wiggled my way to the side of the bed, the cellphone in Ezra's hand began to screech.

"That would be Rani. Again," he sighed and shoved the phone at me with a grimace. "It's for you."

Crap. They mentioned something about her being on a

rampage to find me. My heart twisted. I'd never had a friend care like that. I wanted to ease her panic, I did, but I still avoided calling her back these past couple days. What if I couldn't sell the story? I couldn't explain to a human why I was hiding or that magical beings were trying to kill me...because I was also a magical being.

"Just stick to the plan, princess. It will be fine." A rumpled Kaiden sat up and stretched, his muscles bunching and flexing as his arms rose.

I took the phone from Ezra, if only so I wouldn't be caught staring. One deep breath, and then I answered.

"Tell me where she is or so help me—"

"It's me."

Silence. And then...

"*Eryn! Where the* hell *have you been?*"

I held the phone far from my ear, but we all heard her. She was a wound-up mix of pissed-off and hysterical. My guilt grew with each question she shouted down the line until I thought I'd sink under it.

"I'm so sorry, Rani," I whispered. "I should have called you the moment I felt better. I've been sleeping off this bug for the past few days."

Her ranting stopped, and I glanced over at Ezra who gave me a thumbs up.

"But you're feeling better now?" she asked, her worry making me hate myself even more.

"Yes. Kaiden has taken great care of me."

The rest of the conversation continued at normal volume, and the boys leaned forward to try and listen in. I paced the room to keep out of reach and to keep my nerves in check. Any minute Rani would realize I was lying to her; but I mentioned staying here for the rest of spring break, and she didn't question me. In fact, she sounded downright excited about it.

"You have to tell me what the sex is like when you get back," she squealed.

I stopped pacing. My feet rooted to the floor. Had he heard that? I spared a peek at Kaiden; he'd be smirking if he heard, right?

"I-Uh. I have my own room," I lied. There would be no details of sex because it wouldn't be happening. Ever.

When we finally hung up, with promises to have dinner the night before classes resumed, I felt like I'd run a mile. Who knew lying took so much out of you? Ezra left us to start breakfast and then patrol, and just like that, Kaiden and I were alone again. Three more days of this. Just three more days to get through.

And nights. I pushed that thought aside. Buried it.

"That wasn't so bad, was it?"

I glared because he knew it was. Thankfully, Rani hadn't asked many questions, and the story was easy to keep simple. Less chance of slipping up later.

"Don't look so smug," I told him. "You got what you wanted. I'm living here."

"And it's about time, young lady."

Kaiden cursed and sprung from the bed to slide on a pair of sweatpants. My head swung around, searching for the voice. Was someone *spying* on us? I watched Kaiden make a beeline for the dresser, more annoyed than concerned. He reached up and pulled at the dark cloth covering a mirror.

In the glass was a stern face. The woman was older but had the same eyes and shade of blonde hair as Kaiden. There wasn't a wrinkle to be found on her flawless skin, though I could tell she was older. No laugh lines around her mouth or eyes. Who was she?

"Mother," Kaiden growled, shoulders tense.

Mother? *That* was his mother? The woman who was the

head of the witch faction and member of the tribunal that's haunted me my entire life? I gulped and attempted to sidestep my way into the bathroom but her bird's-eye gaze shifted and ensnared me. She took in everything; my head of knotted curls, Kaiden's T-shirt, and my bare legs. I knew the rumpled sheets on the bed were visible behind me, but that small detail satisfied her it seemed.

"I called to ask about your progress, but I see congratulations are in order. Good."

Congratulations? Did she think we...?

"Mother—"

"Now that the bond is complete, I will prepare your rooms straight away. There is much for you to catch up on, and I'm positive your bond is in need of learning."

Oh gods, she was ordering him home. Us. She wanted *us* to leave and return to the tribunal. I wasn't going to finish school. I wouldn't become a veterinarian. I would be forced to assume my place in their society and...and I was going to be sick. Kaiden looked at me, seeing the terror in my gaze, and whipped back around to face the mirror with a glare. His shadows escaped, fueled by the rage I felt pulsing down the bond.

"We haven't completed the bond, Mother, so you can cease your plotting."

Any other time, I would have taken great pleasure in seeing that level of shock on the face of a member of the tribunal. Right now, I was too focused on not falling apart in front of her.

"*Not bonded?*" she demanded. "I clearly heard otherwise!"

"Eryn is staying here *temporarily* and out of necessity. There are no immediate plans to complete the bond, and we surely won't be returning to the tribunal as soon as it happens."

With small steps, I worked my way closer to the door. Kaiden was going to bat for me. He wasn't going to force me, but she

could force *him*. His mother's gaze, nearly bleached of blue, landed on me once more, and I froze.

"This is not a game, little girl. Your weakness threatens my son and—"

Kaiden stepped in front of me, breaking her stare and hiding me within his shadows. I took in a breath and then another. I had to get out of here. My fear was slowly evaporating over the growing fury her accusations set aflame, but I couldn't shake it completely.

"I told you it was her choice, Mother. I won't allow you to bully her into making it."

There was a squawk of outrage, but I didn't wait around long enough to hear what followed. I scrambled for the door, ignoring Kaiden's calls behind me. The kitchen and living room were empty. Ezra must have already left for patrol. The front door beckoned, promising open skies and room to be free, but I turned down the enticing offer—finally learning that I couldn't escape this. Kaiden's footsteps thundered down the stairs.

"Will you stop running?" he called out.

I spun to face him, tears of frustration clouding my vision. "I'm not! Where in the world would I go where you couldn't find me anyway?"

He nodded, determination hardening his face as his long stride ate up the distance to me. "It's true," he admitted. "I will always come for you. Always."

I closed my eyes against his intense stare. My hand blindly reached behind me, searching until it felt the glass door that led to the large balcony. The coolness of it grounded me.

"Why?" I whispered, anxious to know the truth. "It's just the bond making you want me."

"*Why?*" he asked and stepped forward, gradually corralling me against the sliding door. My eyes popped open when the glass met my back. "Because you're absolutely everything I've

ever wanted and didn't know I needed." He leaned over me, resting his weight on a forearm. His other hand delved into my hair to lightly pull on a coil. "These curls," he breathed like they entranced him. His thumb grazed my cheek on its way down. I frowned, but he tugged at my bottom lip. "This mouth. Gods, this mouth. It doesn't know when to shut up."

My brows flew into my hairline. That wasn't where I thought he was going to take it. Something about kissing me or tasting me maybe. But not that.

He continued, blind to my confusion, "It argues and pushes me. It questions *everything*, driving me crazy until all I want to do is press my lips against it and coax other sounds from its depths."

Oh.

His eyes trailed up my face, lingered on the freckles over the bridge of my nose, to eventually meet my gaze. There was no hiding from the truth he bared in that look, and I didn't know if I could take much more of his honesty.

"You are spirited and fierce—my equal in every way. I don't need the bond to see your loyalty and kind heart, or to know that I would cease to exist if anything ever happened to you."

I slowly shook my head. He couldn't mean all that. "You c-can't possibly...It's the bond's influence."

He smirked, like he knew he had me right where he wanted. "Our bond is in its fledgling stages. Emotions and a heightened sense of one another are the only consequences. I know my own mind, and I've had these thoughts long before I saved your life and we opened this door."

I grappled to find something to hold on to—for some reason that could explain away the pressure in my chest at his words. He couldn't feel that way about me. Gods, he shouldn't admit it so openly either. It forced me to look at him in a different light,

to see what possibly drew me to him as well. I wasn't ready to go there.

"It won't work," I pleaded. "I'm not your equal, Kaiden. I wasn't raised in your world; a world that's tried to kill me my entire life."

His hands cupped my face, keeping me from turning away or closing my eyes. "I'll step down as heir in a heartbeat if you need me to, but I think we can do more good for our people—*our* people—together."

"I-I don't understand."

He pressed a gentle kiss to my forehead, melting a hardened corner of my heart. "We could change everything, Eryn. And not just for nightmares."

I thought I was working with a completed puzzle, but Kaiden just revealed a whole piece that I never knew existed. Power, not the kind from magick. He was offering me the power to decide my future. All I had to do was give myself to him, to the bond, and everything would change.

sixteen

Kaiden

The constant, steady beat of my heart merged with the thrum in my chest until I couldn't tell if it was my heart that matched Eryn's or hers that was in sync with mine. One of her legs was thrown over my waist. I'd woken with my palm against her bare thigh, and the supple feel of the smooth skin was all I'd thought about for the last hour.

An entire hour that I'd laid here, awake, while she slept soundly against me. There should be a rule against this. Technically, it was unavoidable. Pillows were shoved between us each night. We slept under separate blankets. Yet somehow, our bodies found one another. The past two mornings, I woke before the sun to the addictive feel of her touch.

I left before she noticed—knowing our position would only stress her more—but I wanted to spend the day here, wrapped in her delicious scent. Extracting myself was a delicate process, but once again, she slept through the dip of the mattress and

rustling of the soft sheets. I crept out of the bedroom and down the stairs without turning on a light until I reached the kitchen.

French toast was on the menu for this morning, and I got to work gathering my ingredients. My body on autopilot, I thought over the past two days and the strained truce my bond and I seemed to have settled into. Basically, it involved not speaking. Aside from a quiet 'thank you' after Ezra acquired some clothes for her, we hadn't exchanged anything other than awkward silence.

I added milk and cinnamon to the eggs, whisked them, and then mixed in a splash of vanilla. She needed time. That's what I told myself and why I hadn't stalked her around this small apartment for an answer. She hadn't attempted another escape, so I knew we'd made some progress, but was it enough?

"Oh, good morning."

I spun at the sound of her voice, the loaf of bread swinging in my hand. Her little bare feet tried to burrow into the hardwood as I stared. Snapping out of it, I gave her a soft smile and gestured at the chairs.

"Morning. Breakfast will be ready soon if you're hungry."

Instead of taking a seat, she carefully slid around me to the cabinet beside the fridge and reached for a mug. I carried the gallon of milk over, knowing it was her preferred drink of choice in the morning, and our skin brushed at the handle. The tips of my fingers tingled, but she pulled away before the feeling could spread.

I wanted more of it. I waited until she perched on the other side of the island to put her plate down. Then, I held out a fork and smirked as she eyed it, and me, with suspicion. She knew my game, but I didn't care.

"Be brave," I dared her.

With a huff, she snatched the fork from my grasp, managing only slight contact. The small touches were innocent, but I loved

how flustered they made her. Her cheeks were flushed with color, and I felt her interest down the bond, along with a healthy dose of confusion. The reaction to my touch made her worry, and I wished I could alleviate that.

Only time and trust would fix it. Again, I feared what that meant for the end of this week. She had a few more days to make a decision, and I promised myself that I'd respect it. It would be a million times harder to protect her if she wasn't here with me. Her dorm was warded, but also too far for me to get to swiftly if something went wrong, as it always seemed to lately.

"I can feel your anticipation, you know."

Surprised, I met her steady gaze. It was the most I'd heard her voice in days. I hadn't realized how much I missed it.

"You're projecting down the bond," she added. "I thought you were good at blocking your emotions?"

Talking to me *and* acknowledging the bond. Progress.

I cleared my throat. "Sorry, I didn't realize. Stronger emotions are harder to keep locked down sometimes."

She nodded, and the conversation died. Silently, we rinsed our plates and set them in the dishwasher, and I held in my shock when she stepped alongside me to clean the rest of the kitchen. Elbows brushed and hips grazed as we danced around one another in close quarters. She didn't recoil this time, and a part of me preened at the show of trust.

When there was nothing left to keep us occupied, she leaned against the counter with her arms crossed.

"How would we change things?" Her bottom lip was nervously trapped between her teeth, but she didn't shy away as I watched her gather her thoughts. "I know I'm not cut out for this life. I won't fit in. You say you want me for more than just the bond, and maybe that's true, but help me understand why throwing away a quiet, useful life among the humans is worth it."

"First," I held up a finger. "I have to correct you on one thing; you *do* fit in. You're cut out for this life because it's where I am, and together, we just make sense." I braced my hands on the granite behind me. "As to the changes, you've experienced first-hand the consequences of the age-old prejudices our people cling to. My family has fought for many generations to change these beliefs. If you go back far enough in the tribunal records, you'll find my family actually voted *against* the bounty on nightmares."

I both saw and felt her shock. Good. It was time she knew the truth about my family's involvement with hers.

"What about your current relatives?" she asked. "Would they still feel that way if you weren't fated to be with one?"

"Yes," I swore. "And if not, they wouldn't be part of my family for long. As a faction, we've been fighting for a while to change things. I know that's not enough, and I haven't personally done much to protect your kind. More recently, other plights have taken our resources. The siren faction, due to their low numbers and ability to mesmerize, have come under fire. Some of the other heirs and I have been meeting in secret these past couple of years in an attempt to organize ourselves in preparation for our time to make decisions. We want to hit the ground running."

"You all willingly met behind the tribunal's back? That's treason."

"Not *all* of us," I admitted. "And yes, if caught, it's treason. We'd lose our status as heir and any chance at a tribunal seat at best. Death or exile at worst."

"Who isn't a part of these meetings?"

More than I was comfortable with, but only one faction worried me the most right now.

"The djinn for one," I told her and allowed for the implications of that to set in. "They like being in power, so subjecting

the lesser factions to laws and limitations is their favorite pastime."

"That's why they want me dead." She paled.

I nodded. "Our bond pushes them out of power, but ultimately, I think the danger is worth it."

"Because we'd be strong enough to challenge them?"

Now she was getting it.

"And because with our help, your parents, the sirens, and others marginalized by the tribunal won't have to live their lives in fear, fighting every day to carve out a reasonable life for their families."

It sounded like a fairytale—too simple a solution for a problem that's spanned generations. Our lives would always be in some type of danger, especially after we had children, but the only other option was to do nothing. That wasn't who I was, and I didn't think that was who she was either.

I left my side of the bond wide open. She needed to feel my sincerity and the very real fear that came with living this life. She needed the whole picture.

"I'll continue to stay here after spring break."

I couldn't have heard her right. Did she just...?

"I'm not saying I'll complete the bond," she quickly added before I had a chance to slip too far into my fantasies. "I'm still not sure what kind of life I want. The power to change the laws for others, like my parents, is something I've always wished I had, but it comes at a cost."

"Giving in to the bond."

Her chin dipped. "And the danger that comes with it."

I had a feeling she wasn't just talking about the danger from the djinn. She feared *me* and the threat I posed to her heart—to everything she had ever known about how her future would turn out. All it would take was one slip. Just a small crack in her

walls and they would crumble. I'd make sure of it. But I'd also be there to protect her from the fallout.

I only needed a chance to show her how good we could be. A plan took shape, one where she could learn to trust me. It involved some touching and a little coaxing on my part, but maybe we had a chance to turn dreams into reality. A man could hope.

Spring break was over. Tomorrow was Sunday, the official last day, but we had a lot of prep still to do before Eryn could comfortably move in. For one thing, all her clothes were still in her dorm. I could buy her whatever the fuck she wanted, but she refused everything but the basics she was forced to accept this week—and she had the audacity to say she'd pay me back for those.

As if I couldn't take care of my bond. Besides needing to retrieve her personal belongings and supplies for class, she had promised Rani they could have dinner together the last night before classes resumed. Not a care in the world that she could be poisoned again. No. This brave but careless girl thought she could flounce off to the Commons as if everything hadn't completely changed. Ez and I weren't even allowed to sit with them.

How the fuck was I supposed to check her food if I didn't carry her tray, pick her sides, and do everything short of prepare her dinner myself? Thankfully—because I was dangerously close to going full caveman, boinking her on the head, and locking her in our room—a simple topaz around her neck would be enough to warn her of any nearby poisons.

"I can't accept that." She shook her head and leaned away into the armrest of the couch. "It's too expensive, Kaiden."

"Kai," I corrected. "As your boyfriend, it would be weird if you didn't call me Kai."

Her eyes narrowed. "*Fake* boyfriend."

I shrugged. Our budding bond was certainly real, and that was enough. For now.

"Unless you've changed your mind on how we're playing this, you're going to have to let go of that specific chip on your shoulder, princess." I held the necklace up. The fiery crystal contained more orange and red than yellow, a perfect reflection of my bond's temperament. "It serves a practical purpose," I told her and scooched close enough to reach out and brush her curls off her shoulder. "And it's non-negotiable if you want to leave this apartment."

She huffed but finally relented. I hid my smug smile as she turned, giving me her back and lifting her hair enough for me to loop the chain around her neck. The crystal was tiny, small enough to rest comfortably in the hollow of her throat. As such, the chain was just as delicate.

"The stone will change color if any poisons are present in your food or drink." My fingers grazed the sensitive skin on her neck as I made sure the chain remained untangled before I clasped it.

Eryn's hands lay restless in her lap as if she struggled with controlling the urge to reach back and secure it herself. I enjoyed the brief contact it allowed us and took my time. Tiny strands of hair tangled at the back of her neck, and I blew a gentle stream of air to clear them. Her skin pebbled under the cool onslaught, and she shifted in her seat.

"How will I know there's poison if I can't see the stone?" she asked, her nerves carefully concealed.

"It will warm against your skin. Trust me, it will be obvious."

As an heir, I had a topaz on me at all times and was intimately familiar with its warning.

Once the necklace was secure, I moved back so she'd have space to turn around. I casually grabbed the remote from the coffee table and started a random streaming app. Eryn settled into the seat beside me, easily falling into the routine we established a few nights ago. We took turns choosing a movie, usually a favorite or one the other had yet to see. No genre was off-limits.

Tonight, I'd chosen something simple that didn't require much focus to follow along: one of the many Fast and Furious installments. It had enough action to be entertaining and worked with my alternate plan for the night. Touch. I was slowly getting her used to mine. Looping my arm behind her, on the back of the couch, I pressed play.

We hadn't even gotten past the obligatory car chase in the intro before she tried to subtly inch away. My hand came down on her shoulder, stopping her progress.

"We won't convince the world we're a couple if you try to escape every time I touch you."

She was a frozen statue. Caught. "I don't."

"Really, princess?" I snorted. "There's an ocean between us."

She swallowed, her gaze darting down to the length of couch that could be seen between her leg and mine. Then, with a stubborn glare, she practically threw herself across the seat.

"There." Pride filtered down the bond, along with some anticipation.

I smiled at the challenge and closed the distance the rest of the way, pressing my leg against her bare thigh. Her breath hitched, but I turned back to the movie as if all the points our bodies touched weren't slowly driving me mad. My hand on her shoulder, her arm tucked into my side, and our legs pressed

against one another. None of that was even sexual. But fuck, if only I could convince my dick of that.

It was a colossal effort to keep him contained, and still, he swelled. Thirty minutes of tense silence, and a truck going up in flames on the screen, and I decided to increase our torture.

"Hold my hand," I demanded, offering said appendage on my knee, palm up.

A little crease appeared between her brows as she stared at it. "Isn't this enough?"

Ouch. I pushed the sting of her rejection down and buried it under a dwindling layer of confidence.

"You need to get used to the small things," I explained and gently pried one of her clenched fists from her lap. "This is dating 101."

Threading my fingers through hers, I brought our joined hands back to rest on my leg. Every few seconds, I'd rub my thumb over the soft skin of her wrist. It took half the movie, but we finally fell into sync. She melted against me, no longer tense and straight. Her hand didn't grip with misplaced nerves but sat loosely within mine.

Milestone reached. I was perfectly content spending the rest of the night just like this. My dick finally behaved, and her comfort made it easier to relax. That is, until she opened her mouth and blurted out the last thing I thought I'd hear her suggest.

"Should we practice kissing?"

Four words. It only took four little words to break me down to my most basic thoughts. She said kissing, and instantly, my dick stood at attention. There was nothing in my brain but images of her soft lips and memories of how they tasted. I reached for the remote, taking the precious few seconds to pause the movie and get myself under control.

When I trusted that I wouldn't pounce on her like an under-

developed Neanderthal, I turned slightly on the couch. She sat there, as nervous as I'd ever seen her, but completely serious. Her knee bounced as she waited for my answer.

"I'm trying not to be insulted here," I told her, my tone teasing. "Do you think I need practice?"

"No." She shook her head. "You were...fine."

One brow rose. Fine? I was *fine*? Clearly, she needed another demonstration, and she *was* asking for one, wasn't she? I'd show her fine. She closed her eyes and sighed before I could act on my baser instincts. When she looked at me again, her cheeks were tinged pink.

"More than fine," she amended. "What I meant...Shouldn't couples as enamored with each other as we're supposed to be...kiss?"

So that was it. She was still worried that we couldn't sell the story. It was a fair concern, seeing as simple touches were something we had to work on, but I didn't like the idea of her wanting to kiss me only to pacify others.

"No one else needs to know a thing besides that we're together. It's none of their business."

"But Rani will know," she argued, worrying her bottom lip. "There's no way she'll accept that I'm living here and that we're not doing anything. She's already bugging me for details that I refuse to give her."

My grin was slow. I bet I knew what kind of details Rani asked for. The only kind that could get my bond to turn that exact shade of red.

"If she thinks I'm lying, I don't know what she'll do."

I grimaced. Ez already had a theory about that based on how fiercely Rani went after him for details when Eryn disappeared.

"Probably tell the dean I kidnapped you or something." I frowned. "We've kissed before, more than once. Do we really need practice or do you just want to take advantage of me?"

Heat flushed through the bond as she broke eye contact. She coughed, trying to clear her throat. "Those kisses quickly spiraled into something else. Something I don't want to do in front of other people."

"Not into voyeurism, got it."

She smacked my arm. "You know what I mean."

I did. We came together like fire and gasoline, especially when tempers flared. We barely controlled ourselves the few times we kissed, and only because so much was going on at the time. Now? Who knew how far we'd go.

"So, you want to practice kissing but tame it down? Do I have that right?"

One nod. Just that slight sign of permission and I pulled her to me and covered her mouth with my own. A gentle pressure, nothing too demanding. Slow. That was the key to control. My lips brushed hers a couple times, and she sighed, melting into it.

"What's acceptable?" I asked and trailed fingers up her arm. "Can I touch you here?" My thumb brushed over a nipple on its way to cradle her jaw.

She gasped, and I took it as an invitation. My tongue swept inside her parted lips. Claiming. Dominating. She fought back; her little tongue tried in vain to set the pace but eventually gave in and followed my movements. I broke the kiss before her gentle submission broke all my restraints.

"What about here?" I nibbled on her neck while one hand snaked around to grab her ass.

I flexed my hand, kneading the firm flesh and hoping my touch left a mark. That ass was mine. With a growl, I pulled her closer, practically onto my lap, and bit down to hold her still when she squirmed. She straddled one of my legs, panting and wiggling as I marked her neck. I let the delicate skin free with a small *pop*.

"Heavy petting isn't too scandalous. Right?"

Her mouth crashed into mine, lips demanding my attention once more. I let her set the pace for a time, enjoying how she came to life under my touch. Where she ground into my leg was damp and hot, and still, her excitement grew. Her hips rolled and pressed down, triggering the moan she'd been holding back.

Gods, she was perfect. I could listen to her breathy sounds forever and die a lucky man. Her kiss grew more frantic as she reached for her release. I didn't want to stop her, but there was a purpose for this. Reluctantly, I backed off, grasping her hips and stilling them.

"That's our breaking point, I think." She stared at me, lost in a pleasure-filled daze. "If you start writhing against me like that, we'll swiftly find ourselves giving a show."

And what a show it would be. I'd guarantee fireworks. She blinked those emerald eyes, and I stroked my knuckles down her cheek as they slowly cleared. Her blush returned. Embarrassment and lingering arousal flooded her side of the bond, and I found it an oddly satisfying mixture.

"Let me know if you need more practice," I told her with a smirk. "As for tonight, I think I need a cold shower." And to take my dick in hand.

I left her on the couch and went to take care of my own release. Maybe she'd join me, and I could help her finish. Or maybe she'd take care of herself. Either way, I felt like a winner tonight. My little bond *liked* kissing me, even knowing who I was. There was hope for us yet. I didn't bother blocking the happiness trying to escape down the bond. Let her feel it.

seventeen

Eryn

Walking across campus to the Commons, there was something in the air. It lingered like a bad smell—a feeling that something would go very wrong tonight. It was possible my nerves were getting the best of me. Voluntarily locking myself inside for the past week and suddenly strolling out in the open were two sides of very different coins.

Even having Kaiden beside me, his warm hand wrapped tightly around my own, didn't ease the feeling. Was it a fear of being seen? The djinn would resume their attacks once word got out that I survived the poison. Or perhaps my nerves stemmed from the inevitable judgment of my classmates. Dating the TA was sure to cause gossip. Enough to reach the dean even.

I paused outside the dining hall, right in the middle of the path as that stray thought took root. Kaiden and Ezra were forced to stop with me.

"Everything okay?" Kaiden scanned the shadowed courtyard, on alert for any signs of danger. "Have you changed your mind?"

I rolled my eyes; he sounded too pleased with that option. He wanted nothing more than to usher me back into the truck and tuck me safely back behind his wards. And although that sounded better than another attempt on my life, I had to do this. But it was possible I hadn't thought through all of the consequences.

"People are going to think we're dating."

"Uhh." Ezra looked at me like I lost my mind. "I kind of thought that was the point of all this."

Kaiden didn't say anything as he watched and waited for me to elaborate.

"The point was to convince *Rani*," I explained. "If my classmates think I'm dating the TA, they'll assume I'm getting special treatment." Why didn't I think of this before? I would be labeled a cheater, someone willing to sleep their way to good grades. "I could be expelled," I whispered and tried to yank my hand from Kaiden's before anyone saw.

He tightened his hold on me. "I've already taken care of it," he said, very matter-of-fact, and started us toward the Commons again.

"What did you do?" I stumbled alongside him in a confused fog. My education wasn't over? Had Kaiden really thought that far ahead?

"I told the professor I was interested in you, and he agreed to remove me from your class level until next semester due to a potential conflict of interest," he told me with a wink—like it was that simple.

I didn't have too long to stress over it, though. Rani waited ahead, her critical eye taking in our joined hands and evaluating the amount of distance between us as we walked. We must have passed her first test because she smiled wide and skipped forward to loop her arm through mine.

"I can take it from here boys," she smirked. "You've had her long enough."

Then, I was being pulled through the doors before I could even worry whether I had to kiss Kaiden goodbye. I carefully chose my dinner, briefly pausing with each selection to check if my necklace gave any warning that it wasn't safe to consume. My pizza and side salad met the crystal's approval, and I followed my only friend to an empty table near the back.

"I find it strange that your new boytoy couldn't trust you to be out of his sight for a few hours," Rani said, frowning over my shoulder.

I knew what she saw. Probably Kaiden and Ezra finding a table nearby but not too close. They wouldn't want to fail at the laying low portion of tonight's plan. I already bitched to Rani once before about Kaiden being controlling, and his hovering didn't help.

"It's actually all your fault," I said around a mouthful of greasy cheese.

Rani's eyes widened. "My fault?"

I nodded, ready to sell whatever lie I needed to. "Ezra is the one who refused to eat off campus once he heard you'd be here tonight."

Obviously, that wasn't true, but Ezra was obsessed with her enough that it was easily believable. I secretly grinned when I thought about his reaction to me throwing him under the bus.

"Ugh," Rani groaned. "Why do I have to be so irresistible?"

I barked out a laugh. "What a very Ezra thing to say."

My laughter continued as she glared and threw her straw wrapper at me. The playful teasing loosened something inside me, and I thanked the gods for moments like this with a friend to balance out the bad thrown at me lately.

"He's cute," Rani admitted, stealing glances behind me. "But

I deserve more than a playboy, and his reputation precedes him."

She one hundred percent deserved better, but Ezra wasn't all he appeared to be. I learned that much from being around him this past week. He was growing on me.

"Maybe you're different," I suggested. "He's always talking about you."

"I'm sure," she scoffed. "Because I won't give in, and he likes the chase." I opened my mouth, but she kept going. "Look, you're dating his cousin now, so I'm sure we'll be thrown together more often. I'll play nice for your sake, but that's all."

I nodded and thanked her. It wasn't like I expected them to get together. She was right; one night was all Ezra could offer, but not for the reasons she thought. A relationship with a human was impossible for him and not exactly something he could easily explain. The rest of dinner ran smoothly, and I easily dodged her probing questions about my sex life.

I enjoyed myself up until the point when someone triggered my supernatural radar. Little ripples of power were a common enough occurrence that I no longer panicked over them. They were usually so faint that I could tell it was someone passing through. But this...this was a shock to the system. Enough that Rani asked if I was choking. The use of that much power wasn't casual; it was a warning. The jig was up. The djinn knew I was alive.

"I'm fine. Wrong pipe," I assured her, and gathered my trash on the tray. "Why don't we head back, and you can finish telling me whatever it is that has you bouncing in your seat."

A quick peek behind me on our way out confirmed I had at least one shadow as Kaiden disappeared to check the source of that blast. Ezra followed us at a discrete distance until we reached the safety of the dorm and our warded room. Rani prattled non-stop all the way back, but my mind was too

preoccupied with what I needed to pack and how quickly I could do it before Kaiden returned to escort me back to the apartment.

Vivid images of djinn surrounding the truck as we tried to speed off campus distracted me enough that I wasn't sure what I grabbed and shoved into my bag. It's not like I had much anyway.

"Not those!" Rani grabbed the purple shorts from my hand and threw them on my bed. "Have you not listened to a word I've said? The judges said you could remain on the team."

"I don't get what that has to do with me packing them."

I really had tuned her out after she gleefully announced the Zombie Run judges wouldn't disqualify me for having food poisoning and missing the last challenge a few nights ago. To be fair, the games weren't as important as what I had going on.

"You *weren't* listening!" The rest of my team outfit flew at me, spares from Rani's never-ending closet. "I said, our team's next challenge is tonight, along with what's left of teams green and orange. So, get dressed!"

She pranced out the door and down the hall to the restrooms. Now in a full-blown panic, I paced next to my bed and racked my brain for any excuse to get out of this. What would satisfy Rani and keep her off my back? I couldn't feign being sick, and using Kaiden as an excuse would only turn her against him.

The truth was definitely off the table. *Shit.*

A brief warmth in my chest, followed by a knock at the door, revealed a haggard-looking Kaiden. I ushered him inside, where it was safe, casually scanning him for obvious injuries.

"What happened?"

He shook his head and double-checked the room for dangers, despite me already having done so when I arrived.

"Nothing," he grumbled. "No traps and no djinn to be

found." He growled in frustration and hit the window. "*Something* is going down."

With a blast of power that large, I had no doubt.

"Well, we have a new problem to figure out. And fast." I cringed, holding up a purple bandana.

He stared at it, then at my matching outfit, and his eyes narrowed. "Absolutely not! Are you insane?"

I ground my teeth at his tone but tried to remember that we were both on edge. Neither one of us wanted a repeat of the last time I wore these colors.

"Do you have a plan to get us out of it that won't put us back to square one? Further than square one, because if Rani gets suspicious, then our plan for me to continue building my life here is over." I shoved a finger in his chest. "You said you could protect me and that I could get my degree. That was the deal."

I refused to go back into hiding or, worse, be forced to reside with the tribunal for safety. I'd tasted freedom and had a glimpse of what my life could be like, both with and without Kaiden at my side. Dying wasn't part of that plan, but neither was cowering in the dark. Kaiden read the determination in my gaze and challenged it with a glare.

"We stay long enough to complete the challenge, and that's it. Any sign of the djinn, and we're gone."

"Agreed."

"I can't believe we're doing this. Again." His jaw popped as he checked his watch. "It's late enough. Find a sleeping human and let's get you fed. We're not going out there without you at full strength."

This was truly a horrible idea. There were about fifty of us spread wide through the small section of forest; not right on top of one another, but close enough that there was still a small sense of security. Rani vibrated with excitement beside me; she lived for this shit. She squinted against the dark, trying to make out if our stupid piñata was in the tree ahead or if that was a wasp nest. I voted to avoid both.

Tonight's challenge was similar to the last one I participated in. Our "prize" sat hidden somewhere in these trees, and we were tasked with finding it and returning it to the registration tent. Zombies would try to thwart us and avoid our Nerf guns and killer marshmallows. It all seemed so stupid when I thought about what could also be in these woods with us.

Kaiden said there were no djinn to be found, and my power sat fully charged in my belly, ready to go if that proved false, but I couldn't shake the feeling that I was walking into the lion's den. This deep, the ancient trees grew close together, and we were forced further apart. I kept the others in my peripherals and focused on finding that damned piñata and getting out of here.

A thick, ropey fog rolled in around my ankles. It hovered over the ground, seeking, and the frigid temperature that came with it betrayed the source. Dry ice. This was part of the challenge. Further ahead and off to my sides, the fog grew thicker and floated up until I was surrounded. Shouts and co-ed squeals echoed from all around.

The fucking zombies were *in* the fog? Whose bright idea was this?

"Kaiden!" I shouted. "Rani! Anyone?"

My own muffled voice rebounded off the ancient trees as my ability to see decreased. The fog was disorienting and far more powerful than basic dry ice. I had a bad feeling something else was at play here. I pushed harder, moving faster, despite not being able to see, and thanked every lucky star there was when

the fog cleared a few feet later. Standing ahead of me, in an ugly-ass neon green shirt stood a guy. His hair was dark; brown or black I wasn't sure in this lighting, but he appeared my age. Good. I hadn't wandered too far from the games.

I threw a marshmallow with perfect accuracy. It bounced off his chest and landed somewhere in the leaf litter at his feet. He just stood there. Fucker. He was supposed to sit for thirty minutes. That was a grenade and a direct hit. His face was hidden in shadows, so I couldn't tell if he was high or being an intentional dick.

"Hey!" I threw another marshmallow and it bounced harmlessly to the ground. "Dude, you're supposed to die."

Silver glinted in his hand, just to the side of his right leg. Still, he said nothing, only continued to play with whatever he had that captured the scarce moonlight so easily. The hair on my neck prickled as magick reached out with greedy hands. I stumbled back, tripping over roots and debris as the fog once again increased, stemming from the man before me.

His strides easily cleared the obstacles bogging me down, diminishing the small stretch of forest that kept us apart. White surrounded me, blocking out even the bark of the tree at my back. Still, that man came closer. I realized in growing horror that the silver glint in his hand was a knife.

"Who are you?" I called out and tried in vain to become one with the tree.

My magick coiled within me, ready to perform whatever task I asked of it. I tried offensive first, but my projection lacked any real strength, and the thin tendrils of power I sent toward him did nothing more than dissipate with a wave of his hand.

"You should feel honored, bond of Alantes, that I've decided to take care of this myself."

Now, only feet away, I still couldn't tell what color hair this guy had. Dark. Greasy. Unkempt. Those were the adjectives that

came to mind, along with dangerous, djinn, and probably a murderer. My murderer: if I didn't find a way out of this. Hands flat against the tree, I used it to keep me grounded in the fog and gingerly eased around its thick trunk. The guy kept rambling.

"I should have known I couldn't trust anyone else to take care of this." He lunged, pinning me to the tree before I had the chance to bolt. His rancid breath clogged my nostrils as I struggled in his grip. Bruises bloomed beneath his fingers where they gripped my arm, and he grinned. "My father will reward me greatly for this."

Silver flashed, and I screamed, agony spreading from my side into a steady throb of pain. I twisted at the last minute, but the burning told me he succeeded enough. Death hovered in his eyes. This was it. My hands grappled at arms covered in thick leather sleeves. There was no bare skin to find, and my magick floundered inside me, desperate for a release. My attacker grunted, his head falling forward as something hit him from behind.

He doubled his hold on me but turned enough that both of us could see the furious redhead behind him. Rani held a rock in her hand, and a promise of retribution twisted her face into a sneer.

"Let her go, you fucking creep!" She shouted and swung again with the rock. It landed on his upper back, and then again on his shoulder. Too small to reach his head, she mercilessly attacked his body, aiming for whatever soft spots she could find.

The djinn looked more annoyed than deterred, mumbling something insulting about humans as he gathered his magick to him. He was going to use it on Rani, I just knew it, and I couldn't allow that to happen. Seeing this as my only opportunity, I yelled and planted both my palms on his face. At the contact, the floodgates to his mind opened in a brief moment of surprise.

That was all I needed. His mind was a vault; he was obvi-

ously trained in defense against my kind. But there...in the back, a small hairline fracture in his defenses. It was just enough for me to wrangle control, and I held onto it for all I was worth.

"Release me," I demanded, and his grip on me disappeared. "You will stand here, in this very spot, until the sun rises high enough to touch the base of this tree."

He grunted, fighting the web of power slithering through his mind, but I held on. I wouldn't be able to maintain the control for long once I let go of his face, not with the amount of mental strength he had. Hopefully, the command would be enough to hold him until Rani and I got away. With a final, painful breath, I let go and threw myself at Rani.

"Run!"

She resisted at first, determined to beat the guy bloody with her small weapon, but we were wasting time. I had no choice. Using only the smallest strand of magick, I *pushed* at her mind, and Rani fell into step beside me without argument. With one hand pressed against my bleeding side, I dragged us through the forest, listening out for where the other challengers might be. Safety in numbers, even from the djinn.

We saw no others until the checkpoint tent came into view just outside the tree line. I pulled us to a stop, half bent over as I tried to catch my breath. My hand felt sticky, and I knew I left an easy trail for my attacker to follow. Fear over how bad my wound really was blinded me. The idea that the blade was poisoned also froze the breath in my lungs.

"Eryn, what's going on?"

Focus. One problem at a time. There was no talking my way out of this, no explanation I could give her that wouldn't lead to more questions. Keeping one eye out for the djinn, I reached for Rani's hand and gave her a smile, even though I'm sure my lips trembled, and I wasn't at all convincing.

Her mind was wide open and pure. There were no defenses

in place to keep me out, and her only thoughts were about me. She was confused—terrified—but willing to do whatever it took to protect me. It was all too easy to erase her memories of the last few minutes and replace them with false ones. Nothing too complex. The more complicated I made the memories, the higher the chance she would find holes in them later.

I'd just finished planting a false narrative of us searching the trees and coming back empty-handed when the bond in my chest fluttered. Ezra and Kaiden made a beeline for us, worry etched into both of their faces. I shut down my half of the bond as best I could to mask the pain I felt, but I wasn't that successful.

"What happened?" Kaiden asked. "I felt..."

He shared a look with his cousin before Ezra got to work distracting Rani and leading her away from what was about to be a tense conversation.

Once they were out of earshot, I met Kaiden's questioning gaze. "I'm fine."

It was an obvious lie, one that only angered Kaiden more as we made our way to the truck. He didn't ask me anything else, just stewed in silence until Ezra hopped in ten minutes later. I watched out the window as the trees faded from view, thankful to have made it out alive. My side throbbed with each bump on the road.

"Tell me what the fuck happened out there," Kaiden ordered. His shadows leaked around him, darkening the cab even further.

Ezra looked at me around the headrest, but the new lack of light made it hard for him to see anything.

"A djinn attacked," I replied. "Said his father would reward him for my death, tried to kill me, and then scratched me. I'm *fine*."

"What exactly did he say about his father?" Ezra questioned.

So, I broke it down for them. Every step into the fog, each word the djinn spewed, how Rani saved me, and how I in turn had to violate her mind. As I spoke, Kaiden reeled his shadows back, and the overhead light clicked on.

"Tell us again about this scratch." Ezra pointedly looked at my bloody shirt.

It was dark purple, but I guess my wound wouldn't be hard to find if you knew what to look for.

I glared. "Have you never had one, Ezra? I can promise you they're no big deal."

"That's such bullshit," Kaiden growled and swerved into his apartment's parking lot. "I can feel the wound, princess. Right side, correct?" We parked, and he spun around to catch my gaze. "Once we get upstairs, take off that shirt, so I can see what we're dealing with. And no more fucking lies. I swear you're making it impossible not to give you that punishment you've practically begged for since I first met you."

eighteen

Kaiden

I wasn't gentle as I dragged her through the apartment and up the stairs to my room. I should have been. She was stabbed for fuck's sake. A scratch my ass. The dull burning I felt in my own side was probably nothing compared to the pain she endured.

"You still haven't told me how you knew where the scratch was."

Her feet dug into the throw rug, and I stopped pulling long enough to turn and face her. I'd avoided looking before because I didn't trust myself not to lose it, but we were way past that now. My shadows burst free without command to shade the room. Inky tendrils wound their way up her legs, and her little gasp was enough to set my blood on fire.

"My right side is sore," I told her, my tone sharp. "So, I took an educated guess that that's where your wound is."

Sore was an understatement. The spot just above my hip was *throbbing*. I needed to see how bad it was, but my bond had other ideas. She wanted to argue. Arms crossed, she

pouted in that determined but adorable way I usually found appealing. Right now, her attitude made me want to spank that ass until she couldn't walk. Maybe this time I'd actually do it.

I blew out a steady breath. Health first, punishment second.

"That's a bit more than just feeling my emotions, wouldn't you say?"

There was a new undercurrent of fear leaking down the bond that had nothing to do with the most recent djinn attack. The subject of our growing bond was always a touchy one, but there was no time to comfort her about it. Gods help us if that knife was poisoned with more nightshade. I directed my shadows higher, until they wrapped around her hips and chest, leaving a gap where her wound was.

"Pain is a heightened emotion," I explained on my way to the ensuite. My shadows ensured she followed, despite her futile attempts to resist them. "Stop fighting me and get your ass in here."

Seconds later, she stood before me, and I didn't bother asking permission. My fingers curled under the edge of her soaked tank top and pulled it off in one solid motion. Ignoring her scowl, I gently gripped her hips and lifted her onto the counter, putting her breasts right in my face. It was an effort to ignore them and keep her gaze. Her penchant for wearing lacy little scraps over her chest would be the death of me.

"Don't move."

Her brow creased, but she listened as I knelt and rummaged through the cabinets beneath her. Bandages, tape, clean dressings, sterile water; it all went onto the counter. Next, I pulled some purified blue clay, ginger, raw honey, and ground cat's claw. She would need a poultice—likely more than one round.

At the last minute, I grabbed a sterile pack of stitches and tucked them between the supplies in the basket before she

could see. I hoped I wouldn't need them, but the amount of blood on her shirt was enough for me to worry.

"What are you going to do?" Eryn's worried question bounced off the walls of the small room.

I remained where I was, knelt between her legs so that her wound was eye level. Gifted a front-row seat to her rapid breaths and stunning body, I regretted that the first time I had her like this wasn't under different circumstances.

"Whatever needs to be done." I left no room for argument and splashed some of the sterile water onto a thick slice of gauze. "Hold still."

She hissed when the cool liquid hit her hip. I tried to be gentle, but most of the blood had already dried and each swipe of the gauze pulled on sensitive skin no matter how light my touch. With every pass, the dressing changed color to a deeper red, and my bond winced.

Her little pants betrayed her level of pain, even if I hadn't noticed her white-knuckled grip on the marble.

"Easy," I whispered, dropping another soaked cotton square into the sink. "I'm done for now. Catch your breath."

She was going to need it. The wound wasn't as bad as I feared, not an actual puncture. But the knife definitely sliced deeper than a simple pressure bandage could solve. Eryn needed stitches, and I fully expected a battle once I told her.

I waited until her breathing evened out, and her complexion regained some color before reaching for that little pack in the basket. Maybe if I moved quick enough...

"No!" she shouted and would have vaulted off the counter if I hadn't stood. "I know you like control, but absolutely not. Not this time. You are *not* stitching me closed in your *bathroom*."

I leaned in, forcing her against the mirror. A few thick shadows crossed over her thighs just in case. They hovered, ready to restrain if asked.

"The wound is too deep, princess. It's only a couple tiny stitches, and then I'll be done."

"How many?" she demanded and tried to wiggle out from under me.

"It really doesn't—"

"How many stitches, Kaiden?"

I set my palms on either side of her hips. She stopped fighting as I mentally evaluated the task before me. Lying wasn't an option, that wasn't who I was, but fuck she wouldn't like this.

"Six," I conceded. "Possibly eight."

Off she went, fighting with renewed strength and no care for her bleeding hip.

"Eryn," I tried to reason with her, but words were hard when I was so focused on keeping her still. She kicked out, narrowly missing my balls with the point of her shoe. Feisty. Sexy as fuck. But also overreacting just a tad, I thought.

"The hospital can do it," she growled, pissed that she hadn't made any progress to escape.

I shook my head and tightened my shadows. Her bleeding restarted, and it was now heavy enough to scent, filling the small space with a hint of copper.

"It's too risky." I added another band of shadows to her shoulders, lest she try to twist and it opened her wound even more. "I wouldn't be allowed back with you, and I'd have no way to protect you from djinn trying to illusion their way inside. Not to mention, we can't afford the questions."

With my restraints in place, and my hips between her legs, she wasn't going anywhere. I grabbed the small needle and thread and called for my cousin.

"Ezra!"

Eryn paled at the sight of the curved needle, barely longer than the length of my finger to the first knuckle. I lined up

everything I would need beside the sink, just out of reach of her clenched fists.

"Yo, what's up?" Ez popped into the room, took one look at our position, and grinned. "Didn't think you were one to want an audience, cuz."

I glared at his sad attempt at a joke.

"Numb her, please. And then get the fuck out."

Used to my attitude, he prowled forward the few steps and reached a single finger toward Eryn. She stiffened under her bonds but didn't make a sound as Ezra pressed that finger to the side of her wound. I felt a shadow of her relief in my own side and knew she was plenty numb to get to work.

"I'll call if we need another round," I told him and dismissed him with a wave.

My cousin left without a backward glance or new taunting comment. Perhaps he sensed the tension and decided not to poke at it. Unlike him, but there were more pressing matters to tend to. I slowly knelt once more, keeping my movements obvious.

"Will you cooperate?" I asked her. "Or do we have to do this the hard way?"

The knee to my temple took me by surprise. Satisfaction dripped down the bond like a steady faucet, and I sighed.

"Not exactly smart to knock the head of the guy who's about to put a needle through your skin," I tsked and added some shadows over her knees. "I understand your fear, princess, but violence isn't the answer here."

More futile struggles. I wiped away the fresh blood and moved in.

"Wait!" My hand paused millimeters from her skin, and I glanced up. "I-I'm not afraid."

I lifted a brow and pointedly glanced at her shaking grip on the counter. "No?"

She shook her head. "I-I..."

I held perfectly still. The outcome wouldn't change—it couldn't, she needed this—but I refused to begin until I had her consent.

"Eryn." The use of her name and my tone snapped her out of the building panic. "What have I told you? What promise have I kept despite everything?"

"You w-won't hurt me."

"I swear it on our bond." My fixed stare didn't waver. "Trust me to know what you can handle. Trust me to take care of you, princess."

Her tension still tightened every limb, but she took a deep breath, held my gaze, and nodded. I moved before she could change her mind. Thank the gods, I'd had plenty of practice stitching myself and Ezra over the years. I was quick.

She jumped at the first pull of the thread but didn't cry, and I kept a close eye on our bond for any spikes in pain. My first estimate was correct, six stitches, neatly along the curve of her hip. Scarring should be minimal, but the poultice would help just in case.

I mixed my gathered ingredients with hot, sterile water in a small pestle and allowed it time to cool as I cleaned her of any remaining dried blood. When the mixture was at a comfortable temperature, I scooped it into a fresh bandage and taped it down.

"Get ready," I warned, a second before removing my shadows.

She fell forward with a slight squeak, right into my chest. I kept my hold light and open in case she wanted nothing to do with my touch, but she melted into me. Carefully wrapping my arms around her, I kissed the top of her head. I hadn't realized how much of the fear and tension in here was my own. It sat bottled inside me as I focused on her comfort.

"Thank you," I whispered into her hair. "I'm proud of you, princess."

There was some exhaustion and relief on her end at the knowledge that it was all over. What surprised me was the contentment. Was it possible she wanted my touch? By her reaction...I didn't dare hold on to what that could mean, but longing grew inside me anyway.

There was only so much a man could take. Eryn rolled her hips again, her knee grazing my dick as she threw her leg over mine. I thought any latent energy from the attack would manifest in nightmares, not...this. Gods, this was a test in restraint—one I was a touch away from failing.

I had nightly dreams of flipping her over and burying myself in her tight heat, urged on by her innocent writhing and soft moans. With those images in my head, how was I supposed to cope? Feeling around for a spare pillow to use as a buffer, I realized they had all been pushed to the floor.

Fuck. This needed to stop before it went too far. Then again, Eryn welcomed my touch earlier. She basked in it. It was possible she was open to me helping her sate this need, and there was only one way to find out.

"Princess," I whispered into her ear.

Her body answered my call with another roll and press of her damp panties against my hip. I had a flash of worry for her stitches; she could pull them moving like that. I clamped a hand on her thigh and rolled until she lay on her back with me propped on one arm above her. Long lashes fluttered against her cheeks, but she didn't wake. Easing her leg down, I lifted her

long shirt to check the bandage and found no blood. Thank the gods.

I groaned as another wave of heat spiked down the bond. Eryn's entire body tensed like a spring wound too tight. Her moans were broken apart by shallow pants, and I applied light pressure to her lower abdomen when her hips began to writhe against me again. Enough of this.

"Princess," I growled, louder than before.

Her eyes sprang open and met mine in the dark. We said nothing, wrapped in the spell that ensnared us both. Her chest rose and fell as her body backed off the edge. I could tell she was close by the light sheen of sweat on her skin and the way her stomach flexed beneath my palm.

"Do you need assistance?"

A little more of that fog cleared as she answered, "What?"

"I'm assuming you want to finish?" My hand stretched until the tip of my pinky traced low, along the band of her panties. "By the sounds you were making, it wouldn't take much to get you there."

I held my breath as I awaited her answer. The attraction between us flared, so I knew I'd captured her interest. Embarrassment tampered with that lingering need, but I hoped we had built enough trust that she'd give me the green light.

The silence stretched on, unbearable. I felt her indecision, felt the moment her arousal won out, and she folded to her body's demands.

"I need..." she whimpered, and my hand traced a path lower.

"Tell me what you need, princess."

Her panties were soaked. I teased the delicate skin along the edge of the cotton material, and her hips lifted.

"Yesss," she hissed, realizing I already knew how to answer the cues she was giving me. My thumb brushed over her, barely

a graze with the barrier between us. "It doesn't mean anything," she quickly said.

The words hit like barbs directly to my heart. Doesn't mean anything? I scowled at the idea that this was an empty encounter, that anyone could bring her body to life like this. Slipping my hand into her panties, I pressed a finger to her entrance. Her hips jerked, and I slid through the slick proof of her lies.

My scowl smoothed into a smirk when she arched into my touch. "I disagree."

At the hitch in her breath, I added more pressure, easing in just the tip of my finger.

"How so?" she asked, groaning.

"This right here." I pulled out and teased her again before thrusting two fingers inside. "This proves you're not as indifferent as you pretend to be." I captured her mouth, eagerly silencing the moans that spilled past her lips as I crooked those fingers until her legs tensed. "You're so wet for me," I groaned, adding my thumb to the mix.

I used it to circle her clit as I plunged deeper. She clenched around the intrusion and panted into my kiss. Breaking away, I nibbled along her jaw and down the side of her neck. She tipped her head back to give me better access. Further down I went, sucking her straining nipple into my mouth, shirt and all.

"Oh!" she whimpered.

I relished the silky feel of her, the glazed look in her eyes.

"Look at you," I hummed, and strummed my thumb across her clit again.

My chest burned with the urge to rip the flimsy scrap of fabric down her legs and take her for myself. I grunted and instead rubbed my dick against her side like a horny teenager.

"Kaiden," she cried out. "The bond."

I was in control, no matter how much my dick wished I

wasn't. The bond was reacting to our heightened arousal and close contact, but nothing would come of it unless I ignored my conscience and crossed that line.

"Shh. Just feel."

Her legs were long past trembling; they convulsed as she fought to hold back the climax I knew hovered right there. My own loomed heavy and painful with each grind against her. Fuck, I was going to blow in my boxers. I hadn't done that since...well, since I learned how to control myself.

But this girl threw that control out the window. A couple of well-directed thrusts partnered with the silk of my boxers allowed me to free half my length from its constricting prison. The smooth glide of my head against her skin was as close to heaven as I'd ever been. I doubled down on her clit until she arched, angling her hips so that my fingers raked that spot inside her with each thrust.

"Give it to me," I demanded.

Her entire body locked as she came, that perfect pussy clenching down on my fingers. I hardly had enough thought to keep them moving as my own climax hit. Pure pleasure raged through my veins and down the bond to meet the bliss racing at me from her side. It was beyond contentment, it was a split-second feeling of perfection.

Of belonging. The warmth of her against me as we caught our breath felt like home. Until she shattered the illusion with more lies.

"It doesn't mean anything."

I froze, seconds away from wrapping myself around her to bask in our newfound connection. She couldn't mean that. But she did. I felt her pulling away and swiftly shut down my side of the bond before she could catch the pain reverberating through me. I pulled my hand away from her and wiped my sticky fingers on her stomach.

"You can handle clean up, right?" I threw out, and rolled off my side of the bed in search of fresh boxers and a little privacy to lick my wounds.

I allowed myself one glance back to see the proof of what she fought so hard to deny. All I saw was a beautiful goddess, splayed out like an indecent lure as she quickly tried to mask her hurt and confusion at my abrupt manner.

Too bad.

I couldn't nurse my own heart and protect her feelings at the same time. What did it matter anyway? *It didn't mean anything.*

"Careful of the stitches as you clean my cum off your side. Tissues are on the nightstand," I called out, as I stormed into the ensuite and slammed the door.

nineteen

Eryn

Classes resumed with a bang. The teachers didn't care that their audience hadn't mentally returned from break. Endless schedules of tests and assignment deadlines rolled out before me until the end of the semester. I didn't mind. Anything to keep my mind off the turmoil Kaiden was set on drowning me in.

Somewhere between him saving my life—again—and me allowing him to get me off with his fingers—*again*—he joined the hate Eryn train. Well, hate was a strong word. Dislike? He'd probably had enough of me by now.

It shouldn't bother me as much as it did. I wanted him to leave me alone, in terms of our bond, and he finally got the picture. I woke alone in bed the last three mornings and there was no homemade breakfast on the island when I came downstairs. The honeymoon was over. He was done trying to impress me. Good. Great.

It's what I wanted. Really.

If only his attitude didn't change with his lack of interest. I

243

set the textbook down on the towel and brushed the sand out of the binding. Rani begged me for some study time on the beach, an idea half the campus shared today, but she had yet to crack a book. Too busy avoiding Ezra, she spent all her time in the water.

"She won't come up here if she sees you waiting for her," I warned him, not bothering to look away from my notes. "Have you tried playing hard to get?"

He let out a wounded cry and fell next to me. "This *is* hard to get. I don't humble myself for just anyone."

Oh boy. If he thought turning down a few co-eds and offering to take Rani to dinner first was humbling, he was in for a rude awakening. No wonder she wasn't willing to take a chance on him. I saw genuine interest from Ezra, but it was possible *he* couldn't see it. Treating Rani like another notch on his dented bedpost was the wrong way to go about it.

"Let her come to you," I sighed and packed my books. There was no way I could concentrate anymore.

"You think that will work?" he asked. I wanted to slap him but settled for brushing the sand off my legs.

"What have you got to lose?"

Truly nothing. When it came down to it. Whether or not Ezra slept with her wasn't a life-or-death decision, and it surely wouldn't matter whenever his own bond came into the picture. I felt sorry for that girl. Ezra was a handful.

The pair of sunglasses I borrowed from Rani covered a majority of my face as I scanned the student section of the beach. The glaring, late spring sun revealed half-naked bodies glistening with oils and sunblock, a diamond-encrusted sea, and an overall relaxing atmosphere.

But it didn't show the one person I discreetly looked for. I wasn't a glutton for punishment; enough passive-aggressive attitude fueled my days when Kaiden was around, but I couldn't put

my finger on it. A part of me felt at ease in his presence. Was that the new familiarity of the bond or a result of our time spent together? Both?

Regardless, I found myself searching him out despite the very obvious vibe that he didn't want me around.

"He went to patrol the trails." Ezra winked and gestured with his head in the direction I might find his cousin.

I nonchalantly glanced down and picked at my tank top. Stitches didn't make for cute beach attire.

"I was just looking down the beach." The lie was lame, even to me, but Ezra was enough of a gentleman not to call me out on it.

He stood, sending sand everywhere, and shrugged. "I promised to serve my entire share of guard time, but the way I see it, you're safest with your bond." Ezra grabbed my hand and pulled me to my feet. With two hands on my shoulders, he spun me toward the shaded trees. "He went that way. Follow that little flutter in your chest, and I'm sure you'll find him."

I knew it was an excuse to pass me off on Kaiden so he could go flirt, but I wasn't opposed to the idea. I *wanted* to find Kaiden. Gods, the more he pushed me away this week, the more I found myself drawn to him. How messed up was that?

My feet pulled me off the sand and onto the packed earth of the trails without permission from my brain. Honestly, my entire body did what it wanted these days; a rebellion I wasn't in a rush to stop if it got me more orgasms. Yeah, there was definitely something wrong with me.

Tucked away in the shade, the breeze felt cooler, and it went a long way in easing the toasty burn on my skin. Birds chirped to my right, while seagulls loudly fought to the death over a bag of Doritos on my left. Kaiden wasn't too far, maybe a quarter mile further into the trees. Tapping into our bond and following it wasn't nearly as frightening as it had been at first.

It helped that I had a better understanding of the man on the other end. He wasn't the monster that younger me made him out to be. The heir to the witch faction was a good guy, who would have thought? Despite his most recent attitude toward me, he was still out here patrolling.

Honor and duty meant something to him. I wasn't sure about the rest of his faction, especially after that brief encounter with his mother, and I had no plans to ditch my dreams and dive into his world of politics and backstabbing agendas. That didn't mean we couldn't be friends...or more.

Friends who touched and played, who enjoyed one another's company.

Who was I kidding? I liked him. That little admission would have sent me running for the nearest escape route not too long ago, but I knew better now. Emotion strengthened the bond, but nothing would seal it until we crossed that line with no pants on. As long as we didn't have sex, I could remain my own person.

I'd gotten better at controlling my side of the bond, and Kaiden was an expert at keeping his emotions in check. The next four years could work. And after...We'd see about after once I graduated.

My wandering thoughts led me deeper into the trees as I subconsciously followed that flutter in my chest. Sunlight filtered in through the canopy, and a light breeze rustled the higher branches. In the daylight, the forest didn't appear nearly as dangerous as my last few excursions would suggest.

Laughter and the sound of crashing waves still reached me here. Animals frolicked in the undergrowth. Everything was as it should be. Except for the lone pit bull hopping on three legs. The precious puppy gave a pitiful whine and hobbled some more. There was a thick, black collar around his neck, so he obviously wasn't a stray.

Maybe he was one of the campus pets that Rani said

belonged to the veterinary hospital? Before I could reach out with my magick to see what ailed him, he disappeared around the bend.

"Shit," I whispered, afraid to spook him even further. "Wait for me, little guy."

The eighty-pound pupper was far from a baby, but he might as well have been with those big, soulful eyes. I caught another glimpse of him when I turned the corner. He sat on his haunches, tail wagging, and tongue rolled out to the side as he panted. Obviously not injured like I thought, but he still shouldn't be this far out here.

I crouched a few feet away, hand held out, and called to him.

"Do you want to come home with me, buddy? Would you like that?" I inched forward, my calves screaming at the position I held, and reached for my well of power. "I just want to be your friend."

My magick unfurled within me, warm and welcoming. The pit bull growled, his lips receding to show sharp teeth. *That* was odd. Animals loved me. Had my magick scared him? I hadn't even touched him with it yet. Risking another step, I pulled a single strand.

The dog lunged this time with a ferocious growl that jolted me, and I fell back on my ass. Thick goops of saliva dribbled from his jaws as I sat there in absolute shock. I'd never been threatened by an animal. Ever. Even the big ones at the zoo just wanted a good cuddle.

The pit bull took another step, yelped, and scrambled back with his tail tucked between his legs. From my right, Kaiden stalked from the thick brush and lashed at the dog with another shadow. It missed but succeeded in scaring the poor animal further away.

"Don't hurt him!" I shouted, anger flaring. What sick person hurt a *dog*?

Kaiden was close enough for me to hear his mumbled, 'are you fucking kidding me?' and I got to my feet just in time for another shadow to snap like a whip toward the defenseless pup. A cry left my lips as this one made contact...and went right through the pit bull's head. *Through* his head. Like the dog was nothing but smoke and mirrors. Or an illusion.

"Oh," I whispered, still in shock.

A few more strikes were enough to scare off the fake dog, and then Kaiden turned his fury onto me.

"Why do you keep running headfirst after things without thinking?"

He was in my face, blocking out the sun and the rest of the path where the illusion just was. His nostrils flared as he glared down at me, shadows not in check and swirling around us like angry serpents. My pulse raced as the might of his anger poked at my fight-or-flight response. There was no true danger, so my body picked fight.

"How was I supposed to know it was an illusion?" I shouted back, not caving a single step. My lack of remorse set him off.

"Did your parents teach you nothing?" His deep voice was edged with venom. "The djinn create and control illusions, princess. Supernatural 101. These fuckers have tried to kill you multiple times these past months, *and* they make up a majority of the tribunal's hunters." His glare almost burned where it touched me, and he took a step closer. "How the fuck." Another step. "Do you not know how to recognize their magick?"

It was a good question. Spotting illusions wasn't really a problem for me before, but they'd never been concealed within the image of my biggest weakness. I'd also never been as distracted as I was here, with thoughts of Kaiden blurring my usually over-cautious nature. Not that I was going to tell him all that.

"It was an honest mistake," I argued, arms crossed against

his dominant presence. "You're just pissed that you had to save me again." Which, actually, why wouldn't he be upset about that? I could hardly keep myself alive lately. "Thank you, by the way," I grumbled.

Some of his shadows eased, but my apology didn't erase his temper.

"I have no problem saving you, princess. It's having to do it because you refuse to use your intelligence that I find irritating."

"Asshole," I snarled. "Who's to say I wouldn't have figured it out on my own?"

"Before or after getting stabbed again?"

Heat flared in my chest. Anger and insults were practically foreplay for us, but I'd be damned if I gave in to it now.

"I got away." I lifted my chin. Kaiden hadn't saved me that time, I did it myself.

His fingers flexed like they wanted to wrap around my throat and throttle his frustration away. "*After* putting us all in an unnecessarily dangerous situation. And you got consolation stitches."

"Gods," I growled, my own irritation rising to clash with his. He had a comeback for everything.

We faced off, there in the woods, with nature containing our battle of wills. My entire body locked into a defiant, rigid stance; hands balled into fists at my sides and heels sinking into the dirt. Kaiden watched me in that annoying, silent way of his, giving nothing away with the little half smirk twisting the corner of his mouth.

"So bossy," I muttered.

Somehow, he pressed even closer. "You like my bossy."

"Overconfident," I fired off.

"Irresponsible," he replied in kind.

It was a stalemate. Neither one of us was willing to back down, and I didn't like the satisfied glint in his eye. Like some-

how, he won anyway. Twenty minutes later, back at the apartment as I sulked and locked myself in the bedroom, I realized he
might have. He had the last word, after all. I threw myself on the
bed and smothered a scream with my pillow.

I needed a nap. A few hours of unconscious relief to forget
about the tug-of-war Kaiden instilled within me. Part frustration
and part attraction—all parts messed up. I tossed and turned,
twisting the sheets around me like a vise. Sleep didn't come. My
skin felt tight, and the latent anger inside me needed an outlet.

If Kaiden weren't such an ass, I'd ask him in here to help me
out. Probably stumble over my words and make a complete fool
of myself in the process, but it couldn't be that hard. I knew he
was on the edge himself—his bossiness came out the more
turned on he was. Gods, being horny had never been a problem
before he put his hands on me.

It was an emotion I easily pushed aside, but not now. As the
heat built within me, I wiggled. Thighs pressed together, I
shifted and tried to ease the coil in my gut. What was this crap,
and why wouldn't it go away?

The bedroom door swung open as if answering my silent
pleas, but Kaiden stormed past me in a beeline for his desk
across the room. He pulled out the chair and took a seat. No
glance in my direction, no acknowledgment, not a sign that he
even noticed my distress. And I knew I wasn't being silent
about it.

I'd allowed a little heat to escape my side of the bond,
hoping it would taunt him to come in here and solve my
problem without me having to ask. Well, part of that plan
worked. Ignoring me and digging through his bowl of crystals
was not what I had in mind for the other part. I knew he had a
stick up his ass this week, but didn't he still want to touch me?

Another blast of heat down the bond, this one harder, and
his shoulders stiffened. "I'm busy right now, princess."

Busy? He practically nailed me to multiple surfaces with his touch and droned on about how much he wanted to *fuck* me if I'd only let him, but he was *too busy*? Djinn were literally chasing us, and he found the time to finger-fuck me. My ankle might have been broken that one time he slapped my ass and nearly had me screaming, but X-rays could wait. And now? *Now* he wanted to work?

Outrage burned red hot down our connection. I made sure he felt every ounce of it as I clenched the sheets and ground my teeth at his arrogance. Was I only worth touching when it was on his time?

He sighed, placed a blue crystal back in the bowl, and glared at me over his shoulder. "It's nothing personal, and it doesn't mean anything, right?" One brow lifted as he met my gaze and held it until I gave the barest of nods. "So, take care of it yourself."

Did he just suggest I...?

My arousal cooled enough for embarrassment to take over. He wanted me to touch myself while he watched? Or while he was in the room? Either option was not happening. I didn't even touch myself when I was alone. I'd lived with my parents my entire life, in quarters too close for comfort, and the urge to discover what made my body tick was absent my entire life... until he put his hands on me.

His back was to me once more, but I knew he monitored my emotions and reaction. My outrage, thankfully, still ran strong enough to cover my lack of experience, and I played it off.

"Get out," I ordered.

He didn't move an inch. "It's no different than any other time you've done it, and I've seen it all anyway. Just ignore me."

Ignore him. Ha. Fat chance of that. I was highly aware of him even when he wasn't nearby. Even when I slept.

"From what I can tell, it wouldn't take more than a couple

strokes for you to get off," he added, still partly focused on his work.

"I-I don't..." I stuttered and flushed a deep red. I meant to tell him that I refused to do anything while he sat there in the room and played with his toys. I *meant* to sound mature and full of confidence when I ordered him to remove himself from my presence, but it didn't come out like that. "I've nev...I don't..."

Kaiden froze, one hand hovering over the bowl. He straightened in his seat, back going stiff before he turned and gave me his full attention. Those blue eyes speared me with the lust I *knew* was right beneath the surface as his lips split into a devilish smile.

"Princess," he purred, drawing the word out. "Are you telling me you've never touched yourself before?"

twenty

Kaiden

It was inconceivable, but the proof was right in front of me. Her embarrassment and uncertainty were so strong I could taste it. Still blushing red with the lingering arousal she couldn't shake despite the abrupt turn in the conversation, Eryn stared wide-eyed at the wall just past my head.

Avoiding eye contact. *Bingo*.

I wasn't such a pussy that I couldn't admit how much our last encounter had hurt me. Every time I touched her, it meant something. She could deny it all she wanted; I knew the truth. It still sucked, though, to hear her declare otherwise, which made me a little pissy the last few days. Did that mean I'd let this opportunity pass me by? No fucking way.

"I asked you a question." I dropped my tone, tapping into that growl I knew she loved to hear.

Right on cue, she shivered and stopped hiding. It was all there on display, her nerves, and her desire. Her rosy blush spread down her neck to the tops of her breasts peeking over the

rim of her top. Those little shorts had to go, but I took one more moment to admire how long they made her legs look.

I'd sworn to not touch her again unless she admitted that this wasn't all one-sided, but one more taste couldn't hurt.

"How have you never touched yourself?" I asked, genuinely curious.

She wasn't a virgin. I could tell that much, but wasn't self-discovery several steps before sex?

She shook her head like that would get the words to break free. "T-there's never been a time to try. I've always lived or slept right next to someone."

That was a plausible enough reason, but she didn't go searching for that alone time? Wasn't curious? I didn't buy it. It was more likely that the few times she might have tried, it had done nothing for her. Too little experience and not enough incentive to keep going. It was hard to imagine a grown woman not knowing her own body. Time to fix that.

"Do you know how?" I pressed, and her eyes narrowed.

"I'm not stupid," she snapped. "I feel around with my fingers."

I held back a groan at the image she painted and forced myself to stay in the chair. My dick throbbed already. He was definitely paying attention.

"That's right," I nodded. "Light pressure, hard, whatever you like. In circles, rubbing, even a light pinch will work." Her breath caught as I described all the ways my own fingers were familiar with her. I could practically feel her drenching my hand. "I wonder how many of your fingers it would take. If you curl them back, there's a spot I know from experience you find particularly sensitive."

Her chest rose and fell rapidly as her breathing increased. She stared at me, shocked at my words, but not enough to take them and give it a try.

She shyly glanced down, the bed sheets twisting in her little fists. "Never mind."

That wouldn't do. My girl was missing out on the joys of her own body, and I couldn't stand it.

"No, no, princess. We're going to solve this problem right here, right now."

Her head snapped up as I stood and walked over to the end of the bed.

"We?" She swallowed. Her legs lightly trembled at the idea, and I smiled. Perfect.

"I'm going to teach you," I swore, and took a little edge off by feeling on her soft thighs as I pulled at her denim shorts.

The way we were both wound up, this wouldn't take long, but I had to stay in control enough to do as I promised. She didn't resist me as I pushed her back and took her panties off too, flinging them somewhere off to the side. Looking at her spread before me like a buffet begging to be devoured, I put a mental chokehold on my dick and told it to behave. It pushed against my jeans in retaliation.

Fuck, that was uncomfortable.

"Slide your hand down your stomach," I directed her. After a moment's hesitation, she did as I asked. "Slower. Feel how soft you are."

Below her belly button she slowed, her fingers gently reaching. They knew where to go, she only had to trust them. The pad of her middle finger danced lower but faltered just above her pussy. It was pink and swollen, already dripping and ready for us.

That claiming voice in my head demanded I brush her hand aside and show her how it was done, but I silenced it.

"How do you like it?"

She frowned. "I don't know."

I smirked. "When I touch you, how do you like it? Hard presses? Soft brushes? Tell me."

A soft moan escaped, and her hips jerked. "All of it," she panted. "I love everything you do to me."

Fuck! My head dropped, and I clenched my jaw to keep from exploding at her innocent words. She was perfect. Once I scraped control back, I met her half-lidded stare with one of my own.

"Soft then," I whispered. "Start soft."

That middle finger was on the move again, more confident this time. It slipped through her slick lips with no resistance, and her mouth parted on a moan.

"Gentle," I coached. "Rub the tip of your finger down one side of your clit, then back up the other." She did, and her thigh tightened under my palm. I squeezed it in response. "Again." When she couldn't stop her hips from twitching with each downward stroke, I allowed her to progress. "Circles now." Her hand got to work. "Harder. I want to hear how wet you are."

We both lost our breath with her next motions.

"Kaiden," she moaned. "It's not enough."

My dark chuckle made her frown, but she didn't stop. I knew it wasn't enough, but she needed to build the tension before she could shatter it.

"Then slip that finger inside," I dared her. "Feel how tight you are, and follow the pleasure to whatever feels good."

I studied her face, not trusting myself enough to watch what she flaunted right within my reach. I *heard* her add one finger and then another. Her eyes closed under creased brows, and she bit her lip hard enough I thought it would bleed.

"Curl them," I urged her. "Reach for it."

She thrashed her head. Defeat strangled the bond as she told me without words that it wasn't working. She was so close. Fuck, so was I just from watching her. My own fingers brushed

hers as I slid a digit in with her two. Her eyes flew open as a guttural moan fought its way free.

"Put those fingers to work on your clit, princess. I've got you here."

It didn't take long after that. Two circles and a curl of my finger had her shattering into a million pieces. My smug pride didn't last long. I pushed away from her with some mumbled excuse and ran to the shower to finish myself off.

I didn't give her a chance to cheapen what we had done with her denials. The shower stall and steam surrounded me before I even knew that my dick and I were right on the edge.

Eryn

"There. Now you know."

Those were Kaiden's last words, spit almost harshly as he left me and disappeared into the ensuite. Seconds later, I heard the shower running. I wasn't completely naive; I knew what he was doing in there. His arousal saturated our bond, reigniting mine even after what he wrung from my body.

How would he react if I offered to help? He'd never expected anything from me before, but would he if I instigated it? For once, his lack of demands made me want to act. I stripped off the rest of my clothes, double-checking that my bandage was sealed, and crept into the bathroom.

The small space was too foggy to see much besides the marble counters, but I followed the sound of running water until my palms landed on the glass shower. I opened the door

and steam rolled out, clearing enough for me to catch my first real look at Kaiden's cock. Gods above, he was huge.

And thick.

His fist pumped the shaft all the way to the swollen, ruby tip. A small bead of cum called to me where it was smeared just beneath his navel, and a light trail of hair led me right back down. I swallowed. He was close if the sounds of near pain were any indication.

"Feeling brave?" he growled. "Or just here to watch?"

His eyes flared when my tongue darted out to wet my lips. The tip of him was leaking, and I wanted a taste. I reached out, not in control of my own movements, and he groaned again, snapping me out of it. I didn't know what I was doing.

By his less-than-smooth motions, he didn't have much control left, and I wanted to be the one to get him there like he'd done for me. But what if he didn't like it? Kaiden caught my wrist as I pulled away. He tugged me forward. Together, he wrapped our hands around his cock, then guided us up and down, using more pressure than I expected.

I gave a tentative but stronger squeeze, and his knees buckled. For something so smooth and silken to the touch, his cock could take more pressure than I thought possible. At least I didn't have to worry about breaking it.

"Brush your thumb over the head," he whispered harshly, his voice pitched an octave so low that I had to make sure it was really him I held in my hand.

The pad of my thumb traced the slit at the tip of his cock, gathering the thick fluid my grip milked. I brought my hand to my mouth and groaned at the taste. A little salty, but not as bad as I'd heard multiple girls complain about. Before I could second-guess myself, I dropped to my knees.

Down here, the spray of the shower soaked my entire side in

seconds, but I didn't care. I reached for him once more, only for him to stop me.

"We probably shouldn't do this." It looked like it pained him to say it. Was he worried he pressured me into it? He didn't.

"I want to make you feel good," I said, gripping him once more. His hips jerked as I slid a hand up his length.

"Fuck," he moaned, his hand stopping me again. "What I mean is, we *can't* keep doing this if you're going to continue to lie about it meaning something." His entire body shook from holding back, but he didn't release my hand. "Because it fucking does. It means something to me."

That's what had him so on edge this week? I only meant we couldn't complete the bond. It was a defense mechanism and more for myself—to keep my senses when he tried his best to obliterate them. Gods, I hadn't meant to *hurt* him. But I had.

I felt it now, like a tear in the bond. It throbbed in a similar way to a wound. I wasn't ready to sign my life away or to tie myself to him forever, but everything we'd done, including this right here, wasn't an empty action. I was scared to look too closely at what exactly it meant, but it wasn't nothing. I hated that I ever uttered those words out loud.

"Can you admit it?" He asked after what I was sure was a close monitor of my emotions. I nodded. "I need the words, Eryn."

"It means something," I admitted.

He grabbed my hair and wrapped it around his fist. The grip was tight enough to sting as my curls were pulled at the roots, and I cried out as he tipped my head back. His cock sat right in front of me, the tip rubbing around my lips.

"Then open up, princess. Show me what you can do."

With only the head in my mouth, I knew it would be an effort to take him all the way down, but dammit, I was determined to try. He was thick on my tongue, and I lapped at him

like he was my favorite candy before sucking hard, hollowing my cheeks.

A snarl left his throat, and I knew I'd done something right. It was instinct I followed as I licked and nibbled my way to the base. Both my hands wrapped around him next as I took him as deep as I could, swallowing when he hit too far back so I wouldn't gag.

"Princess, you have to stop," he begged and tried to pull me off. I clutched his ass and held on, swallowing again.

My eyes watered, and my jaw ached, but I wasn't letting go until he finished.

"I'm gonna come," he warned.

I brought a hand back to him and squeezed around the base while my tongue lapped at that ridge just under the head. I looked up. His eyes went dark as he came, and the back of my throat was coated with jet after jet as he roared his release. I tried to remember to breathe through my nose, but it was still too much.

Coughing, I pulled off and prayed I hadn't ruined everything by quitting right at the very end. Kaiden sank to his knees in front of me, still trying to catch his breath. Grabbing my head in both hands, he slammed our lips together, forcing my mouth open until our tongues tangled. He didn't seem to mind the taste of himself as he owned me with only a kiss.

"Thank you," he said against my mouth, before resting his forehead against mine.

I felt him smile down the bond and tentatively opened my side enough to allow the barest of touches. I didn't know what bullshit I tried to convince myself of before. This definitely meant something. It meant *everything*.

twenty-one

Kaiden

I stared down at Eryn, watching her sleep. There was a feeling of contentment, of satisfaction I didn't expect to feel without completing the bond. I thought we were a long way off from this —years away—but Eryn's wide-eyed admission hit me right in the center of my chest. This wasn't all one-sided.

She *felt* something for me. It wasn't a love declaration by any means, and me revealing the true depth of my feelings for her would probably unravel all our progress, but...it meant something. Gods, *it meant something*. What though? That was the newest question hounding my every thought.

It's why I wasn't asleep, and instead, watched my bond with this new, excited thrill I couldn't shake. It was why my bag sat packed at the door, ready for the four-hour drive I now *really* didn't want to make because it would mean leaving her side, even for just a short while.

The tribunal called an emergency meeting. All faction seats and their heirs were required to attend. Our enemy would be

there, the one pulling the strings behind Eryn's attacks. I knew who it was the second I saw that illusioned pit bull snarling at my bond yesterday. The damned dog was the calling card of Kol Von Bauer, the heir to the djinn faction.

Combined with Eryn's description of who stabbed her along with what he said, it was a perfect fit. And not at all unexpected. I couldn't make a move against him outright, but his presence was also required at the meeting. Eryn should be safe until I returned. Ezra could handle any low-level hunters still lingering in my absence.

Forcing myself to leave was a harder task than I anticipated, however. A cascade of dark curls fell across the pillow she'd stolen from between us. On her back, Eryn's shirt rode up, revealing her soft green panties and a slice of her toned stomach. The sheets were clenched in her fists, and her face was crumpled in a frown.

Nightmares plagued her as of late, often waking us both with their potency and tendency to make her thrash. I was usually too late to stop them, waking at the same time as her, but not tonight. Tonight, I watched as the terrors in her memories took hold and spun their web of pain. I planned to redirect those thoughts and leave her with other memories to keep her company while I was away.

Before the nightmare grew strong enough to reach me, even through the blocks in our bond, I ran a gentle finger from her shoulder to elbow and whispered her name. Waking her too suddenly could have the opposite effect of what I was trying to do. Her head jerked, one way and then the other. I maintained my gentle touch from her elbow, down her forearm, and into her palm.

"Wake up, princess." Her eyes fluttered behind clenched lids. "You can do it. Follow my voice." Deep emerald orbs, glinting with moonlight and confusion met my steady gaze. "You were

slipping into another nightmare," I told her, my finger still dancing across her skin.

"I thought you'd be gone by now." Her voice was raw with sleep, and the deepness of it did funny things to me. "Shouldn't you have left already?"

I really should have, but I couldn't go after seeing her like that or without leaving her with something to help fight off the darkness in my absence. Who knew how long this meeting would keep me away?

"I have a present for you first." That tiny smile was reward enough and worth whatever punishment awaited me if I was late. "Turn on your stomach."

She hesitated, her trust in me still so new, but eventually rolled and tucked her arms under her pillow. I took a moment to admire the slope of her lower back and where it met the delicious curve of her ass, before rising to my knees and settling over her. She tensed, but the first touches of my hands on the muscles in her shoulders had her melting into the mattress with a groan.

I smirked. "Working some of this tension out of your body might help your mind relax as well."

She responded with another low groan, and my dick jumped behind the fabric that confined it. Working my way down the sides of her spine, I soaked in her little moans of pleasure: both a gift and the most exquisite form of torture. Our bond awoke at the first sign of interest from one or both of us.

It burned in my chest, likely hers as well, and egged us on. I was cautious of its influence but allowed it more rein than usual. Eryn wasn't afraid of it like she was before. That gave us more room to play. I reached the small of her back and dug my thumbs into the tense muscles there. The sounds that left Eryn's lips were needy, desperate.

Her hips lifted the slightest bit. Pushing her shirt higher, I

pressed on those muscles again, testing. She deliberately lifted and wiggled that ass at me. Hint taken, princess.

"Tell me again," I demanded, slipping under the waistband of her panties to get at the muscles there. Another deliberate wiggle and my control broke. I threw myself back and spread her legs. She mewed in response but didn't speak, so I ran a finger down her center. Gods. "You're fucking soaked."

I did it again, making her squirm, but she didn't deny my touch, not even when that finger slipped beneath the near-transparent cotton.

"If you want more, it's going to cost a little honesty." I delved deeper, drenching my finger to the first knuckle. "If you can admit what this means, I'll let you come."

Sliding her panties off, I returned to her wet heat with one fingertip. She writhed and lifted her hips once more in invitation, but nothing slipped past those lips other than her frustrated whines.

"Shall I help you?" I crooned. "Do you need a hint?"

I left her entrance and strummed her clit until she squealed, then backed away, once again content to play far from where she wanted me most.

"K-kaiden. Godsdammit!" She cried when all her squirming got my fingers no closer to her throbbing bundle of nerves.

"Admitting how you feel won't snap the bond in place." I circled her clit, not allowing even the slightest graze. "It's okay to like one another." Muffled curses and unintelligible words were smothered by her pillow. She was close. "What was that?"

She turned her head to the side, those curls covering her face in a wild tangle.

"I like you," she panted.

About damn time. I'd longed to hear those words since I learned her name. Since her picture first slid across my desk. They weren't the exact words I was holding out for, but those

would come in time. My power begged for release, and I let it free.

"Good fucking girl." My shadows pushed on the backs of her thighs until she understood what they wanted. She lifted onto her knees, and they wound around her waist. "Hips up," I commanded, my magick already adjusting her.

I couldn't hold back my deep growl of approval. Face down and that perfect ass propped up on display, her juices dripping down her inner thighs. I'd wanted a taste of her ever since that small sample I got off my fingers in the stairwell. I used my thumbs to spread her open, ready to jump right in.

"What are you doing?" she whimpered, her body tense now.

"Something you're going to love," I told her. I hope she loved it. I would never do something that hurt her. "If I do something you don't like, you can always tell me to stop. I swear on the gods, I will."

I rubbed up and down, spreading that sweet proof of her desire. Leaning in, I allowed my breath to ghost over the most vulnerable part of her. When that didn't push her from fear to curiosity, I blew a steady stream of air right on her clit.

"We can't," she gasped, but there was no power behind her voice. Better still, arousal saturated the bond.

"We can," I hummed and dipped a thumb down to her entrance, pressing. "And I'm gonna, so you better get ready."

My thumb sank all the way inside and rubbed along her walls while I blew once more on her clit. I paused, giving her one more chance to stop me, but that was the last thing on her mind. Her thighs trembled so hard only my shadows kept her up and presented for me.

"Arch your back." She did, and I made her scream with one swipe of my tongue. Her hips curved, trying in vain to escape the now overwhelming touch, and I slapped her ass strong enough

to leave a mark. "Now, princess. Arch your back and leave it there."

Pushing her knees wider, I leaned in and went to work. My hands held her in place as my tongue worked in tandem with my fingers to bring her to the edge again and again. I sucked and nibbled her onto the cusp of an orgasm, then filled her tight channel with a digit until she tightened so much it couldn't move.

I licked up every drop that escaped her. Ignoring her pleas for mercy, I pressed my tongue deep inside her until she clenched around it. Until she tried to escape. Until I couldn't understand the cries coming from her lips—some variation of 'please' and 'I can't take it.' I traced my way back to her clit, and as soon as my lips wrapped around it, she shattered, my name ringing off the walls from the force of her shout.

She rode it out on my tongue until she went limp and bone-less, held up only by my magick. I gently set her back down on her stomach with her legs spread and glistening from my atten-tion. It would be so easy to slide inside her, to break her with round after round of more earth-shattering pleasure.

Instead, I held on tight to my control and forced myself to cover her with a blanket. She was already halfway asleep and hopefully worn out enough that the nightmares wouldn't return tonight. Pulling the blanket up to her shoulders, I brushed her hair to the side and left a light kiss on her cheek.

"I like you too, princess."

My hands clenched around my bag, and I threw myself out the door before I gave in to the urge to take her. Not yet. But hopefully someday soon, she would be all mine.

Eryn

I awoke alone and fully rested for the first time in what felt like forever. My body melted into the plush mattress as I burrowed deeper into the covers, hiding from the early morning glow that lit the room. Rolling over, I rubbed my bare legs against the cool sheets and frowned. I was usually overly hot and wrapped around Kaiden despite all attempts to put distance between us.

Memories from last night converged on me in a rush; Kaiden waking me from a nightmare, his deep voice, his warm body hovering over mine. He gave me a massage and then—his tongue...and his shadows... My body warmed again as I relived every sound and arch he'd wrung from my body.

Gods, and I'd admitted to having feelings for him! There was no taking that back. I waited for the anger or panic to set in, but none did. Did I even want to take it back?

There was no more room for pretending and hiding from myself was impossible. I was loath to admit it, but maybe Kaiden was right. My small admission wouldn't seal our bond even though it *was* one step closer. We were already lots of steps closer. I shoved a pillow over my head to muffle my frustrated groan. I never thought I'd meet him, let alone be comfortable half-naked in his bed. Nothing in my life was going according to plan.

"You're going to be late for breakfast with Rani if you don't get up," Ezra called from the other side of the door, ending with a gentle knock. "I really don't want to start my first encounter with her today already in the doghouse."

I huffed a laugh and dragged myself out of bed to get ready, blushing when I found my discarded panties on the floor where Kaiden must have flung them. Not having him here felt wrong somehow, like I'd gotten used to doing everything with him by

my side. Or at least, I felt safe when he was always around. His lack of presence was noticeable, and I wasn't sure how I felt about it.

My blond bodyguard leaned on the kitchen island as I came downstairs, bouncing like a golden retriever getting ready for his daily walk. Ezra hated being cooped up as much as I did, and any excuse to see Rani was met with too much enthusiasm and a whole lotta lust.

"I'm surprised I'm allowed to go to class," I teased. "I thought for sure Kaiden would tell you to lock me inside until he returned." But really, it was something he would do.

"Your lack of faith in my ability to keep you safe is insulting," Ezra sniffed, and I rolled my eyes.

Grabbing my bag from its spot on the floor near the couch, I followed him out to his car. He knew I didn't doubt him, but Kaiden's need for control was undeniable. Plus, with the recent attempts on my life... the fact my teachers didn't have some made-up doctor's note telling them I was contagious for the next week came as a complete shock to me.

"Then what's the plan?" I asked. I wasn't even sure how long Kaiden would be gone. It was possible that was why I had to maintain my usual schedule. Too much time missing and someone was bound to notice.

Ezra was more than capable of keeping an eye out for illusions, traps, and other pitfalls out to get me. And personally, I had no plans to go wandering in the trees for a very long time. Something always happened when I stepped off campus, and I only needed to be poisoned and stabbed once to get the message. If I could go a week without another attack, I'd call it successful.

"The plan," I asked again when I got no answer.

"Class," Ezra said, pushing his little Miata faster so we

wouldn't be late. "Some training. Getting to see that fiery room-mate of yours."

I grinned at the wistful look in his eye. He had it bad. Poor guy. Rani might never give him the time of day, but it sure was entertaining watching the two of them dance around one another. Campus was crawling with students by the time we arrived, later than I was used to, but the Commons was open, and I still managed to get a full meal in.

Breakfast went smoothly, as did my first two lectures and lunch. Ezra escorted me everywhere, even sitting in the back rows of my classes, and each time he appeared beside me, the twitch in Rani's eye grew. I guess he was taking my advice about playing hard to get seriously because Ezra hadn't said a word to her, not even his usual flirting.

It still drove her nuts that he was around, though. I had to make up another excuse for his constant presence, one of a hundred I'd had to create recently. I hated lying to Rani, but there was no other option. Gods, if she knew how much I was keeping from her, she'd never want to be my friend. She was safer in the dark, no matter how much it strained our friendship in ways she wasn't even aware of. Knowing that didn't make it any easier.

This time, my lie was Kaiden and Ezra had a death in the family, and that was why Kaiden left. I promised to keep an eye on his cousin, which meant allowing his needy ass to follow me everywhere.

"Kai went home for the funeral but not him?" she asked, eyeing Ezra with a new air of disbelief.

"He's estranged from that side of the family," I told her. The lies rolling off my tongue easier the more I was forced to spin them. "He wasn't invited."

I whispered that last part like I was trying to keep Ezra from hearing, and some pity entered Rani's eye. She softened toward

him ever so slightly, and I saw it as a win. Sooner or later, these lies were going to catch up with me. I only hoped I had something to tell Rani when that time came, and that I didn't lose her because of them. But who was I kidding? Secrets were one thing, but lying and the existence of magick? She'd be halfway across the country in an effort to get away from me.

That evening, after finishing my homework, Ezra came sliding through the living room on worn socks and wearing a Cheshire cat grin. He crossed his arms and popped a hip against the kitchen island, content to stare down at me until I gave in to the urge to stab him in the eye.

"What?" I grumbled, forced to break my train of thought surrounding conjugating verbs in a language set on destroying the beliefs of my own mental capabilities.

"It's time to train," he said. No fanfare. No jokes. But still that damn smile. I had no idea what he meant by that and wasn't too sure I wanted to get involved. He seemed far too excited, and my suspicions rose.

"Does your cousin know about your plans for whatever this training entails?"

That grin grew, and it sent off warning alarms in my head. "If it were up to my cousin, you'd be safely locked behind layers of magick and guards forever, where nothing could harm you. You'd live your life at our family's compound, pop out magical babies, and be at the beck and call of dear old Auntie Mira and her nurturing personality. I'm pretty sure you don't want that life."

He was absolutely correct, and he knew it.

"I want to teach you how to be useful. How to properly use those dangerous powers of yours to protect yourself, and most importantly, my cousin."

"Uh, thanks?" Now I wasn't too sure if this was about teaching me to be useful and independent, or because he only

truly cared about Kaiden's safety. If it was the latter...ouch much?

Overall, it didn't take long to convince me to go along with his plan—relying on Kaiden and his cousin for the rest of my life wasn't my goal. Training didn't require us to leave the safety of the condo in the middle of the night or any kind of chanting and potion-making, so I figured it couldn't be that dangerous. And on the plus side, maybe I wouldn't be a sitting duck anymore.

"How much do you know about why your kind was hunted to near extinction?" he asked, and the topic turned serious.

I thought back to all that my parents had taught me. We were hunted because we were powerful, they said. The other factions didn't trust us thanks to the actions of a few bad apples. Swift punishment on the part of the tribunal led to dwindling numbers, a rebellion, and then even more dwindling numbers.

"We can manipulate minds—control them—even supernatural ones trained to keep us out. That terrified the others in power," I replied, feeling like I was reading a passage from a textbook. That's how often I'd heard my parents talk about it.

Ezra nodded, solemn. "That's the gist of it, but there's more to it than that. Nightmares could do more than control minds, they could track them from a distance—could identify them from a mere mental brush."

I frowned. That was new to me. My parents never taught me anything like that or mentioned that it was something they could do. That *anyone* could do. How did something like that work?

"You should be able to identify a source of power, like an illusion, and then follow that use of power back to its caster," he further explained. "One day, you might even be able to control that mind from a distance once you've locked on to it. If you're strong enough."

The idea was terrifying. With an ability like that, it was no wonder the others were afraid of my kind. It didn't matter that most of my people probably didn't have the strength to do something like that. It only took one instance to sow fear, and whoever had done it in the past damned us all. To explain it better, Ezra started by teaching me how to cast a net out with my magick. It was similar to how we sensed other supernaturals nearby, but on a slightly different frequency only I could hear.

That's where I had to figure it out on my own, he didn't exactly have a way to hold my hand through this learning process. I cast out my magick and...nothing. Only silence.

"Not all magick is strong enough to register, as you know, and some go under the radar completely. Illusions are an example of that."

"Then how do I...?" This didn't make any sense.

"You're not looking for magick exactly, but minds while they're *using* magick," he explained. "Try again."

I cast my net wider after still getting nothing from around campus. Along the edges of my reach, there was a small flicker of... something. It was empty, like a void. A shadow of magick.

"Latch onto it," Ezra commanded when I told him about it.

It was harder than it sounded because it moved like smoke. Like something not solid. After several minutes and a growing headache, I caught it and followed it back to an oily mind. One I couldn't read, and that was definitely too far away to control—not that I wanted to—but I knew exactly where the owner of the illusion was. Their location lit up like a bright spot on my mental map.

Ezra smiled, and I released the connection.

"You did great," he said and bent over to double knot his sneakers. "Now it's my turn."

I tried not to think about my role in that person's impending demise. There was no other reason for a djinn or an illusion to

be this close to campus. It was obviously a hunter or someone sent to kill me. Keeping that in mind, it was a little easier to accept going on the offensive. A quick dinner, another round of flashcards, and I passed out the second my head hit the pillow. Using magick was exhausting.

A routine formed over the next couple days, and I grew stronger at what I considered my new trick. Using my magick was like flexing a muscle to build its strength, an ability I could never properly develop while I was on the run. Now, it was all too easy to find a djinn within my reach and send Ezra out to hunt them. I started subconsciously leaving my net out, like a warning system to alert me of *any* magick used within my range.

What I wouldn't give to have known about this ability growing up. It would have saved me and my parents a ton of heartache. There would have been fewer close calls and trauma- tizing memories. It was comforting to know nothing could sneak up on me, and I slept easier knowing I'd have a heads-up if danger came knocking. At least until that warning blared an alarm loud enough to wake me from a dead sleep.

Kaiden was nearby. His flare of power lit up my mind like a firework, mixed in with the icy tendrils I recognized as Ezra's magick. Breaths came too fast for me to calm them, I scanned the room for danger, but the battle wasn't happening inside. I honestly didn't even need my new trick to sense it, any super nearby would know something big was going down.

When had my bond returned? And what followed him back?

twenty-two

Kaiden

This emergency meeting was utter bullshit. Gathering the faction heads and their heirs was completely unnecessary, and I wished I didn't face losing my seat by not coming. The only reason I showed up was because I knew the djinn heir was required to be here as well. *Here.* Not back at campus near my vulnerable bond.

She was safe from his illusions too. That damned pit bull belonging to Kol didn't venture far from its master. It followed him everywhere, both as a deterrent and a smug example of how strong the heir was to maintain a continuous flow of magick with nary a thought.

What a dick.

It wasn't a shock to me-that the order to kill my bond came from the heir to dickdom himself. We'd never gotten along, and the announcement of my pairing with Eryn meant I'd be the winner in our endless battle of who was stronger.

Kol couldn't stand to lose. But especially not to me. Still,

going against a tribunal ruling—nightmares were supposed to be protected now—and the outright risk of attacking another heir's bond? He must be desperate. If caught, his entire faction would suffer for it, putting them so far behind in the power grab that it would take generations for them to catch up.

"I don't like this," my mother whispered harshly from beside me.

We were seated in the meeting hall, waiting for the last tribunal members to trickle in. The room was shaped like an amphitheater, with raised seating for open meetings. Today, only the faction heads and their heirs sat around the large table here at the bottom.

"You've left your bond too far away to defend, and with only that *mongrel* to keep watch over her."

I sighed but kept my face neutral in case others grew interested in our conversation. "Ezra is quite capable of protecting her."

"And you?" she countered. "He's supposed to be protecting *you*. That's his sole purpose in life."

I allowed the slightest roll of my eyes. "I'm perfectly capable of defending myself. And attacks at a sanctioned meeting are punishable by death." She huffed. "What else would you have me do, Mother?"

"Bring your bond home so that she's surrounded by our people and properly protected."

I didn't want to argue about this again, and thankfully, I didn't have to. The meeting had finally begun. Already there was a layer of tension in the room that had nothing to do with the little spat my mother started with me. I searched for the source. The five factions present stared back at one another warily until the head of the oracles stood.

She wasn't the most powerful of us, due to her magick not

being offensive in nature, but her kind's unique skillset allowed for her to be the impartial leader of these meetings.

"Many of my people have seen a disturbing imbalance on the horizon." She surveyed the room with her milky white gaze.

Those eyes always unnerved me, and I sunk into my chair in relief when they stopped on another. The middle-aged man sat almost directly across from me. His hair was stark white, but not from age. His kind always had vibrant hair colors, much like the fish they conversed with beneath the waves. Sirens.

The oracle continued, "A rogue band of your people have been causing a nuisance to the human world. Their actions, if not corrected, threaten exposure for us all."

The siren's fists tightened on the table, causing the scattered scales on his knuckles to reflect the light of the room. Beside him, his heir remained quiet, but I saw the same fury building behind his impartial mask.

"I have made our grievances known for years, and still, you have done nothing to aid us," the siren spoke, his tenor strong and clear in the room. "My people are tired of being silenced, both in this tribunal and out in the world. This rogue band, as you call them, is but a group of the newest generation fighting to make their voices heard. To make Her voice heard."

"Here we go," mouthed the dark-haired vampire on his right.

"Yes, here we go. Might I remind you that I am only in this position of power because I am the head of the oldest known line of my people." The siren glared down at his neighbor. "Your kind are not the only faction that can be *made*. And *I* don't choose who is tapped for that gift."

Most of us—witches, djinn, oracles, and nightmares—were born. Our numbers increased and decreased like any other population of living beings. But the vampires and sirens? They could add to their ranks in other ways. Classically, vampires

could turn humans, but that was a strictly controlled process voted on by this very tribunal.

Sirens could also be made, but they had no say or control over who or when that happened. They claimed the ocean made Her choice. The fucking ocean. The thought of a cognizant body of water made me never want to go to a beach ever again. Honestly, we didn't know what was true or not. Most sirens chose to live in the sea or on isolated islands speckled around the globe. They were extremely secretive and powerful when they wanted to be.

"Are you saying you can't control your people?"

My head snapped to the right as the head of the djinn voiced his question. Kol smiled as he watched his father, and I didn't like the look of it.

"I don't even know *what* rogue band the oracles are referring to or where. My people are spread far and wide. Through every ocean, on every continent. The exact count isn't—"

"Yes, yes," the djinn interrupted. "We know the extent of your lack of leadership. That is precisely my point. An uncontrolled populace of sirens is dangerous. Your powers of compulsion alone rival that of the nightmares, I've always said, and left unchecked you risk the destruction of our entire society."

The siren's eyes widened just as the room erupted, exactly as the djinn intended. He poked at the fear the others had of losing control. Of exposure to humans, which was our greatest threat besides one another. A faction growing too powerful to be checked by the others was exactly what started the hunt and near extinction of the nightmares.

Sirens were deeply involved in the environment and human affairs. More than any other faction besides the vampires, whose food source required them to be involved in more medical matters. Sirens were always trying to save the world, and their

softhearted, hippie attitude allowed them to go overlooked by the tribunal.

But their powers were some of the strongest among us. Their voices could sing you to sleep, lure you from near or far, or put you under a compulsion so strong you would willingly kill yourself. An out-of-control populace with that much power? The tribunal wouldn't stand for it. Was the djinn trying to eradicate yet another faction in their quest to take over? I wouldn't put it past them.

The meeting dragged on with nothing being decided. The head of the siren faction promised to find those causing problems and get them under control, but the threat had been delivered. If he couldn't do it, someone else would.

I dodged my mother's attempts to rekindle our argument and strolled out of the meeting chamber at a casual pace. Any longer away from my bond, and I was liable to snap, but I couldn't let them see that. Kol waited for me at the end of the hall, where I had no choice but to engage with him.

His pleased smirk had my hackles rising. "I'm surprised you were able to drag yourself away from that tight little bond of yours." My growl of warning made him step back with his hands raised. "Touch a nerve?"

"What are you up to?" I asked, a band of shadows building over my hands. I couldn't attack him, not here with witnesses, but the silent threat to Eryn couldn't go unanswered.

"Me?" If possible, Kol's smile grew. "How can I be up to something from all the way over here? You give me too much credit, Alantes."

Eryn was safe, I told myself. Far from here, with my cousin, and locked behind a boundary of strong wards. He couldn't reach her, and his minions were no match for Ez. She would be okay until I got home. He was only trying to rile me.

"Half a credit. For trying," I taunted, moving past him and out into the late afternoon sun.

That fucking meeting took all day. With some luck, I could be back home before midnight. I'd run on less sleep than this before, and resting was inconceivable until I had Eryn tucked into my side and squirming on my fingers. Kol's presence didn't fade as I walked toward the family compound and my awaiting truck.

"I didn't take you for one to pant after my attention, Von Bauer," I called to him. "Share some traits with that drooling illusion of yours?"

"You mean the illusion your little bond wet herself over? Must have hurt to not be her favorite in that encounter."

I spun and found him invading my space, far closer to me than I thought he was. At this distance, I risked more than just physical damage, but being within eyesight of the guards around my faction's property allotted me some protection. Then again, this dick was on his last marble.

"Whatever you're planning, whatever sick plots keep you up at night, they're not going to work. You won't get to her." I vibrated with rage, but that only pleased him more. He soaked it in and grew stronger in its presence.

"I already told you; *I'm* not doing anything. Not from all the way over here." I forced myself to step back, but he wouldn't shut up. "I wouldn't dream of testing your wards anyway, Alantes. Breaking them isn't within my wheelhouse. But my pets are known for their many talents and your bond appears fond of dogs, so..."

Dear gods. Shadows exploded around us, a move that signaled to the watching guards, and allowed me to disappear amid the soundtrack of Kol's maniacal laughter. That fucker. My hands shook as I started my truck and tore out of there, my cell already at my ear and calling Ez.

I had a four-hour drive ahead of me, even breaking all the speed laws in existence. I only hoped I wasn't too late.

"Yo, how'd it go?" Ez answered, his tone relaxed and very much alive.

"Scent hounds!" I shouted down the line. "Kol has scent hounds."

"Fuck!" The curse was followed by the sound of my cousin gathering weapons in the background. "How far out are you?"

"Too far," I growled. "But I don't know how much of a head start they have." I slammed my palm against the dash. Again. And again. I couldn't lose her. I would *not* lose her. "Protect her until I get there, Ez. Promise me."

"Nothing will touch her. You have my word, cuz."

Scent hounds were some of the only creatures able to track their prey through wards. Nothing kept them away except a recall order, and Kol wouldn't give one of those. The hounds were rare, bred sparingly to control who had access to them, and their use was supposed to be tightly leashed by the tribunal. Needing a unanimous vote to release them for a hunt. I'd bet every ounce of my power that the djinn had an unsanctioned breeding pair.

By the time I arrived, my hands were cramped from clutching the steering wheel, and I was half crazy with rage and fear. Ez met me outside, sweat drenching his shirt and breathing more ragged than I'd ever seen him. My warning gave him enough time to lay more wards to keep the hounds from reaching the condo. Those, combined with the traps already laid out, were enough to delay them.

He held them off in the woods, away from any casualties or nosy neighbors, but the strain it took to fuel those wards was wearing on him. Much longer, and the hounds would have broken through and started on the ones around Eryn. They

needed to be put down. I nodded, and wordlessly, we traveled up the path along the cliffs and toward the trees.

The cloying weight of the hound's magick threatened to burn the back of my nose, and I breathed through my mouth.

"How many are there?" I asked, keeping my head on a swivel as we reached the shadows of the deep woods.

"Two that my wards could sense," Ezra replied and pointed.

Off to the right, staring at us from the other side of an invisible line, were the two scent hounds. Their dark fur was matted and wild, accenting their bulk. More than double the size of a normal wolf, their innate psychic magick was so strong it had a physical manifestation around them, appearing similar to my shadows.

Eyes an unnatural red, and fangs I had to double take to believe, I gripped my dagger and cast a sideways glance at my cousin. He was on the last of his reserves. If we were going to make a move, we had to do it now before he was drained.

"Drop the wards," I ordered.

He knew what came next. We didn't have to strategize, didn't have to speak. Falling into a routine as old as we were, Ez dropped the wards and coated the ground with a layer of ice. Just as I suspected, the hounds reacted like a stretched rubber band the second they were free. They lunged forward, claws slipping and grasping for any purchase they could get.

A low band of shadows knocked them off their paws, tail over head, and one landed in front of me, by the grace of the gods. I swung down with my dagger before it could recover, the steel sinking into its eye with little resistance. The hound gave a dying cry, twitched, and lay still.

"Kai!" Ezra called for help.

He stood trapped, unable to lift his arms or cast his magick. Held under the power of the hound, he was a sitting duck. I threw out my shadows, blocking the connection and providing

cover until I could reach him. The hound growled. It knew we were still there, but it couldn't get a lock on us.

"You made eye contact with it, didn't you?" I asked him and clasped his shoulder so he knew where I was.

"Shut up," he grumbled. "You try avoiding two glowing red eyes in the dark. They literally ask to be looked at."

The hound's physic powers only worked if they caught your eye. They ensnared you, making escape impossible, and your death very slow and painful. A beat of silence was the only signal I needed to know Ez was ready. One breath, and I dropped the shadows. My cousin flung a disk of ice with freakish accuracy, slicing through the thick neck of the final hound. The massive head fell one way while the body went the other, and I breathed a sigh of relief.

Until the entire left side of my body felt like it was dipped in acid. My shout of pain echoed over the bodies of the hounds and my cousin's distraught face. We were wrong. There weren't two hounds, but three, and the last one had snuck up behind us. Its claws shredded half my body easier than a knife through tissue paper, and I felt my life's blood gush from the wounds at a speed I knew I couldn't survive.

Ezra leaped over my falling body with a battle cry, revenge burning hot in his eyes. I tried to hold on to consciousness, but it was asking too much of my body. The lack of sleep and loss of blood was a deadly combination, one that finally caught up with me. My last thoughts were of Eryn and a desperate plea for her to survive despite my utter failure in protecting her like I promised.

twenty-three

Eryn

I clutched at my chest, feeling it burn from the inside out. All along one side, from shoulder to hip, I was on fire. Absolute agony raced down my nerves, worse than being stabbed. Worse than the poison that tried to take my life with its deadly burn. I looked down, but there was no visible damage. It wasn't *my* wound.

Was this how it felt for Kaiden when I was hurt? He was usually so good at blocking his side of the bond. The fact that I felt his pain, this *much* pain, meant something was horribly wrong. I climbed out of bed with a spinning head and shaking legs. The surges of power I still felt out there rattled me. I was surprised the earth didn't shake from the force of it.

I checked on my net and followed the twinges to the cliffside deep in the forest. I was familiar with the icy feel of Ezra's power, and I'd recognize Kaiden's anywhere, even as depleted as it was. They surrounded a dwindling pocket of darkness that lashed

out at them with desperate strikes. It faded as the witches pulled their power back within themselves.

Pacing the living room, I mentally tracked them on their journey back and kept an eye out for any surprises within my range. Kaiden's life force flickered like a sputtering candle. I reached out, hoping to protect it, strengthen it somehow, but it was no use. I sensed the second he lost consciousness, and the terror that gripped me was surprising.

It strangled me, making me fumble over my own feet to get to the front door. I opened the many locks, and the thick wood swung open in time for Ezra to stumble in, holding an unrecognizable Kaiden with half his body painted in blood. A ruby puddle formed on the floor around their feet after only seconds of being here.

One of Kaiden's arms was wrapped around Ezra's neck as he used all his strength to drag his cousin the rest of the way inside. I slammed the door shut, reactivating the wards in case there was more of whatever hurt them out there. I followed, helpless, as Ezra dragged Kaiden to the bedroom, careful to not split him open more. Gods. Vomit burned the back of my throat at the sight.

I'd never seen the inside of a person like that.

Things moved too quickly to track. Ezra shouted orders at me that I didn't fully understand. I followed them anyway—grab this crystal or that vial of herbs. Their large stash of potions under the sink vanished at an alarming rate as Ezra did what he could to keep his cousin alive and I was sent to task—boiling water and following the detailed instructions in a potion book to restock whatever didn't require rare ingredients or a spell.

"Sage, stop arguing with me and send the fucking physician! I'll keep him breathing until then."

The mirror shimmered in the corner of my vision, an image of Kaiden's sister blurry from where I sat beside him on the bed.

A healer was necessary for injuries this severe. Half of Kaiden's torso was a tangled mess; shredded skin and muscle; exposed bone; and. So. Much. Blood. I did all I could, maintaining skin contact wherever it was safe to touch to lend my strength, and pouring potions past lax lips.

The bond in my chest was a constant heat—like it was working overtime to hold on. If he survived this, we'd be wound even tighter together. That didn't bother me as much as the thought that he might not make it. My eyes didn't leave him for a second, as if just watching him could keep him anchored here with me. I internally kept watch on that growing bond, so tender and new, ready to tug on it if he started to slip away.

Ezra moved like I'd never seen him move before—swift and controlled. Everything happened too fast. He froze the parts of Kaiden's body that splayed open, but the warm blood melted the ice after a few minutes. His cousin's life force was a sputtering candle, and each time that flame wavered, it threatened to take me with it.

I refused to give up. Every ounce of energy in me went to keeping Kaiden alive. Tense hours later, the physician made it and depleted the majority of his power keeping his faction heir from certain death. Muscles knitted together, blood replenished, and skin closed. There would be faint scars, but considering Kaiden's *organs* had been punctured, scarring was the least of his worries.

Twenty-four hours. It took an entire day of multiple heal-ings, which the physician had to recover from before beginning again, until he was finally satisfied. When he departed, leaving behind strict instructions for rest, Ezra and I sat in a silence born from exhaustion and disbelief. Part of me wasn't sure our efforts would work. By all reason, Kaiden should have died. We were so, so lucky.

"What happened out there?" I asked. I wasn't sure when Ezra

left the condo, and hadn't even known Kaiden was on his way back until I felt the flare of power.

He shook his head—like it would make any of this easier to understand. "Scent hounds," was his whispered reply. "The djinn sent them after you, and Kol, their heir, taunted Kaiden at the meeting about it. He barely got here in time."

The blood rushed from my head, leaving me shaky and even more unsteady. *Scent hounds?* How had the tribunal approved that? I was a faction heir's bond! Technically, a faction heir in my own right now that we'd been granted clemency. Yet they would just send those *things* after me? And for what reason?

"I thought it took a unanimous vote to release the hounds for a hunt?" My voice shook as I realized how close to death I'd actually come without knowing it.

Ezra shook his head. "We think the djinn have an unsanctioned breeding pair." His lip curled in disgust. "Kol Von Bauer is the one pulling the strings, with or without his father's knowledge. He was behind your attacks, the illusions, and the hunters still trying to collect an illegal bounty. If Kaiden hadn't called ahead with a warning and raced like hell to get here, I'm not sure I could have kept you safe on my own."

I didn't blame him. Not against fucking scent hounds. The fact that they both survived was miracle enough and not an easy feat.

"Thank you," I told him, holding his gaze. "I've been beyond selfish and made your life difficult, both of you, but...thank you."

He nodded, a rare moment of severity for him, before leaving to find his own bed, exhaustion causing him to stumble across the hall. The fact that he was willing to go at all told me he thought his cousin was in the clear. I glanced down at the man I'd fought so hard to resist. The better part of this year was spent thinking the worst of him and fighting every attempt he made to get to know me. Despite my actions, he'd protected me

time and time again. He almost *died* for me, and that realization was only just sinking in.

Time blurred as we all recovered. Physically, I was in perfect health, but the amount of energy Kaiden needed was enough to exhaust me. I threw everything I had at him. He could have it all if it meant he'd wake again. I fell in and out of fitful sleep. Each time I woke, I'd check in on that bond in my chest. It hummed softly.

He's okay. I had to remind myself. Despite him being right there, the thought of him slipping away...Pure unfiltered terror gripped me. There it was. The true feelings I hadn't allowed myself to linger over. Somehow, Kaiden snuck himself past my defenses and burrowed into my heart. He rooted himself in there, digging deep.

My heart skipped and froze, sluggishly pumping through the fear that now encompassed my every thought. Every molecule in my body shuddered with it.

If I lost him now...

Beside me, Kaiden shot straight up, and his uninjured arm reached under the pillow to grab a sharp dagger. He held it out in front of him; eyes clear and scanning the room for danger. His healed chest rose and fell in heavy breaths as he completed his search, ending on me sitting beside him.

"Where is it?" he asked, worry clouding the blue in his eyes. "Where's the threat?"

I stared at him, checking every inch of skin I could see to make sure no wounds reopened. Not that there should be anything left to open, not after the healing he had. I quickly peered down at his pillow, still dented with the impression of his head.

"How long has that knife been under there?"

Kaiden lowered said knife and twisted to face me. Concern

still creased his face as he cupped my cheek, forcing me to look at him once more.

"You're terrified," he said, thumb gently brushing my skin. "Tell me what's wrong so I can fix it."

My eyes widened. He'd woken from a bone-deep healing sleep because he'd felt my fear? Barely off death's door, and his first thought was to protect me. To make sure I was all right. That bond between us pulsed, and my chest clenched. I was sure my face was stuck in shock. Seeing him speak—seeing him move like he hadn't been torn to pieces only hours ago...And now he wanted to *fight*, again? Because I was *scared*?

"Eryn," he murmured, eyes capturing mine. His beautiful blue, very alive eyes.

Holy shit. My frozen heart stuttered and then kicked off like a stampede.

"I'm falling in love with you," I whispered. My voice was a ghost, with hardly enough substance to hear, but he caught it.

His smile was slow like a cresting sun breaking through morning fog. "Just figuring that out, are you?"

I stared in silent shock. Panic. Fear. Realizing what I felt and what I just admitted out loud. A very big freak-out was building, and there would be no way to stop it once it arrived. How had I let this happen?

"Would it make you feel better if I still pretended not to know?"

That snapped me out of it. "Still? What do you mean still?"

He laughed, full and open, and the sound eased some of the stricture around my heart. I wasn't sure this was a laughing matter but seeing him do anything besides gasp for air was a massive improvement.

"I've known about your feelings for some time now," he admitted, his chuckle gentle. Pleased. "You're the one who's been

hiding from them. You didn't do a very good job of burying them from me, though."

I scowled. "Well, sorry that I'm not as good as *some people* at blocking my side of the bond."

He laughed again, and I blushed. There was a whirlwind of emotions inside me, spiraling so swiftly I couldn't get a lock on what exactly I felt. Embarrassment rose to the top. This whole time I'd fought against the idea of us, and Kaiden knew all along that it was a farce. He must think I'm an idiot.

"Here." He grasped my hand. "I'll make it even."

The door to his side of the bond opened wide and out flooded every thought, every feeling he'd ever had for me. Excitement. Frustration. Arousal. Irritation. Amusement. *Love*. Tears flooded my eyes until Kaiden blurred in front of me. This entire time, he trusted I'd find my way. All the hurt he'd hidden at my denials and unfounded anger toward him. My mistrust cut him to the core. My smiles he coveted like a personal treasure. He *liked* pissing me off. He let me see it all, pushing some memories through as well for good measure.

My chin wobbled. "Why didn't you tell me?" How did he keep this locked up?

"Because you weren't ready to hear it." He smiled again, a small one. "And you never would have believed me. You'd have thought it was a trick to get you to bond."

He was right. I wouldn't have seen it for anything but manipulation on his part. Even now, I had a hard time trusting all that he showed me, so deep was my fear of bonding. Feelings aside, the thought of allowing that level of control over me still made me wary. Kaiden was so much better at this bond thing than I was already, what would happen once he had wide open access to me?

I shook my head. That was the fear talking. Kaiden had

already proven beyond doubt that he wouldn't hurt me. Why couldn't I trust that and just be happy?

"Easy," he hummed, cupping my cheeks once more. "Nothing has to change. Calm down."

"I'm sorry. I trust you; I do. I swear. It's just—"

"You don't trust yourself," he finished for me. "I can't begin to understand what you've been through or why the idea of our bond makes you feel like that, but I'm here, okay? I'll be here as you figure it out."

I released a shaky breath. Took in another, and let it go as well. Kaiden wrapped an arm around me and drew me close, tucking me into his uninjured side and laying us down. The bond hummed, and he pushed gentle waves of calm down the connection. His fingers trailed lightly over the skin of my arm. Up and down.

The door remained cracked, allowing me to still feel him but not be overwhelmed. Slowly, I relaxed and stepped away from the ledge of panic. Exhaustion rose and hooked into my mind with a finality. There was a long sleep on the horizon—for both of us. Hopefully, the danger that seemed to follow us needed a break as well because we would be beyond vulnerable otherwise.

Before going under, one thought wormed its way past my lips.

"Seriously, how long was that knife under your pillow?"

twenty-four

Kaiden

We tried to let things get back to normal. Easier said than done after nearly dying, but there was really no other option. I wasn't lying when I told Eryn I wanted to help her follow her dreams. I meant every word I said when I promised to protect her while she finished school and became a veterinarian. Things were far more complicated now, but it was what it was.

To change course now would only sever any connection we'd painstakingly built. Locking her up inside my family's compound, even for her own protection, would slowly kill her. I was sure of it. Along with any chance of an us. And so, days at the university continued on while we recovered. Teachers didn't care about trivial excuses after a week of missed classes, despite me being a TA, so Eryn had no choice but to return.

"Rani is beyond suspicious that we keep disappearing." Eryn paced a worn track in the cobblestones outside her lecture hall. "You should have seen the look she gave me when I told her we had the flu. She didn't buy it, which is why I had to agree to this

sleepover tonight to throw her off. What are the chances she actually lets me study instead of grilling me? And that's another thing! Finals are only *weeks* away!"

I stepped in front of her, arms braced against her shoulders to make her stop. She would make herself sick worrying like this. Her anxiety levels had been at an all-time high since her personal revelations, her feelings an added strain to the current mess of our lives, and I was bound and determined to bring my happy bond back.

That started with her having a girls' night with her friend. Ezra was working overtime making sure the campus was clear. We hadn't heard nor seen any evidence that the djinn were in the area. There should be consequences for them using scent hounds, but with no proof, they were likely laying low and plotting their next move.

Whatever. We'd be ready.

I continued the training Ez started with Eryn, having no problem admitting it was a good idea. One or both of us were near her at all times, and I made sure she'd fed last night, replenishing her magick. Come summertime, we could retreat to the family compound to regroup, and be better prepared to return for the fall semester. Until she was ready to bond, this would be our life, but I'd protect her right to choose with everything I had in me.

"Take a deep breath, princess, before you hyperventilate," I teased, trying to keep her calm.

When she only huffed at me in annoyance, I leaned forward and kissed her. Slowly. Lazily. I lightly dragged my tongue across the seam of her mouth, begging for entrance. She clutched at my shirt, halfheartedly pressing her mouth back against mine like she wasn't really present in the moment. That wouldn't do.

Capturing her bottom lip between my teeth, I bit down until she gasped, and then took advantage of her full attention. My

hand caressed up her back and sank into her soft curls as I cradled her head, opening her to the right angle for the slow strokes of my tongue, deep and dominant, just the way she liked it. Arousal vibrated the bond in my chest, and the little whimpers leaving her between gasps for air told me my distraction was working.

"Go have fun with your friend and stop worrying," I whispered against her lips. "That's my job."

One more lingering kiss, and I pulled away. Her eyes were half-lidded, and the emerald behind her thick lashes gleamed with hunger. My answering grin was pure masculine pride as I left her in the capable hands of her approaching friend.

"I need her brain to work tonight, Kai!" Rani called. "You couldn't have turned it to mush *after* she explained the interaction of morphological and biochemical properties of terrestrial plants?"

My grin didn't fade as I shrugged and struck a path out of the courtyard. I planned to circle around and watch them as they ate in the Commons, then discreetly follow as they went back to the dorms. Eryn was right, Rani was getting too suspicious, so subtlety was needed while guarding them tonight.

A half-hour later, Ezra met me outside. Hidden in the shadows of the building across the way, I had a perfect view of the girls as they ate and would clearly see when they left. Until they were safe behind the wards on the dorm, I wouldn't let them out of my sight.

"Sit down, Ez," I growled and pulled my cousin back against the brick. "We don't want her to see you."

"I can't help it, something about her makes me want to stand under the streetlight and peer through the window, you know?"

I gave him a strong side-eye, although I knew he was joking. Ez was as much of a stalker as I was, but even I had to admit, the redhead had him tied up in knots. I'd never seen him like this.

Maybe it was the chase. Or maybe, my cousin had finally met his match. Changing the subject before he created bad poetry about the complexion of her skin—I didn't want to sit through *that* again—I asked for his report.

"Nothing, cuz." He fidgeted and took another quick glance at the girls. I shared his apprehension. "It just doesn't make any sense. Why back off now? Lay low to make sure they weren't caught after releasing their demon dogs, sure. But the tribunal's been silent, so why not press their advantage?"

My thoughts exactly. The loss of their hounds was a hard blow, but not one they couldn't recover from. And if I knew anything about Kol, it was that he had a single-minded determination—to the point of self-destruction—and nothing would stop him as long as Eryn wasn't safely bonded to me. Maybe not even then.

"We stay vigilant," I told him. "There's not much else we can do. An outright move against Kol will be seen as breaking the accords, and I can't risk that."

"The fucker," Ez growled. "He gets to almost kill you, and that's not seen as breaking the accords?"

No one knew about the attacks against me and my bond, outside of my mother and those she most trusted. We had no proof that they weren't the actions of rebelling hunters still after the old bounty. Kol was good at moving under the radar. I wasn't even sure his father knew what he was up to.

I grimaced because we really were between a rock and a hard place. "We win by staying within the rules. I can't afford for my bond with Eryn to be brought into question. There's generations of mistrust of her kind we already have to overcome."

The girls were leaving the Commons, and I stood to follow them, Ez close on my heels. Evening had fallen, leaving the sun to disappear behind the treetops. Campus grew dark way quicker because of the surrounding forest, and the streetlights

flickered to life, creating pockets of light along the path. Eryn and Rani laughed about something, their squeals rebounding off the old buildings, and I smiled.

This was all I wanted for her—happiness. The feeling of contentment in my chest. She warily watched the shadows as they crossed from a heavily lit area to the overgrown path leading up to the dorms, and the fact that she had to look over her shoulder like that made me want to break something. One day, she'd know true peace. I swore it.

Movement in the dark put me on alert, and Ezra stiffened beside me as he noticed it too. Eryn froze. Maybe it was her net of magick or some innate sense of self-preservation, either way, she gripped Rani's arm and moved them at a swifter pace to the back door of the dorm.

My feet ate up the distance between us, but I'd allowed them to get too far ahead. I couldn't get there in time before the man stepped in their path, halting their escape. Words were exchanged, too low for me to hear, but I was running now. I recognized the vampire, had counted him as an ally. Denial surged as I pushed myself harder. Almost there. Ezra cursed, and I knew he figured it out as quickly as I had. How far did Kol's reach go?

"We don't have any money, jackass!" Rani's sass was usually a good deterrent, but this was no ordinary foe she faced.

Dalton wasn't just a vampire, he was the heir, the second strongest of their kind. What the fuck was he doing here? His amber gaze met mine over Eryn's shoulder, and regret shined back at me a second before he lashed out to grab her arm. Fuck! Eryn fought his hold, but supernatural strength wasn't a gift a nightmare possessed.

"Let me go," she demanded, her tone eerily calm.

The scent of lavender saturated the air as Dalton froze, caught under her spell. Good girl. We reached them just in time

to catch Eryn ordering Rani to run. One hand held to the vampire's cheek, Eryn couldn't look away or she risked breaking her hold on him.

"Are you out of your damn mind?" Rani shouted. "Why the hell would you ask me to leave you with the guy who tried to mug us?" Her enraged frown whipped to us as we barreled down on them. "And where did you guys come from?"

"Not now, babe." Ez wrapped an arm around Rani's waist and dragged her a safe distance away.

I carefully approached Eryn. Her arm shook. The strength it took to hold that connection with an heir trained to resist her was astounding. She was incredible. I leaned into our faint bond, pushing what energy I could toward her. There wasn't much else I could do until she let go. Her eyes were wide in a faraway expression, vacant.

"I can't hold him much longer," she said, some emotion returning, and Dalton twitched.

"Then let go, princess," I told her and reached out. "On my count."

The second she broke the connection, Dalton was going to snap. Already, his body vibrated with his contained fury.

"What if I command him to leave?" Eryn offered, voice shaking.

That would be the ideal situation, but I wasn't sure she had the strength to control him like that. One day, with more practice, possibly. But not tonight.

"You hate that aspect of your magick," I reminded her. "My plan will work."

Positioning myself beside her, I readied to push her aside.

"One."

Eryn fell back before I could call my next count. I heard her land on the ground but was too busy jumping in front of her to see if she was okay. Dalton lunged, fangs bared, and I instinc-

tively threw him away with a strong push from my shadows. He flew back and landed in a crouch like a damned cat. Black swirled around me in a whipped frenzy, the threat to my bond too much for me to reign in my magick. Pulling out my dagger, I held it behind me for Eryn, hoping like hell she wouldn't have to use it.

"You don't want to do this, Dalton," I told him. "Whatever he has over you, I can help."

My offer fell on deaf ears. I knew he was going to attack before he sprung. Eryn scrambled behind me, trying to get out of the way but it was too late. I sharpened my shadows into a spear and aimed. A strike through the chest should take him down long enough for us to get the girls out of here, but for the first time in...ever...Ez and I weren't in sync.

As Dalton ran at me, I threw my shadow spear in a perfect arc for the center of his chest. Ezra's magick ran like a wave across the ground to lock around the vampire's feet and encase them in ice. He was doing his job, protecting me. Unfortunately, that small move changed Dalton's trajectory, and my spear struck his heart—a true death for any vampire.

Amber eyes widened and disappeared in a cloud of dust before my mind could catch up with what I saw. Oh, fuck, this was bad. We'd killed an heir. It didn't matter that he struck first or that I hadn't meant to do more than incapacitate him. We had no proof. It was our word against...a pile of dust.

"What the *ever-loving* hell was that?"

Rani stood off to the side, her cellphone held up in a shaking hand as she stared at the three of us the way prey stared at a dangerous predator. The whites of her eyes were wide and filled with fear, and none of us moved as we tried to figure out what to say. Did we lie? I wasn't sure what story I could spin to cover all that she witnessed, but we had to do something. Eryn wouldn't have enough energy to erase this

memory, and I doubted Rani would let her close enough to try it.

"Someone better start talking because I swear to God, I'm going to scream."

"You're already screaming, babe," Ezra joked, palms up. He took an easy step forward, and she shuffled back. "We're not going to hurt you."

She didn't look like she believed us, but she at least put her phone down. Glancing between the three of us and pausing on my shadows that I hadn't bothered to put away, she waved a hand in the air.

"So...go on. Explain."

This was going to be a long fucking night.

***

Eryn

This wasn't a conversation to have outside. There weren't any other students roaming around, but that could change at any moment. Words like "magick" and "supernatural" shouldn't be discussed where just anyone could hear them. Rani didn't want to go back to the dorm, though, and I couldn't blame her.

The fact that she wasn't running away from me, screaming about murder, was as much grace as the gods granted.

"So...you're not human?" she asked, eyeing me like I had a pair of horns hidden in my curls. "And you feed on...dreams? But I've seen you eat pizza."

I kept my smile light, like the one I gave the children at the library I used to volunteer at. Rani scowled, and that smile faltered.

"My kind are called nightmares, but it's a very old term and has no relation to our dispositions. We use the excess energy from human dreams to fuel our magick. No actual harm comes to them and siphoning the excess energy has actually been proven to reduce anxiety for the human. So, we're really helping when you think about it..."

I trailed off as she watched me, and tried not to wince. This was where I lost her. I was sure. Who wanted to be friends with a creature that nommed on humans? No matter how benign.

My voice was soft, "...I eat normal food."

"You said you and your parents were the last," she continued, trying to understand all I had spewed at her. "Because you're so powerful and can control minds and stuff."

This time I did wince. "Yeah. And stuff."

Rani's look turned shrewd. "Have you ever fed on me?"

"No!" I shouted. "I swear. Usually, it's on the night janitor in the library. He sleeps on the job a lot."

Her nose wrinkled as she envisioned the balding man.

"And those two are witches." She pointed at the boys hovering nearby. Ezra waved. "Which is a completely different type of...supernatural."

"It's a lot to take in, I know," I babbled. "But I swear you're safe. It's me they're after and—*ouch!*"

Rani smacked my arm and held her finger up threateningly. "You've been in danger the entire time I've known you."

"Not the *whole* time." She bared her teeth, and my shoulders slumped. "Yes."

"And that time I thought you had food poisoning—it was real poisoning?"

"She was also stabbed!" Ezra called over, and Kaiden smacked him on the back of the head. "What? She still has the stitches."

I thought Rani would explode. Her cheeks were nearly as red as her hair.

"I promise you weren't in any real danger with me around." My babbling was back. "The hunters were never interested in you, and they don't see humans as more than an inconvenience at the best of times."

"I'm more upset that my best friend almost died *more than once*, and I never knew about it!"

My eyes welled. "I'm still your best friend? *Ouch!* Stop hitting me!"

"I don't care if your skin turns pink and you have to dance naked under the full moon every month. I just want to know what's going on with you."

I didn't know any humans who were aware of our world. With no evidence to base it off, I thought she'd run screaming at the idea of other beings out there. I should have given Rani more credit.

"You really don't care?"

The smile she gave me was warm and true. "Bitch, I'd dance naked right beside you." That smile slipped into a snarl as she glared at Ezra. "Not a fucking *word* about seeing me naked or I'll castrate you faster than you can say *witch trials*."

Ezra pouted but wisely kept his mouth shut for once. I offered to walk Rani back to the dorm and still have our sleepover, but she shooed me away.

"Now that I know how dangerous it is, I won't bother you as much about shacking up with your *bond*."

She wiggled her eyebrows, and I scrunched my face in a mock frown. There was still a lot to explain to her about that, about everything, but it didn't have to be right now. Right now, I was content to know she wasn't going anywhere. Thank the gods for best friends.

twenty-five

Eryn

Kaiden and I had the place to ourselves when we returned. Ezra volunteered—demanded really—to be left behind to keep watch over Rani. With me not there, she was in no danger, but he couldn't be swayed. As long as he kept out of sight, it wouldn't hurt. The last thing we needed was for him to freak her out more than she already was.

She hid it well, and I didn't think she lied about still being best friends, but *anyone* would need time to process all she'd seen and learned tonight. Space. I promised myself I'd give her space, even when she hadn't explicitly asked for it.

"Okay, take off your pants. I'll be right back with the supplies."

"What?"

Kaiden's demand pulled me away from everything. I wasn't sure I heard him correctly.

"Did you just tell me to take off my pants?"

He huffed a laugh. "Don't act so affronted, princess. You love

what I do to you when you're"—His gaze branded me as he scanned down to my toes— "half naked. You should see what I can do with absolutely nothing in my way."

My mind blanked. I literally forgot how to speak for a moment because he was, in fact, extremely talented with his hands—and mouth—as I'd already learned.

Mouth dry, I swallowed and tried to reply, "W-why am I taking my pants off?"

"You really weren't listening on the ride over, were you?" His eyes glimmered with amusement.

I tried to think about what he said, but I was too wrapped in my own thoughts. I definitely would have remembered if he told me to take off my clothes. I think.

"Your stitches," he prompted. "Ezra's comment reminded me they need to be removed."

"Right," I ducked my head embarrassed, and he chuckled again, moving closer.

His hand lightly pushed on my shoulder until I backed away. The high mattress behind me pressed against my legs, and he gestured to it.

"Take off your pants and lie on your back."

Not waiting to see if I obeyed, he disappeared into the bathroom. A few moments later, I heard him rummaging around under the sink. I changed directions multiple times, second-guessing myself. Glancing at the slightly closed bathroom door, I hooked my hands in the waistband of my shorts and slid them down my legs.

Before Kaiden came out and caught me in my underwear —a sight he'd already seen multiple times by now—I jumped onto the bed and covered my lower half with a blanket. Hands clasped over my stomach, I stared up at the ceiling like it could open up and swallow my nerves if I begged it to.

"I can feel your panic." Kaiden's voice was suddenly beside me. "You know I'm not going to hurt you."

I cleared my throat. "I was more remembering how it felt to get them put in." A quick peek at the bedside table showed gauze, a jar of sterile water, and a small pair of very sharp scissors. "Shouldn't we wait for Ezra to numb it again?"

Kaiden's large hands settled over mine, his fingers gently wrapping around my wrists to move them higher up. My shirt followed as he folded the material just above my belly button.

"Eryn." His tone demanded my attention, and I turned my head to look at him, lower lip locked in a death grip between my teeth. "This isn't going to hurt, so I don't need Ezra, okay?" I nodded, and he kept moving, as if he knew I'd freak out the second he stopped. "I'm going to lower the blanket now."

The fabric slid halfway down my thighs, and I felt cool air on my hips. The wound had stopped itching long ago. The skin around the small stitches felt tight and pulled often. They definitely needed to come out. But if they didn't hurt when I moved, this shouldn't either, right?

I relaxed my tense muscles and nodded at Kaiden to proceed. I felt his smile through the bond, as impossible as that sounded, and relaxed even more at his approving purr.

"So brave," he whispered and ran a soaked piece of gauze over my hip.

Once my skin was clean and more pliant, he picked up the scissors and a pair of tweezers. My pulse spiked, but I took a breath and told it to calm down. I trusted Kaiden, and he knew what he was doing. His hands didn't shake once as he clipped the little knots loose and pulled them free. There was slight discomfort as the thread got caught in a couple places, but it felt more annoying than painful.

"There," Kaiden said, putting the instruments down. "You can hardly see where they were."

He stared down at me, at my exposed midriff and upper thighs, and swallowed, clearly at war with himself over something else he wanted to say.

"What is it?" I asked. "I can feel your uncertainty. Just ask."

His half-smile set free a horde of butterflies in my stomach. "Look who's getting better at reading me." After another moment of hesitation, he sat on the side of the bed, close enough that I felt the warmth from his leg. "I was just thinking about how much you deserve a reward, but wasn't sure if you would welcome me touching you."

Oh. *Oh.*

"Why wouldn't I welcome your touch?"

His eyes snapped to mine and held. I watched his tongue dip out to wet his bottom lip while a slow burn of arousal uncurled down the bond.

"Do you want me to touch you?" The calluses on his palm tickled the skin of my thigh.

"Why are you asking like it's a bad thing?"

If I couldn't feel his attraction, as strongly as I felt my own, and if I was less confident in how I knew seeing me like this tested his control, I might be insecure. But he *was* holding back.

"I just want you to be sure. Now that the truth is out, and we know where this is headed."

Where this was headed? Why did it always have to come back to the damn bond? I'd acknowledged it, admitted to the fledgling pulse in my chest, and his presence at the other end of it. Was that not enough?

"Isn't there an end game?" he pushed. "Not right away, but eventually?"

I felt myself shutting down, a self-preservation trigger I wasn't even aware of. Kaiden frowned like he could see right through me to the gooey dark center where I attempted to hide.

"Don't do this," he begged, leaning forward to get a better look at me. "Don't go backward."

I shook my head. I wasn't, but talking about bonding wasn't something I was ready to delve into yet.

"You're scared." My heart pounded, and there was a very real chance he could hear it. "You've spent so much time and energy, so much of yourself, fighting it and what you think being bonded means for your future."

His thumb ran soothing circles over my hip bone, right under where the stitches used to be. The easy touches grounded me, and for the first time, I didn't think about running far and fast from this topic. With each pass over my skin, I sank into the mattress, more relaxed. Did he even realize what he was doing?

"I know it will take time for those feelings to change, but part of working through things is talking about them." Kaiden leaned even closer, hovering over me in a way that was both comforting and had my heart beating against its cage for a completely different reason. "What scares you about it?" he asked.

It took a moment for me to find the words, but he didn't rush me. Just kept that thumb moving in slow, tight circles.

"Mainly, that..." I closed my eyes so I could focus. Kaiden wasn't having it. His thumb pressed in, sending a shock down my leg. "Once it's done, it can't be changed," I rushed out. That pressure paused and then resumed a breath later. I dared a look. The blue in his gaze was darker in this light, but they urged me to continue. "What if things are different on the other side? What if *you* are? What if, down the road, we don't see eye to eye when there's no longer a common enemy?"

"Things *will* be different," he admitted.

Well, that was helpful. Not.

"No, don't frown at me. It will be different because it's a choice. When we bond, it will be because we *choose* one another, not because it's safer or because my family pressured us to do it.

I will choose to let you see all of me and all that I am with the knowledge that only you can make me better. Only you can look past the controlling, overthinking, selfish parts of me to the even more greedy man inside that covets you for all the right reasons. Your utter loyalty. Your inner fire and conviction when you're angry. Your huge heart. To the man that wants *you* exactly as you are." Somewhere in his speech, he got closer. That hand left my hip to snake around the back of my neck, anchoring me to him in yet another way. His eyes flicked side to side as he watched my face. "On my life, our bonding is the only thing I can swear you will *never* regret."

I think I stopped breathing entirely. It was possible my lungs had melted and could no longer function. They were now a goopy mess of flesh that *couldn't do their job*. Their one job.

"Then show me," I wheezed, catching him by surprise. As his brows rose, I blushed and backpedaled a bit. "Not...bond, but show me how it could be between us."

Kaiden

How did I ever get so lucky? I wasn't sure I'd done anything in my life to deserve this brave, absolutely captivating woman beneath me, but I was going to make sure I earned every second of her trust. Her fear was palpable, a physical intruder on this moment, but she faced it and offered herself to me despite it.

She wasn't ready to bond, that was fine. I'd wait forever if she asked me to. Right now was my chance to show her what the rest of her life would look like. A lifetime in my bed and forever burrowed in my heart.

I leaned over her and took advantage of that position to slide the soaked purple lace down and off her trembling legs. Doing a double-check on her emotions, I made sure she was still with me before continuing. She watched my every move, eyes wide and slowly darkening with arousal. The feel of them on me sent blood rushing right to the head of my cock, and my pants grew tight.

A condition I'd have to suffer a little longer. This was about her, and what I had planned was more fun anyway. *Show me how it could be between us.* Gods. Did she know how that simple demand wrecked me in all the best ways? I pushed her shirt out of my way, taking her bralette with it over her head. My hands then went straight for a palmful of her perky breasts.

Fuck.

Her breath stuttered as I took a nipple into my mouth and sucked. Hard. My girl liked a little roughness with her gentle touches. Another suck that ended in a bite had her arching off the bed. I wondered if she could come just from me playing like this? I smirked against her skin. An experiment for another day, I couldn't get sidetracked.

Kissing up her chest, I suckled at a spot on her neck that I knew made her squirm. So fucking responsive. It was addictive, and so damn satisfying to feel, both physically and down the bond. I rested the majority of my weight on my elbow by her head but allowed my lower half to settle between her thighs.

I was hard. Like a godsdammed rock, so I knew she felt me, but just in case, I rolled my hips...right...there. Her gasp was like music to my ears, and I did it again.

"Feel that?" I breathed into her ear before nipping the delicate lobe. "That's for you. All of it."

She squirmed wildly beneath me, so I used my free hand to pin her hips against the mattress. The front of my jeans grew wet with every thrust against her, and I was careful to rub the denim

just right against her clit. Giving her just enough friction to make her thighs shake and her moans echo in my ear.

"This is true," I growled and rolled my hips again. "This is real." I surrounded her on two fronts, physical and mental. I opened my side of the bond and made sure to let her feel every admission of love I had contained within me. "Don't deny it," I whispered when she cried out of the barrage of sensations. "Don't hide from it."

I built her up to the edge. Push and pull. Roll my hips, then stop. I wanted her writhing like one brush on her skin would set her off. When she reached that pinnacle, I stopped and flipped us over. The abrupt change in position confused her, and her adorable pout made me even harder. Fuck, my cock was going to fall off at this rate, but it was worth it.

My palms skimmed up the back of her thighs and a gentle nudge had her falling forward. Her palms slammed into the pillow on either side of my head.

"Ride my face, princess," I told her, mouth already watering at the thought of getting to taste her again.

"What?" she shrieked and moved as if to climb off.

We couldn't have that. I held her hips, grip tight, and dragged her the rest of the way over me. Her arms swung in a cute pinwheel as she lost her balance.

"Kai!" she screamed, and I froze. So did she.

She called me Kai. It was the first time I'd heard that name from her lips since she found out the truth of who I was. Pride and smug satisfaction filled my chest.

"Good girls deserve a reward," I groaned and prepared myself for an absolute feast.

My hands tightened on her supple skin, sure to leave little fingerprint bruises, as I spread her legs even more.

"Kai, wait!" She wiggled and tried closing her legs, but it was too late. My head was already there. "Gods, wait!"

I did, only because I didn't want her freaking out. I wanted her screaming for an entirely different reason.

"What is it, princess?"

"I-I don't know what to do with my hands," she mumbled, already out of breath, her thighs shaking as she held herself away from me.

"Grip the headboard," I told her. "And hold on tight."

"B-but—"

The time for talking had passed. I pulled her down and dove right in; lips, teeth, tongue, they all worked together to wring as much pleasure from her as I could. I wanted more. I needed to go *deeper,* but she still kept herself hovering too far away for what I wanted. Her waist was small enough that my arm could easily reach around it to anchor on her hip. With my other hand, I grabbed her thigh and pulled it out, lowering her until I was smothered in her glorious taste.

"Like this," I said, my voice muffled.

I got back to work. My tongue plunged into her damp heat, licking along her walls as far as it could reach while she bucked above me. I ignored the way her thighs gripped my head to focus on the sounds she made. She was close. Good. I wanted more than one tonight. Every muscle grew tense as she came, and I growled my satisfaction while cleaning up every drop.

"Again," I commanded, and she cried out when I started over.

I wasn't worried about her squirming away this time, there was no strength left in her legs for her to try. I was drowning exactly the way I wanted, and only her grip on the headboard kept her semi-upright.

"Too much," she whimpered and tried to wiggle away.

I slapped her ass and wrapped my lips around her clit, flicking my tongue against it in sharp licks. Her squeal made me

smirk, and I sunk a finger into her wetness and curled it against the front of her walls.

"It wasn't a request, princess. You're going to give me one more."

I took my now-saturated finger and inched around to her ass, gently probing between her cheeks. Opening my eyes just in time to see her mouth drop, I wiggled that finger in to the first knuckle. She shook her head, then nodded, then shook her head again. Her muscles clamped on my finger as her back bowed. Only my grip on her hips kept her seated on my face as she rode out another orgasm.

Not even the best upper body strength could keep her upright after that, and I caught her as she slumped against me. Our hearts raced against one another as I pulled her down enough that her head could rest on my shoulder, her face tucked into my neck. My cock screamed its betrayal from its confinement in my jeans, promising to explode if I didn't let it out right now.

I made quick work of my button and zipper, shimmying a bit to release my entire length. It popped up between her legs, but she was far enough down on me that it rested too far to be in danger of slipping inside. Instead, the crown of my head rested halfway between her cheeks. My hips had a mind of their own and began slow, jerking thrusts before I could make them stop.

A few pumps through her slick thighs. A couple brushes of my cock against her ass, and I spilled myself along the skin I'd been gripping only a few moments ago. My moan was one of relief and gratification. Eryn's gentle breaths against my neck told me she was halfway asleep, and I wasn't sure my legs would work right now anyway.

I'd clean us both up when we woke. Snuggling closer to the only woman I'd ever been this vulnerable with, I let sleep claim me.

twenty-six

Eryn

There was something different about waking up in Kai's arms this time. The urge to run wasn't pressing upon me. Usually fueled by an overactive panic response, I closed my walls and put my barriers back up the second I had a chance to overthink things. But today, right now, there was no internal voice screaming at me to move.

We were both naked, and I draped over his chest like a sloth clutching its favorite tree. One leg was hiked up over his hip. His palm clutched my thigh, and a very hard part of him rested near the softest part of me. No fear. Shit, I even entertained the idea of throwing myself the rest of the way over him and testing just how good it would feel to rub along—*okay, calm down.*

My chest pulsed with contentment, the growing bond in there literally humming with satisfaction. We laid skin-to-skin all night, the doors on both sides of the connection wide open. He was burrowed so far inside me now, I wasn't sure how much

more completing the bond would accomplish. My body recognized him as part of itself.

I'd seen inside him, knew him on an intimate level that no words could properly describe. That's what he was trying to explain to me last night. It was how he already felt about me. Once bonded, we'd be like the same soul living in two separate bodies. He couldn't possibly hurt me because it would be like hurting himself.

I was an idiot.

Why had it taken me so long to understand this? I'd seen how my parents were around one another, and my entire life I'd dreamed of finding my bond and feeling the love they so obviously shared. Was my fear so strong that I would let it change the course of my life forever? No. It wasn't.

It was still there, like an annoying voice in the back of my head that yodeled at the most inopportune times. But I chose to ignore it. From this day forward, I wasn't going to live in fear. In fact... glancing down at Kai's peaceful face, I knew exactly what I wanted. The blankets covered a majority of what I needed to see, but the head of Kai's dick rested on his lower abdomen, a pearly drop leaking from the tip.

Gently, I pulled at the comforter and revealed him inch by glorious inch. Gods, there was a lot of him. So focused on trying to please him last time, I hadn't really paid attention to how *big* he was and what that would mean when the time came to fit him inside me. My one and only introduction to sex was many years ago, and I felt lucky to have gotten away with the small pinch and general bland feeling that preceded me losing my virginity.

Until Kai, I hadn't known what it could be like. I didn't know it was possible for my toes to curl and my back to bend in a perfect arch, or that pleasure could be waves of bliss *and* pain—that my body would try to both get away from something and

closer in the same breath. If he could show all that to me, with only his fingers and a wicked mouth, then what would happen when he used *that*?

"If you don't stop looking at it like that, I'm going to flip you over and fill you until my cock tickles that bond in your chest."

Kai stared at me, now fully awake. I bit my lip at the literal *tingling* his words sent south and dared to meet his gaze.

"Don't make promises you can't keep."

The air left him in a *whoosh*. He sat up on one elbow, then his palm, watching me the entire time as he moved with deliberate slowness. It was a chance for me to change my mind if I wanted. When I didn't run, he grinned wolfishly and dove at me. His arms wrapped around my waist, and the world spun as it was flipped upside down.

Ass in the air, Kai carried me over his shoulder into the ensuite, not setting me down until steam billowed from the shower stall. My toes met cool, slick tiles as warm water rushed over my head. I was soaked in seconds. Mouth open in shock, I couldn't drag my eyes away from him as he prowled forward to join me under the spray.

Anticipation was a heady throb between my legs. This was it; I was sure of it. He was going to bond me right here in this damned shower, and if he didn't...well...I might just have to convince him. I watched as he reached out, past my head to the soap dispenser on the wall, and lathered body wash into a handful of bubbles.

Another step closer.

Then, a smooth glide of his palm up the side of my body. Just the outline. He skipped my breast to glide over my collarbone, then up my shoulder and down my back until he reached my ass. It felt great—amazing actually—but his touch was a little more PG than I thought this caveman act would result in. I was scared to speak, afraid that if I said something he would

stop. He loved to taunt, especially when he knew it drove me crazy.

"Is my touch not up to your expectations?" he chuckled, knowing full well it wasn't.

His sly fingers cleaned every inch of me, even dipping between my cheeks. I clawed at his shoulders with a squeak, reminded of what he'd done there last night, and his answering smirk stole my breath.

"Like that, do you?" When he pressed against the tight hole again, my knees buckled. He caught me with a low laugh. "Dirty girl."

There was tension already building in my lower abdomen from a few soft strokes. It was frustrating each time he touched me, and then moved away. My hips followed his fingers, reaching for the missing friction and I swore to the gods if he teased me one more time I was going to stab him. An unhappy growl escaped my lips when those hands made another near pass.

"I haven't even started, and you're already so needy," he murmured, *finally* plunging those fingers between my thighs.

Lights danced behind my closed eyes, and I moaned. There was no stopping my hips. They rolled and jerked—seeking and running from the pleasure he offered. He pressed me back against the wall when my thighs trembled and curved two fingers deep inside.

"*Shit,* Kai," I panted. "I'm so close."

"Slowly," he commanded, controlling exactly how and when my hips could move. "Make it last."

"No," I growled. He was going to kill me; I was sure of it. "I'm ready."

He scooped me up, urging me to wrap my legs around him. The burning tip of him pressed bluntly against me, and he leaned forward to cover my mouth with his. I bit at his lower lip.

Clawed at his back. Bucked my hips. Nothing got him inside me. The soap all over my body made us so *slippery*. The rounded head of his dick grazed my clit, followed immediately by the full length of him.

Again and again. Kai held my ass in both hands and obliterated my body with well-controlled rolls of his hips.

"I'm ready, Kai," I whimpered. "I'm ready."

"Not yet, but you're about to be," he promised and bit down on the tendon in my neck.

The pain of his bite was so sharp it almost immediately bled into pleasure, and I erupted. Wave after wave of my release slammed into me with the strength of a wild storm. My toes tingled, and my legs went numb. Kai had to hold onto me until the feeling came back, and I could once again stand on my own.

"That was one," he whispered in my ear.

One?

How many did he have planned? I needed to be alive for the bonding to work, and that last orgasm hovered right at the edge of making me lose consciousness. Kai reached past me to turn the water off, then wrapped me in one of his oversized towels.

Bunching the cotton in his hands, he worked his way down my body, slowly catching the beaded droplets on my skin and igniting a slow burn in the wake of his touch. Anticipation sent my pulse racing. He knelt on the tile in front of me, deep blue eyes staring with an intensity that would have frightened me before. Now, it only left me breathless as I waited to see what he'd do next. When his tongue darted out to lick my inner thigh, the muscles in my legs quivered. With a chuckle, he nipped me and used the towel to dry the rest.

"I think I already know the answer, but have you done this before?" he asked, hands bringing the towel up around my hips.

I knew he didn't mean *this*—the whole his face between my legs thing—because I most definitely had done this before. With

him. No, he was talking about sex. He didn't seem the type to get jealous about my previous experience, but I was still nervous when I looked down at him and answered.

"Once."

He nodded, like he assumed as much, and stood. The towel came with him until it was draped around my shoulders like a cape. Kai pulled the two ends together and wrapped one over the other until I was bundled in the warm cotton. He then reached over to grab a second one hanging on the rack and wrapped it around his waist.

"What are you doing?" I asked.

He prowled forward and planted his arms on either side of my head, caging me against the wall with a smirk.

"Taking care of you," he breathed and then kissed the tip of my nose. "Go lay down on the bed, I'll be out in a second."

The room was dimly lit. Light from outside fought hard to break in, but only the thin lines around the window shades succeeded. It lent a romantic ambiance to the small space and allowed me to see just enough without taking away the mystery of the shadows. Time stood frozen as I dropped the towel and crawled to the middle of the bed.

This was it. Gods, I really hoped I didn't screw this up somehow. Kai didn't seem to mind my inexperience, but I wanted everything to be perfect. What if I didn't move right or panicked in the middle of everything? I wrung my hands against my lower stomach, then quickly moved them to my sides and grabbed the blankets so I wouldn't look nervous. But a couple minutes of laying like that, and I thought I might look stupid, so they ended up clasped on my stomach again.

"Hey." I jumped at the sound of him so close. How long had he been standing there?

His eyes creased in concern, and I felt him gently probe at my swirling emotions. I tried and failed to lock them down.

"Talk to me?" he asked, stepping closer so I could see him better. His silhouette hovered at the end of the bed, looking down at me and all my exposed skin until goosebumps rose. His warm hand made soothing passes up and down my calf, connecting us and offering me someplace secure to anchor myself.

"I'm fine," I fibbed, and then my legs shook. Traitors.

Kai's hand paused at my ankle as he stared at me. "No, you're not." He bit his lip, "But that's okay."

Up and down my legs, his palms eased the tension from my locked muscles. He seemed perfectly content to stand there and touch me. Just like this. His fingers dug into small knots, breaking them apart before they could truly form, and all the while a steady stream of satisfaction thrummed from his side of the bond. I wasn't sure how much time passed like this, but eventually, my tension eased. Embarrassment quickly filled the silence.

"I don't know why I'm so nervous," I whispered. If he could see my face, it would be unrecognizable in its color. Cherry red. Gods, I really had issues, didn't I?

I spent so long avoiding this moment while also secretly dreaming about it, that now I didn't actually know what to do. How did I handle this nerve-bending tension and excitement all at once? Kai's palms pressed into the mattress beside my head as he crawled over me. He kept his body safely hovering over mine, only the faint brush of his towel touching my skin.

"It's because you know that once we do this, there's no going back. You're mine." His eyes softened. "Just as I'll be yours."

I nodded, my gaze fixed on his. Yes. That. Belonging to *him*. Us belonging to each other. All of it. The thought sent a thrill down my spine, and I wiggled. Kai smirked, like he could feel my need finally pushing ahead of my apprehension.

"Do you want this?" he asked. It was an olive branch. A get out of jail free card, if I needed it.

I nodded again, and he tsked, "Say the words, so there's no confusion."

"Yes," I whispered. "I want this."

He inhaled and ran his nose up the length of my neck. "The things I'm going to do to you, princess."

Promises, promises.

But then he stepped away and cool air replaced where he once was. Returning to the foot of the bed, he dropped his towel and stood before me, unashamed and utterly delicious.

"Take a deep breath," he commanded. "And when you're ready, just nod. I'll handle the rest."

I did as he said. One focused breath, then two. I wanted to do this. I was ready. I gave a subtle, but sure nod, and a ghostly touch wrapped around my ankles. Kai's shadows brushed cool kisses over my skin, gently nudging the inside of my legs. I frowned and looked away from them to see Kai holding back a grin.

He raised a brow, and his shadows tapped on me again. Ah. I got the message. With a shy grin, I slowly spread my legs apart, stopping when I thought my feet were far enough. My knees still touched, and a thick sliver of shadows played a game of peek-a-boo over them. Peering at me one minute, then diving down to tickle my skin the next.

"A little more," Kai encouraged.

I opened them an inch. "There?" He shook his head, and my knees separated just enough to see him standing between them. "How about there?"

The damn shadow started wagging back and forth like a finger telling me no, and Kai chuckled. "I think we can do better than that. Don't you?"

My mouth went dry in anticipation, and I swallowed. "We?"

Multiple bands of his magick caressed my thighs as they slowly circled around them. With gentle, playful tugs, they opened me fully until there was nowhere left to hide. Kai stood there, arms crossed, watching as his shadows positioned me just the way he wanted. The look of hunger on his face filled me with confidence, and I relaxed even more. Something bumped me, and I glanced down to see a condom and a small bottle of lube rolling over the mattress with the outward press of my leg.

"Eyes on me, princess," Kai instructed. "Don't worry about those right now."

My knees were bent and pushed wide, heels resting on the edge of the mattress. A brave glance down my body showed Kai's large cock perfectly lined up, all he had to do was push forward. But instead of reaching for the condom, his hands gripped my inner thighs and squeezed.

The muscles only slightly resisted, and he kept rubbing them until they obeyed his command to relax. If he kept looking at me like that...One hand left my thigh to dig into the crease of my hip. His thumb stretched over, running through the proof of my arousal to swirl around my clit, and just that small touch was almost too much after what we had done in the shower. I grabbed his wrist to stop him.

"I'm still a little sensitive," I said, and he smiled.

"I know."

No warning. No more slow, introductory touches. Kai dove right in and shattered all coherent thoughts with a well-planned strike against my senses. Two fingers plunged inside me while that thumb kept featherlight circles on my clit. Shadows held my ankles hostage, so no matter how I arched, my ass wasn't going anywhere.

There was a mouth on one nipple and a pinch of fingers on the other. Wet suction and teeth. Pinch and pull. Persistent fingertips against that spot on my walls, and I was gone. My toes

curled when the waves kept going, easing off only for Kai to add a third finger to the mix.

"One more."

I shook my head. "I'll die."

Kai laughed against my neck but didn't slow his touch. "You can take it."

I always thought he believed in me a little too much. Still, despite my protests, my release was building again. This one was going to knock me out, I just knew it.

"If this... is some kind of punishment... for making you wait so long to bond...well played..." I gasped.

Kai leaned over, making sure to catch my eye before he answered. "You're tiny, and it's been a while," he said, scissoring those fingers as if to make a point. "You're going to need all the help you can get to take me."

Well, when he put it that way.

It didn't take long for me to come again. Kai built off the back of my second orgasm and sent me screaming headfirst into the third. That shower was well and truly wasted because my body was covered in a light sheen of sweat, and even my wet hair felt like it needed to be washed again. As I lay there catching my breath, I watched him tear open the wrapper and slide the condom down his long length.

He tossed the foil square somewhere over his shoulder and grabbed the bottle of lube, applying a generous amount. Wrapping his fist around himself, he worked his hand up and down. The sound it made...The way he looked at me while bringing obvious pleasure to himself...It was almost indecent. Gods, but it made me squirm in all the best ways.

Gripping the base of his cock, Kai rubbed his thick head along my slit, bluntly pressing in with a roll of his hips. He pulled back and moved forward again. Stretching me. Filling

me. Going so slow I had no choice but to feel every single inch of him.

"Easy, I'll go easy," he said, his breath tickling the damp hair at my temple.

I didn't mean to tense up. His shallow thrusts were gentle, each one easing him further inside, but damn was it getting crowded in here. I cried out at the sting when he flexed his hips a final time and buried himself to the hilt.

"Are you okay?" His hands roughly cupped my cheek. "Tell me if it hurts, princess."

It felt like he was in my ribs. He froze above me, not daring to move as I tried to find words to describe what I felt. Static. I couldn't grasp anything. Our eyes locked, and I tried to explain all the turmoil in my head with a few blinks. Able to read me better than I could myself, Kai pulled out, flipped me over, and in one move, pulled my hips up and slid all the way back inside.

"I knew I'd fit," he growled. "You were made for me."

He ground small circles against my ass, lighting up nerves inside me I didn't even know were there. From this angle, there was no pain. We fit together like perfect puzzle pieces, and I rocked back against him with a moan. Kai curved his body along my back, gripped my hips in a bruising hold, and began to *move*.

He'd withdraw almost all the way before pushing in once more, the head of his cock bottoming out with each thrust. My body clutched at him tightly, like it didn't want him to leave. Like it could draw him in so deep that we'd become one. The bond in my chest was a wildfire. Overheating pulses of his pleasure and mine spiked when he slipped his hand beneath me to stroke my clit. I couldn't control how I clenched around him in response.

"Fuck, Eryn. *Princess*," he groaned.

It was building again. My fists ripped at the sheets as I fought to hold on. The bond stretched tight, burning like a thousand suns until I thought it would burst from between us as a

visual livewire. There was a pounding in my head so strong I almost wondered if it was real. Deep. Kai was so damn deep.

My face was pressed into the mattress, and I wildly bit at it as pleasure stacked level upon level. My sensitive skin, the sparks Kai drew from within me, his finger flicking across my clit, all of it swirled together—coiling tighter and tighter.

"I need you to fall with me," Kai begged, voice ragged as he tried to hold on.

A familiar, cool strand of magick squeezed between us and made its way down my back. I knew what he was about to do but there was no preparing for it. Kai was an ass man, and as I was coming to find out, I was more than okay with the benefits of that. The blunt shadow brushed between my cheeks, pressing, pressing...

The tightness in my core snapped and together we fell over the edge, our voices crying out in one sound. Something happened between us. Somewhere between one breath and the next; a bridge opened in my mind, and waiting at the other end, was Kai. He wasn't *physically* there, of course, but it was him. All of him. His emotions and dreams—his thoughts.

I knew all my crazy had to be screaming at him from my side as well, but it didn't seem to bother him. His warm breath bathed the back of my neck as he caught his breath. Arms still clasped around me, cock softening inside me...I'd never felt more at peace.

You are so fucking beautiful.

My eyes widened as the echo of his voice lingered in my mind.

Kai?

His chuckle vibrated my back.

Surprise.

I laughed, and it jostled him, still half hard inside me. Wincing at the movement of now tender muscles, I wiggled to

try and get comfortable again. My legs had absolutely no feeling, so me and those abused muscles were stuck here for a moment.

Did I hurt you?

His concern made me smile...and it was an unexpected turn-on. Well then, I didn't think I'd have to do much convincing to get my body up and awake for round two.

Can we do that again?

Blatant male satisfaction blasted down the bridge as Kai ground against my ass.

Maybe give me a second to catch my breath and turn the bass down in my head, I teased.

I might die if my heart didn't slow down and calm itself. That pounding I heard hadn't gone away. It was worse.

That isn't you.

"Ezra, stop fucking banging on my door!" Kai shouted over his shoulder. "We're obviously a little busy in here!"

Oh. Maybe that wasn't my pulse racing in my ears then. Honest mistake.

The bedroom door burst open with a fling of splintered wood, and then Ezra was there, standing only a foot away. He didn't appear to care that we were both buck-ass naked and connected by a cock, but I still dropped over the other side of the bed to hide all my personal bits. His distorted shape was clear over the mattress, moving back and forth in an agitated dance, and there was something white in his hand.

"You better have a good fucking reason to—"

Ezra frantically waved a piece of paper in the air. "She's gone! They took her!"

twenty-seven

Kaiden

I pushed my cousin out so that Eryn could run into the bathroom. I then grabbed my towel from the floor and cinched it around my waist before letting one very rude, very soon-to-be homeless witch, back inside. I hadn't even had time to process what just happened. One second Eryn was squirming in my arms, an absolute fucking dream, and now I was here, half-naked, trying to calm a panicked Ezra.

He was losing it. Incoherent and ranting about not under-standing how it happened. How *what* happened? I still wasn't sure what was on that paper he clutched either.

"Ez, Ezra! Calm down, man." I forced my legs into a pair of pants and tracked him as he paced near the door.

The mirror on my dresser took that moment to also make itself known and began to vibrate. The edges of the black cloth covering it waved but it didn't fall. Fuck, did no one want me to enjoy my bonding? It finally fucking happened, and we couldn't even bask. Or do it fifty more times.

"They took her," he said again, desperate.

"Who?" I asked, ignoring the mirror. Whoever it was could call back. "They took who?"

All of us were right here. Eryn's head peered out of a cracked bathroom door; another towel wrapped around her body. Her worry mingled with mine as we watched my cousin unravel.

"Rani!" His voice was strained. "Kol has her. It's all in the letter."

I snatched the letter in question, tearing a corner. Thankfully, it didn't damage the message. It was a ransom note. Whoever was watching us that night I killed Dalton—or however else Kol got his information—told him that Rani was important. She wasn't just an ordinary human. He might not know that she was now aware of our world, but that bit of knowledge wouldn't really matter in his plans. He only needed to know that using Rani as bait would lure out the prey he'd been trying so hard to snare.

I slowly turned to look at Eryn. Her face was pale, but fury burned in her eyes. The emerald I so loved to taunt into igniting was already shimmering with tears. She heard.

"We have to go get her, cuz," Ez pleaded. "She doesn't stand a chance against them."

I nodded, already forming a plan. The letter demanded Eryn come alone to retrieve her roommate, but that wasn't going to happen. She wasn't even going to leave this apartment. I fully anticipated a fight on my hands when I told her she couldn't join our hunting trip, but I'd be damned if I let her fall into Kol's grubby hands after all we'd survived to keep her out of them.

"Dress up, Ez. We move out in ten."

My cousin disappeared to strap on every weapon he could find, and to shove our bag of explosive potions into the truck. I pretended to ignore Eryn as she swiftly made her way to the closet and then back in the bathroom to change. Let her get

dressed, she wasn't stepping one fucking foot further than the living room.

The mirror began its rattle again, and I ripped the cloth off with a snarl, "What?"

My mother's pristinely held-together image took shape, and I knew before she spoke that even more shit was about to be thrown our way. She only sat that still when anger filled every inch of her body until it locked up like a mannequin.

"Mother, I don't really have the time right now—"

"Did you, or did you not kill the vampire heir?"

Fuuuuuck. Now really wasn't the moment to get into all that. Out of the corner of my eye, I watched Eryn leave the bathroom, but she kept out of sight and silent. Smart girl. My mother would have no qualms of shifting her animosity to her once she finished with me.

"It was self-defense," I tried to explain. "He attacked us first."

Colorful curses filled the room from her side of the mirror, and my brows rose. I didn't think I'd ever heard my mother lose her composure quite like that. She was always a picture of pure poise, even when she was flaying you alive with her scorn.

"I know I didn't raise you to be that stupid," she snapped. "You know better. And now Kol Von Bauer is claiming before the tribunal that he was there and witness to your *unprompted attack*. He's calling for a trial!"

Things just kept getting better. In fact, this was probably Kol's plan all along. Maybe not Dalton's death, per se, but incriminating me in front of the other factions; definitely. That Dalton was no longer alive to prove he'd been coerced into attacking was just another nail in my coffin. Without proof, I was as good as dead, and so was Eryn.

I had to get her to the compound. With our bond complete, my family would protect her. There was still a risk my death

would tear her apart from the inside, but with how new it was, I hoped she'd survive.

"What if we can offer the tribunal proof that it was self-defense?" Eryn asked, stepping up beside me.

She met my mother's glare straight on, and I sent a feeling of pride down our newly forged bond. *This* was the partnership I dreamed of, and I couldn't have asked for a better half.

"Short of bringing the vampire back from the dead, which isn't possible, little girl, I'm not sure what kind of credible proof you could offer," my mother sneered.

"Would a video work?" Eryn countered, and if I thought my mother wanted to strangle me before, she certainly considered it now.

"You allowed yourself to be *filmed*?"

I met Eryn's gaze, sending a little telepathic message along with my jumbled mix of emotions.

What are you up to?

I wasn't aware of any video from that night. Too focused on the betrayal and keeping her safe, I fucked up. Although, if that video could prove I was innocent, it was an acceptable mistake. This time. But I would have to be more careful in the future.

Eryn raised a brow but didn't respond to my message. I understood what she wanted anyway. Opening the black cloth I still clutched in my fist, I readied to sever the connection with my mother.

"*Don't you dare*," she warned.

Too late.

"I'll get you your proof," I swore.

The fabric fluttered over the mirror and settled in one dark sheet, covering the glass and silencing my mother's outraged screeches. I let out a breath, releasing the extra stress that call added on my already pressured shoulders, and then spun to look at Eryn.

"Please tell me you weren't bluffing."

She shook her head. "Rani was filming that night," she answered, voice choking on her friend's name. "I don't know whether it's the proof we need, but it's the only record of what happened that might counter the lies spun against you."

This brilliant, genius girl. I swooped down and laid a gentle kiss on her lips. Maybe she'd see the intelligence in my plan and could be reasoned with. Doubtful, but a guy could hope. Ezra wasn't going to like the abrupt change either, but what I had in mind was the best we had to work with. In the living room, Ezra waited by the front door. His anxiety was beyond obvious, as was his outrage when I told him my plan.

"I'm going after her, cuz." He bared his teeth and made to push past me.

I shoulder-checked him and added a little extra buffer with my shadows. They were going to get a lot of use tonight, I was positive.

"You are *my* second," I said, carefully controlling my tone. "That means you do as I say. If you can't follow my orders, Ez, you're doing more harm than good."

He was loyal down to his bones; I had no doubt about that. Rani worked her way under his skin, but he knew what he had to do. He clenched his jaw and offered me one more pleading glance, but I held firm. The temperature of the room lowered until I saw my breath. Still, I wouldn't bend. With a final dip of his chin, he conceded, and I clasped his shoulder.

"Get the phone safely behind these wards, and then come join me. We'll destroy them together."

The plan was for me to go to the exchange point—the spot where Kol thought Eryn would give herself up for her friend. But my bond wasn't going to be there. Using my shadows for coverage, I would whisk Rani away, probably back here where it

was safe, and then I'd return to reap absolute carnage on those who dared to threaten me and those I cared about.

At the same time, Ezra was to go to the dorms to find the phone so we could secure the proof needed to save my life. If, by chance, Rani had her phone on her, then I'd kill two birds with one stone and have them both back here behind the wards. If I was lucky, I'd kill far more than two birds tonight. There was just one more thing I had to do.

Nowhere in that plan did I hear what I would be doing. Eryn finally spoke down that mental bridge, her voice disarmingly calm.

I recognized the beginning stages of rage building in her, and knew I needed to end this before it became a full argument. We didn't have the time. But telling her what to do and expecting obedience wouldn't work with her. I didn't think she had an obedient bone in her body, not even when I had her naked and beneath me. Especially not then.

"You're going to stay here," I told her, preparing a thick band of my shadows for what came next. I settled it over the door, sealing her inside. This wasn't going to go over well, but it couldn't be helped.

"No, I'm not," she argued.

"It's a trap," I tried reasoning with her, but she wouldn't hear it. "A very specific trap. For *you*."

"I'm aware, but if this Kol asshole wants to kidnap my friend just to get me to introduce myself, then I'll fucking go and say hello!"

She tried to fake me out and run around me. It was cute but unsuccessful. My legs and arms were much longer than hers, there was no way she was getting past.

"You've actually already met him. He's the one who stabbed you."

She froze, and a slow, maniacal glare spread across her face. "Even better."

We were running out of time, and it was obvious Eryn wasn't going to back down. Forced to use more of my shadows, I wound them around her and essentially tied her to a chair. Her screams of rage echoed in the empty condo and drowned out my apologies. She'd forgive me. Eventually. When I returned with her best friend.

Until then, I left a kiss on her forehead and stepped through the thick shadows still over the front door. My magick would hold until I traveled too far out of reach, which would be almost to the meeting point on the edge of campus. I hoped that was enough time for her to calm down and see reason.

Miracle. I needed a miracle.

twenty-eight

Eryn

I was going to kill him. First, I was going to save him and maybe kiss him, but then most definitely kill him. The back of my head throbbed as I raced toward the docks. Breaths choppy because I had no time to warm up before launching into a full-on sprint, I thanked the gods Kai's place was closer to the beach than it was to campus.

I tracked him all the way out here, following the pulse of his shadows in my mind until they suddenly snuffed out, along with the ones he left behind to keep me away. The dull pain lingering in my skull was the only clue I had for what might have happened. I knew going alone was a bad idea, and I should have fought harder to be included in their plans.

Damn him and his overprotective instincts. And damn me for failing to break free sooner. I smelled the ocean before I saw it, and this late at night it appeared as a wall of complete darkness that roared a daring challenge to come closer.

The full moon highlighted three figures huddled around a

couple of jet skis, as well as one prone body on the sand. My heart stopped. Kai didn't move, but I knew he was alive. That connection between us was still strong and wide open. Not for the first time, I cursed myself for letting him block me with his shadows so easily.

Talk to me, Kai, I shouted down the bond. *Tell me you're okay.*

No answer. Crouched behind the sand dunes near the boardwalk, I couldn't make out what the djinn were saying, only the faint echoes of their laughter made it to me over the sound of crashing waves.

Think, think, think.

I couldn't take on that many by myself, not without a distraction. Even Kai's shadows hadn't helped him. Getting to him and Rani on my own wasn't an option. Creeping backward, I spun around with the intent of finding Ezra, but the enemy found me first.

"Would you look at that," the djinn crowed. "Just the little birdie I was looking for."

Covered from wrist to ankle, he sported a black turtleneck, pants, and a pair of leather gloves. Full serial killer getup.

"Well, someone was prepared," I muttered, and the djinn grinned.

"I've done my research."

"Yay for you," I deadpanned.

Fury made me brave. My usual MO was to fade into the background, to go unnoticed. Be docile. That flew out the window when they kidnapped my best friend and threatened my bonded. My glare only made the djinn laugh as he shoved me toward the beach.

"Be a good birdie and I won't have to tie you up."

The next several minutes were a blur of motion and vague landmarks. An inflatable raft tied to one of the jet skis. The tossing of my unconscious bond onto said raft. The spray of salt

water on my cheek. Thousands of stars. A giant boat. I tried to take in as much detail as I could, but there was no way around it. We were screwed.

Two beefy goons hauled Kai out of the raft and onto the boat. I winced at the sound and shoved their hands away when they reached for me next. Everyone wore gloves. Guess there was a secret memo about me shared among their little fan club. Goodie. The boat rocked on steady waves as I searched what I could see of the deck for any sign of Rani.

The front of the boat wasn't visible from here, and no one stood at the wheel one level above our heads. Kai lay in a heap at my feet and four djinn surrounded us, including the one who kept calling me birdie. I rested a gentle hand on Kai's shoulder and tried to nudge him awake.

"Hey! No touching!"

Yanked away, my arms were wrenched behind my back as the door to the cabin opened. Everyone seemed to hold their breath as the man of the hour stepped on deck. Even the boat stilled as if the very waves were his to command. Or maybe it was an illusion like the now-familiar pit bull that trotted out beside him. I'd never hurt an animal, real or not, but if that dog took one more step toward Kai, I would eviscerate it.

Under the light of the moon, it was easy to make out Kol's features. His hair was black and oily, with slimy strands hanging down to his ears. He stood maybe a couple of inches shorter than Kai, and had one eye that was slightly wider than the other. He wore jeans, a fitted shirt, and nice sneakers—why the hell was everyone so terrified of him?

"What is the meaning of this?" he shouted, voice carrying across the open water.

His men frowned at one another, and the silence stretched an uncomfortable amount. Finally, one of them got the courage to answer.

"You said to get them on the boat."

"Alive!" Kol hissed, and his pit bull snarled. "I said to bring them to me alive."

There was very real fear in these men at his reaction. The one holding me actually shook, and his clammy fingers kept slipping off my elbows.

"Sir, he *is* alive."

Kol paused and gave Kai a long second glance, pursed his lips, and then looked at me. Whatever he saw on my face convinced him—perhaps my lack of tears. Surely Kai's bonded would be out of her mind with grief if he were dead.

"Get them below and let me know the second he wakes." That glare turned into a smug smile as I was led past him. "This will be no fun if our guest of honor isn't aware of the festivities."

Yup, that was definitely the same asshole who stabbed me. I didn't put up a fight as they shoved me down the cramped stairs, through narrow halls, and into a humid room. I strained my neck but saw no sign of Rani anywhere on this damned boat. Aside from what looked like a closet or a possible bathroom, there was nowhere else down here to hide her. Kai was tossed on the bed that took up most of the space, and I was left to stumble in beside him. I spun to face the djinn just before he shut the door.

"Where's my friend?" I demanded. "We held up our part of the trade."

Technically, we were both caught rather than giving ourselves up, but hopefully, they weren't sticklers for the details. At the very least, I hoped they'd let her go. What did they need with a human? The djinn looked annoyed that I questioned him, but I'd scream the walls of this boat down until I got answers if I had to. I opened my mouth to do just that when he finally responded.

"We tossed her overboard the second we had the Alantes

heir." *And then he shrugged.* Like admitting to killing someone was an everyday occurrence.

Like Rani's life didn't mean anything. Each breath sawed my chest in half, and it took all my concentration to keep the air moving so I didn't pass out. Rani was a strong swimmer, but tossed in the middle of the ocean, at night, this far from shore? I didn't want to believe it, even though an absolutely wrecked voice in my head screamed that she couldn't have made it.

They killed her. The first friend I ever had. A true and loyal soul who had so much to offer— snuffed out. Rage like I'd never felt simmered in my gut, igniting a well of power I'd allowed to lay dormant. One I'd refused to tap into my entire life for fear of discovery. I burrowed into it now. I took my time drawing my magick from its deep slumber. Too much too fast and I'd alert everyone on this boat to my plans.

I scooched beside Kai on the bed, carefully drawing his head into my lap. There was a lump at the base of his skull, but no blood. Gently, so gently, I pushed on our bond and brushed the hair from his forehead. A little skin contact and some hope, that was all I could offer. While I prayed for that to work, I sent my magick out.

Only the smallest tendril, undetectable unless you knew to look for it. That stream of magick raced for the guarded mind surrounded by a wall of ice currently searching a dorm on campus. I gave a solid knock to that barricade, hoping now wasn't one of the times Ezra chose to be stubborn. I had a plan, and I needed his help if we were all going to make it out of this in one piece.

Kaiden

The pain was enough to make me think my skull was split open, but there was a sense of calm running under the agony. My chest thrummed with contentment, and I sighed. Wherever I was, despite the pounding in the back of my head, I was safe. Fingers threaded through my hair and down my cheeks. The scent of lavender filled my nose. The bed rocked to and fro in a gentle lullaby that called for me to let go and return to sleep.

Wait.

My bed didn't rock. Not unless I had my bond under me and a whole lot of time to play. And lavender usually meant danger —either Eryn having to use her magic, or Ezra had left a damn candle lit again. The fingers in my hair paused when I frowned, and the lack of touch made my head hurt even worse. Fuck.

Come back.

"Kai?"

No. All at once, the fog lifted from my mind, and I sat up. I clenched my eyes as vomit burned the back of my throat, and my head swam. What the hell did that guy hit me with? My hand instinctively reached for the tender spot below my left ear. Last I remembered, I was zeroing in on the group of djinn down on the beach.

Hidden in my shadows, the plan was to let the time for our meet-up pass and then follow them to wherever they were holding Rani. But one of them got the jump on me instead. One minute, spy kid, and the next, lights out.

How long was I down for? It couldn't have been too long. And how was Eryn *here*? I didn't need to open my eyes to know it was her beside me. There was no way they got past my wards, which meant...

"Please tell me we're home in bed, and I fell asleep watching a movie," I whispered, deadly calm.

"Well, we're in a bed but—listen, there's not much time."

I held up my hand, eyes squinting open despite how it made

everything spin. It was dark, and abnormally humid. I wasn't sure if I was moving because I was dizzy or if the room was actually unstable.

"I'm going to give you one last chance to tell me you *didn't* sneak out after me. That we *aren't* both captured by the guy who almost succeeded in killing you not once, or twice, but *three* times, and that you aren't once again at the mercy of a mother-fucking psycho."

Silence. My shadows grew restless with every roll of what was now obviously a ship, and *not* my living room couch, and I opened my eyes fully to see Eryn sitting on a dingy little bed beside me. Her eyes glowed, an iridescent green like a cat caught in the beam of a flashlight. Lavender was still heady in the air—I'd be suffocating on it if it wasn't my favorite fucking scent in the world.

"You can be mad at me later," she started.

"Oh, I'm going to be mad at you right fucking now, princess. I can be mad and get us out of this at the same time. Multitasking."

I can't fucking believe she didn't listen to me. Actually, strike that. I one hundred percent should have expected it, and I had. What I didn't account for was being knocked out and waking to find not only myself trapped but my bonded as well. Of course she came after me. She was going to whether I was in danger or not, it's who she was.

But, *fuck*, I wasn't used to feeling like this. Out of control. Like every step I made was the wrong one. I had to get us out of this. We were obviously out on the ocean, but if I could get up top and see how far from shore...Possibly drive the boat back if there weren't many djinn on board... We had options. I could work with options.

"Are you done being a control freak and trying to figure this all out on your own, or can I tell you my plan now?"

Eryn stared at me with the grumpy frown I loved so much, the one that made the spot between her eyebrows furrow and her delectable lips pout. My girl had a plan.

I grinned, pride filling me all the way up. "All right, let's hear it."

"I reached out to Ezra," she said, and my brows flew up.

"Like, you called him from my cellphone that you secretly snuck in here with us?"

She smirked and tapped the side of her head. "Like, I'm done pretending to be powerless because I'm scared of what might happen when I show the world I'm not." She reached out and grabbed my hand, easing her fingers between mine. "I'm not scared anymore, Kai."

I swallowed past the lump growing in my throat. "No?"

She shook her head, and I got another look at those eyes, so full of magick and confidence. "Ask me why."

"Why?"

She leaned forward and placed her lips on mine. It was tender and slow, like what our first kiss would have been had I not ravished her against that stairwell wall. What I always dreamed our first kiss would be. Her lips were soft and plump and yielded with the slightest bit of pressure. I tasted her slowly this time, losing myself in the swirl of her tongue on the roof of my mouth and the little gasp she made when I grabbed her by the waist and pulled her close.

Her small hands clutched at my shoulders, nails digging in and leaving behind the sweetest burn. I could stay here forever, but a large wave and the room tilting sideways was a harsh reminder that now wasn't the time.

"What was that plan, princess?" I whispered against her lips. "Tell me, and if it gets us out of here, then maybe I'll go easy on you for not listening and putting yourself in danger." I rubbed

my finger over the deep crease in her brow. "Glare later. Explain now."

She did, and with every word, my pride for her grew. So did my fear. I wasn't aware that Kol was on this boat. Four djinn was no problem when I wasn't caught by surprise with a knock to the head. But four djinn, Kol, *and* his damn pit bull? I wasn't liking those odds.

"If we can get the guard close enough for me to touch, I'll ensnare him," Eryn explained again. "That's one less dude on their side and more buffer for us."

"It's also a major distraction for you," I argued. "Your attention will be split. That's too dangerous."

She crossed her arms. "I can always command him to jump overboard. One less distraction."

I chuckled; she was fucking adorable when she tried to be vicious, but my girl didn't have a mean bone in her body. It was all well and fun to *plan* to hurt someone. Actually following through with it and living with the consequences was a different matter entirely.

"I don't want that on your conscience." I cupped her chin when she tried to look away. Tears filled her eyes, but they didn't fall. "Could you live with yourself if he didn't make it back on board and drowned?"

"They killed Rani." Her admission was followed by a spike of sorrow down the bond. She'd been hiding it behind adrenaline and rage, but it was there. "One of the hunters told me they tossed her overboard once they had you. So yes, turnabout is fair play when you murder my best friend."

Gods. Rani didn't deserve any of this. I knew Eryn blamed herself, but I was the one at fault. I played my games instead of being truthful about who I was. I allowed us all to get so involved in the human world when I knew the dangers that were

after us. And most of all, I allowed my confidence to overshadow the obvious actions I should have taken to protect our friend.

I pulled Eryn close and tucked her into my chest. "I'm so sorry," I murmured into her curls. "I know that doesn't mean much, but they will pay for what they've done. I'll make sure of it."

I held her as the boat rocked and the night wore on. Any minute, one of Kol's men would come down here and check on us, and this little bubble of calm would be broken. Eryn would have to tap into more power than she'd ever used before and potentially commit acts that would leave scars on her kind heart.

It was ultimately up to her. She was my partner, my bonded. We were stronger together, and it was just about time to show these fuckers what happened when you messed with us...but part of me would mourn the sweet girl I knew would be left behind in the process.

twenty-nine

Eryn

I'd never used this much magick before. It was in small quantities, hardly enough to register, but still. I had feelers out in a hundred different directions—just call me Medusa. If it were visible, I was sure my magick would look like a bunch of writhing snakes coming out of my head. That's what it felt like.

There was so much to keep track of. I kept a steady watch on the djinn nearby and made sure they didn't call out for any reinforcements. Ezra was a constant light in the back of my mind as I followed him on my mental map. Even Kol's damn pit bull had a special place on my radar. I never felt so betrayed by an animal before, even one who wasn't real. It left a sour taste in my mouth.

"Hey," Kai whispered, pulling me from my plotting. "It's going to be okay."

His reassurances were sweet, but he couldn't guarantee we'd make it out of this. With every hour that passed, I grew less

confident in my plans. So much could go wrong, and everything relied on my ability to...use my abilities.

You're not supposed to be talking out loud, remember? I admonished, and he grinned.

I much prefer this type of communication with you anyway.

I rolled my eyes as he winked.

Flirt.

The boat rocked a little too roughly, and we nearly fell off the bed. Loose knickknacks were tossed about the room, new projectiles only the latest in bad signs. The change in weather provided a new level of complications for our escape, and I only hoped we could enact our plans before things got too bad out there. There was a storm coming, in more ways than one, and what would be left when the skies cleared remained to be seen.

They're steering us back in.

Kai stared out the small window as another angry slap of water crashed against it. Raging waves and wind weren't ideal conditions to escape in, but if it brought us back to shore, it made part of my plan easier at least. Ezra wouldn't have to swim to us, for one. The entire room tilted to the right, and this time I did fall off the bed, thumping against the wall loudly enough that our captures were sure to notice. Shit. They definitely heard that. I pulled on the back of Kai's shirt and scrambled back onto the bed.

You're supposed to be unconscious, I mentally warned. *They're coming.*

Part one of the plan: surprise attack. We knew Kol was waiting for Kai to wake so he could showboat his glee at one of his evil schemes finally working. The only way we were getting out of this room was to be paraded in front of him and his goons. We'd be outnumbered and at their mercy, stuck on a boat in the middle of the ocean, and none of that led to a happy ever after. Just ask my best friend.

Thinking about Rani filled me with sorrow and an over-whelming amount of rage. I was doing this for her just as much as myself. She deserved revenge, and I was going to get it for her.

Focus, princess. I met Kai's stare as he haphazardly draped himself over the side of the bed. *Don't let your emotions cloud your senses. I can't do this without you.*

I nodded, but it was hard. Everything simmered inside me, ready to explode at the smallest opportunity. I felt very much like the storm growing outside, and it took all my control to hold back. A rush of calm flooded the bond as Kai buried his head in the moldy sheets. He pushed another surge toward me until I thought clearly once again.

Thanks, I squeezed out before the door slammed open against the wall.

The boat rolled as the djinn appeared, an annoyed glower forming on his face when he saw Kai still "unconscious." I tugged on my bond's arm, looking for all the world like I was trying to get him on the bed and failing spectacularly. Trying to keep my balance while the storm did its worst helped add credibility to our act. I was out of breath and red in the face, my curls hiding the calculated gleam in my eyes.

"Can you help, or are you just going to stand and watch?" I snarled and leaned into the next shift of the waves.

The djinn sneered at me but cursed and moved down like he was about to help. It put him in perfect range and easily distracted. I waited until his hands were both occupied—sorry Kai—before slipping my fingers onto the back of his bare neck, the only skin accidentally exposed. His reaction was instantaneous.

He jackknifed, face frozen in a mask of horror as my magick sank deep into his subconscious. Kai moved without my having to ask, trapping the djinn's arms and holding him until I got a firm grasp on his mind. It was easier than with the vampire heir,

but still difficult. He'd had some training on keeping my kind out.

I doubled down, worming through cracks in his defenses and planting triggers I could use later if I needed to debilitate him. Tossing him overboard was still an option, but Kai was right when he warned I might not be able to live with myself after. When I knew the djinn was well and truly mine, I nodded, and Kai released him.

Unseeing eyes stared at the wall above my head. When I released him, he would look and act as normal, but with my directions guiding his every move.

That's a solid trap you have him in, princess. I'm impressed.

I smiled at the pride I felt from Kai's side of the bond and took a second to pat myself on the back. Step one was complete, and so far, so good. Thunder camouflaged the sound of Kai breaking the lock on the window. He stuck his head outside, drenching his hair in seconds, but he nodded at whatever he saw. The djinn guard stood silent and unseeing through it all.

There's a small ledge right outside, Kai called, then shook the water from his hair like a dog. *You should be able to get to the driver from here.*

Then why are you frowning?

This was good news. We had one djinn under our control, and once I got to whoever was at the wheel, we basically controlled the boat. But Kai's frown and the growing concern I felt told me he was second-guessing our plan. We were running out of time.

It's dangerous.

I rolled my eyes. This whole thing was dangerous. My entire life has been one giant ball of danger, and I'd just rolled with it. Right now wasn't any different. It couldn't be. If we focused on what could go wrong, we'd screw ourselves, overthinking every

choice and hesitating when the slightest pause could mean failure. There was no turning back.

Kai's fear wasn't something he could hide, not from me. It was choking and thick, an exact mirror to what I felt when I thought of losing him to the asshole pirating this whole situation. But we had the element of surprise, and we had to move. Refusing to answer his overprotective pleas to think about this, I released the djinn and sent him out of the room.

There's no turning back now.

I ignored Kai's glare and closed my eyes, tapping into my net. Ezra wasn't far. The strong flicker of power I saw pacing along the shore told me he was in position and just waiting for us to get within range. Movement on the ship warned us a second before my enthralled djinn returned with a friend in tow.

The new guard glared at both of us as he ducked into the room. He had no idea the trap that was waiting for him, and my fingers practically vibrated with nerves. Like his comrades, he was covered head to toe with no exposed skin aside from his face. I could work with that. Just a little closer.

Easy, Kai warned with a side-eye toward me. *You're practically smiling.*

Oops. I fixed a scowl on my face and tried not to jump out of my skin as the djinn slunk closer.

"No fucking funny business," he warned, obviously meaning Kai. "Any shadows, and I'll knock out your pretty little bond."

He stepped toward me in a warning, and Kai's fists clenched. Gods, I hoped he kept it under control. Being knocked out would put a huge damper on my plans. Completely demolish them, actually. The level of hate stemming from Kai's side of the bond had to be a record, but he kept his magick tightly leashed. I felt it whipping around inside him, stronger than the storm outside and just as impatient.

A feeling, that was all I needed. Just a little thrum on the

bond, not even a word, and it was time to act. Kai struck, using the barest hint of magick to knock the djinn off balance. Combined with the unsteady waves and his friend under my thrall, the new guard was forced to his knees before me in a matter of seconds.

Hurry, Kai pleaded. *They felt that.*

The djinn struggled, but a band of shadows over his mouth silenced him, and my enthralled buddy kept a firm grip on the back of his neck. A few brushed fingers over his cheek were all it took. I was in. This guy either hadn't trained as hard or wasn't very good at mental exercises because there were almost no barriers keeping me out. I planted the same traps I left in the other and locked down his thoughts as my own before releasing him.

Just in time too.

When backup arrived, having felt Kai's flicker in power, the enthralled djinn had my bonded strung between them and turned to face their comrades in mock surprise. Things went a little off-script after that. We had hoped Kol would want to brag to Kai in private, leaving me in the cabin and able to sneak out through the window.

That's not exactly what happened. Apparently, the psycho wanted a show. Escorted out of the bowels of the boat and onto the rain-drenched deck, I squinted against the wind that threatened to topple us with one well-placed breeze. The rain was at least little more than a mist. The waves on the other hand....huge. Why the hell were we on the deck? And could I get a life jacket?

The shore loomed gloomy and gray in the distance, a long pier sticking out like a sore thumb to greet us, but the ocean tossed too much for us to safely dock, so we sat idling while the creep in front of us played his little games. My second look at the djinn heir was no more flattering than the first. In fact, he looked

worse. Soaking wet and half-deranged, he twitched before us like a junkie overdue for his fix.

He's deteriorated so much since I last saw him. Kai's shock wasn't necessarily a good thing.

Crazy didn't mean easy to manipulate. It meant unpredictable. The enemy we dealt with now wasn't a familiar one, so we were operating in the dark when it came to assuming his reactions.

We stick with the plan, I urged.

We didn't have time to come up with something new. Half the djinn on the boat were under my control. A little distraction, a slip of the wrist on the driver, and I could have the boat on solid ground in time for Ezra to come save the day. I felt him chomping at the bit out there, not used to being on the sidelines when his cousin was in danger.

"Finally," Kol preened, ignoring the way the boat fought with everything it had not to capsize. "We've come full circle."

The pit bull I once thought was cute and fluffy sat on its haunches beside its master, dry as a bone. The dreary mist went right through it like the illusion wasn't as strong as usual. Like its manipulator wasn't at full strength. Strange.

Those teeth will shred through you, half-strength or not. Don't touch.

I fought a glare. I wasn't stupid. No touchy the doggy. Kinda common sense when said doggy was nothing more than a mental representation of its psychotic owner.

"I've waited a long time for this," Kol continued, oblivious to our internal banter. "*You* are particularly hard to get a hold of for a breed that's almost...extinct."

Kai lunged but didn't get far. I gave the guards free rein to react as normal, choosing to conserve my magick for when the fight really began. That meant keeping up appearances. The

djinn landed a solid fist to Kai's gut, and I winced as the phantom pain shot down the bond.

Sorry.

Kai coughed and straightened in their hold. I readied myself to flip that mental switch if they so much as hinted at striking him again, but Kol waved them away. Free to stand on our own, we kept a wary eye open.

"Why are you doing this?" Kai asked. "You could start a war."

Kol laughed like the idea was preposterous. "Not if I kill you before anyone finds out."

What? That didn't even make sense. Did it? My heart began to race as fear sank its claws into me for the first time since I set foot on this boat. It was one thing to have my life threatened multiple times. It was another thing entirely to find out the guy trying to kill me was actually after my bonded. I guess I was just the consolation prize. My magick pulsed.

Breathe, princess. Nothing is going to happen to me. You've got a plan, remember?

Damn right, I had a plan. With a mental nudge, I directed one of the djinn under my thrall to climb up to the steering platform. We had to get to shore if we had any hope of making it out of this alive. Besides the ocean actively trying to kill us, I didn't think Kol had much restraint left in him.

"I find it hard to believe your father is very supportive of this plot of yours," Kai replied, cool as a cucumber on the outside. He casually leaned on the cabin door behind him, the best distraction. "He's worked hard for the power your faction now holds. Why throw it all away?"

Another deranged laugh from Kol. "Our people won't have that power for much longer if my *father* has anything to say about it. He wanted me to let it go, you know? He wanted to let the heir of our rival faction bond a fucking nightmare and become more powerful than me. Disgusting."

364

"Tell us how you really feel," I grumbled, and Kol shot me a glare.

"*You,*" he sneered. "If it weren't for you, the djinn wouldn't be at risk of losing everything!"

His pit bull snarled, teeth bared and drooling thick saliva. The boat tilted steeply, tossing me and Kai to the side along with everyone else not holding on to something. There was a sharp scream, and the driver fell from above to land in a heap in front of me. He groaned, and I reached out to touch him—having his mind under my control was crucial, whether or not he'd be able to get up—but the boat slanted in the opposite direction and the djinn slid away.

"What are you doing?" Kol shouted up at the djinn now driving the boat in a straight shot for the shore.

I laughed. No amount of cursing his lineage was going to make him stop, not when it was my magick that fueled his every move. Kai dove to the side, avoiding one of the guards not under my thrall. Shadows burst free when he found himself suddenly surrounded by six more. An illusion, but which one was real?

Stop worrying about me and get your ass to safety! Kai shouted, then disappeared behind a cloud of black.

His disappearance jolted me from my staring in time to avoid a mouthful of teeth inches away from my face. Across the deck, Kol smirked with glee as he set his pit bull after me. I scrambled backward, slipping over the wet surface. There were no weapons within reach to save me, not that anything physical would stop the attack from coming.

I rolled when the dog lunged, and then rolled again when the boat crested a large wave and landed back down harshly enough to knock the air from my lungs. Kai threw something, a fucking flashlight, at Kol and it was enough of a distraction for me to put some distance between me and the viscous illusion.

I climbed the metal ladder in front of me, one slick bar after

another, until I crouched on the swaying platform with my enthralled djinn. Reaching with my magick, I tugged on the other connection I made, stopping the other guard in his tracks as he snuck up behind Kai. He switched directions, immediately coming to stand at the bottom of the ladder.

"Ok, let's see how good your illusion holds up against his," I said to myself.

It wasn't much of a stretch to control the djinn's magick, not when I was in his head like I was. It's not like I was casting the illusion, just controlling the part of *his* brain that was capable of doing it. The pit bull prowled closer; eyes locked on the guard like he recognized him as the enemy now. With a strong push, I made the djinn conjure a large python.

My cackle was drowned out by the sound of the engine as that massive snake wrapped around the pit bull and squeezed. I left the djinn to fight that battle while I scanned the deck below me. Swaths of shadows hid Kai from view, but I easily made out the shore in front of us. It was close—too close. Impact imminent kind of close.

Kai!

I only had time to scream his name before the bottom of the boat hit land and sent us airborne. It felt like flying. The speed at which we shot through the air, the sky so thick with clouds and close enough to touch, even the feel of the rain on my skin —none of it warned of the pain coming when we landed.

And it was coming. We had seconds. Oh gods, this was going to hurt. The ground grew closer, and I knew not even the packed sand would cushion the breaking of our bones. I gave a final glance to Kai, hoping to see him one last time. His green eyes were wide with fear, but I felt nothing but love and determination from the bond.

I've got you, he promised and reached for me with his shadows.

Darkness. I was enveloped by a familiar, cool touch as my other senses were completely smothered. Sight and sound disappeared. For a heartbeat, I was weightless, and time slowed. This was it. At least I wouldn't have to see the end coming. Kai's chuckle in my mind was comforting as I raced toward a broken body, but his warm embrace caught me by surprise.

So little faith, he teased. *As if I'd let anything happen to you, not after finally being able to call you mine.*

thirty

Kaiden

I wasn't sure it would work. It was pure instinct to reach out with my shadows, but I'd never used them like this before. They naturally sought out my bonded and effortlessly wound around her as she fell from the platform. Drawing her to me, I held on tight.

I've got you, princess.

Rain and wind merged together into lethal knives that peppered my defenses like heat-seeking missiles. I pushed more energy into thickening the outer layer of shadows, but they found me anyway. Fuck, how was the storm still getting through? In the middle of the madness, Eryn fit perfectly in my arms, her head tucked into my neck, and her little hands clenched on my chest. I squeezed her back, wishing I could wrap my entire body around hers to cushion the blow I knew we couldn't completely outrun.

My magick flowed from me in a continuous stream. I gave it full reign and emptied every drop from my reserves trying to

strengthen the cloud I enveloped us in. The fear in Eryn's eyes before she fell was mirrored in my very soul. She didn't think we were going to make it. I tried to flood our bond with as much love and confidence as I could muster, determined that if these were, in fact, our final moments, she wouldn't feel a thing besides the happiness our bond filled me with, and the peace within me at finally being able to say *mine*.

The boat hovered in the air for what felt like a lifetime. Wrapped in my magick, we were weightless and blind, cut off from the view of the impending crash. Sounds were muffled as my shadows finally did as I asked and thickened. Magick pulled everything from me, tugging at the smallest drops hiding in my core and then hungrily searching for more at the other end of the bond. I shut that shit down. My strength would have to be enough. Eryn wouldn't be drained because I wasn't strong enough to protect us.

There was world shaking and a high-pitched ringing. We hit *hard*, and I clutched Eryn tighter, terrified she'd be thrown from my arms and I'd never find her again. I spoke to her through it all, repeatedly professing my love in case they were the last words I'd ever say.

I love you too. Came her heartbreaking reply, and then it all went silent.

Small things registered at first, like the fact we were alive. Well, that was a big thing. The *best* thing. I cut the drain of magick, leaving only enough to maintain the sphere of shadows around us. With my chest no longer throbbing, it was easier to check in with the rest of my body. No broken bones or intense pain. Exhaustion made me dizzy, and my muscles were locked around Eryn like concrete, but so far so good.

Are you okay, princess?

I checked in, making sure no phantom pain came from her

side. She wiggled in my arms, as reluctant to let go as I was but time wasn't on our side.

Eryn, I pleaded, *talk to me.* I needed to know, needed to hear her speak.

"I'm okay," she mumbled into my neck.

Thank the gods.

Slowly, I released my shadows. I kept a layer around us, protection from the unknown, but it was me being over-cautious. Surviving a boat crash wouldn't sound nearly as cool if we were stabbed or mauled by a pit bull immediately after.

Smoke merged with my shadows as I took in the crash site. The deck was split down the middle, half buried in the sand, and completely on its side. Eryn and I were tucked into a solid corner near the damaged cabin door at the center of it all. The framework of the boat had protected us, and I let out a sigh of relief as I took in the rest of our surroundings.

The djinn were still alive if their moans of pain and movements were anything to go by. Kol lay in a crumpled heap, half dangling over the side of the highest intact wall. His illusioned pet shook its head and got to its feet, ready to protect its master even while he was half-conscious. I wasn't sure which of the guards stirring were under Eryn's control, but only one was too out of commission to worry about.

"*Where is she?*"

The last of my magick dropped as Ezra crested the wreckage. His platinum blond hair shone like a beacon under the dim light of the moon, and the lingering storm clouds moved across his face as he scanned the wreck for the one person he wouldn't find. Fuck. Eryn scrambled off me and cautiously approached my cousin with her hands held up.

"She wasn't on the boat," she said, calmly. "We haven't had a chance to ask...what exactly happened."

Her sorrow was debilitating, but she expertly hid it from

Ezra. His frenzied demeanor eased to the calculated strategist I was used to seeing as he took in the scene, registering small details I knew even *I* missed and categorized them in order of importance. There was a reason he was my second, and it wasn't just his loyalty. When Ezra's gaze landed on Kol, I prepared myself for an explosion of power.

"Then let's find out where she is, shall we?"

Fuck. *Fuck.* I shared a glance of panic with Eryn and then scrambled to get over there before everything went to shit... more than it already was. How did I tell him Rani was dead? Normally, it wasn't something I'd shy away from, giving my cousin tough news. I'd spent our entire childhood shielding him from the bad stuff and buffering what I could. I'd had plenty of practice.

But this...this was different. Rani meant something to him. I wasn't sure what exactly, but I knew I'd never seen my cousin act like this before. He didn't even seem worried that *I* almost died, and he took his protection of me very seriously.

"Where is she, you fucker?" Ezra shouted, stopping at the first djinn.

The broken deck of the boat was already slick and treacherous to navigate, but my cousin's magick made it downright deadly. Ice coated every surface as it burst from him in uncontrolled waves. The frozen crystals inched their way up the legs of the battered djinn, and he moaned in pain.

Ez lifted his foot. "Last chance to talk before I start smashing."

Too far to grab him, and my power on empty, I couldn't stop him even if I tried. This was about to get real bloody real fast.

"Ezra!" I shouted, and my cousin paused. "There are protocols to follow."

There were ways to do this. As much as I wanted to see these guys dead, that would cause more trouble than I could

handle. Already I was being questioned for the murder of one faction heir. Kol's death, and that of his men, would only seal my fate...and Eryn's. For a second, I wasn't sure if my order was enough to stop him, but reason won out, and my cousin stepped away.

One breath, that's the only warning I got before Ezra threw his head back to the sky and screamed. Magick exploded out in front of him like a bomb, encasing the djinn up to their necks. All of them. At once. Kol's pit bull illusion wavered and disappeared as the last of his energy finally depleted.

We have to tell him, Eryn said, her broken heart written all over her face.

I knew she was right, but for once, I didn't know how to do it. I didn't know how to intentionally hurt my cousin. Not like this. We weren't even completely sure *what* had happened to Rani. The words of one vindictive djinn weren't what I wanted him to hear, even if they were the truth.

Let him question one of the guards under your thrall, I told her. *You can make them speak the truth, and then we'll know for sure.*

She nodded and pointed Ezra toward a fully conscious, frozen djinn in the sand. He warily watched us as we carefully climbed out of the wreckage and crossed the short distance to where he was thrown. That my cousin's magick reached him all the way over here...

Eryn took over before the djinn had a chance to spew his venom, and we watched his eyes glaze. Lavender mixed with the scent of sea salt and brine as she expertly pulled the truth from the depths of his mind.

"Speak," she ordered. "What did you do with the human you held captive in exchange for us?"

Ezra's fists clenched at Rani being referred to as "the human," and I put a hand on his shoulder to ground him. I wished I hadn't drained my magick keeping us alive, my

shadows would be more than useful now when my cousin completely lost it.

"We tossed her over the second we had the Alantes heir."

Ice froze the palm of my hand as Ezra's fury spiked, but I held on. His entire body shook, but he said nothing. Did nothing. Just stared at the djinn like he could put a hole through his head with force of will alone.

"She could have swum to shore," Eryn offered, and I knew it was also her last hope that Rani might have made it.

The djinn shook his head, still in a daze. "We tied her up good and snug."

Ez didn't get a chance to retaliate. I felt the surge of power through the bond before it left Eryn on a soul-deep cry of pain. The djinn's head fell to the side, his face lax and all intelligence gone from behind his eyes. She pulverized his mind. I wouldn't have been surprised if liquid leaked out from his ears.

Princess...

I crouched behind her, afraid she wouldn't accept my touch right now, but she spun and buried her face in my chest. Her tears blended with the ocean spray that still soaked my shirt as I cupped the back of her head, tangling my fingers in her damp curls. I rocked her, there on the beach, and mourned the loss of our friend.

Ezra was a statue beside us. Tears didn't fall from his eyes but instead froze on his face and then floated off on the breeze. He stared at the rolling ocean, its rage matching ours with its cresting waves and roaring undertows. I expected him to detonate, to drop to his knees and scream beside us, to...*something*. But he was locked down and calculated—how he got when he fell into his killing calm.

"She isn't dead," he whispered, and I almost didn't hear him.

"Ezra—"

"*She isn't dead*. I would know."

I didn't want to argue about this. Forcing my cousin to accept that Rani was tied up and tossed overboard in the middle of the ocean wasn't on my list of things to do, *ever*. I felt like a dick for just thinking about it. But he had to accept she was gone. We could get revenge, we could...do something. I didn't know. Fuck. Why couldn't I have protected her?

"Don't look at me like that, cuz." Ezra's eyes were pleading. "I'm telling you, she's out there. I can feel her."

"That's not possible," I said as gently as I could.

Actually...

I glanced down at Eryn as she stirred and leaned back with a frown. She wiped the tears from her cheeks as I tucked a stray curl behind her ear with a shaking hand, waiting for her to sort through her emotions. Too much was flying at me at once: confusion, hope, disbelief, and more confusion. She finally peered up at me with a wobbly smile.

I returned it. *Whatever has you feeling like that has to be a good thing, right?*

I don't want to get his hopes up, she said, worrying her bottom lip, *or mine.*

Gods, we were a mess. The small circle we'd created this year was fractured and missing a huge piece. Something we wouldn't easily recover from, but any bit of hope was better than nothing.

"Just tell me," Ez pleaded, looking at Eryn with a longing I recognized all too well. "You feel her too, don't you?"

She nodded. "I don't understand it, but...she's on my map."

It was possible that Eryn's familiarity with Rani's mind made it so she could track her. And I guessed it was also possible that by some miracle she had survived being thrown overboard. All of these were big *ifs*, though. I wasn't sure how I would hold them together if their hopes turned out to be nothing but that.

"What are we going to do about the others?" I asked, gesturing back to the boat where Ezra's magick kept the other

djinn from escaping or attacking. "We still have this mess to clean up."

I wanted to run after this lead as much as they did, but the humans would be scouring this beach soon, drawn in by the storm and wreckage. We had to clean this up or all our lives were forfeit. Exposure wouldn't let us hunt for Rani any faster.

"I'm not sure," Eryn said. "We need them for proof, I guess, right?"

That was the last thing I wanted to think about with my bond in my arms, and my hopeful cousin hanging on by a thread. Fuck Kol and everything he'd caused. If I could have killed him and gotten away with it, I would have. Just for the principle of it all. If it were only my life on the line, we wouldn't even be questioning what to do right now.

Ez dug into his pocket, paused, and then pulled out a thin phone. He stared down at it, that mask of his cracking for just a moment before he handed it over.

"Everything we need is on there," he said.

He'd had that the entire time. Rani's phone...

I swallowed over the lump in my throat. "Hold onto it for me."

He nodded and slipped it back into his pocket, then turned as Eryn marched over to the boat. What was she up to? I wasn't worried for her safety, not with Ezra's magick locking everything down, but her ability to process all this? Definitely. I gave one more glance to the dead djinn in the sand at my feet. She didn't need anything else on her conscience.

thirty-one

Eryn

Nothing made sense anymore—not the storm that came and went from out of nowhere, the djinn that I'm pretty sure I just killed in a blind rage, and definitely not the fact that I could somehow *feel* Rani on my mental map. Feel her, like she was *alive*. I held onto that hope and fought every muscle in my body that wanted to force me to run down this beach in search of her.

We had to clean up first. As much as finding my best friend should have been my first priority, I recognized the danger we were still smack in the middle of. Humans couldn't learn about what happened tonight. A washed-up ship in a freak storm— that was the story we needed them to spin. Kind of hard to do that when there were four non-human bodies on board, completely encased in ice.

Climbing onto the ruined deck, I took in the damage for the first time. I hadn't gotten a good look before. How had we survived this?

Skill, princess. Kai's voice filled my mind with muted amusement. *And a lot of luck.*

I thought it leaned more on the side of luck. I strangled the sob that built at the thought of what could have happened if Kai's shadows hadn't shielded us. My chin quaked at the conjured imagery of him broken across the back bow, and a warm hand slipped into mine, soothing my runaway thoughts.

We're okay, he said, and I held onto his words.

We *were* okay, but Rani wasn't. She was somewhere out there, probably hurt and terrified. I shook myself and mentally ran through my options. We could kill them all, but that created a bigger problem to deal with later. It would be incredibly suspicious for the heir who had accused Kai of murder to suddenly end up...also murdered.

"He's going to be a problem," I said aloud, pointing to Kol.

His face was a mess of bruises. No pit bull in sight, thankfully, and his eyes were half-closed. I wasn't even sure he was aware that we stood in front of him. The other djinn—only one still had my magick wrapped around his brain—-were at various levels of alertness. What was to keep them from spinning their own stories to the tribunal? The three of us stared at the four of them, none of us with a plan.

"We can't kill them," Kai said, stating the obvious. "Don't look at me like that, Ez, you know we can't."

No...but...there was another way to put them out of commission. A plan unfolded before me, complicated and risky. There was a lot that could go wrong, and I wasn't even sure I could do it. The muscles in my shoulders grew tense as the weight of my decision began to register. It wasn't just our future on the line here if the tribunal ever found out...

The stories of my childhood warned against the very thing I thought about doing. I'd already killed someone with my magick, something I knew was going to come back to haunt me,

but to go against everything my parents taught me was almost as hard. It was like a fail-safe built within me. Before I could talk myself out of it, I approached Kol.

Ezra and Kai tensed and stepped up in case the djinn suddenly broke free and tried to cut my throat. Or whatever. Overprotective, the both of them. I had plenty of power left to do what needed to be done. It was strange, acknowledging the untapped stores resting at my core. They rivaled what I knew lurked inside Kai at any given moment, and he was the most powerful super I'd ever come across.

I was stalling.

I shook out my hands and gathered my magick. Unspooling threads of it, I pulled more than ever before, then added a little extra—just in case. It was going to take a lot to get through Kol's defenses, and I had to be precise. The very tips of my fingers touched the heir's temples, and I fell. Deep into his mind, even deeper into my power, I pushed past layers of blockades and mental defenses that were as complex as my own.

This was an entire lifetime's worth of work. Some of these walls were probably laid in childhood, and yet, I found ways around them. Through them. I smashed them the fuck down with surgical precision. My hair lifted off my neck, exposing sensitive skin to the humid air. Static raised goosebumps on my arms. This was almost too much power, it blinded me as I forced it to bend to my will. I wondered what it looked like from the outside.

Your eyes are black, Kai answered. *It's kind of hot.*

I snorted. He would find that attractive.

A few more slices through Kol's psyche, and I severed his ability to ever find his way back. For the rest of his days, as long as he breathed, he would be unable to function as heir ever again. If he could do more than babble nonsense it would be a good day for him.

I basically obliterated his mind.

Vomit flooded my throat as I pulled back and away from the tangled mess that was left. I turned just in time to be sick over the side of the boat. I never wanted to do that again, but my work wasn't done. There were three more djinn to deal with. Breaking them wasn't necessary, and I wasn't sure I had it in me to do it again anyway.

With shaking knees, I floated to each of my victims, my magick on a tight leash lest it try to take more liberties now that it was free. I erased the events of tonight and whatever I could find that led up to it. In their place, I planted ideas that their heir was unraveling.

Kol was insane, obsessed with killing Kaiden Alantes and his bond. He would do anything to stay in power, including frame the fellow heir for murder and try to kidnap the protected nightmare. I installed thoughts of doubt and negligence and wrapped them all up in a pretty bow that ended with the djinn laying an illusion around the boat until their people could get here to clean it all up. The guard I killed would have to be lost at sea because there was no other way to hide how he died.

Three birds, one stone.

Between their testimonies, the now-broken Kol, and the video on Rani's phone, we should be in the clear. I tried to find a way around the guilt, but despite the djinn deserving everything I'd just done, regret and shame tried to dig their claws into me. I had to push them into a little mental box and hide them in a dark corner to be examined later. After tons of therapy and puppy cuddles. Definitely some chocolate.

And sex, Kai added.

I glared at him, but a small smile pulled at my lips. I was going to be okay; he'd make sure of it.

The morning sun was slow to rise, and that fucking sucked because I needed its light to help find my best friend. Storm clouds created a gray haze as we ran down the beach, hands shielding our eyes against the random gusts that swept over us. Rani's glow was new and...different. An aquamarine color. It pulsed on the edge of my map near a well of power so deep I almost wondered if I was hallucinating.

Over a mile from where we had crashed the boat, this stretch of shore was private property and belonged to the fancy houses on the overlooking cliffs, with their private stairs cut into the rockface. She was somewhere over here; I just knew it. Ezra kept pace beside me, his eagle eyes scanning the water in case there was a splash of red floating somewhere out there.

I double-checked my map, we had to be getting close.

"There!" Ezra shouted, flinging sand in my face as he took off toward a pale, crumpled form in the distance.

Kai and I fought to keep up, and I slid the last few feet on my knees, sobs escaping at seeing Rani half-soaked and caked in dried salt but very much alive. Rope lay in chopped pieces around her, with some thick chunks still covering her chest. Crabs and a few seagulls picked at them, almost like they were helping, but they scuttled away at our approach. Her chest rose and fell in steady breaths, and her eyes moved behind closed lids. She was alive! Against all odds, and by the grace of the gods, she was *alive.*

"I told you," Ezra cried. "I fucking told you!"

He reached for her, his hands shaking with relief and adrenaline, only to yank them back at the first brush against her skin. I stilled, worry now battling with my relief.

"What's wrong?" I asked. What could possibly go wrong now?

Ezra touched her again, a gentle hand on her arm, and shook his head in wonder. Kai's confusion blended with mine, but there was an undercurrent of something else: suspicion. My patience was on its final legs. I wanted nothing more than to throw my arms around Rani and squeeze until I was sure she was real.

She was now cradled in Ezra's bare arms, his damp shirt removed to try and cover as much of my friend's cold body as he could. She was paler than usual, causing her hair and lashes to stand out in stark contrast to the rest of her. Hypothermia probably set in a while ago. We needed to get her to a hospital, but no one was moving like we were at risk of losing her...again.

"Someone fucking tell me what's going on before I go postal."

Ezra didn't look at me when he answered, too busy staring at Rani like she'd disappear if he so much as blinked.

"She isn't human."

What? I took a harder look at my friend. There was nothing different about her. She was pale and limp and alive, which by all accounts should be impossible, but there had to be a rational explanation. Just jumping from human to supernatural was a stretch. Wasn't it? Doubt crept in when Kai didn't contradict him. It was weird that I could suddenly see her with my magick...but that...gods, my head hurt.

"Vampires aren't the only supernatural that can be made," Kai said, sending calming waves down the bond to keep me from hyperventilating. "No one really knows how it happens for sirens."

"Sirens?" I gasped and then looked at Rani again. Were those faint scales I saw on her knuckles or just a trick of the morning

light? Maybe it was wishful thinking. I *wanted* an explanation, right?

"There's no other way she could survive drowning," Ezra added and pointed at the rope. "She was obviously bound. She couldn't have survived as a human. It also explains why I felt her. How I knew."

None of this made any fucking sense. My best friend couldn't be a siren. All the evidence in the world couldn't...It didn't...

Easy. Kai wrapped his arms around me and squeezed. *Breathe for me, princess. Come on, in through your nose.*

I forced air into my lungs and then back out. Kai's arms gave me something solid to focus on, and I clutched at him for all I was worth. It was all too much. The past twenty-four hours drained me of any strength I had left to deal with the dreadful surprises life tossed at my face. Yes, my best friend was alive, but she was utterly changed. How would she feel when she woke? Would it even stick, or could she turn back human if she stayed out of the water for a while?

I wasn't sure how any of this worked or how to even begin to navigate what it meant for the future. Rani was going to wake afraid and alone, and I would be no help to her.

She won't be alone, Kai told me. *Look.*

I unclenched my eyes and peered over. There was pink in her cheeks now as her body warmed. Her hand clutched a fistful of Ezra's hair, and her head was tucked in against his shoulder as he held her like she was something precious. They fit together— perfect puzzle pieces.

He won't let anything happen to her; the same way I'd never let anything happen to you.

I shook my head. *We're bonded. It's different.*

Is it?

I shook my head again like that would knock my thoughts in order and make it all make sense. All the clues were there, and I

focused on trying to put them together. The way Ezra looked at her as if she was his entire world. The way he went feral at trying to find her and was ready to destroy everything in his path when he couldn't. How he *felt* her and knew she was alive before I saw her on my map. Holy gods...even before all that. His attraction to her and slight obsession. How she claimed she couldn't stand him, but her gaze always followed him when he was around. They...I think they were...

Bonds. Kai smiled, his relief mirroring my own.

I remember him telling me he worried that Ezra would never have one, because he was half-human. Turns out, nature had a way all along.

She's going to eat him alive, I giggled, and Kai laughed with me.

I tried to envision a future with the four of us here, where our worlds first collided. In my mind, the fantasy unfolded. Years rolled out before me in a blur of college classes and movie nights. Arguments in the living room over what to watch next, while Kai cooked something delicious in the kitchen. Rani and I giggling about overprotective bonds and the best ways to drive them crazy. Holy shit, was she going to give Ezra absolute hell, but I couldn't wait to watch them fall in love.

Excitement grew at the thought of her and I graduating, with our bonds standing proud in the audience. The unwavering support when the time came to meet our respective families, and the absolute joy on my parents' faces when they met the girl I loved like a sister. Rani and I in beautiful dresses as we married our bonds in the human way, as we built our lives and fought each and every day for the happiness we deserved.

It was the life I'd always dreamed about, the one I prayed for late at night when only my deepest wishes kept me sane. There was a lot still to do before these dreams could become reality, and I wasn't foolish enough to think our battle with the djinn

was over. Far from it. Treacherous roads dotted our journey, but we'd be ready for them.

I had plans—ones that needed to be modified to fit the man at my side, and a best friend who needed *my* support this time. Updating my parents would be a *delight*, but I knew they would be happy for me and respect my decision.

Maybe I could even convince them to rejoin society. Being fully bonded meant my immunity and protection extended to them now, as far as the tribunal was concerned. The djinn were another concern entirely but they wouldn't be attacking anytime soon. And when they did, we would be ready.

Despite it all, the future was bright. Ezra cradled Rani closer, and I swore I could see the love pouring out of him. Bonds. It was the most powerful magick there was. Nothing could stand in its way.

It's really going to be okay, isn't it?

Kai left a tender kiss on my forehead, his love streaming down to me bright like the sun finally cresting the clouds.

As long as you keep looking at me like that, princess, everything will be all right.

To find out what the djinn have planned and to get updates on our favorite couple, keep an eye out for book 2! The love story will center around Rani and Ezra in
SIREN BOUND